Susan Madison was born in Oxford and lives there now, following spells in Paris and Tennessee. A novelist of considerable experience, her previous novel, *The Colour of Hope*, marked an exciting new direction in her writing career.

Also by Susan Madison

THE COLOUR OF HOPE

and published by Corgi Books

TOUCHING THE SKY

Susan Madison

CORGI BOOKS

TOUCHING THE SKY
A CORGI BOOK : 0 552 14773 7

First publication in Great Britain

PRINTING HISTORY
Corgi edition published 2002

1 3 5 7 9 10 8 6 4 2

Set in 11/13pt Sabon by
Falcon Oast Graphic Art Ltd.

Corgi Books are published by Transworld Publishers,
61–63 Uxbridge Road, London W5 5SA,
a division of The Random House Group Ltd,
in Australia by Random House Australia (Pty) Ltd,
20 Alfred Street, Milsons Point, Sydney, NSW 2061, Australia,
in New Zealand by Random House New Zealand Ltd,
18 Poland Road, Glenfield, Auckland 10, New Zealand
and in South Africa by Random House (Pty) Ltd,
Endulini, 5a Jubilee Road, Parktown 2193, South Africa.

Printed and bound in Great Britain by
Cox & Wyman Ltd, Reading, Berkshire.

To my daughter-in-law
GINA BERTSCH
who has taught me so much

Acknowledgements

There are a number of people I would like to thank in connection with this book, among them:

Dr David Daintree, of Jane Franklin Hall, University of Tasmania, for many things, especially the freedom to concentrate on my work.

Tim Anderson, also of Jane Franklin, for the mountaineering bits.

Selina Walker, my editor, for her enthusiastic encouragement.

Jim Napier, for expert chauffeuring, bad puns and general devotion to the cause.

Anne Thomas, for support in Vermont.

Lars Petersen, for the telephonic brainwave.

Mark Lucas and Araminta Whitley, my marvellous agents, for once again providing constant and inspired motivation, and to Celia Hayley for her dedicated input.

And especially John Donaldson, who was so suddenly thrown in at the deep end yet managed to keep his head above water with forbearance and love.

And ever has it been that love knows not its own depth
until the hour of separation.

Khalil Gibran *The Prophet*

TOUCHING THE SKY

PROLOGUE

'*I am waiting for my true love*,' Melissa Hart wrote in her journal on January 1st of the year she turned fifteen. The journal, leather-bound, its heavy cream pages edged along the top with gold, was a Christmas present from her grandmother, and young though she was, she knew that what she held in her hands was quality, was exceptional. At the time, she had not been aware that the pages were wove-laid, the endpapers were hand-marbled, though she could tell that the journal required something of significance from her. But what? Bookish, lonely, she pondered the question for some time. What she really wished to say was *I want to be loved*, but the thought that her father might find and read the journal was too intimidating. Eventually, feeling both solemn and pretentious, feeling that she really had nothing else to say, she pushed her heavy pale hair back behind her ears and, bending over the page, wrote in a careful italic script which she had practiced beforehand: '*I am waiting for my true love.*'

She did not imagine that some day a prince would show up at the door with a glass slipper in his hand, or cut through a hedge of thorns to wake her with a kiss. But, as she listened to her father's cold voice in the living room below, her mother's subdued responses, she was possessed by the sustaining conviction that somewhere ahead of her lay choices, dreams, magical possibilities.

Somewhere . . . but not here. From an early age she had been aware of the sour currents which swirled between her parents. 'Do you love me, Daddy?' she had asked once, four years old, her hand on his knee, anxious, placatory.

He had put down his drink and stared at her without smiling. 'I'm afraid I don't,' he said.

Her mother had gasped, an ugly flush on her cheeks. 'David . . . So cruel.' She caressed Melissa's thick mop of white-gold curls. '*I* love you, sweetheart.'

But it was her father's love she craved.

Years later, traveling round Europe after graduation, lounging on a beach in Portugal, marveling at the ancient stones of the Forum in Rome, learning London, Melissa sometimes caught sight of what she expected true love to be. They were no more than brief glimpses, a bright expansion of normality, but they remained in her memory like a sip of champagne from someone else's glass.

After art school, she found a job in a New York gallery. She had discovered by then that she preferred to look rather than to do. As long as you did not get too close, art might disturb but it did not damage, it challenged but it could not wound. Selling pictures, not painting them, she waited for her true love to appear. She had always assumed that when he did, other things would automatically follow: setting up house, having children, growing old together. A straightforward life, marked by recognizable milestones. But it had not been like that. From the first moment her lover walked into the gallery where they were showing his work, she had been captivated by the electricity which snapped and crackled around him. It was not until it was too late that she

14

discovered she had fallen totally, hopelessly, in love with a man who did not believe in milestones.

His violent mood swings, the nightmares, the tempestuous scenes which were so much part of their shared life, left her out of her depth. Gradually she pieced together some of his sad and bitter history – the death of his parents in the ovens of Auschwitz, a childhood of being shunted between Red Cross centers and unloving relatives – but the knowledge did not make him any easier to deal with. And though she loved him passionately, she sometimes felt as though she was suffocating, *drowning* in someone else's pain.

Remembering this now as they walked home through the midnight streets, she wondered wearily why nobody ever explained that the hard part was what came *after* you found your true love.

'Did you enjoy the party?' she said.

'Not at all.'

'You always say that.'

'And it's always true. The last four hours were a complete waste of time. What shallow, artificial *poseurs* those people are.' He scowled. 'So many egos, all trying to impress you with their new novel, their new painting, their new car, their new wife. I felt as though I was being smothered.'

She laughed. 'You looked like you were having a ball.'

He did not answer.

After a while, she reached for his hand. 'Nice to hear that Rachel Friedkin's pregnant at last.'

'Why is it nice?'

'They've been trying for so long.'

'They are stupid people. Careless, unthinking . . .' He pulled away from her, and set off down the street at such a pace that she had to hurry to keep up with him.

'What's careless about it?'

'The world is already full of children,' he said. 'Starving children, diseased children, tortured children.' He shook his head. 'Terrible, terrible. Babies dying from lack of water, little kids going blind or being blown up by mines, teenagers forced into armies to kill other children. Why should these people wish to have more when there are already too many?'

'The Friedkins' children aren't likely to be starving or diseased.'

'That is such a blind, idiotic, *egocentric* comment.' He swung round so fiercely that she stumbled into the gutter. 'How do you *know*? How can you be *sure*? Can you guarantee happiness for Rachel's child?'

'Of course not, but—'

'Or even for your own, if you were ever foolish enough to have any?'

'Nobody can guarantee anything.' She was gripped by apprehension. 'But theirs must have a pretty good chance of growing up happily.'

'What if Rachel and Zeke should die in a car crash?' he demanded. 'What if Zeke abandons Rachel? Or Rachel falls in love with another man and runs away? Or the child is born disabled, or is crippled in an accident? Or abducted by a madman?'

'Why should such things happen?'

'Look around you. Read the papers. They happen all the time.'

'You're being melodramatic,' she said. 'As usual.'

He suddenly smiled. 'You are right.' He took her by the shoulders and kissed the tip of her nose. 'You are always right, my darling, my sweetheart.'

She leaned against him. His skin smelled of lemons and clay. To love, to be loved: there could be no greater

16

happiness. 'I adore you,' she murmured, looking up at him. The street light above his head shone through the tight wildness of his curly hair.

He held her away from him, his expression serious. 'Melissa, my little honeybee,' he said. 'If you were to tell me you were pregnant, I would not be happy.'

'Why not?'

'Because I will not take the risk that any child of mine would have the kind of life I have lived.'

'But we'd do everything possible to make sure that it was happy and cared for.' We would, she thought, feeling slightly breathless, make sure it knew how much it was wanted. And, above all, loved.

'I'm sure my parents thought exactly the same as you,' he said. 'Unfortunately it doesn't work like that.' He let go of her and walked on.

'Why do you always have to be so cynical?' There were tears in her eyes now as she ran again to catch up with him.

'I mean it, Melissa,' he said. 'If you become pregnant, you will have to have the baby on your own because I can't, I *won't* have anything to do with it. Don't expect me to change my mind on this.'

'You'd think differently, I know you would, if it was yours.'

He stopped again. 'Think of it, Melissa. Think of the consequences. With a baby, we should have to find a bigger place to live, another studio for me to work in. There would be noise and crying and diapers and ugly plastic toys everywhere. There would be extra expense and less income. There would be no sleep, no peace.'

'I see,' she said coldly. 'So all this high-minded crap about not bringing a child into a hostile world is just to disguise the fact that you're basically just another selfish bastard.'

17

'Why am I selfish? Why should I have a baby if I don't want to? Where does it say that I *have* to be a father?' He pressed both hands to his chest. The skin round his large pale eyes crinkled as he smiled crookedly. 'Besides, do I really look like someone's father?'

As so often, she was defeated by the logic of his argument. 'But what if I want to be a mother?'

'Then you must find another man.'

Looking at the expression on his face, she realized that choices were being made for her, choices she had been attempting to avoid for the past few weeks. She tried again. 'What would you say if I *was* pregnant?'

'I would say you must get rid of this child, or go somewhere else, anywhere else. Do not tell me about it, don't try to persuade me to change my mind. I don't want to know.' He turned and took her into his arms, smoothing her hair away from her forehead. 'Oh, Melissa,' he murmured. 'Such hair. Like moonlight. Like melted pearls or silver water.' His voice was suddenly unsteady. 'Don't torment me with such talk. I've seen too many traumatized children in my life. Too many eyes filled with pain.'

'Yes, but—'

He took her hand and held it tightly. 'The sound of a child crying . . . I cannot stand to hear it. Even if it's only over a cut finger or a lost toy. I simply cannot do it. Not now. Not ever.'

With the heaviness of a stone sinking into a pond, she knew that he meant every word.

Two weeks later, having done what she had to do, she waited for an afternoon when he was absent, then walked out of their apartment for good. No fuss, no scenes. She did not even leave him a note. What was the point? Heart raw with sorrow, she had already packed a single bag: a few clothes, some books and photographs, three or four treasured possessions – the icon he had given her, a small wooden carving, an embroidered cloth.

For the last time she looked round the place where for three years she had been so happy. And now, so very sad. She was twenty-two years old; this part of her life was over.

Stepping into the passage, she closed the door behind her.

CHAPTER ONE

Pulling into the short driveway which ran up one side of her house, Mel Sherman opened the car door. Instead of getting out, she sat for a moment, listening to the sounds of early summer: shouts from the schoolyard three blocks away, the swish, swish of the lawn sprinkler, wood pigeons droning in the trees at the end of her backyard, someone mowing grass.

Across the road, Brian Stiller, widower and former army colonel, was up a ladder, doing something to his screens. Her own house gleamed in the late morning sun: strawberry-pink paintwork, white gingerbread trim, black shutters. On the porch, the two old rockers offered an invitation to sit down and visit for a while. The red flowers of the japonica hedge glowed. Roses, lilacs, lavender, poured fragrance into the air.

Every time she came home, she remembered her first sight of the house. She had driven into the historic little town of Butterfield searching for nothing more than coffee and a sandwich and then, on impulse, instead of heading back to the freeway, had begun aimlessly roaming the streets which led off the Common. Often, since, she had wondered what it was about the place which had made her pause in her flight. Why Butterfield? Why not any of the other picturesque places she had driven through over the past few days?

Whatever the reason, she had abruptly abandoned her journey to nowhere. Parking behind the First Federal building, she had stepped out of her car into long-established air, tradition, continuity. Into a sense of time not just enclosed but cherished. Walking along the main street, past the porticoed town hall, the cemetery with its hand-carved slate gravestones, past the old schoolhouse, past the bookshop and the Methodist church, across the Common, she had begun to prowl the residential streets, recognizing that this was a place where she might find sanctuary. She passed a wealth of elegant old places: Cape Cods, saltboxes, former mansions turned into discreet offices or B & Bs. And then, on Maple Street, she had seen the house – *this* house – with the FOR SALE sign, half hidden by the overgrown hedge along the front of the yard. Within an hour of that first glimpse, she was being shown around.

'Have you ever bought a property before?' the realtor asked, made uneasy by her youth and obvious inexperience.

'No.' Mel was transfixed by the corniced ceilings, the cracked leaded lights, the brick fireplaces and scuffed wooden paneling.

'This is definitely a fixer-upper, you do realize that, don't you? I mean, you couldn't live in it without extensive modernization. The plumbing's about a hundred years out of date, so's the wiring. You'd have to have the roof done – rain's been coming through for years – and half the shutters would need to be replaced.'

'I can see that.'

'The siding,' said the woman helplessly. 'A lot of it's rotten.'

21

'I don't care. I love the house. I'm going to buy it.' She would use the money left by her grandmother, which for two years had been sitting untouched in her bank account. Then all of it would be hers: the semicircular porch, the rounded turrets on either corner of the house, the pink dogwood which matched what was left of the paintwork.

That was twenty-five years ago. Now the house stood ordered and serene behind its neatly trimmed hedges of azalea and rhododendron. It had taken her nearly five therapeutic years, doing much of the work herself, to turn it from near-derelict to habitable, to restore its former grace and make it into a home.

Getting out of the car, she crunched across the gravel towards the back porch and up the steps to the kitchen door. The overgrown apple tree at the edge of the lawn was already laden with ripening fruit which flavored the air with the sweet scent of cider. She put her shopping bags down on the table and turned on the heat under the coffee pot. There was a small stain on the otherwise immaculate stainless steel draining board; she got out the Ajax and rubbed at it with a pad until it disappeared. A dead wasp lay on the window sill and, frowning, she tore off a sheet of paper towel and carefully disposed of it in the garbage. While the coffee heated, she methodically put away the groceries, multigrain loaf in the earthenware crock beside the refrigerator, cans in the cupboard to the left of the range, vegetables in the racks in the old-fashioned larder. Finally, she listened to the messages on the answering machine.

Sarah Mahoney from the Library Committee. The auto garage. Lisa.

She poured herself a cup of coffee and went upstairs to her bedroom. She took off her skirt and blouse and hung them in the closet before she pulled back the quilt and

22

folded it neatly at the end of the bed. Stretching out on the bed, waiting for the caffeine rush to kick in, she closed her eyes. If she had had the slightest inkling of how exhausting the preparations for the Koslowski show would prove, she might never have embarked on the project. And yet, at the same time, it was the most exciting enterprise she had ever been involved with. Galen Koslowski, one of the leading contemporary sculptors, agreeing to display his work in a small art gallery in Vermont? *Her* gallery? Sometimes she could hardly believe it.

Eighteen months ago, she had been leafing idly through *Art Today* when his face had leaped at her from the pages, set in the middle of an article describing a retrospective of his work to be held shortly. In San Francisco. He looked older than he had the last time she saw him, and almost respectable, almost Establishment in a pale linen jacket worn over a dark T-shirt, his wild hair tamed, brushed close to his head. Long ago, she had come to Butterfield looking for a sanctuary, in search of peace. She had made her bargains and been more or less content. But, reading the article, she had been struck by the thought that peace is never more than relative, and often comes with a price tag attached. She had not fully realized just how much she missed the excitement of working close to the creative edge, being right at the heart of where it all happened. Looking at Koslowski's photograph that day, she had been overwhelmed by nostalgia. And abruptly she had thought: 'Why not?'

It seemed so outrageous a notion, yet so right, that she had sucked in a sharp breath, then thought once more: 'Why not Vermont? *Why not the Vernon Gallery?*'

She had called Koslowski's agent and put the idea to him. The man had laughed. 'I'm sorry, Mrs . . . uh . . . Sherman, but no way. Absolutely out of the question.'

23

'Why?'

'Vermont?' She could almost see the derisive expression on his face. 'Are you kidding?'

'I don't want to mount an all-embracing retrospective,' she said coldly. 'I'm talking about a selection of his work.'

'Are you, indeed?' His tone was sardonic. 'And what possible benefit is a well-known artist going to get out of a show in a – if you don't mind my saying – a one-horse provincial gallery like yours?'

'I do mind you saying,' Mel retorted. 'No contemporary artist can afford to turn down the chance to show his work. And any exhibition, whatever the size of the gallery where it's held, must enhance the reputation of the artist concerned.'

'In Vermont? Yeah, right . . .'

'A smaller gallery like mine can often be more productive in the long run than a larger one. You may not be aware of this, stuck down there in New York where the art scene hasn't moved on in twenty years . . .'

'Say *what*?'

'. . . but hand-selling the artist to potential purchasers is one of the most constructive ways to make sales. And it's something I'm particularly good at.'

'Am I convinced?' The agent pretended to consider. 'No, I don't think I am.'

'OK. I'll give you some more.' Mel's confidence increased as she talked. 'My two most recent shows, Arthur Herbert, the miniaturist, and Keno Wasaki, the watercolorist, were both sell-outs.'

The agent grunted.

'And then there's Mirja Kopler . . .'

'What about her?' He sounded interested now.

'Mirja, as you're obviously aware, was a complete unknown from Augusta, Maine, until last year, when her first show got so much attention from the critics that she was immediately snapped up by a New York agent – not, I should point out, *you* – and she's now selling her work for eye-watering prices.'

'So?' the agent said rudely.

'Mirja was my personal discovery,' Mel said. 'I was the one who gave her that first exhibition. I saw her work in a local art shop and recognized immediately that she was one to watch. And I've been proven right, I'm sure you'd agree. In fact, you'd be an idiot if you didn't.'

'OK, I'm beginning to be convinced,' the agent said. 'Only prob is, somebody already discovered Koslowski.'

'This is true.' Mel took a deep breath. 'Pity about his kooky reputation.'

'His reputation is second to none. Do you have any idea what kind of price he goes for these days?'

'So he's well-known and sought after. But the way I heard it, a lot of the major galleries won't show him any more.'

'Yeah.' There was a silence in which Mel could almost hear the agent's brain ticking over. 'He's a great guy, in himself,' he said finally. 'Give you the gold fillings from his teeth, if you needed them. But when it comes to his work, the guy's a total retentive. Just hates to part with anything.'

'Maybe that's because he knows his work can always be improved.'

'Yeah, but sometimes you just gotta let go. Trouble with Galen is, he tries to impose all these conditions, can you believe that? Gotta display it in the right light, can't have anything else within ten feet of it, needs to be set at just the right height, gotta choose the right background. I mean, these are wealthy art collectors he's talking to, not some kindergarten in Nebraska. Some of them get so sick of it, they just cancel their checks and tell him to go fuck himself.'

'As a business ploy, it's certainly trail-blazing.'

'It's like he's defying them to appreciate his work, like he actually doesn't give a rat's ass whether they value it or not.' He sighed. 'I guess you have to remember his background, the Holocaust, entire family wiped out, all that. Poor guy still has nightmares about it.'

She remembered steamy New York nights, being woken by screams, sobs, bone-shaking shudders. Too young, too ignorant, too sheltered, she had not known how to handle it.

'I'm sure Mr Koslowski himself will see the sense of displaying in my gallery,' she said. 'We have a growing reputation. And between ourselves, Vermont's far enough away from New York that he can't go barging into people's apartments the way I heard he did last year, trying to take a piece back because they weren't treating it right.'

'What a flake,' said the agent. 'I mean, I love the guy, don't get me wrong, he comes round to my house sometimes for supper, gets down on the floor and plays with the kids – he *loves* kids – makes up these wild stories, draws them pictures, they can't get enough of him. But he doesn't seem to have a friggin' *clue* what makes buyers tick.'

Mel tried to envisage the sculptor in a shaggy sweater and work-stained pants, an arm round each of the children, their eyes large with wonder at the fantasy he was creating for them. She cleared her throat authoritatively. 'Discuss my proposal with him, will you? See what he says.'

'I'll try, Mrs Sherman. Just don't expect any miracles.'

I don't want miracles, she thought, putting down the phone, just *this* miracle.

And, against all the odds, the difficult-to-please Koslowski had accepted her proposal. In an attempt to assert his authority, the agent had then tried to hedge the exhibition round with all sorts of insurances and guarantees, but, having got what she wanted, Mel had happily agreed to everything.

Ever since, in addition to the day-to-day running of the gallery, she and Carla Payne, her assistant, had worked all the hours God gave. The lengthy negotiations required to get the Koslowski exhibits to Vermont were bad enough, but as the time drew nearer they spent hours talking up the event, making scores of phone calls, wooing the press, calling in favors, finding strings to pull, calling clients who would be interested, others who would certainly buy.

Now, with all the arrangements finally in place, they could afford to wind down for a while. The event was scheduled for the beginning of October, and until the time came there was not much more they could do, so Mel was taking some time off, leaving Carla to handle things.

She finished her cooling coffee, then lay with her hands behind her head. In a while, she would go and pull a few therapeutic weeds in the garden, deadhead the roses, maybe mow the grass or clip the hedge, but for the moment she was content to absorb the quiet of this pale, peaceful room, the first she had refurbished once the old fixer-upper was hers. Creamy Chinese rugs lay on the sanded pine floor. Bleached linen curtains hung at the windows which overlooked the back of the house, the furniture was white-painted wicker, even her grandmother's creaky old rocking chair was white. The only color came from the two big vases of flowers set in the corners of the room and the icon which hung between the windows, calm and lovely.

She napped for half an hour, then got up and pulled on

jeans, a faded blue T-shirt and an old pair of sneakers. Downstairs, she ran her hand over the rounded contours of the small sculpture on her bureau, a curved column of polished rosewood no more than eighteen inches high, which only gradually revealed itself to the viewer as a virginal female torso, the breasts, buttocks and belly barely defined. As always, she was both comforted and disturbed by it, by the memories it resurrected.

She went out onto the wooden porch which ran across the front of the house, letting the screen door swing shut behind her. A bluejay was clinging to the trunk of the big shade tree like a piece of jewellery but it arrowed away as she came down the steps. Kneeling on the familiar grass of her front yard, she plunged her fork into the earth. In the still afternoon air, she heard the sound of Brian Stiller's front door. It had become an unvarying routine whenever he realized she was home. Creak of the screen door opening. Slam as it swung shut again. Nervous little cough. Purposeful footsteps across the road. Click of the white picket gate. She wished he would get the message that she was fine on her own, that she did not need anyone else.

Another cough. 'How's things, Mel?'

'Just fine, Brian, thanks.' Resigned, she sat back on her heels, holding her small garden fork in one gloved hand.

'I was thinking,' he said. 'Maybe sometime you'd like me to dig up that ground at the end of your yard. It'd make a great vegetable patch.'

'I don't have time to look after it.'

'I'd be glad to do it for you.'

'I don't think so, thanks all the same.'

Brian had lost his wife to breast cancer at the same time that Eric had died three years ago, and since then had tried to adopt a protective attitude towards Mel, reminding her when to put snow tires on her car, offering to clean

28

out her gutters or do yard work, even buy groceries for her.

'Are you sure?' He looked crestfallen.

'Absolutely.'

'How's it going at the gallery?' he said.

'Busy.' Because she knew he was lonely, she gave him a big smile. 'Up to our eyes with arrangements for a major exhibition.'

'Good, good.' Reluctantly, he stepped away from her. 'Don't forget, anything you need, I'm just across the road.'

'Thanks, Brian.'

When he closed the gate behind him, she glanced at her watch. She had a couple more hours before she need stop. Pruning, clipping, plunging her fingers into the earth, reaching for roses, she was aware of something very close to happiness.

Later, she went upstairs to shower and dress. In the bathroom, she examined the reflection of her unused body in the glass. Full breasts, rounded hips, small waist, strong and shapely legs. She touched the scar which ran below her left breast almost to her hip. Her arms were sun-tanned, the skin shiny where they flowed into the roundness of her shoulders. With her gym-toned figure, her thick silver-blond hair, she did not look bad, she thought. Dispassionately she noted the way her stomach had begun to sag, however tightly she pulled it in. *I am no longer young*, she thought. *I shall never be young again.* What had happened to the girl, the young woman, she used to be? Where had this new version of herself come from? *I am forty-seven*, she told herself, smoothing her hands over her hips, pinching the flab below her ribs, *how can I expect to look like a girl*? More importantly, *Why should I want to*?

29

Once, travelling in Europe with Eric, she had found herself in some famous hot-spring-fed bathhouse in Budapest, surrounded by naked women. Most were older than she was but some were younger, and all were massive of belly and thigh, breast and buttock. She was suddenly aware of her own lack of womanliness. This is what real women look like, she had thought then, women who have lived, struggled, borne children and raised them. This carelessly abundant flesh is what women come to. It should not be denied, but rejoiced in.

Yet she kept on watching what she ate, going regularly to the gym, even though she hated the smell of the place and the unspoken desire of the other middle-aged women there to remove the very signs of what they were. What she disliked most, perhaps, was the feeling she had that only by punishing her body could she stave off the sentence of . . . not of death, which might almost have been bearable, but of something worse.

Loneliness.

CHAPTER TWO

Mel had first met Lisa Andersen at the Mahoneys' spring party three months earlier, when Sarah, taking her by the arm, had steered her across the room, saying, 'You *must* come and say hello to our little newcomer.'

Mel had been reluctant. 'Why must I?'

'Oh now, Mel. Don't be so unsociable. Besides, you're bound to like her: she's artistic too.'

God, not one of those women who painted flowers on velvet, or made shell pictures, macramé lampshades. Mel tried to pull her arm away, but Sarah in hostess-mode was relentless.

'You probably already know Lisa's husband,' she said. 'Ben Andersen? His family's had a house up by the lake for years.'

'The Andersens are my neighbors up there.' Mel was interested despite herself.

'Well, little Lisa and Ben have been living in New York until recently. Moved up here three or four months ago, renting the old Adams house. Lisa, dear . . .' Sarah's voice turned creamy, '. . . this is Melissa Sherman.'

'Lisa Tan.' The girl who held out her hand to Mel was as tiny and vivid as a humming bird. In Sarah's highly

31

polished living room, she had seemed like a creature from another world.

'I think you two are going to get along really well,' Sarah cooed. 'So much in common . . . both so artistic.' She turned. 'Oh, look. There's the judge. I must go ask him about . . .' She faded away, leaving Mel and Lisa together.

'What do *you* think?' Lisa said. She wore a peacock-blue scarf and a yellow linen shift which glowed like sunshine.

'What about?'

'Us getting along.'

'If we're both ar*tist*ic,' Mel said, 'not a chance.' She drank from the glass of wine she was holding. 'Do you make macramé lampshades?'

'Not if I can possibly help it.'

'Paint on velvet? Fretwork? Patchwork cushions?'

Lisa grinned. 'I'm a potter.'

'Lisa Tan . . .' Mel said slowly. 'Hasn't Rita Bernhard got one of your pieces?'

'That's right.'

'I own the local art gallery.'

'That converted barn place on the way to Middlebury?'

'That's right.'

'From the road, it looks really interesting. All those weird stone sculptures out front.'

'They're by Ted Zimmerman, a local guy.'

'I keep meaning to stop and look at them more closely.'

'They're worth it. Come in when you've done that, and I'll give you a coffee.'

'It's a deal.' Lisa raised her glass of punch, watching Mel over the rim. 'You wouldn't believe how many people I've been told since I got here that I'm going to get along fine with.'

32

'And have you?'

'Not so far.'

'Funny. You don't look like a social misfit.'

'I guess I just haven't developed a small-town mentality yet.' Lisa widened her eyes, which were so dark that it was difficult to distinguish the pupil. 'But perhaps I shouldn't be saying that.'

'Because I might have?'

Lisa put her head on one side and grinned. 'Small-town? I don't think so. Nicole Farhi suit, Manolo Blahnik shoes, hundred-and-fifty-dollar hair cut – doesn't shriek small-town to me.'

'Good,' Mel said drily.

'I'm being way too personal. Ben's always telling me to watch what I say, in case I offend someone.'

'Which one is Ben?'

'The good-looking hunk over there, by the bookcase.'

The man she indicated was leaning against the wall at the far end of the room, looking through a book which he had obviously taken from the shelves behind him. One shoulder was hunched, as though he was trying to shut out the sight and sound of Sarah Mahoney's guests.

Mel realized that she had seen him many times before, up at the lake, rowing vigorously across the water, shopping in the little supermarket at Hallams Cove, fishing from the dock in front of the Andersen house. She was struck by the impression he gave now not simply of wishing he were elsewhere, but of actually occupying an alternative space. 'He doesn't seem to be enjoying himself very much,' she said.

Lisa rolled her eyes. 'My poor husband. He's just come back from Peru so this is a bit of a contrast . . . And he hates parties anyway. I practically had to hire a tractor to drag him here tonight.'

As though he knew they were talking about him, he glanced up from his book. Despite Lisa's description, he was not particularly good-looking. His deeply tanned face was topped by short untidy curls of an indeterminate color, each one tipped with gold, as though bleached by exposure to the sun; his eyebrows were thick and so blond that they were almost white. But when he looked at his wife, a smile of extraordinary beauty lit up his face.

'Golly,' Mel said.

'I know!' Lisa laughed. 'From the very first time he did that to me, I was a goner.' She looked up at Mel. 'And which one of the dozens of guys standing round gawping at you is *your* husband?'

'I'm . . . My husband's dead.' Even after three years, Mel could not bring herself to use the word 'widow'.

'With all those panting males, it doesn't look to me as though you'd have much problem finding—' Lisa stopped short. Color rushed into her face. 'Oh my God, what am I saying? That was a terribly insensitive thing to . . . I mean, I don't know how long you've been on your own or anything . . . I'm so sorry.'

'That's OK.' Mel changed the subject. 'Sarah said you'd been here for three or four months. How come I haven't seen you around before?'

'Ben's been away a lot. And I'm so scared of running into the folk I'm supposed to get along fine with that I stay home most of the time.' Lisa put a hand to her mouth. 'Oops! Probably shouldn't have said that either. Actually, I'm being unfair. I've met some really great people.' A grin spilled across her face. 'Most of them from my childbirth class.'

Mel's eyes dropped to Lisa's tiny waist. 'I'd never have guessed.'

'I probably shouldn't be spreading the news just yet, but I'm so thrilled I can't keep it to myself.'

'When are you due?'

'October.'

'And it's March now.' Mel did the mental arithmetic.

'I know,' Lisa said. 'Just over two months. But I'm – *we're* – really excited about it.'

'What are you hoping for?'

'Who cares, as long as it's healthy?'

'What does Ben do?'

'He climbs mountains,' Lisa said.

Mel looked over at him again. Joanne Mayfield was talking to him now, flirting outrageously, while he stood with the book he had taken from the shelves still in his hand, nodding politely. 'And what does he do when he's not doing that?'

'Climbs even more mountains.'

'And in between?'

'Does a number of different things to fund his mountain-climbing. Odd jobs, mostly. Carpentry. Construction work. Rigging.' Lisa had smiled ruefully. 'Anything that'll give him enough money to go off again. Sometimes he leads walking tours. Treks. Guides people who want to go mountain-climbing. Mountains are what he does.'

Later, finding herself alongside him, Mel had introduced herself. Close to, she glimpsed in his deepset eyes an almost chilling remoteness, as though he were used to more alien landscapes and wider horizons. 'I'm Melissa Sherman,' she said. 'We bought our cabin by the lake from your mother.'

He did not smile, which disconcerted her. 'I've seen you up there.'

'Are you enjoying your move to Butterfield?'

He nodded. 'I don't like living in New York.'

'Nor do I,' she had said. And suddenly wondered if that was still true.

'Really?' He raised disbelieving eyebrows. 'You look like the sort who'd—'

'Do I?' She had turned away.

The Adams fruit farm had flourished for three generations, but with the death of their father and then their last surviving brother, the Adams sisters had been unable to keep the business going. Gradually they had sold off parcels of land to the developers, and now the original house, the barn beside it and a few scrawny apple trees were all that remained of the original acres. In return for fixing it up a little, Ben and Lisa Andersen were able to rent the place for a nominal sum.

As Mel swept round the gracious graveled driveway, Lisa came to the doorway of the barn and waved. Despite being almost five months pregnant, she looked like a little girl, from the shiny black pigtails on either side of her head to the vivid colors of her clothes.

As Mel stepped out of her car, Lisa gestured at her own sea-green smock and melon-colored shorts. 'How come you always look so darned chic?' she said. 'Even in chinos and a tee you look like a million dollars.'

'And you look twice that.' Mel handed Lisa a bag. 'I had to go to Burlington this morning and I simply couldn't resist this.'

'Another present? You're always bringing me stuff.'

Mel followed Lisa through the dark front half of the barn which still contained the paraphernalia left behind by the Adams sisters: an ancient wooden cart, various farming implements, a broken box of asphalt tiles, rusty window screens. Garden tools, a couple of dusty mountain bikes, coils of hosepipe, flowerpots, sacks of compost and woodchips filled the cobwebbed corners, but in the light-filled space beyond sun streamed in through the back wall, its wooden planks now replaced by glass. A Mozart piano concerto spilled softly from speakers on the plain plaster walls, which Lisa had painted in wonderful muted shades of old rose, faded blue, dusky lavender.

Most of the studio was devoted to Lisa's wheels, her bins of clays, pails of slip and bowls of hand-mixed glaze, and the tools she used to shape and refine the pots she threw. Tables and shelving of matching maple lined the walls; the ceiling was wood too, set with large square skylights. Earthenware pots from the garden center stood here and there, blue, green, turquoise, holding bamboo stakes, rolls of graph paper, a feather duster. A couple of kilns stood against the far wall; the rest of the space was occupied by racks of paints and jars of brushes. One of the walls was cork-lined, pinned with color charts and design sketches. A large open closet held boxes of expensive white porcelain.

'Help yourself.' Lisa nodded at the long counter where a coffee-maker stood gently burping beside a double sink of stainless steel. A small refrigerator was set beneath the counter. 'There's cream in the icebox. I even made some of those butterscotch brownies you like.'

'A New York gal making cookies? Something's wrong somewhere.'

'Hey, when in Rome . . . Ben's brought me up here to live in the country so I gotta be a country wife, right?'

'Yeah,' Mel said. 'And I have to say you got it down pat. Every time I see you these days, I think sheesh, there's a *real* Vermonter, family must've been here for generations.'

'I'll be churning my own butter any day now.' Unwrapping tissue paper, Lisa pulled out a baby-sized pair of bib-fronted dungarees. 'Oh, Mel, so *cute*.'

'It was the gingham heart on the front of the bib which sold me on them,' said Mel.

'They're really sweet. And they'll be perfect with the size zero high-tops I bought last week.'

'High-tops? For a baby?'

'Crazy, isn't it? The way babies grow, it'll only be in them for about a week, but I just had to have them.' Lisa held the overalls up against her swollen belly. 'Mind you, these are a *teensy* bit small for me, but if I slimmed down a bit . . .'

'Lose any more weight and you'll disappear altogether.'

'Lose? I wish. I daren't put on another gram. I'm getting awful close to the maximum the gynecologist allowed me, and there's more than four months still to go.'

'OK,' Mel said. 'If that's how you feel, keep them for the baby.'

'Mel, thanks *so* much.' Lisa reached upwards for Mel's cheek and kissed her. Suddenly shy, she rubbed the checked heart on the front of the dungarees. 'It's been really great, you know, having you as my surrogate mom.'

Mel could never have explained to Lisa exactly how much the coming baby meant to her. She searched her friend's face. 'So . . . is everything OK?'

Lisa tapped her teeth with the end of a paintbrush as she stared at the small wilderness of trees and tangled undergrowth outside the window. 'Being alone so much sometimes gets me down. I knew when I married him that Ben was never going to be the conventional husband, wearing a suit, working nine to five. I mean I *knew* that. It's what I loved about him, right? That he'd be off, climbing mountains, trekking, stuff like that.' She shook her head from side to side so that her pigtails bounced. 'It's just that now, with the baby and all, I wish he wouldn't.'

'Why do you let him go?'

'Let?' Lisa laughed. 'He's an adult, Mel. He does what he needs to do. I wouldn't begin to try to stop him.'

'Tell him how you feel.'

'I can't. When he's climbing, he needs to focus a hundred per cent on what he's doing. Fretting about me could quite literally mean the difference between life and death.'

'Maybe he could find something less dangerous to do, something nearer home.'

'Maybe he could. And maybe he'd be miserable. I wouldn't want that. Mountain-climbing is like a fix for him. The ultimate challenge. It's not for me to veto it. I don't even want to.' She looked down at her coffee cup and added quietly, 'Besides, the only one who could stop him climbing is himself. For me to try would be like trying to . . . to tame a panther.'

'Panthers can be tamed.'

'But then they wouldn't be panthers.' A dimple showed in Lisa's cheek. 'The way Ben talks about it, the discomfort, the danger, I've realized that being scared shitless on a regular basis is what keeps him functioning.'

'Mad.'

'Not if pitting himself against the odds, and winning, is how he . . . validates himself. Up in the high mountains he knows exactly who he is.'

'But not when he's with his wife?'

'He lost a cousin when he was just a kid, in some kind of biking accident. He doesn't talk about it much but I know he still blames himself, even though it wasn't his fault. So as far as I'm concerned, if climbing mountains is what Ben needs, then that's what he must do. I'm happy about that because I love him and I want him to be happy too. It's only sometimes that I wish . . . God, this

39

sounds so pathetic . . . I wish he wanted to be here with me, with us, instead of out there . . .'

'It's not pathetic at all.'

'Oh Mel, it *is*. I hate the way these clinging-vine, fragile-little-woman sort of things have taken me over. I really hate it.'

'Pregnant women are allowed to cling a bit, aren't they?'

'Not this one.' Lisa grinned.

It was strange, Mel thought, that she had become so close to Lisa whereas Lisa's husband remained almost unknown, as inaccessible as the mountains he loved.

'And on top of that, I really miss New York, that exhilarating sense of living on the edge, standing close to the abyss.' Lisa clasped her arms around her chest, staring out at the orchard with its unpruned fruit bushes and knobby-trunked apple trees. 'Trouble is, when he's away, I get so *frightened*. Not just for him, but for me, too. I lie in bed thinking what I'd do if something happened to him, how I'd cope. Whether I should be bringing a baby into the world if there's a chance it might not have a father.'

Mel felt suddenly cold. 'Come on, honey,' she said quickly. 'Nothing's going to happen to him.'

Lisa forced a smile. 'OK. That's enough griping. Wanna hear some good news?'

'You bet.'

'I sold a piece yesterday.'

'That's terrific! Which one?'

'You haven't seen it. There's this little gallery which some woman runs out of her brownstone on the Upper East Side, and she called me to say someone had bought it. By the time she's taken her commission, there won't be a lot left, but at least it's a sale.'

'With many more to come, I just know.'

'You won't want to see my latest ar*tist*ic project, will you?'

'No,' Mel said firmly.

'Oh, go on. You'll love it.' Lisa grinned as she picked up a plate by the edges and showed it to Mel. 'It's a wedding gift, from the groom's parents, for a couple down in Texas. They want a dozen of everything – plates, soup bowls, side plates, dessert bowls. Plus serving dishes and platters. What do you think of that?'

'Great.' Mel's tone was deliberately non-committal.

'The people are called Peacocke.'

'Which would explain all the darling blues and greens and feathers and stuff.'

'OK, if you don't like that, what about this?' Lisa indicated a white platter with a delicate design of lady-bugs and poppies painted round the rim.

'Oh, please . . .' Mel put a hand over her eyes.

'It's for a customer in Chicago who's got a hang-up about ladybugs. Lots of women have, apparently. Supposed to be sexual, the black spots, though I'm just as happy I can't see the connection.' Lisa waggled her fingers. 'Her husband commissioned it for her fortieth birthday.'

Mel gave an exasperated sigh. 'You know how much I admire what you've achieved, setting up your own business and all . . .'

'But . . . ?'

'*But* you're an extremely talented potter. That's what you should be concentrating on. Not wasting time on crap like this.'

'At least it brings in good money while I wait for people to discover how extremely talented I am.'

'They will, Lisa. Be patient. There's been a lot of interest in those pieces of yours in the gallery.'

'But no actual sales.'

'Two.'

'You. And Rita Bernhard. Both of you are my friends. It doesn't count.'

'Three, with this New York sale. And incidentally, Rita and her husband are very knowledgeable collectors. If they buy a piece by Lisa Tan, believe me, the word will spread.' Mel frowned at the platter. 'Think you'll be able to carry on working once the baby comes?'

'I've no idea. What I hear, it's unbelievable how much time one small human being can take up.'

'Only at the beginning. Listen, honey. If you get down again, don't keep it to yourself. Call me up and come round for a meal one evening.'

'I'll do that.' Lisa began jamming paintbrushes into a coffee jar which stood beside the sink Ben had set into the counter. 'Mel . . . I didn't mean to badmouth Ben. I know you'd love him if you got to know him.'

'I'm sure I'd adore him. Pity he's not around long enough for me to find out.'

'What it all boils down to is that I love him. Simple as that,' Lisa said. 'Now, I've had my turn, tell me what's going on with you.'

Mel grinned. 'Not much, apart from living, breathing, sleeping, dreaming Koslowski.'

'I still can't figure out how you managed to get a guy like that to show his work up here. Quite a coup, Mel. Is he going to come up to open the show for you?'

'I haven't asked him to.' Mel smoothed her hair behind her ear. 'Koslowski may be ready for Butterfield, but I bet Butterfield's not ready for Koslowski.' She gathered her things together. 'I better get moving.'

Walking her back to her car, Lisa put her head on one side. 'I hope you don't mind my asking, but why didn't you ever have kids? You'd have made a wonderful mom.'

'I . . .' Her face flushing, Mel said, 'Eric – my husband – felt he was too old to start a family.'

'I guess that's the way it goes, sometimes.'

'Right.'

But driving back to Maple Street, Mel felt a painful rush of guilt. She should have been honest. She should have admitted to Lisa that it was not Eric's fault there had been no children. Not his fault at all. But even after all these years, she still could not talk about, could scarcely think about the child she had once carried within her, and had then, quite deliberately, destroyed.

CHAPTER THREE

Night was beginning to drift across the mountains as Ben Andersen turned off the highway onto the road through the woods. However many times he drove these quiet lanes between the deep thickets of white birch and sugar maple, he always experienced a lift of the heart as the crowding trees pushed close to the edge of the road and blotted out the sky.

At Parris, he drove slowly over the covered bridge, the wheels of his old Jeep rattling across the planked roadway. Strips of daylight leaked between the rough wooden sides and up through the gaps between the boards. Summer heat had already narrowed the creek below the bridge; soon it would be reduced to a mere trickle between dry stones.

Further along the dirt road, he pulled up. Turning off his engine, he got out and stretched. He'd set off early, driven all the way to Brattleboro, spent the day refitting a kitchen in a restored Victorian house up there. The home-owner was exacting, knew precisely how he wanted it to look, and because he was paying for top-quality materials, wanted top-quality craftsmanship to go with them.

Which is exactly what he's getting, Ben thought. He enjoyed the challenge of fitting wood together, matching the grain, planing down the surfaces until they felt like silk under his fingers. Standing back and thinking: that's a job well done. And when he'd finished that, there would undoubtedly be more work. Kim Bernhard had asked him to drop by his house on his way home, to discuss a further project.

When he looked back at the years he had spent in New York, they now seemed like a punishment, a rite of passage, something to be endured. The money had been good, excellent in fact, more than enough to subsidize his climbing: not many people had his particular skills and construction bosses were prepared to pay well for a good ironworker, a man who could walk the steel, work eight hundred feet up in the air with nothing more than rubber-soled sneakers, a tool belt and an unshakable faith that he wouldn't fly. It was exhilarating being up there, so far above the rest of the world. It was quite different from being in the mountains; it was something he found impossible to describe to other people, even to Lisa, something that belonged only to himself.

He breathed in the good smells of leaf and earth and fresh air. God, he loved it here. The freedom, the space, the constantly changing beauty. If he was ever injured badly enough to stop him from serious climbing, then living in this place wouldn't be that much of a hardship.

He stretched again, feeling his shoulder muscles tighten and relax. Silence is never absolute, yet up here it seemed to have been distilled down to an essence of the faintest murmuring of leaves, tiny movements in the undergrowth, the call of a bird, the clear run of water over rocks. He drew a deep breath, feeling his habitual restlessness begin to dissolve. He'd only been back from Switzerland for five days, and already the urge to get up into the high mountains possessed him again.

There was a rustle behind him and he turned carefully, not wanting to scare anything away. Between the trees, stone walls half buried in leaf litter started up only to end in a scatter of tumbled rocks. The air was muggy with the last of the day's heat and clouds of no-see-ums danced tirelessly under the leaves. Beyond, where sunlight slanted into a clearing of sumac and bayberry, he saw a deer step out of the shadows and start to nose at the leaves, searching for the tender roots. Suddenly it raised its head and stared in his direction, liquid nose quivering, ears twitching at the possibility of danger. Slowly he drew in another deep breath, filling his lungs with the scent of the forest.

Yes, he'd almost be willing to settle for this.

The Bernhard house was big, built on the hill above the dam, out of glass and white glazed brick. Way below, the reservoir glittered among the surrounding trees, flat as a golden coin in the setting sun.

'What a view!' Ben said when Kim opened the door to him.

'We're lucky.' Kim was a big man, with plentiful hair and an attractively creased face. Ben usually saw him wearing a hard hat and a business suit, but today he was in corduroy trousers and a rollneck cashmere sweater. 'And I knew a few people. I doubt if we'd be able to build it today, they've slapped on so many restrictions.'

'I should probably disapprove,' Ben said.

'Probably.' Kim winked. 'Come on in.' He led the way through a plant-filled atrium to a wide space which looked like a gallery. There were several velvet-covered couches in jewel colors: ruby, amethyst, topaz. The white walls were hung with paintings and marble plinths held sculptures and statuary. 'You're looking well, Ben. Very fit.'

'I've been training,' Ben said. 'I'm off climbing again soon.'

'Where this time?'

'Alaska. Climbing Denali with a couple of friends.'

'Denali?'

'Mt McKinley.'

'Is that difficult?'

'The rangers like to tell you that it's killed more climbers than the Eiger.'

'I'm surprised you haven't climbed it before.'

'I have. Twice. But both times we had to turn back before we topped out. You can get some horrendous weather up there. Conditions are often worse than at the North Pole.'

Bernhard showed him into a large room which was part office, part studio. One end was cosily masculine, carpeted in dark blue, with a desk standing in front of a booklined wall, and some leather club chairs set round a low table holding a number of specialist magazines: yachting, design, gourmet food. Architectural prints hung on the walls, interspersed with photographs of buildings which Ben guessed had been designed by Kim. At the other end of the long space, two drafting tables were set back-to-back on a riverstone floor, in front of tall windows which looked down over the dam. On an L-shaped wooden counter dividing the two halves of the room stood models of various buildings, ranging from a lakeside cottage to a shopping center.

'So, third time lucky . . .' Kim waved Ben into a leather director's chair on one side of the large desk and folded himself into a high-backed padded chair on the other.

'I hope so. It could be good experience for the future.'

'Talking of which, how exactly do you see the future?' Kim laced his hands behind his head and leaned back.

As a lifetime of climbing, Ben thought. High peaks, adventure, the purity of striving. And Lisa to come home to. What else could there be? He lifted his shoulders in a shrug. 'Other mountains.' He didn't expect a non-climber to understand.

'Right.' Bernhard stared at him with a slight smile then pushed over a roll of blueprints. 'Reason I asked you to drop by . . . here's the deal. I don't know if you can read these things, but these are some preliminary sketches for a big new winter sports center we've been commissioned to build.'

'We?'

'My firm of architects. Bernhard Associates. This is going to be a prestige commercial operation and I'm going to need all the advice I can get. Not on the bricks and mortar aspect, obviously.'

'On what, then?'

'Thing is, Ben, you're a sports-oriented guy. I'm not. Sailing, a bit of tennis, that's about my mark. Not just sports, but you're an expert in your field.'

'Not really. Just a—'

'Come on, Ben. This last year, I've had to get into the specialist magazines, including mountaineering and rock-climbing stuff, in order to have some idea of what's going to be required for this project, how best to approach it. Your name comes up all the time. Point is, I want to take advantage of your expertise.'

'Mountaineering? Is that what you're talking about?'

'That, and other things. What I'd like is to bring you in on this project by retaining you as our sports consultant. What do you say?'

Ben felt uneasy. This was exactly the kind of job Lisa had hoped he would find when they moved up here.

Bernhard gave Ben a hard stare. 'If I looked around, I'd

probably find plenty of other people who could give me the same advice as you can. But because I've worked with you before, I know you're reliable, and that you never do less than the best you're capable of – which is considerable.'

Ben hated to hear people talk about him in this way. 'Consultancy?' He couldn't help the chilly edge to his voice. 'I don't know. I'm a practical sort of person. I'm used to working with my hands, I like getting up a sweat.'

'I know that. And there'd be no reason why you'd need to give that up. But I'm pretty sure, a guy like you, you're not going to be satisfied with construction work and basic – or even skilled – carpentry for the rest of your life.' Bernhard picked up an alabaster egg which sat in front of him and held it lightly in his hand. 'Leisure time and how to fill it: that's going to be one of the major challenges of the twenty-first century. Sports centers, dedicated activity sites: there's an ever-growing demand for such places. You should tap into that. You have all the necessary qualifications – and I'm prepared to pay a generous retainer to get them.'

'I'm not interested in being stuck in an office all day.'

'Who said anything about an office? Half the time you'd be on site. Then you'd have to research other centers across the country, find out what works for them and what doesn't. If this project goes well, there'll undoubtedly be others. The people behind this have big plans – you could carve out a very nice little niche for yourself. Best of all, you'd still have the flexibility to take off for the wild blue yonder whenever you needed to.'

'I'd have to think about it.'

Kim grinned at him. 'Meaning, in your head, you've already turned the idea down.'

Ben shifted in his chair. 'Not necessarily.'

'Truth is, you'd be doing us a big favor if you came on board. It'd give us quite a lot of prestige if you were in on the project.'

'Prestige? Me?' Ben looked around as though expecting to see someone else. 'You've got the wrong guy.' Alarm bells were ringing inside his head. He could see that, on paper, what Kim was offering was perfect for him. But if he accepted Bernhard's offer, he would be allowing himself to be shackled. Because whatever Bernhard said now, how much of a free agent would he really be? He thought of the high mountains, snow pluming from the peaks like smoke in the constant winds, the bite of the air. Up there, you were responsible only to yourself. Down here, he would be accountable to God knew how many other people, all kinds of bureaucracy to deal with, paperwork, records to keep.

He shook his head. 'I'm the wrong man,' he said again.

'Think about it for a while before you decide, Ben. It could be a mutually beneficial arrangement.'

'How so?'

'Sponsorship deals for you, just for starters.'

'I'll give it some thought.' Ben pushed back his chair. 'I'd better get back.'

He drove home slowly. Lisa had told him that Mel Sherman was dropping by today and he wanted to be sure she was gone before he arrived. Women like that made him uneasy, all diamond rings and designer clothes, that brittle air of having just come from the beauty parlor. Difficult to imagine what Mel Sherman looked like first thing in the morning, with no make-up and her hair all mussed. He grinned. She probably slept with her hair in a net, the way his grandmother used to.

Not like Lisa, his gorgeous lovely Lisa. His wife. God, he was lucky. As soon as he walked into the Soho loft where he'd been invited to dinner, he'd noticed her, been mesmerized by the way her hair shone like water when she moved her head. Encountering her obsidian gaze across the table between the candle flames, a sense of recognition caught him in the pit of the stomach. Before he left that evening he'd obtained her phone number, but though he called her every day for the next week, he could never find her at home. He didn't want to leave messages on her answering machine: for all he knew, she was sitting in her apartment monitoring calls, not wanting to take one from him.

Two weeks later, as he stepped onto the Manhattan sidewalk from the construction site, he saw her coming towards him.

'Hello, Ben,' she said. She glanced at the mess of mixers and girders, rusting iron and JCBs behind him, the ten-meter rods of concrete being driven into the ground, huge bundles of timber and steel being hauled up by the tower crane high on the roof, all the chaos of a new building going up in a restricted space.

'Do you work down here?' he said.

'No. I came by because Monique told me *you* did.'

'Monique?'

'Our hostess at that dinner party,' she said. 'The painter.'

'Oh yeah . . . I don't really know her, just met her through a friend.' He moved his shoulders under his black T-shirt. She was wearing a sleeveless crimson dress and elaborate silver earrings. The color of her lipstick exactly matched her dress. There was dirt under his fingernails; when he pushed back his hard hat, he could feel the gritty cement dust in his hair, a crust of grime and sweat on his skin. He had felt gross and ungainly next to her. Delicately, afraid to sully her, he had encircled her bare

51

arm with his thumb and finger, feeling the sparrow bones under her skin. He smiled and watched her features dissolve as though she were under water.

'How are you, Ben?'

'I've called you dozens of times and you've never been in.' He put a hand against the wall to steady himself. Had she really said – or implied – that she had come all the way down here just to see him?

She rolled her eyes at him. 'Darn it. If I'd only known, I'd have cancelled everything and stayed home.'

When she smiled, the skin beneath her eyes pouched up. He couldn't remember when he had last seen anyone so beautiful, so absolutely . . . right. The future settled around his heart. 'I wanted to ask you out,' he said.

'And?'

'I still want to.'

'So what's stopping you?'

If she dropped her gaze, he thought, she would surely see his heart leaping with joy beneath his T-shirt. With more than joy. 'Will you have dinner with me?'

'Yes.'

'When?'

'How about tomorrow?'

'Tomorrow?'

One of his workmates shouted down from the scaffolding high above. Someone gave a long appreciative whistle.

Lisa glanced upwards and waved, then looked back at him. 'Or the day after.' She put her head on one side. 'Unless you're busy, of course.'

It couldn't be this easy. He'd expected her to make some vague response about next week, to say that she would call him and fix a time, and he'd never hear from her again. 'Make it tomorrow,' he said, and was surprised that his voice managed to sound so normal. He couldn't unlock his eyes from hers.

That first date, he'd picked her up from her apartment. She was wearing a turquoise silk dress with a high collar, and long turquoise earrings, jade bracelets on her slim arms. It was a cold wet evening, the pavements slick with rain, wind gusting between the buildings. They'd ended up at a small Italian restaurant; with sudden clarity, he recalled opening the door from the dark street to warmth and light, ushering her into smells of garlic and rosemary and wine, still unable to believe his luck.

He felt an enveloping sense of urgency, a compulsion to learn her. 'I want to know everything about you,' he said, across the checked tablecloth. 'Absolutely everything.'

'How long have you got?' she asked.

He reached across and took her hand. 'The rest of my life.'

She smiled. Pulled her hand away from his. Looked down at the table. 'No, really.'

'Tell me about your family.'

She shrugged. 'Not much to tell. My mom had cancer and died when I was six. And my dad: he's Chinese, and he's blind.'

'I see,' he said, not knowing how to respond, and was immediately mortified.

Then Lisa laughed. 'Which is more than Dad can do,' she said. 'Anyway, after my mom died, a cousin of my mother's came to live with us in Brooklyn. She wasn't my mom, but she acted as though she was. It was kind of disorienting for a six-year-old. I was an only child, which made it even worse.' She lifted her head and stared at him, her eyes black and profound, and he thought he could see in their depths the confused little girl she must once have been. She shrugged. 'That's *my* family. What about yours?'

53

'A brother, two parents. Very dull, really.' He felt immediately guilty. 'No, I have a great family. I love them and I'm sure they love me back.' It wasn't quite true. Ever since the accident, he'd felt that he had forfeited the right to their love.

'But . . . ?' she said.

'But what?'

'There's a skeleton in your cupboard, I can tell. What is it, a mad aunt up in the attic? A second cousin doing time in Alcatraz?'

He lifted his hands. 'No skeletons.'

'What does your father do?'

'He was a linguistics prof. He died last year. My mom's a pharmacist.'

'My dad is a piano-tuner. He's very . . . I suppose distant is the word. Or self-sufficient. Perhaps he's had to be, being blind, having to fend for himself. And for me, too, once my mom died.' She put a finger on his hand so delicately it was like air blowing over his skin. 'You're an ironworker or something, aren't you?'

'Not in any permanent sense. I do it because it pays well, gives me the freedom to do what I really want to do.'

'And what's that?' When she looked at him, he was conscious of happiness swelling under his ribs.

He smiled at her and watched her face melt. 'Climb mountains.'

'What's it like, working up there above the city?'

'Great.' He wondered how much she would understand. 'It's like climbing. You get the same feeling of exhilaration.'

'Do you need special skills?'

'A head for heights, mostly. A steady nerve. People do fall – I saw a man who fell forty stories once. Not good.' He turned his face away, remembering the pulpy look of

54

the body, orange mud pushing up between the fingers, black blood oozing from the guy's ears, mouth. The stillness was the worst thing, knowing there was nothing there, nobody left inside the T-shirt and trousers which lay spreadeagled on the ground.

'I can imagine.' Lisa shuddered.

'Even so, even though you know there's always a chance of flying – falling, that is – there's such a sense of freedom up there, such a terrific high . . .' He shook his head at her. 'I can't describe it.'

'That's something which, whatever else you do, nobody can ever take away from you,' she said quietly and he realized that she had instinctively understood all the things he hadn't said. He knew in that moment that he had to spend the rest of his life with her.

He reached across the table and took her hand. 'Tell me three things you like.'

'Yellow roses. Silver spoons. Black coffee.'

'Colored things.'

'How about you, what do you like?'

'Water. Rocks. Mountains, above everything.'

'Elemental things.'

'That's right.' He curled his hand round her small fingers. 'But I like you more than any of them.'

'Am I elemental?'

'Totally. Completely.' Laughing, he said, 'The five elements: earth, air, fire, water. And Lisa.'

Later, dropping her back at her apartment building, he said, 'Will you marry me?' He had never felt so reckless – or so sure.

She laughed too, turning her head away from him in a gesture he already coveted. 'You don't know me.'

'I know enough.'

'I don't want to get married.'

'But if you did, would you consider me?'

One hand on the door leading into the lobby of the building, she turned her head and looked at him. He could see lights reflected in her dark eyes, and a tiny double image of himself. 'Maybe,' she said.

The next day he sent her a dozen yellow roses; the day after that, a bag of coffee beans; the following week, a pair of silver spoons he had found in an antique shop in the Village.

She sent him a bottle of Evian water. And a postcard of Mt Everest. She gave him a piece of rock studded with shining crystals. They surveyed each other's terrain like explorers.

She invited him round for supper at her apartment. Bone white walls, black ash table and chairs, a black flokati rug on white-painted boards, a single red rose in a glass vase. It couldn't have been more of a contrast with his parents' overstuffed object-laden decor.

'I warn you, I can't cook anything except pasta,' she said.

'Must be your Chinese ancestry,' he said. 'My sister-in-law has this great recipe for pesto sauce. Want to try it?'

'Sure.'

'I should warn you that it's very very sexy. One mouthful, and anything could happen.'

'I'm up for that,' she said, holding his gaze with her own, breathing in through her mouth before she pressed her teeth into her lower lip and looked away.

Together they pounded up pine nuts and fresh basil, grated long strips of Parmesan cheese, added the rough green oil he had bought in the delicatessen round the corner from her place. Watching her small strong fingers peeling garlic, he was overcome with love. The aroma seemed to him the very essence of passion; he knew that he would never again smell garlic without thinking of her.

'Mmm,' she said, dipping a spoon into the oily sauce over the fettucine she cooked for them, closing her eyes in rapture. 'Oh, Ben, this is perfection. This is . . . *orgasmic*.'

'What did I tell you?'

Later, eyeing him over the rim of her wine glass, she said, 'I wonder what's going to happen.'

'How do you mean?'

'You said anything could, if we made this sauce.'

'Better believe it,' he said, his voice hoarse.

She had stuck candles into a rough stone bowl full of colored glass beads. For dessert there were ripe pears. They sat at right angles to each other, eating with their elbows on the table, gazing into each other's eyes, where reflections from the candles danced. She peeled him a pear, dipped it into her glass of white wine, held it delicately between her teeth. She moved towards him until their mouths met and he bit off the half she offered him, their lips brushing together in a frisson so delicate that it felt like the touch of a feather. Juice ran from the corner of her mouth into the hollow at the base of her neck and he leaned forward to lick it away.

She arched her neck, closing her eyes. 'Ben,' she said faintly. 'Ben . . .' Her mouth, still glistening with oil, was grave.

He flicked his tongue over her lips, tasting garlic and pear juice. 'I love you,' He took her hand and pressed it to his heart. 'For always and for ever, I love you.'

Opening her eyes, she smiled. 'Shall we go to bed?'

Lying on the hard futon which served as both couch and bed, Ben wrapped his arms round her and pulled her so hard against his chest that she gasped. 'Are you sure?' he said, lifting her little white T-shirt.

'Yes.' She fitted herself under him.

'Are you really *really* sure?'

'Absolutely.'

He had pressed his fingers against the tight bones of her back, so fragile, it seemed to him, that they would snap like breadsticks if he was too rough with her. Her hair smelled of coconut and garlic. He put his head between her small slightly asymmetrical breasts and drew the scent of her deep into himself. Under his hand, her skin had felt as soft as nectarines. She gazed at him with childlike seriousness when he came into her for the first time, catching her breath, holding him hard against her. 'Yes,' she said softly, when he came, when she came. Her smile was rapturous. 'Yes.'

He knew what she would say when he told her about Kim Bernhard's proposal. He smiled, thinking about it. She would launch herself at him, her face one big beam of delight. Fly into his arms, the bump of the baby keeping them apart, cover his face with kisses.

'Oh darling, that's *marvellous*!' she would say. 'That's *terrific*. When do you start?'

He loved her so much. He wanted to make her happy. But once he'd told her, he would have no option but to accept the job and the limitations that went along with it. Loss of freedom. Loss of the mountains. Loss of the high pure moments of achievement when he could stand above the world and know that no-one possessed him, no-one could doubt him, that for those moments, his only allegiance was to himself.

He wouldn't tell her. Not just yet. Not until he'd been up to the cabin and had a chance to think about it some more.

'Honey, I'm home,' he called in the deep voice that always made her laugh, coming in through the front door, leaving his keys on the stand in the hall. He could smell new paint, roasting chicken, fresh-baked cookies.

'Sweetie!' She stood for a moment at the door of the kitchen then ran into his arms.

There was a smudge of yellow paint on her cheek, a streak of it in her hair. He picked her up and whirled her round, then kissed her mouth. 'Oof!' he said, carefully setting her down again. 'I shan't be able to do that much longer. You weigh a ton.'

'I'm eating like a horse at the moment.' She took his hand and drew him behind her into the kitchen. She opened the refrigerator and removed a bottle of Coors. 'Here you are. Want a glass?'

He shook his head, removed the cap, raised the bottle to his lips. Pulling out a chair, he sat down at the table. 'So, how was your day?'

'Fine. I put a second coat on the baby's room. Had a nap. Made some cookies for Mel.'

'And how was she?' he asked, not really caring.

'Good. She brought this cute pair of overalls for the baby. Look . . .' She picked them up from the back of a chair and showed him.

'Very generous.'

'I know. She's almost as excited about the baby as we are. I guess – poor Mel – this is as close to having a grand-baby as she'll ever get.'

'Her husband wasn't keen on kids, is that right?'

'Or maybe she just didn't want *his* children.'

'Can't say I blame her. I used to see him up at the cabin in the summer and he always seemed to be a bit of a jerk. Don't know why she put up with him, if you want the truth, smart lady like that.'

Lisa leaned her face on her hands and wrinkled her nose at him. 'At the risk of sounding like an old

59

married couple – how was *your* day, sweetheart?'

'Great. Worked on the kitchen in that restoration I'm doing – did a great job, if I say it myself. It's going to be really something when we've finished. I love working in wood.' He reached behind him to the refrigerator and without getting up, hoicked out another Coors. 'And how are you feeling, darling?'

'Just peachy. The backache, the nausea, the heartburn – I *love* it.' She pressed her fists into the small of her back and arched her spine.

'Aren't there things to make all that easier?'

'Probably. Unless you happen to have a doctor who, whenever I mention any of that stuff, tells me it's a woman's lot.' Lisa clucked her tongue. 'Can you imagine? That is the twenty-first century, for heaven's sake.'

'Brad Patterson may be a bit old-fashioned but everybody says he's a good gynae man.'

'Yeah, well, I'll tell you right now that the second Andersen baby will be going to another doctor.'

'Next time . . . God, I hadn't thought beyond this one.'

'We want more than one, don't we?'

'Yes, but . . .' He wanted to savor this baby, this first child. 'As long as they look like you, we want dozens.' He tipped the bottle of beer towards his mouth. 'But let's get this one sorted out first, shall we?'

'I just thought that while we're at it, we might as well go for the deuce. Or even the treble.'

'At least the house is big enough.' He got up. 'What do you want me to do?'

'Make a salad. Everything else is ready.'

He kissed the top of her head. 'You are just the cutest thing I've ever seen in my entire life.'

'That's sweet of you, honey, but I caught sight of myself in the mirror when I stepped out of the shower this morning, and I know better. Swollen boobs and huge belly. I look like a sow.'

Ben tore lettuce into a bowl. 'There's not the slightest resemblance.' He reached for oil and vinegar, garlic, mustard. He pretended to examine her face. 'Except maybe just a little round the nose.'

Lisa took plates out of the rack and found cutlery. 'Thanks a lot.' She put a hand-thrown bowl of cherry tomatoes in the center of the table. 'The really great news, according to my childbirth group, is that it doesn't end after the baby arrives. Not only does it take weeks to get back into shape, but there's stretch marks and diapers and no sleep for years and years. I can't wait.'

'It'll be worth it.'

'I know that.' Lisa threw back her head and laughed. 'I can't imagine why I'm being such a grouch, when this is what I've looked forward to all my life. Being pregnant, being a mommy. All that. I've never wanted anything else, really. God, Ben our first baby . . . it's the most exciting thing in the entire world.'

'And then some.'

'Someone to love. Someone who'll love me. I know I've got you, but that's different. A baby means absolute and unconditional love. And I so much want to do all the things with her – or him – that my mom never got to do with me. Play games, walk her to school, teach her to ride a bike, tell her I love her.' She bit her lip, smiling. 'I hope I'm not going to be one of those obsessive mothers who never stops talking about how brilliant their child is – but I'm afraid I will be.' She pulled a pair of oven gloves shaped like penguins over her hands and opened the oven door. 'If I start making the baby recite poems or play its little violin for visitors, bat me round the head, won't you?' She lifted out a roasting dish and put it on the table. 'Promise.'

61

'No way. I may even start looking out for a baby-sized instrument or a book of poems next time I'm in Burlington.'

'You're going to be as bad as me.'

'Much much worse.' Ben smiled at her.

Later, they did the dishes. Lisa washed while Ben dried and put away. As the light faded from the sky, moths and mosquitoes began to tap and flutter against the window screens. In the darkening glass, he could see their reflections. A perfect domestic scene, he thought. A perfect marriage. We're set fair, the two of us. I am so damned lucky.

Chapter Four

On her way home from Lisa's place, Mel stopped by the Mayfields' house.

'Knock, knock,' she said loudly, walking into the untidy hallway, its once-polished broad-planked floor almost invisible beneath a layer of schoolbags and running shoes, piles of books and outgrown clothing which Joanne was always going to give to the Goodwill or the hospital, if she could ever find the time. A row of hooks held coats and jackets, scarves, baseball caps, a bowler hat which Tom, Joanne's eldest, had bought at a barn sale years before, backpacks, a pair of binoculars. She paused at the doorway to the living room, which smelled of burned toast and spaghetti sauce and old dog.

'Hi, Mel.' Twelve-year-old Jamie, Joanne's younger son, looked up from his book. Gargery, the family's ancient basset, lifted his head from Jamie's knee and gazed at her with mournful red-rimmed eyes.

Mel planted a kiss on top of Jamie's head, and caressed the rough spikes of his hair. 'Before I go find your mom, bring me up to speed.'

'Lucy's in her bedroom having a fit 'cause Mom won't let her go to the Prom with some guy on the softball team. Tom's out in the garage making a bomb—'

63

'A bomb?'

'Not a real one, it's for the film he's making with Lee and Sam and those guys. And Mom's in the kitchen setting fire to everything and wishing she was dead.'

'So just another day in Paradise . . .'

'You got it.'

Mel had to restrain herself from putting her arms round him and hugging him until he squeaked. 'I think I'm too old for hugs,' he'd told her last time she had tried, looking very serious. 'Though I don't expect I'd mind too much on very special occasions like Christmas or birthdays.'

'What're you reading?' she asked.

He held up his book. '*Lord of the Flies.*'

'Enjoying it?'

He pushed his round glasses further up his nose. 'I don't think enjoy is the right word,' he said. 'But it's very interesting.'

'Think you'd behave like those kids, if you were in similar circumstances?'

'Probably.'

'*Lord* means you're at L again. What's next?'

He frowned, showing the dimple in his cheek. 'I can't decide. Mom suggested *Moby Dick* or *Mansfield Park*: which would you go for?'

'*Moby Dick*, this time round. Save *Mansfield Park* for next time you get to M.'

'That's what I thought.' He looked down at the page. 'And before you ask, yes, I did offer to help Mom, and I laid the table for supper without even being told.'

'You're a star.' Mel went down the short passage which led to the kitchen at the back of the house. Joanne Mayfield, her closest friend, had lived in this big old house for the past fifteen years, ten of them without Gordon, her husband, who had moved out when Jamie was two and gone to live in Connecticut with his then personal assistant. She rapped at the open door, through which she could hear Joanne cursing loudly. 'May I come in?'

'Who is it?'

'The Wicked Witch of the West.'

'In that case, yes.'

Mel went in. 'Oh God,' groaned Joanne. 'Look at you. Thin, tanned, gorgeous. Now I feel even worse.'

Mel held out the chilled bottle of Chardonnay she had bought at the liquor store on the way over.

'On the other hand, maybe I feel better.' Joanne indicated a bottle standing on the counter. 'That one's already half empty.'

'Or still half full.'

'I'm in a half-empty mood,' said Joanne sourly.

The big old-fashioned room had such a pall of blue smoke hanging under the ceiling that Mel's eyes had begun to water. 'What happened?' she said.

'That damn toaster. I put a couple of slices of bread in and the darned thing wouldn't turn off, wouldn't pop up. By the time I thought to pull the plug out of the wall, it was like being down a coalmine in here.' Joanne wiped an arm across her forehead. 'And I've just had a humdinger of a row with Lucy about the jerk who wants to take her to the Junior Prom. I said no way, not with the reputation he's got, thank you very much, so now I've ruined my daughter's life for ever and she might as well slit her wrists since there's nothing left worth living for.'

'And I hear Tom's making a bomb in the garage.'

'That movie!' Joanne said. 'What idiot gave Sam a camcorder for his birthday? If they don't hurry up and put it to bed or can it or whatever it is they do with films, I'll be slitting my wrists too.'

Mel put the wine she had brought in the refrigerator and found herself a glass. 'Sit down for a while,' she said. 'The kids can wait for supper. And darling Jamie's laid the table for you.'

'Lucy made a salad, too. I think she was hoping to soften me up before she mentioned Hank.'

Joanne was three years older than Mel but today, in her loose shirt, worn over a droopy denim skirt and Birkenstocks, she seemed younger. Refilling her glass, she pressed her fingers against her temples. 'What a day. Apart from the spaghetti sauce which, because of the toaster, I forgot was on the stove so it burned, this morning Jamie snuck into Lucy's room to play some stupid game on her computer, which he knows he's not supposed to do, and managed to wipe out the assignment she'd been working on for the past week, so you can imagine the screaming and yelling that's been going on ever since, even before the Junior Prom came up.'

'Lucy's always had healthy lungs.'

'And Eezi-Flo tear ducts. Plus it's been one of those days at the bookshop.' Joanne shook her head. 'First Wendy took sick and couldn't come in this morning. Then there was a Grade A fuck-up over a delivery of books for the high school. And on top of that, it turned into Dissatisfied Customer Day. I had three of them ranting at me at different times, including some snotty-nosed woman who actually started screaming aloud, almost howling, if you can believe, when she found out her order hadn't arrived, even though she only came in yesterday and I told her then that the chances were pretty slim since every kid in the known universe is trying to get hold of the latest Harry Potter.' She leaned forward and scooped up a handful of nuts from an opened packet on the table. 'I know I shouldn't be eating these, after the way the Cruella De Vil who takes my exercise class stared at my thighs, but the hell with her. I deserve a spot of self-indulgence after the way she put us through it tonight.'

'You've been to your Body Shapers group, have you?'

'Can't you tell?'

'Minute I walked in.'

Joanne ran her hands over her broad hips and smiled at Mel. 'Not all of us are born a perfect size six, you know. And movie-star looks to go with.' She looked at Mel over the rim of her glass. 'Do you realize it's nearly ten years since I opened the bookstore?'

'My God, so it is. I can hardly believe it.'

'I always meant to have a party, invite everyone who's ever bought a book from me, but . . .' She shrugged. '. . . I know I won't get round to it.'

'You must. I'll help. Besides, don't forget there's a certain birthday coming up.'

'Oh Christ. Don't remind me. The Big F – that's all I need.'

'I never thought the bookshop would last so long, the number of times you've threatened to sell up and go and do something – and I quote – "really interesting" with your life,' Mel said. 'I'm really proud of you, Jo, for sticking at it, especially with the divorce and three kids and everything.'

'What *I'm* proud of is that I've managed to keep afloat – just – for so long. Ten whole years . . . wow!'

'Remember how nervous you were when you took it over from Don Cunningham?'

'Remember cleaning the crud off those acres of shelves?'

'Remember the mouse nests in the stock room?'

'And the half-chewed sandwiches hidden behind the books!'

The two of them laughed. 'I guess the poor old boy kept putting them down and then forgetting where he'd left them.'

'He wasn't that old,' Joanne said. 'In fact, if you hosed him down and spruced him up, he was quite presentable.'

'Joanne, he *smelled*.'

'It wasn't a dirty smell so much as a . . .' Joanne chose her words carefully, '. . . as an intensely male smell.'

'Oh, *please* . . .'

'I'd never have done any of it without you, you know that, don't you?' Joanne grinned. 'Ten years! Gawd, it's about time I got stuck into something else.'

'You're always saying that.'

'Maybe this time I mean it.'

'C'mon, Jo. Of course you don't. For one thing, you've only just got the bookshop the way you want it. And what about that Japanese garden you've been making at the front? If I'd had the faintest idea you were planning to move on, I certainly wouldn't have wasted so much of my free time toting bags of gravel and heaving boulders around for you.'

'Thing is, you have to reinvent yourself every now and then.' Joanne scooped up another handful of nuts and tossed them into her mouth.

'Only if you don't like what you already are.' Mel hated sudden change. 'Anyway, what would you do instead?'

'If I had the money, I'd travel. But since I don't, maybe a health-food store would be good. Butterfield could certainly use one. At the moment you have to drive twenty miles just to buy a pound of organic apples.'

'Health food?' Mel burst out laughing. 'You can't be serious.'

'Why not?'

'What in God's name do you know about healthy eating?'

'More than you imagine,' Joanne said. 'Lucy and Tom are both health freaks.'

'But the bookstore . . . People round here rely on you to tell them what to read. And what about the discussion groups? All those people travelling into town on Tuesdays and Thursdays to talk books. And your competitions. And the kids' clubs.'

'Hey, I dreamed of running my own bookstore since I was about six, even though I knew I'd never make any money at it. But it's starting to drive me crazy, what with all the competition from the chains, the Internet and so on. And I've got other dreams. Could be it's time for me to move on to the next one.' Joanne pushed her fingers through her wild hair. 'We need to live as many lives as we can.'

'One's more than enough for me.'

'Not for me, babe.'

'And your new life is *health* food?'

The door burst open and Lucy came in. Her eyes and nose were damply red. There was a backpack slung over one shoulder. 'I'm going down to Hartford to live with Dad,' she announced.

'Does he know?' Joanne asked.

'I'm not staying in this house another moment.'

'That's a shame. I thought we'd call in a pizza, since I burned the spaghetti sauce. But hey, a girl's gotta do what a girl's gotta do.' Joanne smiled at her daughter. 'I don't think Dad'll let you go to the Prom with Hank Summers, though, any more than I will. Especially after I call him and tell him about what happened to Anna Kirchner.'

'*Mom!*' Tears welled. 'You're so *mean*. Sometimes I really hate you.'

'Sorry, hon. I've met too many guys like Hank to risk my precious daughter's happiness.'

'You don't give a *rip* about my happiness – oh, hi, Mel,' Lucy said, suddenly turning back into the nicely raised adolescent she usually was. 'How's it going?'

'Just fine,' Mel said.

'I saw an article in the *New York Times* about that girl, Mirja something, you discovered,' Lucy said. 'It even mentioned you.'

'Yeah, I was pretty pleased about that.'

Lucy scowled at her mother. 'If I decided to stick around, how long before this pizza arrives?'

'You can call them yourself. It'll take them thirty, forty minutes to deliver, give me a chance to have a civilized chat with Mel. You can order whatever you like.'

'OK,' Lucy said ungraciously.

When she had gone, Mel whispered, 'What *did* happen to Anna Kirchner?'

'Basically the bastard raped her. And then insisted it was consensual. Her family're immigrants, much too embarrassed to do anything about it.'

'What a jerk.'

'Precisely.' Joanne raised her glass. 'Talking of the gallery, let's not forget that it's coming up to some kind of an anniversary too.'

'Nearly four years.'

'No thanks to your late husband.'

The two women stared at each other for a moment, then Joanne sniffed loudly. 'Face it, Mel. He wouldn't let you set up the gallery, even after you got the money from your mom. You practically had to wait until he'd died. You could have been ten years down the line by now, well on your way to bigger things than a gallery in a small town in darkest Vermont. You've got dreams too, Mel. I know you have . . .'

Yes, she had dreams. But few of them were ever likely

70

to come true. 'I guess our lives *did* kind of revolve around Eric.' She attempted a smile. 'He used to call himself the senior partner.'

'The senior fucking partner? Get a life.' Joanne eased her broad back against the wooden chair.

'Let's not go there again.' As so often recently, when Mel thought about her marriage her hands started to tremble. *I'm afraid I don't* – why did she now keep hearing her father's indifferent voice, when for years she had managed to push the incident to the back of her mind? *Do you love me, Daddy?* It was a question that expected, even demanded, the answer yes. She drank more wine, felt the cool passage of it curl around her brain.

'Time you found someone else, girl.' Joanne gave her hoarse laugh. 'Good-looking broad like you. Three years is a long time to go without.'

'How do you know I have?'

'Because you'd have told me if you were getting some.'

'Don't count on it.'

'You *would*. That's exactly why women are superior to men. Because they can *share*. *And* they live longer.'

'What's that got to do with anything?'

'It's a known fact,' Joanne said. 'Women live longer than men. Especially single ones. Because they can fart in bed if they want to. Because they can eat what they like, when they like. Because they don't have some selfish jerk constantly whining about where his clean underwear's got to. Jeez . . . When I meet a new guy, there's one thing I tell him right at the start.'

'What's that?'

'I don't do windows. Or socks. Above all, no god-damned jockey shorts.' She shook her heavy bosoms and pouted sexily. 'I'm strictly a good-time gal.'

As Mel started to laugh, wine caught in her throat,

71

came down her nose, choking her, spattering the front of her shirt.

'God,' Joanne said in mock-disgust, 'what a Martha Stewart moment *that* was.'

Mel found a tissue, wiped her eyes, her nose. Leaning across, she squeezed Joanne's hand. 'I don't know what I'd do without you. Ever the best of friends, eh Jo?'

'You said it. Or rather, Charles Dickens did.'

'Mom, does this look like a bomb?' The door from the garage was pushed open, and Tom came in, followed by three of his friends from school. 'Hi, Mel.' He held up a spherical object.

'Hi, Mrs Sherman,' chorused the others.

'Looks more like one of those bath bombs,' Lee said.

'Or a big gray tomato,' said Sam.

'More like a basketball,' the fourth boy said. 'Which is exactly what it is.'

'What do you think, Mom?'

'Honey, my Symbionese Liberation Army days are long gone. I've no idea what a bomb's supposed to look like.'

'What do *you* think, Mel?' asked Tom.

'It does look a bit like something out of a comic strip.'

'How about if you wrote BOMB on it?' said Joanne. 'Then people would know exactly what it was.'

'Oh, yeah, like Russian revolutionaries always labelled their bombs,' said Tom scornfully.

'So they wouldn't get them mixed up with their tomatoes,' said Lee.

'Or their balls,' said Sam snickering, one eye on the two women.

'Guys, we need to rethink this,' the fourth boy said. The sound of an electronic rendering of Beethoven's 'Ode to Joy' came from the pocket of his jeans. 'Oh shit, that'll be my mom wanting to know why I'm not home.'

72

'I better go too,' said Sam. He looked at Tom. 'See you later, OK?' Another cellphone rang, this one giving them a tinny burst of the Hallelujah Chorus before its owner could locate it.

'*Not* OK,' said Joanne. 'Today's a week night and you've got homework to do.'

'*Mom* . . .' Muttering and grumbling, the boys moved back into the garage, slamming the door behind them.

'I wish they wouldn't *do* that,' said Joanne, holding her head.

'It's the mobile phones welded to their ears that I can't get used to.'

'Sign of the times,' Joanne said. 'And talking of signs, how's Lisa doing?'

'I saw her this afternoon. She's a bit depressed at the moment.'

'She came into the shop the other day and bought yet another book on how to be the perfect mother. I've never seen anyone so keen to be a parent. Him too, I have to say. Little do they know what awaits them.' Joanne poured more wine into their glasses. 'God, it seems like centuries since I was that dewy-eyed.' She pushed ineffectually at her untidy hair. 'All set for Boston?'

'You bet.'

'The big kids are watching the house while I'm gone – God knows how that'll work out. And Jamie's taking the bus down to Hartford,' Joanne grimaced. 'He really misses his father at the moment.'

'He's such a sweet kid.'

'I don't know how much longer that'll be true. Did you see the zit on his chin? I fear we're moving rapidly into adolescence. The thought of going through all that again makes me shudder.'

Mel leaned back and eyed her friend. 'Ever thought of getting back together with Gordon?'

'Are you kidding?'

'You two always seem to get on really well. Better than a lot of married couples we know.'

'Living with Gordon again would be a fate only marginally better than death.'

'You know that's not true.'

Joanne gave her a sardonic look. 'I'd rather talk about the trip next week. Are we using your car this time?'

'It's more likely to get us there and back than yours is. By the way, I'm going up to the cabin the day after to-morrow. Want to come along?'

'Gaahd, no.'

'You could bring Jamie, if you like.'

'I don't.'

'It's beautiful up there, and you know it.'

'Maybe you're forgetting that last time you lured me up, there was a spider the size of the Ritz in the shower, and I was nearly chewed to death by a rabid squirrel.'

'One tiny money spider, as you very well know, and a woodchuck, which ran for its life as soon as it saw you.'

'It was probably trying to get warm.'

'There are heaters in every room, Joanne. Besides, it's June now. You'll be gasping with the heat.'

'Not in the evenings, I won't.'

'So, we'll light a fire. Joanne, *please* come with me.'

'I'll come up sometime.' Joanne saw Mel's expression and her voice softened. She put her hand over Mel's. 'Next time, sweetie. I promise. Just not this time, OK?'

But it's *this* time I want you, Mel thought. It's *this* time that I'll be lonely. This and all the other times I go up to the lake on my own. 'I'd do it for you, if you asked,' she said.

'Which just shows you're a much nicer person than I am.'

Jamie came in. 'Mom, *Friends* just came on and it's the one where Ross—'

'Yeah, yeah,' Joanne said. 'Go see if your sister called the Pizza Palace yet.'

The telephone rang. From the living room came the sound of the opening sequence of *Friends*. Gargery came lumbering in and, with a deep sigh, laid his heavy head on Mel's knee and began drooling on her chinos.

'He's totally disgusting, isn't he, poor old thing?' Joanne said.

Mel got up, trying not to look revolted. 'Time to go, I think.'

Back home, she laid a fire in the big hearth; even in summer, Vermont evenings could be chilly. She set a bowl of salad on the square coffee table, laid smoked salmon on rounds of fresh multigrain bread, put out a dish of chicken and rice. A plate, a linen napkin, cutlery. Salt and pepper. A crystal vase containing two cream-colored roses from the garden stood at one corner, the petals slowly opening in the heat.

She looked at the table with her head on one side, checking and rechecking that everything was exactly where it ought to be. Perfect. Beautiful. She picked up the fork and squinted along it, did the same with the knife. There was a faint mark on the blade and her heart began to bump apprehensively around in her chest as she guiltily rubbed at it with a paper napkin.

It would have been much easier to sit at the kitchen table and read a book while she ate. But self-sufficient though she was, she had not yet grown used to being on her own. Eric had given her a framework within which to operate. Without him, she was often seized with an uneasy sense of displacement, as though she were not quite here, as though she hung suspended between the past and the unknown future, unattached and unrooted, waiting for something to overtake her. Which was why she forced herself to continue the elaborate rituals of domestic perfection: light the fire, lay the table, keep the linen starched and the furniture polished. Pattern gave a shape to her life.

Though she enjoyed the cheerful chaos in which Joanne lived, she was always glad to return to the calm orderliness of her own house. She looked about her at the gracious well-appointed room, then stared up at the portrait above the hearth.

'I hate that thing,' Joanne had said, last time she came round. 'Talk about the Bitch Goddess from Hell. Why on earth don't you take it down?'

'That's Eric's grandmother.'

'I don't care if it's *God's* grandmother.' Joanne had raised her eyebrows. 'I hate to be the one to remind you, sweetie, but Eric is dead, and has been for over three years. Haven't you cottoned on to the fact that you're a free woman now and you can do what the hell you like? Look at this place. You haven't even shifted the furniture around, changed the drapes, *any*thing.'

'I think about it, but whenever I do, I can hear Eric disapproving.'

'Eric had a friggin' Ph.D in Disapproval.' Joanne made a face. 'I can see that the room's esthetically pleasing, a calm oasis in the midst of a busy life and all that *House & Garden* crap. But it's exactly like it was when he was alive. I always feel that any minute he's going to come through the door and start plumping up the sofa cushions, the way he used to when he wanted visitors to leave.' She shook her head. 'Pure Rip Van Winkle.'

'Sometimes I wouldn't mind going to sleep for a hundred years.'

'All you'd need then would be a handsome prince to waken you with a kiss.'

Recalling the conversation, Mel lifted a forkful of chicken and rice to her mouth and thoughtfully chewed it. Joanne was right: the portrait was hideous. But keeping things as they were was a way of holding back the chaos which she felt might otherwise overwhelm her. She glanced at *First Love*, the rosewood statue in its place between the windows. For reasons he had been unable to articulate, Eric had disliked it and until his death she had kept it in one of the guest bedrooms. Now, it offered her a kind of solace.

She went to bed early. Over the past few weeks, she had found it increasingly difficult to sleep. When she did so, she dreamed of tears and ice and dark wings beating, of time passing, of an anonymous and overwhelming despair. Waking, she would recall Galen's night-time terrors. Was this what it had been like for him? Had he too been beset by black dreams which wove through his mind like ribbons? Perhaps if she had been able to love him less and understand him more, they would still have been together.

In the darkness beyond her windows, she could hear the wind sighing through the branches of the apple tree and the occasional thud as unripe fruit dropped to the ground. The sound reminded her of visits to her grandparents' farm in Maine. She had always appreciated the ceremonious way each season embraced its own rituals, required its own observances: the birthing of lambs, the planting of vegetables, picking fruit to put up as preserves, drying lavender for the ribbon-tied muslin bags her grandmother made afresh each year. Ritual meant order, and in order, she had understood even then, lay safety.

Her life now was ordered too. Neat and tidy. She had a home, good friends, a successful business. Listening to the wind, she wondered why, in that case, she so often felt like breaking down and weeping, why she was consumed by a corrosive sense of waste.

CHAPTER FIVE

Another sleepless night.

In the end, it was easier to get up than to toss and turn. Having dressed quickly, Mel balanced on her hip the box of groceries she had packed the previous night and picked up the black leather backpack waiting by the back door, took them out to the car. It was cold, and still dark. Shivering, she set off for the lake, wishing she had been able to persuade Joanne to come along.

It was not until she turned off the highway onto the country roads that the sky began to lighten. By the time she was inching the car down the narrow track towards the cabin, the lake was like a pool of fire, reflecting the rising sun.

Because of her preoccupation with the Koslowski exhibition, this was the first time that she had been up here since the spring, and she wrinkled her nose at the musty neglected smell of the place. Everything was covered in dust, there were cobwebs in the corners, stray feathers and dead leaves had blown through from the deck out in back. But beyond the high floor-to-ceiling windows, the world looked fresh and clean. The lake shimmered, swallows skimmed the surface of the water, and the line of trees on the further shore was very green.

Mel opened all the windows and doors to let in the fresh air, took the rugs outside and hung them over the deck rail, began to sweep and dust. She swilled a selection of dead insects down the kitchen sink, polished the wooden furniture, picked an armful of lilac branches from the straggling bush which grew under the windows on one side of the cabin, and set them in a heavy earthenware pot.

It had originally been a poky little guest annexe for the Andersen house next door, but Eric had had the place completely gutted and extended. The roof had been heightened so that now the great room soared like the nave of a church towards heavy timber cross-beams thirty feet above the ground. Two large squashy sofas, covered with cheap Indian-cotton spreads, dominated the floor. Between them and the raised hearth was a low table made from a slab of cherrywood. A long run of shelves covered the lower part of one timbered wall and held an eclectic mix of books, lake-washed stones, photographs, ceramics, carved wooden bowls. The scent of woodsmoke permeated the air.

Cleaning ashes out of the big fireplace, Mel knocked over a glass bowl full of pine cones which stood on the stone hearth. Before she could grab it, the bowl had fallen and broken, scattering pine cones and dozens of glass fragments across the polished floor. She felt herself flush: Eric would be furious. Eric would be— but Eric was no longer here, could not heap blame and criticism upon her, could not make her suffer the withdrawal of his love before finally offering forgiveness. Picking up the pieces, she remembered, as sharply clear as though it had been that same morning, how he had bought the bowl in Venice, on their honeymoon. He had looked at dozens before finally settling on one, haggling about the price, being embarrassing.

'It's for you, darling,' he had said, when the purchase was finally completed. 'For us, for our house.' He had beamed at her and because the transaction had taken so long, she did not like to say that actually she preferred the bowl streaked with blue and red, rather than this muddy brown and green one. Often she had wondered if that honeymoon had set the shape of their marriage: wondered, too, why she had found it so difficult to speak up, to indicate in various different ways that she had a point of view, a mind of her own, a set of personal criteria. Perhaps because of the age gap between them, almost from the beginning their relationship had resembled that of parent and wayward child. *Do you love me, Daddy? I've been a good girl, Daddy* . . .

Suddenly, she was weeping. She pressed the palms of her hands to her face. How had it come about that so much of their married life had consisted of Eric leading and her following? What had happened to that fine strong feeling of being in control which had seized her as she signed her check for the house on Maple Street? She had felt certain then that, after so much loss, there would finally be gain. And there had been. Yes, there had. Eric, Joanne, Lisa, the gallery . . .

Bittersweet, unbidden, another memory from their honeymoon came back to her. Her younger self, leaning from the window of their hotel overlooking a small canal, Eric only half awake in the bed behind her, the smell of decay. A young man stepping from the shadows on the other side, walking across the bridge which spanned the narrow waterway below her. Some movement must have caught his attention; looking up, he had smiled, lifting a hand, beckoning to her, calling, *'Ciao, bella!'* She remembered it still, the softness of the morning air, the piercing sense of standing on the threshold of something

81

splendid, the knowledge that it was there for her to reach out and touch. His crisp hair. The whiteness of his shirt. She had been seized with the absurd desire to run after him, to link her arm in his and go with him. Then Eric had called sleepily from the bed, telling her to shut the window, he was cold, and she had turned away.

The first time she had come up to the lake after Eric's death, she had still been trying to come to terms with his absence. So much of him was here: books, clothes, fishing tackle, wet-weather gear. Beer steins and matchbooks, unfamiliar underwear, ancient sweatshirts and even a curious tweed hat with a feather in the brim which she had never seen before and could not imagine him wearing. During the first days of her widowhood, she could fix on nothing except the fact that he was dead. Even the simple act of brushing her hair or lifting a cup of coffee seemed too much for her. Because it felt frivolous, even sinful, to swallow food, she had been resentful of the way her body continued to need sustenance, and tried to deny it.

Eventually Joanne, armed with tissues and whisky, had taken the initiative. In the days prior to the funeral, she fielded telephone calls and discussed with the minister the hymns to be sung and which friends should be asked to deliver eulogies and readings. On Mel's behalf, she accepted the pies and dishes and bowls of salad which friends and neighbors brought to the door, talked soothingly to them as they stood there awkward or distressed.

It was Joanne who drove her to the funeral service and sat beside her in the front pew. Held her hand. Guided her into throwing the first clod of earth onto the descending coffin. Stood at her side afterwards, whispered encouragement while people mouthed kind meaningless platitudes.

It was Joanne, too, who packed up Eric's clothes, removed his shaving things from their bathroom, took away the leather toilet bag, the bottles of aftershave and Floris cologne, the feathered hat, the many pairs of hand-made shoes. She put into boxes his walking boots, the albums of childhood photographs, the pipe racks and college-crested humidor, the pair of silver-initialled ivory-backed hairbrushes which Mel had given him as a wedding present, the useless necessary paraphernalia of a life.

'I wouldn't be able to manage without you,' Mel said weakly.

'Of course you would,' Joanne said.

She had listened patiently as Mel talked about Eric. 'We had a good marriage,' Mel said, over and over. 'A wonderful marriage.'

'You were a great couple, honey.'

Mel began to weep again. 'How shall I cope on my own?'

'You have to carry on with your life,' Joanne held her close. 'You can't change anything. You can't bring him back. Sounds harsh, sweetie, but there's nothing else you *can* do except move on.'

'I can't imagine life without him,' Mel moaned.

'You've got the gallery,' said Joanne. 'You've got me.'

Mel smiled tearfully.

'What are you going to do about the cabin?' Joanne asked.

'I don't know.'

'Why don't you go up there? Take a break for a few days.'

'It was Eric's cabin, not mine,' Mel said, and realized how silly that sounded. And even as she spoke, she had envisaged space, distance, rocks and water, green trees pushing skywards, and big birds flapping under the winter sun. Up by the lake, there would be room to think. Room to put herself back together. 'I don't want to go up there without him.'

'Don't be such a wuss,' Joanne had said, finally losing patience, and her sudden irritation had mobilized Mel where sympathy had not.

Ben was down by the shore, cementing in the last of the flat pieces of stone which he was laying to form a little terrace at the water's edge. This place was so full of memories for him that it was impossible not to remember the ghosts. How it had once been. The weekends, the barbecues, the laughter. And how abruptly it had all come to an end.

He straightened up, his back muscles tense from bending over.

Don't think about that.

Think instead about the baby.

Sometimes he was almost overwhelmed by Lisa's pregnancy. He couldn't properly absorb the fact of what lay inside the frail walls of her stomach. When he felt the fluttering kicks, the sudden movements, he found it hard to believe that they belonged to another individual. A separate person. His child. It still astonished him that out of the act of lovemaking, someone else would emerge. He longed for that moment. He was impatient for their new life to begin, yet at the same time he was scared. Lisa seemed instinctively to know what she was doing, what her role was. All he could do was watch the gradual unfolding of a chain of events over which he had not the slightest control.

He'd not imagined that Lisa would get pregnant so soon. There'd always seemed to be time for that later, somewhere in a vague future. But in four months from now, they would never again be just two: they would become three. For always. The demands they made on each other would be different. They would become different people. Parents. Not individuals, but part of a family.

He carried over another spadeful of cement and tamped it down between the flat rocks. Fitting the stone flags together, smoothing the cement, soothed as always by using his hands, he envisaged his child – *their* child – leaping into the lake, the way he and Rory used to, the water pluming above his head, sinking down, down through the green to the lake bottom, water bubbling round him, the pressure on his ears, and each time the tiny thrill of fear that he would never float up to the surface again, before bursting free, the sun warm on his wet head, the kids shrieking, his father throwing a ball, Mom and Aunt Evie waving from the porch, holding up a pitcher of home-made lemonade, the pearly opacity of it, slices of lemon floating on top, sprigs of mint from the herb bed beside the house, sugar slowly settling at the bottom of the tall glasses. Such golden days, such long heedless hours, edged with heat and idleness and the knowledge that school was out and summer would last for ever.

He loaded one last trowelful of cement and wedged it between the rocks. Standing at the water's edge, he looked across to the wooded shore on the far side. There was movement at the corner of his eye and, turning his head, he saw Mel Sherman wading in the water. Fuck. It was too late to pretend he hadn't seen her.

'Hi,' she called.

It was an effort to answer. 'Hi.' If his voice sounded false and unwelcoming, too bad. That was how he felt.

She'd tied her hair into a knot on the top of her head. The first time he'd seen her, he'd thought it was white until he'd seen it in the light, the palest of golds, the precise color of corn silk. She waded towards him, up to her knees in the lake.

'Water's cold,' she said.

'Hasn't heated up yet.'

'Never does,' she said. 'I didn't realize you were going to be here.'

'Lisa's visiting her father.' He stared at her for a moment. 'Guess I'd better go in, take a shower.'

'Me too. I've been for a hike and thought I'd cool off in the lake, but it's much too cold for swimming.'

'Right.' He lifted a hand and walked up to the house. Later, he decided, he would sit on the porch with a glass of wine and start psyching himself up for Alaska. Lisa was driving up the day after tomorrow – meanwhile, it had become part of his ritual of preparation before a big climb to spend a couple of days up here alone. Go over his arrangements again. And again. Check it all out in his mind before he got to the mountain. And check it again.

It was shady in the house, the rooms quiet in the warm hush before evening closed in. Ben smelled the familiar scent of the place: old wood, lake water, garlic, ash, the ghosts of a thousand shared meals. He had been coming here for as long as he could remember: he imagined he would continue to do so for the rest of his life.

Lying in the hammock strung up on the porch, his thoughts drifted between past and present. Denali would be a big climb, and a hard one. Their third attempt. For Joe's sake, he hoped they managed to top out this time. He drank from his glass of lemonade, chewed on the sprig of mint he'd added, the way his mother always used to, when they were young. The scent of pine mingled with the smell of the rosemary bush, laden now with flowers the color of butterflies. His father had planted it years ago and the pungent, almost aggressive odor had become part of the summer. '*There's rosemary*,' Dad had said, staring at them all, his gaze lingering longest on Ben. '*That's for remembrance.*'

Ben thought of Aunt Evie, hippie, flower child, bangles and beads, a scarf tied round her flowing hair, the scent of marijuana in her skirts. Half a lifetime away – and yet it still felt as though it had been only yesterday. He supposed that he would never stop missing Rory, his bright, clever, good-at-everything cousin, always laughing, one of those kids that everyone loved. Nobody knew who his father was – and nobody ever asked.

They'd done everything together. Neil was older and had other friends in the neighborhood, but all summer long, Ben and Rory were inseparable. He remembered grabbing handfuls of cornflakes from the cereal box, the sun coming in through the kitchen window and turning Rory's copper hair into fire, the adults down by the water, the feel of a whole summer day in front of them.

And then their birthdays, his and Rory's, a week apart. They'd always celebrated together, midway between the two. The summer they turned twelve, they'd both been given mountain bikes. There'd been cake and candles, barbecued chicken and hot dogs, Mom's homemade ice cream, the whole family singing Happy Birthday, Aunt Evie dancing barefoot on the deck, a glass of wine in her hand.

He felt the familiar tremor of disaster. Rory in front of him, freewheeling down the hill, hands in the air like a competitor in the Tour de France, yellow top, black cycling shorts, green bike, rounding the turn at the foot of Windrock Hill, his own voice screaming to take care, be careful, screech of brakes, tinkle of glass, a horn blaring, knowing already, as he came to the bend, what he would find. Oh God, it had been so awful, blood everywhere,

Rory lying at the edge of the road, his . . . his *brains*, and the driver of the truck bending over him, and the terrible heart-tearing knowledge that Rory was dead.

It wasn't his fault. Mom and Dad had told him so, over and over. 'It wasn't your fault, Ben. You're not to blame yourself.' They'd sent him to someone, a grief counselor, who'd said the same thing. But he knew better. He was supposed to look out for Rory. And he hadn't.

When he'd told Lisa about it, she'd asked him if he'd cried, and he had laughed. 'Big boys don't cry,' he'd said wryly. 'That's what my father used to tell us when we were kids.'

You don't cry, not even when your best friend, your cousin, has died. Unless you're alone, in bed huddled under the covers in the dark. Once Neil had climbed into his bunk and held him awkwardly, had repeated that it wasn't his fault, Rory had never done what he was supposed to. He could still remember the shape of his brother's bony chest against his back.

There was nothing he could do to change what had happened. He knew that. He'd gone over it a thousand times. Ten thousand times. It hadn't been his fault. Except that he could not free himself from the conviction that if he looked hard enough, he would find the clue, the key, the one essential detail which could – *would* – have made all the difference.

The water was as flat as a mirror when Mel stepped out onto the deck the following morning. Under her bare feet the wooden boards were cool, pearled with dew; the early sun was still hidden behind light clouds, turning the lake the color of ashes. Heat and humidity were already thickening the air, although there were still faint streamers of mist above the surface of the lake. She looked to her left

88

across the stretch of stony grass and pine-needled forest floor separating her from the Andersen house. Beyond it, the lake opened out and the mountains thrust into the sky. Although the sun was not yet shining here, shafts of light illuminated the higher slopes.

She dressed in soft jogging pants, a cotton singlet, a fleece. Pulled her hair into a band to keep it off her neck. Laced up her hiking boots, filled her day pack with a waterproof jacket, water in a plastic bottle, a couple of apples, some dried figs and a candy bar, then set off up the steep track which led away from the lake and up the side of the hill.

Two hours later, she was clear of the trees and had come out at the top of Fitch's Gulley. From here, she could see the hills spreading away from her, green blending to hazy blue and topaz before merging with a golden sky. She was sweating after the upward hike; her body felt loose and easy. And alive. She put her hands on her hips and breathed in the sharp clear air. A long way below her she could hear voices. She hoped no-one would appear, obliging her to smile at them, speak. She had come here for solitude, not to be sociable. Taking one last deep breath, she set off along the stony track which led further across the ridge of the hill. The going was rougher here and she had to watch her step: it would be all too easy to twist an ankle or damage a knee.

By the time she reached the big boulders which marked the summit of the notch, the sun was high, and the clouds had drifted onwards, leaving the sky empty and blue. Water trickled over rocks somewhere among the trees; a hawk circled overhead, uttering harsh sounds. Otherwise it was silent. She sat down with her back against a boulder and closed her eyes. Up here, alone, there was a chance to look inside oneself. Lisa had once said about Ben: *up in the high mountains, he knows exactly who he is*. Yes, Mel could appreciate how that could be.

Peace settled on her. She could have sat there for ever, forgotten her responsibilities, turned into a rock or a tree. And then, when she was almost asleep, she heard someone jogging up the track, feet pounding, breathing harsh. Frowning, she opened her eyes and saw Ben Andersen staring at her, annoyance clear on his face.

'How did you get here?' he asked.

'The same way as you did, I imagine.' She too was annoyed, hoping he would go.

'I hadn't figured you for—' He stopped.

'For what? The outdoorsy kind?'

'That's not what I was going to say.'

'Or did you think I wasn't fit enough?' Mel got to her feet.

You'd love him if you got to know him, Lisa had said. Yeah, right. Someone who clearly thought that anyone over forty was overdue for a retirement home? She tightened the band round the plume of hair at the back of her head, picked up her water bottle, tilted it to her lips. She swallowed, felt chilly drops rolls slowly down her neck onto the exposed skin above her breasts. She stared at Ben, matching his hostile glance with her own. 'Guess I'll start back,' she said.

As she passed him, she waved her fingers. 'See you.'

When she reached Fitch's Gulley, there was no sign of anyone else. She swung down the track, enjoying the looseness of the muscles under her skin, the easy way her long legs moved to the rhythm of her stride. She was halfway down to lake level when she turned a bend and saw ahead of her a woman and two little kids. As Mel drew nearer, the smaller one suddenly tripped and fell awkwardly onto his arm. For a moment there was silence,

90

then he started to howl while his mother tried to calm him.

Mel hurried closer. 'Anything I can do?' she asked.

'I don't know.' The woman looked distressed. The kid was screaming at the top of his voice. 'Sssh, Timmy, let me see what you've done.' She took hold of his arm. 'Looks like he's sprained his wrist.'

'It does seem a bit swollen,' Mel said. The wrist was bluey-white now, and limp.

'Or maybe even broken it.'

'Fingers *hurt*,' sobbed Timmy.

His mother retrieved a cellphone from her pocket and began jabbing at the numbers. 'I'll try to get hold of my husband, he's fishing down at the dock in Hallams Cove.'

Timmy went on screaming, his small body shaking with sobs which were growing more hysterical by the second.

'It doesn't seem too serious,' Mel said, keeping her voice calm. She looked back up the track, wondering if Ben would be taking this same path down. He might have a better idea of what to do.

'I'm always meaning to take a course in first aid,' said Timmy's mother, 'but I never seem to get round to it.'

'I could run and find Daddy,' the elder boy said. 'I'm good at running.'

'Best to stay with me, hon.' His mother bent over Timmy. 'You can walk OK, can't you?'

He nodded, his sobs winding down a little, becoming tearful gasps. 'But it *hurts* . . .'

'I'll come with you,' said Mel. 'I could drive you to Hallams Cove so you can find your husband. It might be a good idea to see a doctor.'

'Hopefully it's just a sprain,' said the woman.

To Mel's relief, Ben Andersen appeared further up the track. He stopped at the sight of them, frowning, then came quickly towards them. Running on the spot, assessing the situation, he ignored Mel, his eyes flicking from the mother to her sons. He smiled at Timmy. 'Looks like someone had a bit of an accident here.'

'I fell over,' Timmy said.

'What's your name?'

'T-Tim.'

'What'd you do, Tim? Trip over an ant?'

'*No*.' Timmy spoke on a burst of breath, insulted that anyone should think a big boy like him would be so dumb. 'There was this rock . . .'

'He put out his arm to stop himself falling,' explained his mother.

'Bang your head too, did you?'

Timmy shook his head.

'Mind if I take a look?' As he spoke, Ben gently grasped the little boy's wrist in his big palm. 'Can you feel that?'

Timmy nodded.

'Want to wriggle those fingers for me?'

Gingerly Timmy did so, anticipating pain. 'My arm hurts.'

'I'm not surprised, a knock like that.' Ben touched the swollen skin of the little wrist, watching the boy wince. 'Know what time it is when your clock strikes thirteen?'

'What?' Despite himself, Timmy was interested.

'Time to get a new clock.'

'I know a better one than that,' said Timmy's brother. 'Why did the kangaroo get arrested?'

'Why?' Ben said, touching each of Timmy's fingers in turn.

'Because it kept jumping the lights.'

'What's warm and yellow and very dangerous?' said Timmy quickly, the wrist temporarily forgotten.

'Shark-infested custard,' Timmy's brother said. 'Everyone knows that one.'

'I didn't,' said Ben. He looked at the mother. 'We need to splint the wrist – it's almost certainly fractured – and get him to the casualty department of the local hospital. Until then, you should keep Tim quiet – if that's possible – and go on checking his hand for sensation and movement until a doctor's seen him.'

'Lord,' said the woman. 'All he did was trip over a stone . . .'

Ben looked down at Timmy's brother. 'Want to help me find a couple of straight sticks so we can keep Tim's wrist safe till he gets to the hospital?'

'You bet!' The older boy was excited. He joined Ben in searching through the undergrowth at the side of the track.

'That's a big help,' Ben said. 'Tim's lucky to have a big brother like you.'

'Am not,' Timmy said, but without conviction. By now he had stopped crying.

Ben strapped up his forearm with a roll of bandage from his rucksack, then hoisted him onto his shoulders. 'You'll be fine,' he said. 'Just won't be able to go swimming for a while.'

'I hate swimming,' Tim said.

'That's OK, then.'

Once the little family had been dispatched, Mel had no choice but to walk back to the cabin with Ben at her side.

'You were really great with that kid,' she said.

Ben grunted.

'He almost forgot he'd hurt himself.'

'If they're not seriously injured, kids are pretty easy to distract.'

'You've obviously had some experience.'

'I've got two nephews.'

Where their paths diverged, he nodded at her and walked away to his mother's house without speaking or looking back.

'Ben . . . ?'

He looked up with annoyance. She was standing at the foot of the steps up to the porch, wearing crisp white linen shorts and a rose-colored blouse.

'Hi,' he said, conscious of the fact that his singlet was torn and faded, and there was a rip in his cut-offs.

'Um . . .' She raised a hand to smooth her already smooth hair. The sapphire ring she wore was the same color as her eyes. 'Uh . . . I brought a steak up from town with me, but there's far too much for one person. If you haven't got other plans, I could cook supper for you.'

No, was his first thought. I don't want to waste my time making polite conversation about nothing in particular. You're not my sort and I'm not yours. But sensing, to his surprise, something needy about her, something unsure, he hesitated for a fraction too long and then it was too late to make an excuse, even though she'd given him the opportunity. 'OK,' he said ungraciously. And then, belatedly, 'Thank you.'

'In about an hour?' She put her head on one side, the pale hair falling across her cheek to reveal neat pearl studs in her ears. He remembered the slow slide of the water-drops down her neck, the way they had lingered on her sunburned skin.

'I'll bring a bottle,' he said. Dammit. He'd have to change before he went over.

'Just come as you are,' she said, then walked away between the trees.

*　*　*

Putting together a salad, placing baking potatoes in the oven, Mel wondered what on earth had possessed her. The challenge, perhaps. Or a sense of duty to Lisa – in which case, why hadn't she simply suggested that he come over for a drink? But if she was honest, she knew she needed company. Someone with whom to pass the time. Someone who would, even if only for a little while, give her a break from regret.

You'd love him if you got to know him . . . I don't think so. She could not imagine anything she wanted to do less, right then, than to eat dinner with dour Ben Andersen. Especially when she had come up here for some peace. Apart from anything else, he seemed incapable of forming sentences of more than three words. Maybe he wouldn't stay too long. Maybe she could get him talking about mountains, pass the time that way.

What a waste of an evening. He pulled his least un-crumpled polo shirt over his head, found a pair of reasonably clean jeans. Walking across to the Sherman place, he decided that if he could get her talking about her art gallery, he could sit and look interested and let his mind wander.

He walked along the deck and stepped through the open glass doors into the great room. 'Wow!' he said, his bad mood abruptly forgotten.

She was at the kitchen worktop, holding a glass of wine in her hand. 'Like it?'

He stared up at the roof beams thirty feet above his head. 'This is fantastic. Amazing. When I was a kid, this was just a cramped little overflow guest cabin.' Sometimes, on warm midsummer nights, his mother and aunt had allowed him and Neil and Rory to sleep here: he recalled that strange and dangerous feeling of separation, the adults in one house, the three boys alone over here, while the night grew darker and things began to shriek and howl in the woods or on the lake.

'My husband called in an architect,' Mel said. She gestured at her glass. 'Wine? Beer? Something stronger?'

'Beer is fine.'

'It's in the fridge. Help yourself.' She pointed. 'How do you like your steak?'

'Medium rare.' Holding the cold bottle in his hand, he stood on the deck, looking at the water. The sun was sinking behind the hills in a blaze of vermilion and gold. Near to the shore, a pair of loons were bobbing and diving in and out of water the color of flamingo feathers. Further out was the black shape of a boat with a hunched figure holding a line. He remembered other summers, him and Rory fishing for the eels which were supposed to lurk in their thousands just below the surface. Never did catch one, but it was fun trying. And the sound of music drifting towards them from the house, Dad sitting on the porch steps with a pipe in his mouth, reading the paper, Mom and Aunt Evie laughing in the kitchen. Scenes from a life which had abruptly slipped away from him.

'May I look round?' he said.

'Of course.'

He started up the stairs, scarcely recognizing the space above. The room where he and Neil and Rory used to shudder with delicious fear as the night sounds began was now a sleeping platform, divided from the great room by a railing of finely turned full-bellied balustrades, each one individual, each made of a different wood: maple, butternut, oak, hornbeam, hickory, yew, others he didn't recognize.

'Beautiful, aren't they?' she said. She was standing by the big hearth, watching him.

'Where did you get them?'

'I had them specially made. Originally there was just a pine rail there, but a year or so ago I came across this man, a superb craftsman, an artist, really. He carved them for me.'

He reached out to caress the smoothly polished surfaces. I could have made those, he thought.

'I love the way he's brought out the different grains, don't you?' Her voice sounded different now, eager and unguarded. 'I was lucky that he had access to supplies from a timber merchant who specialized in imported woods. Rosewood, amboyna, cedar – such lovely names.' She walked across the room and stood below him on the bottom step, her pale hair gleaming like an unfamiliar flower in the gathering dusk. She had changed into a blue linen shirt and a string of pearls that seemed to be the same color as her hair. He was embarrassed by her beauty.

'I've been trying to persuade him to do some pieces for my gallery.' She held up a glass of wine and he saw the ruby glow of it in the light from the tall thin candles she'd put on the table behind her. 'Wine with your steak? Or will you stick with the beer?'

'Wine would be good.'

'OK. Supper's ready when you are.'

Reluctantly he came down to her level. She'd made some kind of peppery sauce to go with the steak, sprinkled chopped chives over the potatoes. He was aware of a grace in her, an absolute need for even the simple things to be right. To be perfect.

He could not think of a single thing to say.

When he had gone, moving through the trees towards the

97

light burning in the living room of his own place, Mel went up to the bedroom platform feeling exhausted. He had insisted on helping with the dishes, he had made coffee, he had been perfectly pleasant, managed to keep the conversation going. But she hoped she would not have to spend too long alone with him again. He only seemed to lose his inward gaze when he spoke of Lisa and the coming baby. There, at least, they had found common ground.

She sighed. If she had not seen the way he dealt with Timmy's broken wrist, she would have found Lisa's choice of husband almost inexplicable. And yet, at the same time, she would have said that there was something haunted about him. It occurred to her that, locked away inside him, an entirely different person might be waiting for release.

CHAPTER SIX

He stood at the bottom of the back steps and watched Lisa for a moment. Lying in the big old hammock strung across the porch, she wore her usual brilliant palette of colors: yellow shorts and a bright blue cotton smock, a green scarf tied round her black hair. Such a contrast to Mel Sherman's pearls and neatly pressed shorts. One bare foot rested on the floorboards, the toenails a dark silvery blue which shimmered against her tan. The muscles in her slim brown leg alternately flexed and relaxed as she pushed herself back and forth.

Her eyes were closed: he wondered if she had managed to sleep a little. She and the baby inside her. Did babies sleep when their mothers did? He remembered his father bringing the hammock home from the chandler's store in Hallams Cove, screwing in the big hooks from which it swung, one into the pale blue siding of the house (Williamsburg blue, his mother called it) and the second into one of the upright posts, and how the three boys had squabbled over who got to be the first to try it out.

'Neil gets first dibs, because he's the eldest,' his father had finally decreed, 'then Ben. And Rory last, because he's the youngest.'

'That's not fair,' ten-year-old Ben had protested, and

99

Rory chimed in, 'especially when it's not our fault we're younger than Neil.'

'I agree.' Professor Andersen had smiled at his children. 'Which is why Neil goes first, but Ben gets longer in the hammock.'

Ben had thought this one through and nodded. 'Neat,' he said, making a face at Neil.

'What about me?' Rory demanded.

'You get a longer turn than Ben.'

'That's not fair,' said Ben immediately.

'That's *definitely* not fair,' Neil had said, his breaking voice hoarse with indignation. 'It's not *my* fault I was born first.'

'Those are my terms. Take them or leave them.'

'Otherwise that hammock's going right back to the store,' added their mother, though nobody believed her for a moment.

The blue paint had long since faded to a dull grey, the hooks had rusted, but the holiday house was otherwise little changed and the hammock still swung where it had twenty years before.

He whispered Lisa's name, and she opened her eyes. Sweat glistened on her upper lip and rounded cheekbones.

'Hi,' he said.

She turned her gaze to him. 'Hi, darling. Had a nice day?'

He nodded. 'But it's good to be back.' He smiled at her.

'God, you're beautiful.' Her voice was still edged with sleep.

'You too.' He reached for her hand and held it against his cheek. The heat hung above them, trapped in the spider webs draped over the wooden planks of the porch roof. 'How come your fingers are so cold?'

'Poor circulation.'

'I'm going to wash up,' he said. 'Then get a drink. Want anything?'

'Iced tea, please. There's a pitcher in the icebox.' She smiled at him tiredly. 'A stiff martini would be a lot more fun, but hey, I'm pregnant.'

'I'll have iced tea too, keep you company.'

'That's sweet of you, darling, but you know you hate the stuff. Have your usual martini.'

'I'll wave it under your nose – or would that be too sadistic?'

'It would, but do it anyway. It's as near as I'm going to get to alcohol for a while.' When she smiled, coffee-colored shadows pouched beneath her eyes.

He pushed a Frank Sinatra CD into the player and stood for a moment listening as the music washed against the wooden walls, the comfortable time-worn furniture, the beamed ceiling. He took bottles out of the refrigerator and fixed himself a drink, then poured iced tea into a glass, added a lemon slice and a sprig of mint. Handing it to Lisa, he sat down in one of the battered wicker rocking chairs which furnished the porch.

The two of them watched the water turn golden and then orange as the sun sank behind the mountains; in the house, Sinatra sang of love. Ben stared at the softly moving water. 'Isn't it beautiful?' he said.

'Isn't it *dead*?'

It was an old argument between them. 'Would you honestly rather have the big city than this?' he said.

'Where's the excitement? The energy? In New York, we used to be out every night, at the theatre or the movies or meeting friends or going to concerts or just hanging out, watching the world go by.'

'We never had time to be still.'

'Honey, I'm twenty-six. I don't *want* to be still. There's

101

time enough for that when I'm *old*. At the moment I want to be out there, living my life, not moldering in some rural backwater.'

'*This* is life,' he said, bewildered.

"If you're dead from the neck up, I guess it is. I want to be with my friends, with people who can talk, people who *do* things, people who're in touch with what's happening, who don't give a damn whether the weather's hotter this fall than last or how the rutabaga crop is doing.' Her voice softened and she reached a hand towards him. 'Sorry, sweetheart. I'm feeling kind of cranky.'

'Are you sure you're OK?'

'Fine. I'm fine. Tired, that's all.'

'I hope you haven't been overdoing it.'

'I promise you I've never been so lazy in my entire life.' She yawned, delicate as a mouse.

'As long as you aren't working too hard.'

'Honey. I'm *OK*.'

'We don't want to take any risks.'

'As if I would.' She shook her glass so the ice cubes rattled thickly against the side. 'The only thing I wish now is that you could find some kind of job that would really use your skills.'

Now was the moment to tell her about Kim Bernhard's offer. Ben opened his mouth to say that it looked like the very job she had in mind had just fallen into his lap. But if he told her, and then decided not to take up the offer, she might find it hard to forgive him. Much better to think about it for a while longer, then tell her. Or not.

'I hoped we'd have more time to spend together,' she was saying. 'But you're away climbing just as much as you ever were. If not more.'

'Climbing's what I *do*.'

'It doesn't have to be.'

He took a deep breath. 'I've told you I'd stop climbing if you asked me to.' He wanted to mean what he said, but he knew he did not.

'It has to be your decision, not mine.'

'I hate it when we argue.'

'Me too.' She sighed. 'I can't wait for the baby to come, but sometimes I wish there had been more time for us to be just the two of us, to *learn* each other.'

It was exactly what he had thought when she told him she was pregnant, and what, despite the rush of excitement which hit him whenever he visualized the baby, he still thought.

'I've been happy from the first moment I saw you,' he said quietly.

'Thing is,' she said, 'before I was pregnant, I didn't mind you going away. I mean, I did, of course I did, I missed you and worried about you, but it . . . didn't matter so much. Now . . .' She laid a hand over her tight belly. 'Now it does.'

Pinpricks of light were beginning to appear between the trees, their long bright reflections glinting across the dark water. He went and knelt beside her. 'Lisa, I mean it. If you want me to stop climbing, I will.'

She ruffled his hair. 'What? Give up all that challenge and adventure? All that dicing with death?'

'Yes,' he said, intrepidly, hoping he sounded as though he meant it. 'Except . . .'

'Except what?'

'I don't think I could ever drop it entirely.'

'I don't think I'd ever want you to.'

'I wish I wasn't going to Alaska,' he said, knowing he didn't wish anything of the kind.

'So do I.' Her mouth crimped slightly.

'You mustn't worry. You've met Joe and Ross. They're

103

good guys to climb with. Dependable. And this climb's very important to Joe: he's never summited Denali and he needs to if he's going to be able to establish himself as one of the elite climbers so he can set up his own expedition business.'

'That worries me. It makes him much more likely to take risks.'

'Joe doesn't take risks.'

'He *does*, Ben. You told me yourself about the time he tried to race some other guys up some frozen ice falls or something and fell off.'

'That was when he was younger. He's got a family now. He's much more careful these days.'

'Oh darling, I shouldn't say this, but . . . I wish you wouldn't go.'

'It's only for three weeks, more or less.'

Squeezing his hand, she said, 'I've never asked you before but . . . don't go this time. *Please.*'

Pregnant women tended to overreact; he remembered how Neil's wife had once completely lost it over something totally trivial: a spill down the front of her new sweater, something like that. He spoke soothingly, anxious to calm Lisa. 'Darling, I set this up with Joe and Ross over a year ago, long before we knew about the baby. We've all been planning it for months. I can't let the others down, at this stage.'

'I know.' She lifted her shoulders and let them drop. 'And I knew all about the climbing before we got married, so why am I complaining now?'

'Sweetheart,' he said, relieved. He got up and brushed his mouth softly over her lips. What would he say if she came right out and asked him not to climb again? Actually said the words: 'Stop climbing.' Would he be able to? He thought again of the uncompromising mountains,

104

the harmony of exhilaration and fear, the purity of the paradox that since death was always a possibility, it was the one place where he felt truly alive.

'One of the ladies from my prenatal class showed me an article about you in the *Boston Globe*,' she said.

'Yeah?' He remembered that particular journalist, the way the guy had sweated, kept slanting his questions in an effort to make Ben sound like some brainless jock.

'You didn't tell me about it,' Lisa said.

'What's to tell?'

'You're my husband,' she said. 'I ought to be aware that you're a hero. Why didn't you tell me about rescuing that little girl who fell off the cliffs? According to the magazine, she'd have died if you hadn't risked your life to get her.'

'I thought everyone had forgotten about that,' he said dismissively, uncomfortable.

'I bet the kid hasn't. Nor her mom.' Lisa took his hand. 'I'm so proud of you, honey.'

'It was years ago.'

'And there was someone else, who had a heart attack . . .'

'I was working for the Mountain Rescue Service. It was pure chance that I was the one on call at the time.'

'That's not what this article said. "Only someone with the skill and selfless daring of a man like Ben Andersen could have brought off such a complicated rescue." And I quote.'

'Yeah.'

'You don't want to talk about it.'

'Right.'

There was a long pause. 'So . . . when do you leave on Monday?' Lisa said finally.

'Our flight takes off from Boston first thing in the

morning. I have to hook up with the others the day before, which means I'll . . .' He lifted his glass and swallowed the last of his drink. '. . . I'll have to leave here on Sunday morning.'

'The day after *tomorrow*?'

'Yes.'

'But that's a whole day less than I realized.' She wrapped her arms around her chest and bent over, staring at the floor. Her voice was very low when she spoke again. 'Suppose you fall. Suppose you're caught in a blizzard and you die, like those people on Everest did, a few years back.'

'That's not going to happen.'

'You can't be certain, can you?'

'Of course I can't.' He felt a stir of impatience. 'Nobody can. But I've got far too much to live for. You. The baby. Our whole future. You don't think I'm going to risk all that, do you?'

'Can you imagine how I feel when you're gone, thinking of you clinging by your fingertips to a bit of rock, or hanging over a crevice—'

'Crevasse.'

'Who gives a shit,' she said, her voice rising. 'Crevice, crevasse, if you fall down one you're still dead.'

He tried to lighten the suddenly charged atmosphere. 'People get rescued from crevasses all the time.'

'Some of them.'

'*Most* of them.' He reached for her hand but she snatched it away.

'Sometimes it just seems so fucking *futile*,' she said. 'So bloody stupid.'

'Not to me.'

Her face set, she shook her head. 'Oh God, what's the point in getting upset with you?'

'Darling.' He seized her hand again and this time she let him hold it. 'I'll be thinking about you all the time I'm away, and if I know you're anxious and upset, I'm going to be worrying myself. Nothing's going to happen. I always believe one hundred per cent – one hundred and ten per cent – that everything will be absolutely fine. You shouldn't climb if you don't believe that. And *you've* got to believe it too.'

'Just promise me one thing,' she said.

'Anything.'

'This is the last climb until the baby comes, OK?' Her voice wavered. 'Promise me, Ben.'

'I absolutely promise.' He squeezed her hands. Smiled at her. 'Our first baby . . . it's the most exciting thing that'll ever happen to us. I hate being away from you. If I could have gotten out of this . . .'

'If some other pal of yours calls up, you say no, right?' she said.

'Cross my heart.'

'Practice,' she said. 'Say no. Say it a hundred times.'

'No, no, no, no, no,' he began, then stopped as he saw the tears start to roll down her face. 'Oh, honey,' he whispered.

She heeled away the tears with the back of her hand and managed a little smile. 'I'll start wearing frilly aprons and baking tuna-and-noodle casseroles if I'm not careful.'

'I can't wait,' he said. 'Especially if there's nothing under the frilly apron.'

The sun had gone now and mountain shadows were crowding across the lake, turning the water black. The air smelled of leaf-turn and rain. In the warm dusk, the peepers began to call. 'Want to go indoors, or eat out here?' he asked.

'Either place, it's so darn hot.' Clumsied by her bulk,

Lisa tipped out of the hammock. 'Maybe I'll go and cool off in the lake. Wish we had air conditioning.' She padded across the porch to the wide doors leading into the sitting room. The old floorboards creaked. 'On second thoughts, it's too much effort to walk down to the water.'

Overcome with love and remorse, he put his arm lightly around her. 'I adore you,' he murmured into her hair.

She stood stiffly inside his embrace. 'What are we eating tonight?'

'How about the famous Andersen hamburgers? Or the famous Andersen barbecued steak? I can light the barbecue, easy. Or there's pork chops in the freezer – I can fix them, if you like.'

'I'd be just as happy with the famous Andersen canned tomato soup. Cold. There's some in the refrigerator.'

'You're in luck, lady. I'm the best opener of cans in the business.'

'Why else do you think I went for you?' She smiled at him.

'My performance in the sack?'

'That might have had something to do with it.'

'Is soup going to be enough for you? You're supposed to be eating for two.'

'I'm not sure I can even eat for one.' Lisa held her stomach between her hands. There was a small frown between her eyebrows. 'I don't think I could keep anything down.'

'Guess it goes with the territory.'

'I feel wrong,' she said.

'How do you mean?'

'It's like there's something . . .' She shook her head. '. . . Not quite right.'

'But you had a scan just after I got back from Switzerland and that was, what, a week and a half ago. There was nothing wrong then.'

She shrugged. 'I've got another appointment next week. But I don't think the doctor could care less.'

He hugged her briefly. 'I'm sorry you're going through so much of this on your own.'

She moved away from him. 'I don't have a lot of choice, do I?'

Later, they cuddled up on the sofa, dipping their spoons into a half-gallon of rocky road ice cream and watching the news on the TV. Lisa was curled inside his arm, while one of Ben's hands rested on her belly. The baby was dormant this evening: he missed the usual kicks and shoves.

'I almost forgot,' he said suddenly.

'Forgot what?'

He disentangled himself from her. 'Just a minute.' He went into the kitchen. 'Look what I bought.' He held up a little box.

'What is it?'

'I was on my lunch break and I saw this in the window of an antique store.'

Lisa lifted the lid and took out a baby's rattle.

'It's English,' Ben said. 'Coral and silver. A hundred and fifty years old, the sales clerk told me.'

'It's absolutely beautiful.' Lisa reached up and stroked his cheek. 'Oh darling . . . I'm sorry I've been giving you a hard time.'

'I can just see the baby with it, can't you? Lying in its bassinet, holding it the way they do, so tight you feel you'd have to break their fingers to make them let go.'

Lisa shook the silver bells on their coral ring. 'It's lovely, Ben.'

'Our baby . . .'

'What do you think it'll be when it grows up?' she said.

'President of the United States. Bound to be. Plus Olympic gold medallist and award-winning musician.'

'You left out decorated war hero.'

'Oscar winner.'

'And best-selling novelist.'

'All that and more.'

'I kind of think, if it's a boy, that it'll be tall and rangy, like you, curly-haired and good at sport,' Lisa said.

'If it's a girl, she'll be like you,' said Ben. 'With the cutest dimples.'

'Who can twist her daddy round her little finger.'

'That's what little girls are for, isn't it?' He touched one of the silver bells. 'Any further thoughts on names?'

'If it's a girl, I still think Rosemary's good, after my mom. We're not doing well on boys, though.'

'What about Rory?' he said suddenly.

'Because of your cousin?'

'Partly.'

'Is it short for something?'

'Don't think so. My aunt used to say it was Gaelic for red.'

'Rory,' Lisa said, considering. 'I like it. OK. If we don't come up with something else, we'll go for Rory, if it's a boy, and Rosemary if it's a girl.'

Ben thought about his possible daughter, his maybe-son, and felt a sudden tightening of his throat. 'It's going to be so . . .' There simply weren't the right words. 'Amazing,' he said in the end.

Lisa kneeled up beside him. Reaching towards him, she closed her eyes. Soft as petals, her fingers began to map his face, traveling across the planes of his cheeks, tracing the bony ridges of his eye sockets, the curve of his mouth, the jut of his nose.

'It must be so awful for my dad, being blind,' she said.

'Imagine not having the faintest idea what your child looks like.'

Ben shut his own eyes for a moment, trying to envisage a world of perpetual darkness, then grabbed one of her hands and brought it to his mouth. 'Would you have fallen in love with me if you hadn't been able to see me?' he asked.

'Definitely.'

'Why?'

'Your smell,' she murmured, eyes still closed. She pressed her face against his cheek. 'You have such a good smell.'

'It must be that new aftershave.'

Her small hands cupped either side of his jaw. 'I mean you smell like a good man.'

He pulled her towards him. 'I would be totally lost without you,' he said. 'You know that?'

Opening her eyes, she shook her head. 'As I would be without you.'

Logs crumbled softly in the fireplace and Ben leaned forward to throw another one on the embers. He put his arm round her shoulders. 'You're the most beautiful thing I've ever seen in my life.' He leaned towards her. 'Always will be. In fact, I'd kiss you right this second . . .'

'What's stopping you?'

'The disgusting smudge of tomato soup right slap bang in the middle of your upper lip.'

'Ueugh! Gross!' Lisa dabbed at her mouth with a piece of kitchen towel. 'Since I got pregnant I seem to have turned into a real slob.'

'You may be a slob,' Ben said, 'but you're my slob. For life.'

Sometimes, cupping himself around her compact body at night, watching her dress in the morning, he was

111

overcome with the same sense of splendor that he felt on completing a climb. The smell which lingered at the roots of her hair, the beads of sweat in her armpits when they had made love, the sight of her tiny panties hanging in the bathroom, aroused in him a kind of ecstasy. The way her clothes fitted her body, the serious look on her face as she brushed her hair, the color of her skin or the shape of her mouth would flash into his mind at intervals during the day and he would know with finality that this, *this*, was all he would ever want.

On Sunday morning, he hugged her tightly, pushing her against the side of the car, though the bump of her pregnancy kept them apart. Looking at the fragile bones of her arms and the stretch of her slender neck, he was seized with a vague sense of apprehension. Bending down, he kissed her soft mouth, felt the press of her breasts against his shirt. 'I love you so much it hurts,' he murmured.

Lisa stared deep into his eyes. She ran her tongue seductively over her lips. 'I don't suppose you want to get into the back seat for a quickie, do you?'

Behind them, the bus to Butterfield revved its engine and the driver lightly hooted. Ben laughed and pulled her closer. 'Don't tempt me,' he said. 'Just wait till I get home again.'

She nuzzled into the space below his ear, standing on tiptoe to reach it. He could feel tears on her cheek. 'I wish . . . I so much wish you wouldn't go.' Breaking away from him, she stood shivering in the early morning air.

'You'll be all right, won't you? All on your own.'

'I'll be fine.' She held him by the arms. She pressed her hands against her swollen stomach. 'It's just . . . sometimes I have this terrible fear that there's something not quite right in here.'

112

'If you're seriously worried, you should go see Brad Patterson. Don't take any chances.'

'Nor you, Ben Andersen.'

'I always take good care.'

'Take extra special care. This time it's not just for my sake.'

'For both your sakes.'

Her face was serious. 'If anything happens to you,' she said, 'it won't be you who suffers, it'll be us. Me and our baby. We'll have to spend the rest of our lives without you.'

Anxious now to be off, he bent and kissed her hair. 'Nothing's going to happen.'

'I wish you weren't going, Ben,' she said again.

'Me too.' He was surprised this time at how much he meant it. 'I left my contact number on your pillow.'

'OK.'

The bus inched forward slightly and the driver stamped on his brakes with a whoosh of squeaky air. 'I love you,' Ben said.

'Love you too, dreamboat.' She leaned forward and kissed his mouth hard so that he felt her teeth under her soft lips. 'Love you too.'

CHAPTER SEVEN

'Remember when we used to take the kids down to see the Christmas windows?' Joanne said, halfway to Boston.

'I always loved that.'

'Me too, except . . . Oh, God, remember that time we lost Lucy in Filene's Basement?'

'How could I forget? The *noise* you made . . . even those women ripping bargains out of each other's hands stopped for a second or two.'

'The whole scenario flashed before my eyes,' said Joanne. 'Some filthy pervert carrying her off to inflict God only knew what unspeakable fantasies on her before strangling her and throwing her poor little corpse . . .' Joanne choked. 'Jeez.'

'And after all that, she was only in the john!'

'One good thing about not having kids, Mel, is you miss out on the nightmares of the imagination you suffer when they're out of your sight.'

'Very true.'

'It's not so bad when there's someone else to share the angst with.' Joanne sighed. 'I still feel guilty about the divorce.'

'You shouldn't, Jo. All of your kids are really nice people. You've done a wonderful job on them.'

'I couldn't have done it without you. Their dad wasn't around, but they always had you if they wanted to talk to someone who wasn't me.'

'I guess I stood in for that maiden aunt who's always popping up in Victorian novels.'

'Maiden?' Joanne glanced at Mel quizzically. 'Hardly. You were married to dear Eric at the time.'

'Speaking figuratively.'

'Anyway, maiden aunts were always tatting and getting the vapors, weren't they? I don't remember you doing too much of that.'

'I might have tatted, if I'd had the faintest idea how.'

They drove along in silence for a while. 'Want to stop for coffee?' Joanne asked. 'I see a Dairy Queen coming up.'

'Coffee, and maybe some of those doughnut holes.'

'Yes please. I love eating something which theoretically doesn't exist.'

'There's a non-existentialist thought.'

'Oh, so droll.'

The shared years hung between them, so many questions asked and answered, so much common experience, so much information confided, strand after strand, linking the two of them together with an indestructible bond.

Joanne started rooting around in the glove compartment where Mel kept tapes, then held one up. 'Do you really listen to this crap?'

'What is it?'

'Albinoni and some of his talent-free friends doing their tinkly baroque thing. God, I don't know which I hate most: awful Albinoni or bloody Boccherini. And that other guy who always gets lumped in with them.

'Pachelbel.'

'That's right, poxy Pachelbel. Who in their right mind would actually go into a store and buy a tape like that? It's pure musak.'

'I gather you don't like it.' Mel pulled out to overtake a transporter. The rocky tree-covered slopes on either side of the freeway were leveling out now, and the traffic was thickening as they drew close to the city. 'It was Eric's.'

'In that case . . .' Joanne lowered the window and tossed out the tape.

'Excuse me . . .' Involuntarily Mel stamped on the brake. 'Did you just throw my tape out of the car?'

'Too right.'

'I can't believe you did that.'

'And I can't believe you still keep this old stuff in the car.'

'That was a waste of a perfectly good tape.'

'Relax, darlin'. I'll pay you for it if it'll make you feel better.'

'That's not the point,' said Mel. 'It was *Eric's*. He always played it when we drove anywhere.'

'My case rests.'

'That was a bit of my past.' Mel thought of Eric humming along to the music. A few times she had brought some Schubert lieder along, a Mahler symphony, but he would frown, say he couldn't concentrate on driving with that stuff playing. She would offer to take the wheel but he refused. '*Not after you nearly hit that milk truck, darling,*' and though she would protest that the truck had ignored a red light and that anyway, she *hadn't* hit it, he would simply pat her knee, tell her that he was only thinking of what was best for her.

'Got to look forward, sweetheart, not back,' Joanne said, as though she could read Mel's mind.

'It's a darn good thing we're friends,' said Mel crossly.

116

'For both of us.' Joanne pushed her sunglasses further up her nose. 'Where we going to eat tonight?'

'The usual place, I thought.'

'Why don't we try something different for a change?'

Because I don't want different, Mel thought. 'But we always go to Momma Rosa's.'

'We started going there a hundred years ago but the food's gone right down since then and anyway, it's not even Momma Rosa's any more, it's Glad-to-be-Gay LaVerne's.'

'Remember last time, when I asked if he did zabaglione?' Mel started giggling. 'The way he drew himself up and said, "But dahling, zabaglione is *soooo* yesterday." His face!'

'God, yes. That man could sneer for America.'

Laughter bubbled up between them. 'Until then, I thought it was only fashion that went out of style,' Mel said. 'Not food as well.'

'I'm not sure if you noticed, but last time we were there, I nearly took a bite out of his butt,' Joanne said, scarlet with laughter. 'When he passed our table in that purple crushed-velvet jumpsuit and matching scarf . . .'

'Oh Lord, yes.'

'. . . I swear I thought he was a serving of blueberry pie.'

'Joanne, you are so ridiculous!' Mel clutched the wheel, her face creased with merriment.

Joanne smiled. 'I love to see you laugh. You don't laugh nearly as much as you should. Which doesn't answer the important question of where we're going to eat tonight.'

'I know another place,' Mel said hesitantly. 'It's Russian.'

'Great,' said Joanne. 'Russians seem to cater for people with my kind of appetite.'

'It might not be there any more, of course. But I remember it as being pretty good.'

Back then, Mel would not have cared whether it was good or bad. It was enough to be up from New York for the weekend with Galen. To be sitting opposite him in the crowded little room, candles on the red-embroidered tablecloths, a tureen of soup between them, chunks of black bread in a basket, filled dumplings.

'My grandmother was from Russia,' he had said. 'She used to make *pirozhki* like these.' He pushed one into her mouth and laid his finger across her lips as she chewed. 'Is it good, Melissa?'

'Very good.'

He had ladled soup the color of antique garnets, thick with meat and cabbage, into a bowl, then added a dollop of sour cream from the dish the waiter had brought.

She had picked up her spoon. 'What is it?'

'*Borzcht*. Taste. You will love it.'

And although she had always disliked the taste of beets, he was right, she *had* loved it, had accepted more, dipped the black bread into it, marveling at the richness of the life he had introduced her to. She watched him eat, her true love, her lover. 'It's wonderful,' she had said. 'Everything's wonderful.'

They spent the afternoon apart, Joanne checking out the bookshops, Mel visiting a couple of the galleries. At six they met up in their shared hotel room and went out to find the Russian restaurant. To Mel's surprise it was still there, scarcely changed since her previous visit, twenty-five years before. The same muddy brown paintwork, the same yellowed ceiling and steamed-up windows, the same rich smells coming from the kitchen. Their waitress, a girl of seventeen or so, had fair braids tied up on top of her

118

head with scarlet ribbons, and a full skirt of thick red wool with a white blouse tucked into it.

Mel ordered the same dishes she had eaten last time and Joanne added blinis and fish. 'And a couple of glasses of vodka first,' she said. 'I'll have the pepper vodka and my friend will have . . . ?'

'Strawberry,' Mel said. 'Just because it sounds nice.'

'Doesn't it, though. Can I try some of yours?'

'Of course.'

They drank two glasses each before the *borzcht* arrived. 'God, this stuff goes straight to your head,' Mel said, as the waitress placed a thick white soup dish between them, offered them black bread and tiny curls of butter.

'Not to mention other parts.' Joanne put her glass down noisily on the table and leaned on her elbows. 'OK, so who was he?'

'Sorry?'

'Mel, ever since we walked through the door you've had this goofy expression on your face, like love's young dream just came true. Don't pretend you didn't come here with some really special guy – I recognize the signs.'

Mel played with the little glass in front of her. 'We were just good friends.'

Before Joanne could respond, the waitress came back and looked at their empty glasses. 'More vodka?'

'What flavors have you got that we haven't tried yet?' Joanne said. Her hair was coming loose from the tortoiseshell combs she had pushed into it and her cheeks shone with heat.

'Peach, raspberry, coffee, lemon, mint . . .' The girl reeled off half a dozen more.

'I'll try the peach,' Joanne said. 'And for my friend, the orange.'

'No,' Mel said. 'I've had enough.'

'Go on. Live a little, darlin'. Can't be a maiden aunt all your life.'

When their fresh drinks had been brought, Joanne spooned soup into her mouth, and took a mouthful of bread. 'This is totally delicious,' she said. Then, without pause, added, 'So . . . was this guy Russian?'

The pure alcohol they had drunk was getting to Mel. When she shook her head, tiny flashes sparked at the corners of her eyes. 'Polish,' she said.

'Did you know him before or after you got married to Eric?'

'Before, of course.' Mel took a sip of the little glass of orange vodka which the waitress had brought. Joanne and I have been friends for years, she thought, and I have never before suggested we eat here, never mentioned him until now, even though she has asked. 'But he was just someone I worked with for a while,' she said quickly.

'Shit. And I thought at last I was going to hear something about your mysterious past.' Joanne slathered butter onto a piece of the black bread. 'Can I ask you something?'

'No.'

'You always say no.'

'And you always ask anyway.'

'Have you ever been in love? I mean really really searingly in love.'

For a moment Mel was silent. 'Yes,' she said eventually. But love did not come anywhere near describing the scalding emotions of that lost time. The pounding of her nerves beneath the skin, the pulsing at her wrists, the electricity which tingled in her fingers. She had walked through the days without feeling the ground under her feet; if she reached out, she could have touched the sky. At the end of each day, she remembered nothing of what had passed since she woke, except for him. Only him. Only his face. His smile. His name. His touch.

Would she fall as hopelessly in love with him, were they to meet again?

'What was he like?'

'He was . . .' What had he been? Warm and strong and angry. Fierce and gentle. A man of contrasts. A man she had not known how to handle. Which was why, from then on, she had made sure that she never again took on anything she could not control. 'He was everything, really,' she said simply. 'He was what you said, a special guy.'

'So not Eric, then.'

'Knock it off, Joanne.'

'Sorry, sorry. What was his name?'

His name . . . even after all these years the shape of it was still bright in her mind and at the back of her tongue.

'His name doesn't matter,' she said.

'Hey, come on, Miss Melissa. we're friends, remember?' Joanne swallowed what was left in her glass and signalled the waitress. 'What happened to him?'

When Mel shook her head, Joanne raised her eyebrows. 'So you went for Eric. Because you loved him, naturally.'

'Yes.'

'Just as a matter of interest, how was he in bed?' Joanne widened her eyes. 'You know something? In all the years we've been friends, we've never talked about sex.'

'*I* haven't talked about sex,' said Mel. '*You* never stop.'

'So . . . what's the answer to the bed question? Did you moan with passion when he touched you? Did you ache for him when he left for work? Did he make your body come alive?'

'Why do you have to reduce everything to sex, Ms Mayfield?'

Joanne stretched out a pleading hand. 'He wasn't your

121

first fuck, was he? Please, please tell me you and this other man were screwing. I couldn't bear it if—'

'Joanne, you're my best friend, but I'm damned if my love life is any of your business.'

Joanne wiped her mouth on her napkin. 'Go on, honey, tell me. Please.'

Mel looked away, across the room. A couple had just come in, holding hands, glancing at each other in that world-excluding self-sufficient way that lovers do. He was white-haired, in his early sixties, she maybe ten years younger. What would I do if Galen walked through the door, Mel wondered. Would he even recognize me?

'You going to answer the question or not?' Joanne said.

Mel took a deep breath. She did not want to discuss this. Not with Joanne. Not with anyone. Especially not with herself. And yet the urge, the need, to tear the string from her tightly wrapped past was almost irresistible. 'You're going to be a really obnoxious old lady, you know that?' she said. 'You'll go to parties and get absolutely smashed out of your skull and say the most outrageous things, and spill stuff down your front and . . .'

'And when I stand up to go, I'll leave a little damp patch where I've been sitting.'

'Hasn't anyone told you?' Mel said. 'You already do.' The two of them rocked with laughter.

The waitress took away their soup bowls and brought blinis stuffed with caviar, a platter of smoked fish. When she had gone, Joanne put down her knife and fork and leaned forward. 'This is a serious question, hon. I didn't know you back then, but it's obvious that you could have gone anywhere, done anything, had anyone. So why Eric, the master of the subtle put-down, cushion-shaker extraordinaire, almost old enough to be your father?'

'You've got a real obsession about him, you know

that?' Mel said. 'What is it with you? I'm beginning to wonder if you had the hots for him.'

'You must be joking.' Joanne shuddered dramatically. 'So why?'

'If you really must know . . .' Mel swallowed the words thick as stones in her throat. 'I was . . . I was trying to get over an . . . an abortion.'

'*What?*'

'You heard.'

'An *abortion*?' Joanne stared at her disbelievingly. 'I've known you for – what is it? God knows how many years – and you've never hinted at, not a whisper of – of such a thing. And now suddenly you come out with it, calm as you please.'

'I'm not calm,' Mel said. 'Oh no. Not at all. Not in the very least.'

'Why didn't you ever tell me?'

If the truth be told, Mel thought, I wish I had not told you now.

The waitress brought two more tiny glasses of vodka. Joanne raised hers and sniffed at it. 'An abortion,' she said. 'I don't think I've ever been so surprised in my life.' She dipped a finger into the glass and tasted it. 'Peppermint, I think. Unless she's brought me mouthwash by mistake.'

Mel looked down into her own glass.

'Was the . . . was it his?' Joanne said. 'The Russian guy's?'

'Polish.'

'Whatever. Was it his?'

Mel changed the subject. 'Did I tell you I invited Ben Andersen round for supper last time I was up at the lake?'

'Ben Andersen?' Joanne pulled the combs out of her wild hair, letting it fall around her flushed face. Sweat stood on her upper lip. 'Hey, now you're *really* cooking with gas!'

'He was there on his own, so I suggested we shared a steak.'

'And how did it go?'

'Very sticky. Believe me, this is a man completely lacking any of the social graces.'

'What about other kinds of graces?' Joanne worked her eyebrows suggestively.

'Joanne, that was *not* why I invited him over. Apart from anything else, he's a happily married man, he's young enough to be my son – and I don't think I've ever been more grateful to see someone leave.'

'I was thinking of giving Lisa a baby shower, down at the bookstore. Any thoughts?'

'Why at the store?'

'It could be kind of fun to hold it in the kids' section. Have everyone sit on those little chairs or the beanbags or something. Give them kiddy food to eat along with their coffee, make it like a children's party.'

'I should think she'd absolutely love it.'

'She's already signed Junior up for the storytime sessions on Tuesday mornings, if you can believe it.'

Mel laughed affectionately. 'She just can't wait to be a mother.' Nor could I, she thought.

'Point is, I don't want to butt in on your territory. I know you two are very close and if you were planning on having one for her, I'll just leave it lay.'

'I was, but I thought I might wait just a bit longer. If you like, we could host it together.'

'It seems such ages since I was buying stuff for my lot,' Joanne said wistfully. 'God knows when I'm going to get to be a granny for real, and they have such cute baby things nowadays. I saw this tiny little body warmer in

LL Bean's the other day: I couldn't keep my hands off it, so it's in my hall closet waiting for Baby Andersen right now.'

'Between the two of us, we're going to spoil that child.'

'That's what grannies are for.'

'You're right. By the way, I'm going up to the lake again – any chance you'd come along, with or without any of the kids?'

'Not for at least another week, hon. We're stocktaking, and then I have to go down to New York, meet some wholesalers.' Joanne looked at Mel's disappointed face. 'But I absolutely promise I'll come up soon. OK?'

Joanne lifted her head and groaned. 'Jesus,' she said, dropping back onto the pillow and putting an arm across her eyes. 'What happened? I feel like a herd of wild horses is galloping around inside my skull.'

'Too much vodka.' Showered and dressed, Mel was unsympathetic.

'What?' Joanne pressed a hand to her forehead.

'You drank rather a lot of it last night.'

'So did you.'

'But not as much as you.' Mel counted off on her fingers. 'You had the pepper, the peach, the raspberry, the coffee, and another pepper, plus half of the three I ordered. Which is why I feel great, and you don't.'

'You're such a goddamned prig.'

'You play, you pay,' Mel said. 'Want me to call room service, get them to send up a pot of coffee?'

'Make that a cauldron.'

'Here.' Mel handed her a glass of water and two paracetamols.

Joanne swallowed them and closed her eyes. 'I swear that is the very last time I ever touch spirits.'

125

'I believe you, darlin'.'

When the coffee arrived, Mel poured a cup and placed it beside her friend's bed. 'Best thing I can do is go out for a stroll and come back for you later.'

'How much later?'

'A couple of hours.'

'Fine. Great.' Joanne turned on her side and whimpered. 'Promise me you'll never let me get within ten feet of a bottle again,' she moaned.

'OK.'

'Honey, last night . . .'

'What about it?'

'You . . . I know you don't want to discuss it – but you did say you'd had an abortion, didn't you? I mean, I didn't dream it, did I?'

Mel walked around in the sunshine until she found a restaurant which had outdoor tables separated from the street by box plants set into green-painted tubs. With an extra large cappuccino and a chocolate croissant in front of her, she sipped coffee and read the newspapers, something she rarely had time to do at home. She realized for the first time just how fraught the last few months had been, how hard she had been working. It was good to be away from Butterfield. Because Eric had not liked traveling, she had hardly ever left home during the years of her marriage, apart from visits to Boston or New York and a trip to Europe to celebrate their tenth anniversary.

When she returned to their hotel room, Joanne was up and packed. 'I feel much better,' she said. 'Just don't explode any firecrackers near me.'

'I promise.'

'What I feel like is some soup,' said Joanne. 'Minestrone or something, to settle my stomach.'

'Nancy always makes a huge lunch,' Mel said. 'You won't be able to eat any of it if you start scarfing down minestrone.'

'I won't be able to eat any of it if I don't,' said Joanne. 'And I don't want to miss out if she serves up those soft-shell crabs she's so good at.'

'I saw an Italian restaurant about two blocks away,' Mel said. 'Let's go.'

As they were passing a small terrace of stores and restaurants, Joanne stopped. Old-fashioned iron railings separated the sidewalk from steps which led down to what must once have been the basements of the buildings. 'Oh my God!' she exclaimed. 'It's gorgeous.'

'What is?'

'Down there.' She began to step down a short stone staircase which ended in a flagged walkway fronting a quartet of little stores. 'The hat shop.'

Mel followed her. The hat shop was a narrow one-room place sandwiched between a dollhouse shop and a store specializing in books on military history. The glass front of the fourth shop was painted black and could have sold anything.

The store window contained a single hat, set on an antique cherrywood hat form. It was ravishingly beautiful, made of pale lilac straw and swathed in lavender chiffon, with a tiny bunch of silk violets lying delicately on the brim. Set opposite, on the other side of the window, was a small glass vase containing a bunch of real violets. 'Look,' Joanne breathed. 'It's absolutely perfect.'

'For a society wedding, yes,' Mel said. 'Or some blue-blood charity tea.'

'It goes perfectly with that scarf you're wearing – and that amethyst necklace that used to belong to your mother. Oh Mel, you just have to buy it.'

'People don't wear hats like that in Butterfield.'

'Start a new trend. Why not? Give Sarah Mahoney something to be bitchy about. You'd look so wonderful, wafting about in lilac chiffon, that you wouldn't give a damn what she said.'

'It's pretty, but it's not really . . .'

Joanne took her arm. 'Buy it,' she said firmly.

'But I'd never use it.'

'You can wear it to my funeral.'

'We've always agreed that I'll be dead long before you. Anyway, I've never been much for hats.'

'Time you started.' Joanne pushed open the shop door.

A sad-looking woman was standing at the back, staring thoughtfully at a wide-brimmed hat of green velvet which was balanced over her raised hand.

'That hat in the window,' Joanne said. 'My friend would like to try it on.'

'No, she wouldn't,' protested Mel.

'It's gorgeous, isn't it?' Carefully the woman set down the green velvet hat and went over to remove the straw one from the window. 'Did you read about me in the paper last week?'

'No. We're visiting from Vermont.'

'They did a feature on my hats,' said the woman. She pulled out a chair covered in white plush and when Mel had seated herself, settled the lilac hat carefully on her head.

'Beautiful,' she said. 'Especially with your blond hair.'

'I don't know . . .' Mel turned her head this way and that. Eric would have laughed himself sick but in fact the hat was rather flattering.

'It's wonderful with your eyes,' Joanne said.

'It does bring out their unusual color,' the hat-shop lady agreed. Darting to the rear of the shop, she came back with two more silk flowers of a deep blue. She pushed them in among the violets. 'Let me just . . .' With a threaded needle, she added three or four tiny stitches. 'There . . . that's really perfect. What do you think?'

'She'll have it,' said Joanne.

'Will she?' Mel said.

'No question.'

'You look lovely in it,' the hat-shop lady said.

Lovely? Mel raised her hand and adjusted the hat, brought it forward a little. I was never lovely, she thought. I was young – and that was loveliness enough. *His hands parting my thighs, his face looking down at me, the serious mouth telling me I was luscious, I was perfect, he adored me, his muse, his inspiration.* She suddenly wanted to weep. The woman in the foolish beautiful hat who gazed back at her from the mirror was a stranger, someone she had never known, but might have liked. Who am I? she thought. Where am I going? The familiar feeling of dislocation rushed over her, the sense of waste. 'All right,' she said. 'I'll take it.'

The hat-shop lady brought out a hatbox printed with violets and began to rustle tissue paper into it, but Joanne had seen something else. 'My mother had a hatbox just like this,' she said, holding up a box of lilac silk edged with purple leather. 'I haven't seen one of those for years.'

'I found it at a flea market. It dates back to the Twenties,' said the woman.

'It's lovely. Is it for sale?'

'Well . . .' The woman hesitated. 'It *is* sort of made for that hat, isn't it? As a matter of fact, the box inspired it so I guess they should stay together.'

'I can't possibly afford—' Mel began, but Joanne interrupted her.

'I'll pay for the box, darling, if you buy the hat.'

The woman went to the window and brought out the vase of violets. 'Take these too,' she said. 'They're sweet violets. Such a wonderful scent.' She tied them up in a purple ribbon and put them in a see-through bag, then wrapped the hat in violet tissue paper. 'There you are: a souvenir of Boston.'

Mel looked up at Joanne. 'Of friendship,' she said.

CHAPTER EIGHT

The Cessna air-taxi disgorged them onto the rutted-snow landing strip known as Kahiltna International Airport. Standing out into the cold air, Ben stared up at the vertical granite cliffs and the icefields far above them, transfixed by the sheer dwarfing splendor of the landscape. As always when he came to the high hills, he was made uncomfortably aware of the insignificance of mankind.

Gearing up, he and Ross and Joe began the tedious slog from the airstrip up to the lower glaciers, seven thousand feet above them, and, beyond that, the camp at fourteen thousand three hundred feet. They took it slowly; they'd allowed themselves a week to acclimatize to the higher altitudes. The days were sunfilled, the nights frosty but clear.

'This keeps up, we'll be OK to summit,' Joe panted, as they paused to drink water from their bottles. 'God, I'll be glad to have this one under my belt.'

'I'm not sure I care that much about summiting,' Ben said slowly.

The other two stared at him in surprise. 'Then why you here, man?' asked Ross, setting off again.

'I do care, of course I do. But climbing, it's not so much

about . . . achieving, it's more about doing.' The feeling was one which had been growing on him recently.

'Yeah, right,' Joe said. 'And what I want to do this time is top out.'

'Me too.' Ross, a couple of years younger than the others, nodded vehement agreement. 'You wouldn't believe how much dough I already dropped on this trip.'

'Same for all of us,' said Ben.

Ross wrinkled his forehead, looking quizzical. 'Which is why there's no way I'm gonna go back and tell my girl-friend I decided not to bother summiting after all. Or at least *trying*.'

Arrived at the camp, they registered their expedition, as required, under the name The Three Musketeers, then set up their tent in one of the snow bunkers built by previous climbers. It was cold, with an intermittent wind, but the skies were still clear; they were hopeful of leaving soon. Despite that, climbers coming into the camp from higher up were pessimistic about their chances, talking of ferocious winds and worse than Arctic conditions. Everyone agreed that a big storm was on the way.

'That's OK.' Joe grinned at his team. 'We'll just hang tough till it blows itself out.'

'Nothing to it,' said Ross.

But after sitting about for two days of good weather and sunshine, not doing much beyond checking gear they'd already checked a hundred times, they began to discuss the feasibility of pushing on. Joe was developing a chest infection and was anxious to start off before it got any worse. 'It looks OK up there to me,' he said, standing outside the tent and gazing upwards. 'I say we chance it.'

'What do you think, Benny boy?' asked Ross.

'I agree.' Ben examined the peaks gleaming white

132

against the blue sky. 'If it gets too bad, we can always come down again.'

Despite headshakes from other climbers, they began the climb that afternoon. The going was tough but not excessively so. They were at seventeen thousand feet by nightfall and set up their tent, anchoring it to the slope with snow pickets and an elaborate web of ropes in case conditions deteriorated. The next day they made two climbs up to nineteen thousand feet, double-carrying food and fuel which they stashed in case of emergency, before climbing down again to their tent.

That night the storm hit.

Three days later, it was still raging. Dense clouds swirled about the higher peaks and tumbled down the mountain, blotting out the sky. The noise of the wind, continuous and disorienting, battered their minds into numbness. The snow froze as it fell, pounding against the sides of their tent. Stormed in, they stayed inside. When they were forced by physical need, they got up to use the bags and pee bottles stacked in the tent's vestibule, otherwise they lay in their sleeping bags, trying to keep warm. At first, the inactivity didn't faze them: all three were philosophical about it, knowing that waiting for the weather was part of high-altitude climbing. They'd experienced worse conditions than this.

But, as the hours passed, the enforced confinement to a space barely wider than three large beach towels began to get to them. Acceptance gave way to irritation, tempers frayed. The way Ross sniffed every minute or two was getting on Ben's nerves. And several times Joe had kicked away Ben's encroaching sleeping bag with unnecessary force.

'Keep your fucking feet out of my space,' he'd yelled

133

last time. 'Jesus, it's bad enough that I'm stuck in a fucking tent after I worked my butt off all year to pay for this trip, without some moron trying to grab more than his share of territory.'

'Hey, I'm sorry,' Ben said. 'It was an accident, OK?'

'OK,' muttered Joe, looking away. 'Guess I'm getting cabin fever. Sure didn't plan on spending my vacation in a soggy tent with two of the ugliest guys I ever laid eyes on.'

'Wouldn't matter so much if you looked like Julia Roberts,' Ross said.

'You're just jealous,' Ben said. He lay on his side in his sleeping bag, concentrating on reserving his energy, trying to look on the bright side. At least the storm meant they could rest after the gruelling climb up to this height. 'Nobody's ever going to vote *you* Mr Pecs, like they did me.'

The three of them hooted, remembering a drunken evening spent with fellow mountaineers at a base camp in Peru, which had ended with everyone stripped down to their jockeys.

The main thing bothering Ben was the fact that Joe's cough was growing steadily worse with the cold and the altitude. He wasn't about to say so, but, looking at his friend, he began to have doubts about the wisdom of pressing on.

'You don't sound good,' he said, after sitting through a prolonged bout of coughing.

'You said it,' agreed Ross. 'Chest like that, you shouldn't be climbing any higher.'

'Turn around, is that what you're saying?' Joe demanded. 'No way. I've been preparing for this climb for a year and I'm damned if I'm giving up just yet.'

'If you're not fit, man—'

'Fit? I'm fitter than either of you two.' Joe pounded his chest. 'I've climbed with worse than this.'

Ben knew it was true because he'd been there. But that didn't make it any more advisable for Joe to be on the mountain if he was in poor shape. He remembered Lisa's anxiety about Joe's recklessness and his own reassurances. Life at over fourteen thousand feet had been tough but bearable; up here, at seventeen thousand feet, the situation was markedly different. The air was thinner, the cold more intense, the dangers more acute. He worried most about altitude sickness: Joe had already suffered a bout last time they'd climbed together. As the days passed, he monitored his friend's condition with an anxious eye.

Joe coughed again, a gurgling wheeze that made the other two glance at him with concern.

'Jesus, man,' Ross said. 'You sound like a fucking cement mixer.'

'Feel like one, too.' Joe's laugh ended in a rattling, long-drawn cough.

Ben coughed too, felt the premonitory wheeze in his own lungs. He tried to tamp down his fear that it was the onset of altitude sickness. It couldn't be. Aware of the dangers of pushing up too high, too fast, they'd been careful all along, taken their time.

Ross pretended to dodge. 'Christ,' he said. His lips were cracked and bleeding with the cold, his grin white in his frost-glittering beard. 'Keep your germs to yourself, OK? Little suckers nearly got me that time.'

Outside, the wind screamed, buffeting the frail nylon walls of their shelter. The Kevlar poles bucked and bowed under the strain but, built to withstand hurricane-force winds, mercifully held. For now. The tent might not prove adequate protection if the howling energy of the wind outside got any worse. The gale could easily rip it right off the ridge, leaving them without any shelter at all.

Joe coughed again. Shivered. Another cough. A longer spasm of shivering. Ben's fingertips were raw; his feet numb. Although he was wearing every garment he'd brought with him, expensive cold-weather gear designed to keep out the chill, he still could not stop shivering. His throat ached alarmingly.

He knew, too, that despite the hard training all three of them had put in over the past twelve months, their physical fitness was deteriorating with every hour they spent incarcerated here. Tomorrow, if things didn't lighten up a little, they'd have to seriously consider trying to battle down through the storm to the camp and either give up or start over. They all knew that the people who survived the high mountains were the ones who knew when to about-face and climb down instead of up, yet the summit beckoned irresistibly. To stand on top of the highest peak in North America, knowing they'd got there under their own steam, knowing they'd fought against the elements, called on every last ounce of their strength, battled fatigue, nausea, thirst, pain . . . that was why they'd worked so hard for the past year, that was what they were searching for. The ultimate moment. The *achievement*.

They couldn't give up now.

Fighting a low-grade headache, Ben thought about Lisa. With the wind screaming all round him, the constant boom and rumble of the ice, the vicious whip of the tent, he remembered how he'd been invited by a far more senior climber to join an attempt on Everest next year. At first he'd been elated at the possibility of scaling the highest mountain in the world in such illustrious company.

'Prestige for you,' Lisa said, when they talked it over. 'If you went, it would mean you could virtually name your price.'

'True.' But he didn't think of the mountains as a means to a better job or increased pay.

'Isn't climbing Everest something you've always wanted to do?'

'Once maybe. Before the baby.' He'd rubbed the bristles on his jaw. 'Now I'm not so sure. When I was younger, perhaps.' He wanted to add that he didn't climb simply to get to the top. To add another notch to his mountaineering belt. Mountains weren't trophies. He climbed for the sake of climbing. 'But these days, Everest's almost like walking through Central Park.'

She'd laughed at him.

'It's true. I've thought about it a lot recently,' he'd said. 'And I wonder if maybe it's better not to conquer it. Better for me, personally, I mean.'

'Why?' She hadn't understood. 'How?'

'Because if I summited, if I got up there to the very top of the world, what would I do next? What challenge would there be left? People set themselves all these absurd goals – youngest to do this, first American to do that – but Everest has to be the pinnacle, in more ways than one. I get up there and I'm thirty-one, thirty-two years old, and there's nothing left for me to climb. Maybe it's best to leave it as a symbol of something I could have gone for, rather than to risk failing – or succeeding.'

He could still recall the expression on her face when he called the guy back and refused the invitation, the mixture of disbelief, reprieve and – he hadn't imagined it – disappointment.

He coughed again, an action which required ten times as much effort as it would have done at lower altitudes. Every breath of super-dry air that he took in exacerbated

137

the inflamed tissue of his throat. Liquid bubbled at the base of his lungs. He was beginning to feel uneasy. Survival in these conditions depended on weighing up the odds and making a calculated decision. If he and Joe were both in the preliminary stages of pulmonary edema, then they would have no choice but to descend, regardless of how they felt about it.

A huge gust of wind buffeted the tent and the sides of the dome were sucked outward and then in. The poles bowed inwards, moaning as they did so.

'Wow,' said Joe. 'What do you reckon, eighty knots?'

'Eighty-five,' Ross said. 'Minimum. Go out in that and you really will freeze your balls off.'

At least for the moment the satellite telephone was working and Ben had been able to keep in touch with Lisa, though the noise on the mountain had all but drowned out the sound of her voice. He was afraid, however, that as they climbed higher it would become increasingly difficult to get hold of her, and that worried him: last time they had spoken, she had sounded so fragile. She'd said that something didn't feel right. But then Neil's wife had said the same thing when she was six months pregnant with Jeff, and in the end it had turned out to be nothing more than trapped wind.

'Guys,' he said. 'It's time to get the stove going.'

'Do we have to?' groaned Joe. 'Damned fumes. My lungs are already coated with carbon. Makes me nauseous just to think about it.' He turned his head and retched. 'Me too,' said Ross.

'We have to get something warm inside us.' Ben struggled to sit upright, his body shaking with the cold. 'Tea. Soup. Noodles. What do you want?'

'I don't feel hungry. My throat hurts too much to swallow.'

'We have to eat. No way we'll top out if we don't keep our strength up.' Speaking was becoming an effort.

'You're right,' Joe said. He stared at the others from the shelter of his sleeping bag and Ben could see him trying to pull himself together, get back to being the strong one, the ambitious one. 'After missing out last time, I'm not leaving here until I set foot on that fucking summit.'

'Tell you what's keeping me going right now,' said Ross.

'What's that?'

'My grandchildren.'

'Grandchildren?' scoffed Joe. 'What are you, twenty-nine years old? Did you lose it, or what?'

'You don't have any *kids* yet,' Ben said kindly. He tried to lick his cracked lips and tasted blood.

'Hell, he doesn't even have a wife.'

'No, really. I had to spend hours when I was a kid listening to my old grandpappy tell us how he won the war, what a hero he'd been, show us his medals, all that crap,' said Ross. 'I figure I'm owed. One of these days it'll be me boring the pants off everyone, and those little tykes who'll have to sit round and listen to me. That's why I gotta get to the top this time.'

'Third time lucky,' said Joe.

'Tough bastard like you,' Ben said. 'You'll make it.'

'You bet I will. Can't let those grandkids off the hook, right?'

Ben wheezed a laugh. He himself couldn't think further than the coming baby. Grandchildren seemed immeasurably far away.

Between them, they managed to light the stove, boil some melted snow water for tea, force down one of the prepacked meals they'd brought with them. The food revived them a little. Later, relieving himself in the vestibule, Ben sensed that the force of the wind had

139

lessened. He unzipped the tent and poked his head out into the raging darkness. To his surprise, he saw that there were a few stars shining up there in the immense cold. Stars. The weather must be clearing. He stumbled back to the others.

'Guess what: looks like it's clearing up,' he said. 'If the weather stays good, we might just make it to the top tomorrow.'

'It'd mean an early start.'

'Or we could leave a couple of hours from now, maybe.'

'If it keeps on clearing, why not?'

'Think we can do it?' asked Ross. 'You two don't exactly look in prime condition.'

'We have to,' said Joe. 'If the gale dies down, I vote we go all out, make a dash for the top.'

'Specially since the weather guys were just saying on the radio that we might not see clear skies again for three or four weeks,' Ross said.

'Let's start packing our gear now,' Ben said. 'Just in case.'

Revitalized by the change in conditions, they packed their loads and checked their gear. The wind continued to abate. When they looked outside at ten thirty that night, although the temperature was still bitingly cold, the clouds had been swept away and the skies were clear.

Ben put a last phone call through to Lisa, told her he was fine, that, if all went well, he might be back earlier than he had thought.

'Good luck, sweetheart,' she said.

'I miss you.'

'Mmm. Come back as soon as you can.'

'Don't worry. I love you, my darling. Both of you.'

'Love you back.'

The other two were ready. 'OK, guys,' Joe said. 'This is it. The Musketeers are on their way.'

'All for one . . .' Ross said.

'. . . and one for all,' finished Ben.

The three of them looked at each other silently for a moment, then shook hands.

CHAPTER NINE

'I'm not doing any work, apart from wedging clay.' Lisa said, when Mel called her.

'So you might as well be up by the lake, where it's cooler. And I'd enjoy the company.'

'Me too.'

They had driven up earlier in the afternoon. Now, sitting on the deck of the Andersen house, a glass of iced tea in her hand, Lisa said, 'I can understand why you and Ben like it here so much. The lake and everything. It'll be great for kids. Ben's laid a kind of diving ledge, too.'

'Mmm.' Mel could see them too, those children who would leap into the water, the happy shrieks, barbecues, picnics.

'Mind you,' Lisa continued, 'I'll need a while to get used to people who take fifteen minutes to think up an answer to a question like "Isn't it a nice day?"'

'Different strokes, hon.' Mel tilted her glass, smelling mint and lemon. 'Ben's in Alaska right now, isn't he?'

'Yeah. I really miss him but at least he can keep in touch by satellite phone.'

'How's it all going?'

'They've finished the acclimatization period – getting used to the altitude – and are into the serious climbing.'

'He's OK, is he?'

'Just about. He called last night. They're stuck in a storm, apparently. He said the windchill factor up there can get as low as a hundred below, and the wind is hurricane force. And there he is with his buddies, crouched in a tent halfway up a mountain.' She shook her head.

'It sounds horrendous.' said Mel. He had sat opposite her, drinking red wine, staring at her with those distant eyes of his, candles casting shadows on the lean planes of his face, and though she had asked him, he had told her nothing of the thrill and desperation he must surely feel in situations like this.

'Horrendous is part of the fun,' said Lisa. 'He's up there not in spite of the danger, but *because* of it. It's part of his need to escape.'

'From you?'

Lisa laughed. 'I hope not. If you ask me, it's from the guilt at the death of that cousin of his I told you about.'

'It can't have been his fault.'

'Of course it wasn't. But deep down, he still feels it was.'

'I thought you said he was only eleven when that happened.'

'Eleven, twelve, in there.'

Not as long as her own guilt had lasted. Mel stood up. 'I'm right next door if you need any help. Just yell.'

The next morning, before setting off for a hike up the mountain, Mel strolled over to the Andersen house. 'Everything all right?'

'Fine.'

'No more of those funny feelings you were talking about in the car?'

143

Lisa made a face. 'I don't know, really. So where are you going?'

'Up to the Falls.'

'Wish I had the energy to tag along.' Today Lisa was wearing a green linen top over royal blue shorts, with a yellow scarf over her black hair. 'Instead, I just slung the hammock out in the yard and I'm gonna veg out, grab those rays when they show. I'm still bushed from yesterday.'

'What've you been doing?'

'After you went back to your place, I got a severe attack of the nesting instinct and spent about three hours scrubbing down the kitchen – turned out the cupboards, cleaned out the drawers, washed the floor, laundered the drapes and the dish towels, you name it.'

'A lazy morning today, then. And here's something to think about while you enjoy it. I've been mulling over an idea I've had for setting up an exhibition of crafts. I don't mean like those places you see in the tourist towns – something much more demanding than that. I know all sorts of people whose work is worth showing. Quilters and paper-makers and workers in wood. Even potters.'

'It may be crafty, but will it be artistic?' Lisa rounded her eyes. 'Sarah Mahoney will want to know.'

'That's the whole point.' Mel said. 'I want to challenge the assumptions of people like Sarah about the boundaries between art and crafts. Your pots, for instance – which are they?'

'I certainly don't think of them as simply craftwork.'

'We'll talk about it when I get back.'

A scatter of pine needles had drifted up against the door of the cabin by the time Mel returned. She had cut short her hike: the temperature had risen and by midday, the

144

heat pressing down on the top of her head, sullen, almost unbreathable, made conditions unpleasant, even up in the cooler forest. As she shucked off her boots, she could hear the murmur of the lake. She poured water from the refrigerator and carried it out onto the terrace. Her body was pleasantly tired: she could feel the movement of each separate energized muscle, as though the mountain air still bubbled through her blood.

Clouds were building up behind the hills, purple and black, spreading towards the lower ground. There would be an electric storm later, maybe even some rain. Leaning forward and looking to her left, she could see the Andersen house. Laundry fluttered from a clothes line: beyond it was the hammock. Smudges of green and blue, a patch of yellow. Lisa was enjoying the heat – or perhaps dealing with it the best way she could, by doing nothing. Mel had read somewhere that pregnant women were always five degrees hotter than anyone else, whatever the temperature.

She went upstairs and changed into a swimsuit, found a towel, went outside. The heavy pine-scented air under the trees was as thick as syrup as she walked down to the water's edge. Yearning for the cool water on her over-heated skin, she plunged into the lake and began to swim towards the farther shore. After just a few minutes, however, she began to shiver. The water was cool, then cold, then icy. She turned over on her back and let the sun's rays, dimmed by the thin cloud, warm her until the cold beneath was too much and she ran gasping out into the heat again.

Back in the house, she pulled a T-shirt on over her chilled body, poured more water and drank it down. It was too hot to do much. Lying sprawled on the sofa, she could see a shard of glass from the bowl she had broken last time she was here. As she bent to retrieve it, she saw on the bottom shelf of the bookcase the catalogue of an exhibition of Naive Art which she had given Eric to celebrate their tenth wedding anniversary. She remembered how he had torn the wrapping paper from the gift and stared at it uncomprehendingly. 'Naive Art?' He had raised his eyebrows. 'Is this my sort of thing?'

'That exhibition,' she said quickly, too quickly, 'it's where we first met,' and saw how swiftly he had pretended that of course he remembered. Laughing, he had reached for her hand, spoken knowledgeably of Grandma Moses, L. S. Lowry, American Gothic, the Middle European tradition, said how much he had always enjoyed primitive painters.

She pulled it from the shelf and saw that it was still sealed inside the protective film in which it had arrived. He had never even bothered to open it.

She picked up a book which lay on the coffee table in front of her. Not really a book, more of an album, its stiffened cover made of coarse paper, its spine and corners reinforced in soft chocolate leather. Inside, the pages were uneven, rough cut, each one unique, each one handmade using petals, leaves, threads of linen, silk ribbon. It had been created by Rowena Clyde, a woman artist who lived with her painter husband up in the hills behind Butterfield. Mel lifted it to her nose, sniffing the good animal smell of leather, and thought of the journal her grandmother had given her years ago. Where was it now? She had written in it once, something self-conscious about waiting for her true love, and never opened it again.

Restless, she got up again, poured more water, walked out onto the deck. Maybe she would go over and see how Lisa was doing. She looked between the trees and saw that Lisa was still in the hammock, which hung motionless.

Mel frowned. There was something odd here, something not quite right. In the hour or more since she had last looked, Lisa had not moved at all. Mel came down the wooden steps, then hesitated. Should she go across? What business was it of hers if Lisa wanted to sleep the day away? Pregnant women got tired very easily.

Yet, although unwilling to interfere, about to turn back into the house, she felt uneasy. Stepping down from the porch, she walked slowly through the growth of tree and bush which divided the two cabins. By now, storm clouds were racing across the sky and the wind was rising, ruffling the surface of the lake. However tired she might be, it was odd that Lisa did not sense the dropping temperature and wake up.

'Lisa?' Mel called as she approached. Her bare feet winced from sharp-pointed rocks and the roughness of fir cones. Under the trees where Lisa swung, the grass was discolored, not summer-green but a reddish brown, like autumn leaves.

'Lisa, honey? Are you OK?' Closer to, the immobility of the young woman seemed even more abnormal. Fractions of a second passed while Mel's brain digested what she was seeing. Blood, a crimson glisten on the stained grass, bright drops falling. Then she began to run.

'No,' she said aloud. 'Please, no.'

Her brain absorbed possibilities, spinning through a series of disconnected thoughts. *The baby. Loss. Pain. Ben. The baby. Lisa.*

She bent over the hammock. Lisa's face was as pale as cream, limbs set, body inert. One arm hung stiffly over the edge of the hammock . . . *and time instead of spinning was suddenly suspended her vision expanding to include everything not just the still body but everything a line of ants the fraying end of a knot in the strings of the*

147

hammock a chip in the blue polish on Lisa's middle toe
the complicated whorls of a pine cone on the ground
the racing clouds a bird in the pine trees everything
not the baby please not the baby . . .

She could feel her heart jumping under her breast. 'Lisa!' she screamed, the elongated sound floating up into the blue air. 'Lisa!'

In that hard still moment, it seemed very clear Lisa was dead. Yet Mel knew that could not possibly be. She pressed her palm hard to her chest, drew in a few deep breaths, heard the bird above her head, its cry drawn-out and thin, then put the back of her hand to Lisa's cheek. It was still warm. So was her bare shoulder. Bracing herself, she leaned down and laid the side of her head against the girl's breast. Deep inside Lisa's body she could hear the slow thud of a heartbeat. The flood of relief was so strong that she felt faint. Was it Lisa's or the baby's?

About to run for the phone, she saw Lisa's eyelids flutter and her eyes slowly open.

Involuntarily Mel stepped back, raising a hand to her mouth. 'Oh, my God,' she whispered.

'Help me . . .' Lisa's mouth scarcely moved as she formed the words.

'Are you in pain?' Mel seized Lisa's hand and held it tightly.

Lisa moved her head from one side to the other. 'Cramps,' she murmured. One thin hand moved towards her belly and then fell back. A faint blush of color appeared in her face and was gone again. 'My baby . . .'

'I'll call nine-one-one.' Mel looked up at the Andersen house.

'No phone . . .'

'I'll call from my place.'

'I'm bleeding.' Lisa shifted slightly and her face creased

148

as though a hand had violently squeezed it. At the same time, there was a liquid gushing sound from between her legs and her body spasmed. She closed her eyes.

Clots of fresh blood were oozing from between her thighs, seeping between the spaces of the hammock, falling in bright red globules onto the grass. The ground beneath was dark with dried blood. Such a lot of it. More, it seemed, than Lisa's small body could possibly have contained, or could afford to lose. How long had she been bleeding?

Miscarriage, Mel thought. Lisa was having a miscarriage. Facts, half-digested from general reading but never really concentrated on, crowded her brain. I can't remember, she thought. Towels. Compresses. Tourniquets. What am I supposed to do? I ought to know but I don't.

She touched Lisa's arm. 'I'll be right back, honey,' she said. 'I'm going to telephone. Try and keep absolutely still.'

Lisa's pale lips moved but no sound emerged.

Mel ran. Her brain seemed paralyzed and at the same time buzzing with questions. One in six pregnancies miscarry, wasn't that what she'd read? Would it be best to bring her car as close as she could to the hammock, get Lisa into it, rush back to Butterfield? That could take two or three hours. Lisa had looked so . . . so *dead*. The shock of it made her fingers so clumsy that it took her three tries to dial.

A calm female voice answered. Stumbling over herself, Mel tried to explain what had happened.

'Please verify your phone number and address,' the voice said.

Mel did so. 'She needs to get to a hospital immediately,' she said urgently.

'How many weeks pregnant is she?'

149

'I don't . . . five, five and a half. Months, that is.' Mel tried to do the calculations but her brain seemed unequal to the simple task of multiplying by four.

'Twenty, twenty-two weeks?'

The woman on the other end of the line seemed not to have grasped the urgency of the situation. 'Send someone quickly, please,' entreated Mel. 'She has to get to the hospital. She's lost a huge amount of blood.'

'Could you bring her in yourself?'

'I don't think I dare move her. There's so much blood,' Mel said, squeezing her eyes shut against the picture of Lisa's body. 'Clots of it. I don't know anything about miscarriages but that's what this looks like.'

'If you'll hold, I'll see what's available.'

'Hurry,' Mel said. 'I don't like leaving her alone. Tell me what to do.'

After what seemed like a lifetime, the operator came back to her. 'A helicopter will be with you as soon as possible. Is there somewhere it could touch down?'

Mel tried to think. 'Yes, there's a field about half a mile away – but you'd have to come up and get her from here. She's at the old Andersen place.'

'While you're waiting, you could try to contain the blood loss.'

'She's – I'm not sure if she's lost the baby or not but—' Mel had visions of the fetus moving down the birth canal, a dark mass of crimson tissue, pushing its way inexorably into the world. More blood, the palely violent colors of the body's secret places, pink and purple and blue. She saw the tiny dome of a half-formed head, flipper limbs, small clutching fingers. A rudimentary face. She shook her head to rid it of the images. 'Hurry!' she begged. The sight of fresh blood, Lisa's blood, was terrifying. Disorienting. Again, she felt faint.

150

'They're on their way,' said the woman. 'Don't let her move about.' She hung up.

Ben, Mel thought, replacing the handset. She had to notify Ben, let him know what had happened. But how? She paused for a moment. Was he even contactable? He must be, if he was in touch with Lisa. Running back to Lisa under the pine trees, she tried not to think of the child, Lisa's child, *our* child. For a second, past and present fused. *My* child.

Lisa was still bleeding heavily. Sensing Mel at her side, she opened her eyes.

'I've lost the baby,' she said clearly.

'You don't know that.' Mel took one of the limp hands in hers and began to chafe the cold fingers.

'It's dead.' Lisa tried to raise her head to look down at her belly. 'My baby.'

'Keep still,' urged Mel.

'Why? My baby's dead.' Tears formed in Lisa's eyes and slowly moved down the sides of her face. 'My precious baby.'

'You can't be sure,' Mel said.

'I can. I am.' Lisa's body convulsed and she squeezed her thighs tightly together. More blood dripped onto the pine needles below the hammock.

'The emergency services are on their way,' said Mel. She listened for the thock-thock of the helicopter's rotators against the air, but the wind was too strong to hear anything except the tossing branches of the trees.

'It's my fault.'

'Don't be silly,' Mel said sharply.

'I shouldn't have cleaned the house last night.' The words were scarcely audible. 'I shouldn't have tried to work. I should have rested more.'

In the distance, above the roar of the wind, Mel heard

151

a hammering of the stormy air. 'That's the helicopter,' she said.

'Too late.' Lisa closed her eyes and the tears continued to seep from under her lids, each one weighted with loss.

Mel's own throat was constricted as she held the younger woman's cold hand in the circle of her own. Above her, the treetops bent and swayed as the ERS chopper turned looking for somewhere to touch down. She did not look up at it. Instead, she bent her head and squeezed her eyes shut while sobs welled up inside her, wave after wave.

A doctor came into the passage from the recovery room. He was a man some fifteen years younger than herself but already worn down by responsibility for lives other than his own. There was a mask around his neck; his green scrubs were dotted with what Mel knew must be blood. Lisa's blood? The baby's? She pushed herself up from the vinyl-covered sofa on which she had been waiting, bracing herself for what he had to say.

'We've stabilized her,' he said, glancing down at the clipboard he carried.

'She looks . . . she was so pale.'

'She's lost a great deal of blood. They've given her one transfusion already, but she may need another.'

'And the baby? She lost it, didn't she?'

'I'm afraid so. Are you her mother?'

'Her neighbor. Her friend.' Grief burned behind Mel's eyes, not just for Lisa but also for the dead child who had been alive but had not made it into the world. 'Her mother died when she was young.'

'Do you know when she had her last ultrasound?'

'I can't remember. It must have been, what, a couple of weeks ago.'

'Mmm.' The doctor stared down at his notes. 'Unfortunately Dr Patterson is out of town this weekend.' He looked at Mel. 'Not that he could have made any difference to what happened.'

'I was right there when it . . .' Mel could not rid herself of the image of the still figure lying under the trees. 'If only I'd realized earlier that there was something wrong, I might have been able to do something.'

He shook his head. 'There was nothing you could have done.'

'But if I'd called the ERS sooner, it might have . . .' said Mel, a frantic sweat breaking out under her arms, guilt choking her.

'For the record, Lisa's baby has been dead for about two weeks.'

'What? But surely . . .'

'What happened today was a natural process, the body's response to an irregularity of some kind. A death in the womb often occurs for a very good reason.'

'A *good* reason? Whatever the reason, how can the loss of a wanted baby be *good*?'

'The fetus may have been abnormal in some way. This is her first pregnancy, isn't it?'

Mel nodded. All this time Lisa's baby had been dead? She had been carrying around a dead child for two weeks? The information was too difficult, too appalling, for her to process.

'It happens,' the doctor said. He patted her arm. 'Especially with first babies.'

'That doesn't make it any better.'

He smiled at her. 'She'll be all right, I promise you.' He straightened up. 'For the record, we've cleaned her up, done a D and C. She's young and healthy. There's no reason why she shouldn't try again as soon as she feels like it.'

153

'Try again?' Mel frowned.

'For another baby.'

'But that's so . . .' Anger leaped inside her. '. . . such a *thoughtless* thing to say.'

A complicated expression passed across his face. For a moment he stared at her. 'Yes,' he said eventually. 'I suppose it was. I should know better. When you see so many women, it's easy to forget the trauma each one of them is going through.' He sighed, looked down at the floor for a moment, then back at Mel. 'I apologize, Mrs . . . uh . . .'

'Sherman.'

'Mrs Sherman. I shouldn't have been so insensitive. Let me put it a little differently. Lisa will be emotionally traumatized by this, and who can blame her. However, if she wants to get pregnant again, then she shouldn't have any trouble doing so.'

It was not very much but it was at least a recognition of Lisa's humanity.

'Can I see her?' Mel asked.

'She's still in recovery,' he said. 'An hour or two more should do it. Why don't you find the canteen, have a cup of coffee or something?'

'When can she go home?'

'Best to keep her here for a couple more days. After that – as long as she takes care of herself and has plenty of rest, she should be OK.' He smiled at her again, the smile less broad now, less professional. As she turned to go, he said, 'Mrs Sherman . . .'

'Yes?'

'My wife miscarried our first child. I don't think a day passes when she doesn't grieve for him.'

'What about you?'

He passed a hand over his face. 'Me too,' he said.

154

For a moment Mel stood without moving. Then she nodded slowly. 'Thank you for telling me.'

Later, Mel was allowed into the recovery room. Exhaustion sat on her shoulders, as though she had been carrying an invisible burden around with her for years. She stood beside the high hospital bed, holding Lisa's hand. Such a small hand, almost square, with its blunt potter's fingers and short-clipped nails. Such a cold hand, too, despite the heat inside the room.

Fear and shock crashed around inside her skull. Lisa looked so frail, the black lashes lying on her pale cheeks, the blue-veined eyelids seeming almost transparent. The fragility of life, the everyday proximity to extinction, had never struck Mel so forcibly as now. She wanted Lisa to be strong again, to see color in her white face. She wanted to see her laugh, watch her eyes light up as she made some outrageous remark.

Lisa stirred a little. Her skin had lost its earlier deathly pallor, but she was still pale. 'Ben,' she moaned. Her eyes were closed, her voice still fogged with the effects of the anesthetic.

Mel leaned close to Lisa's ear. 'I'll be back later but I'm going to go home now and try to track him down,' she said, enunciating clearly, hoping the words would reach her friend's troubled heart. 'I'll find him for you, Lisa.'

She spent some time searching Lisa's home, looking for anything that could conceivably be an Alaskan phone number. The cork bulletin boards in the kitchen and in Lisa's studio held only cards from a couple of cab services, flyers promising pizza deliveries within thirty minutes, a takeaway menu from Butterfield's single Chinese restaurant, Mel's own number, the local cinema. She pulled out drawers, moved piles of newspapers, opened books. She went through an address book she found in the living room, opened the nightstands on either side of the double bed upstairs. Nothing.

Possessed by an increasing sense of urgency, she got up before dawn the next day and drove back to the lake through early morning mists. In the Andersen house, everything was as it had been just a few short hours before: the iced-tea glasses from the morning had been rinsed and left upside down on the draining board, an empty coffee cup still stood on the counter, along with the remains of a salad. It jolted her to realize that so much had happened in such a short space of time. Outside, the hammock still swung between the trees; even in the early morning light she could make out the discolored ground beneath it and, without any warning, she found herself shaken again by a grief so severe that she could scarcely draw enough breath into her lungs. 'Oh God,' she moaned. 'Oh God.' She felt as though her heart were being torn into pieces. Doubled up, clutching at a chairback for support, she waited for the spasm to pass, feeling tears burn her face as she wept for Lisa and for her own unacknowledged loss.

Back at the Andersen house by the lake, she finally found what she was looking for. On the double bed was a small bottle of Je Reviens scent, and a Post-it note cut into the shape of a heart, scrawled with the words *Je reviens aussi. Until then, you can reach me on this number. Je t'aime.*

Mel read the message several times. This small glimpse into the private side of Lisa's marriage moved her in a way she could not quite define. She had grown used to believing that Ben was an irresponsible husband. Now she envisaged him laying the perfume on the pillow, smiling his fabulous smile as he thought of Lisa finding it. Try as she might, she could not help imagining them together, his big hands on Lisa's small body, her black hair spilling over his chest, the two of them reaching for each other, love enclosing them in a glow of rapture.

She wrenched her mind back to the number in her hand and began the long and tedious business of trying to make contact via satellite radio with a man halfway up a mountain in Alaska.

CHAPTER TEN

They had been climbing by the light of their head-torches since eleven o'clock the night before. It was slow going in the corrosive chill, but, as dawn rose, they were making their way up the final headwall. All around them was a thick layer of rolling white cumulus, pierced here and there by the topmost peaks of Mt Huntington and the slender spire of the Mooses Tooth. The sky was immense, the color of rose-tinted honey, changing slowly and magnificently through peach and melon to blue.

Ben stood drinking in the beauty around him, then turned and followed Joe and Ross up the final thousand feet until the three of them stood on the summit. The sun blazed down from a sky of a blue so profound that it was like staring into eternity. The wind was mercifully silent. The moment of purity that he craved when he was earth-bound overtook him like an orgasm: tears stood in his eyes and, pushing back his goggles, he brushed them away with the back of his mitten. He knew that if he stretched out his hand, he could have touched the sky. It saddened him that this ethereal moment of absolute integrity, unspoilable, incorruptible, was one he would never be able to share with Lisa. This was a view only those who

158

ventured to twenty thousand feet or more above sea level would ever see.

Joe fell on his knees in the snow and threw his arms wide. 'We made it!' he exulted. 'We fucking made it!' His voice was hoarse and he collapsed in an extended bout of coughing.

Ross rolled over and over in the snow, kicking out his legs. 'Oh thank you,' he shouted gleefully up at the sky. 'Thank you!'

'Uh-oh,' said Ben. 'Those poor grandchildren!'

The storm promised by the weathermen held off, and they were able to make good time back to their camp at seventeen thousand feet. But by the time they reached it the wind was getting up again, and Joe's condition had suddenly begun to deteriorate. When Ben lit the stove, he hacked, bent double, clutching at his stomach, 'Oh man,' he gasped and keeled over, bile spewing from his mouth.

'Oh, my God,' said Ross. His face was grey with fatigue. 'Edema.'

'We have to get him down lower than this.'

'How?'

'Any way we can.' Ben shook his head, grimacing. 'He needs to be way further down the mountain. If we stay up here, he'll die. Simple as that.'

'Hey, I'm whipped out, man.' Eyes closed, Ross gulped hot tea.

'Yeah.' Ben sank back against his backpack. After the efforts of the past eighteen hours, the thought of sleep was irresistible. Outside the wind howled, and the tent shook.

'I gotta have some rest before we go on,' Ross said.

'Two hours, OK? And then we're out of here.'

'I'm fine,' Joe croaked. 'I can go down by myself.'

'Dream on,' Ben said. 'Think I'm going to let you go

159

down alone? But first we've got to get some fluid inside you.'

'My throat's too sore to swallow.'

'Too bad.' Ben crouched over the stove, melting snow, adding cubes of chocolate. Joe needed both fluid and sugar: this was one way to make sure he had both.

An hour later, Joe had ingested most of the warm liquid and was looking a little better. Exhausted, Ben swallowed the last dregs from his own mug and wondered whether he was being overcautious. Maybe they should risk staying there overnight and getting down in the morning, when all three of them would be rested. But another look at Joe convinced him that they didn't have that much time to spare.

In the corner of the tent, the sat phone buzzed faintly. Ross looked at it. 'Christ, I hope that's not my mother.' He picked up. 'Yes,' he said. 'Yeah. Mrs Who?' His eyes swiveled to Ben. 'For you, man.'

'Who is it? Lisa?'

'Not unless she's calling herself Mrs Sherman these days.'

'Mrs Sher—' Ben's heart felt as though it had stopped beating. The foretaste of disaster struck him with a pain like a skewer being inserted into his brain, so that he cried aloud as Ross handed him the receiver. 'Yeah?'

'Ben?'

'Yeah. Yes.'

'It's Mel Sherman here.'

'What's happened?' A burning rush of anxiety swept over him. He swayed, almost overcome by cold and exhaustion.

'It's Lisa. She's . . .'

'She's what?'

'She's had a miscarriage.' Her voice came and went.

'Oh Jesus. Sweet Jesus.' Ben's nose and throat had blocked up and he could scarcely breathe. 'What happened, for Chrissake?' He looked at the other two men. 'Lisa . . . she's lost the baby.'

'Oh, man, I'm sorry.' Ross reached out and held Ben's ankle for a brief moment. 'What a fucking bummer, man.'

Ben's head felt like a balloon. His heart was beating so fast he was afraid he would pass out.

Mel's voice wavered slightly. 'I'm so very—'

'My wife . . . how's my wife?'

'She's still in the hospital. For observation.'

'Is she all right?'

'She's . . .' Mel's voice faded again. Phrases emerged through the storm of digital static. '. . . very weak . . . loss of blood . . . no chance . . .'

'*What?*'

'. . . meet you at Boston if you tell me when you'll get here.' The sentence was clear this time, reverberating in the frost-lined tent. Ben was aware of the other two staring at him, their faces gaunt.

'I can't just walk off the fucking mountain at a moment's notice, you know,' he said, anxiety roughening his voice.

'You should be here. Lisa needs you.'

'I know. I know that, for Chrissakes.' He felt as though someone had gripped his heart between a pair of pincers and was squeezing them slowly shut. Tears came into his eyes and froze on his lower eyelashes. 'Oh, my God, I can't believe this, Mel. I can't get my head round . . .'

'What? I can't hear you.'

He pressed his hand against the bridge of his nose in an effort to stem the tears. 'I can't get away.'

'What?'

'I'm snowed in. I can't—'

'Hello? Hello? I can't hear you. Ben? Are you still there?' Her voice faded again, receding away from him into the brutal mountains.

'Lisa,' he screamed. 'Lisa . . . she's OK, isn't she?'

But there was no answer and though he pushed at the keys, banged the damn machine with his fist, he couldn't get it working. 'Fucking thing,' he yelled. 'Fucking piece of crap. I cart it all the way up here so I can keep in touch with my wife, and it doesn't work worth a shit.' He stared at them with savage eyes. 'My wife . . .'

'Oh man,' Ross said.

'Jeez, I'm sorry.' Joe lifted a hand in Ben's direction and dropped it again.

Ben smeared his face with a half-frozen hand. Pulling down the hood of his parka, pushing his feet into his yellow plastic Koflax boots, he tugged down the tent zipper and struggled out into the clamor of the storm. A screaming confusion of barbarous cold and whirling snow greeted him. Each flake slammed into his face with the force of flung pebbles. The sound of the wind had risen to a continuous shriek. Several times its sheer force knocked him to his knees in the snow.

Lisa . . .

An hour later, the new storm had turned into a blizzard. Ben had been unable to rest, though he knew he would need all his strength to help guide Joe safely down the mountain. He couldn't stop thinking about Lisa's small body, torn apart by pain. He groaned aloud. She had wanted the baby so very much. What grief she must be feeling, and he not there to hold her close, kiss her cheeks, tell her it would be OK, it would be all right, they could try again. He should have been there, he knew that.

162

She'd told him she had a bad feeling about this trip and she'd been right. He looked over at Joe, who seemed semi-comatose. If they couldn't rouse him sufficiently, it was going to be a real problem to get him down to a level at which his oxygen-starved body could start to recover. People died of edema, both pulmonary and cerebral, very easily, very quickly. It was vital that they get him down to the relative safety of the camp three thousand feet below.

They set off, Ross and Ben assisting Joe as best they could. Roped between them, and moving on instinct as much as anything else, Joe managed to stagger along under his own steam, but the mind-numbing effects of oxygen deprivation caused his legs to give under him from time to time, pitching him to the ground. The first part of the route followed a ridge as sharp as a blade of scissors, with a two-thousand-foot drop on one side, a three-thousand-foot drop on the other. The slightest inattention could lead to a terminal plunge. At first another couple was ahead of them, dimly visible through the snow, but then the clouds came rolling down again, leaving them entirely alone in a landscape where they could barely see each other in the whiteout.

Struggling, laboring, all of them overextended, they finally made it off the ridge to the flatter ground which led on down to the camp below.

They were going to make it, Ben thought. It was going to be OK. And as soon as he'd delivered Joe to the medical tent he was out of there, heading back to Vermont as fast as he could.

'Oh, fuck!' Suddenly Ross, who was in the lead, stepped onto fresh powder and, in doing so, broke through a thin snow bridge above one of the many narrow crevasses which riddled the terrain. 'Fuck,' he yelled again as he fell, disappearing into the crevasse.

Joe, scarcely aware of his surroundings, was yanked after him, his weight pulling Ben down too. Acting on instinct, Ben stamped his feet firmly into the snow and sank the shaft of his ice axe next to his boot before frantically wrapping the remaining rope around the shaft, making it strong enough to hold. He hoped.

'Joe!' he yelled. 'Are you OK?'

Whether it was the adrenaline engendered by the fall, or the lower altitude, Joe seemed suddenly more awake.

'Yeah. I'm anchored,' he called.

'How far down?'

'Maybe twenty feet.'

'And Ross?'

'I'm OK too,' Ross said, his voice fainter. 'Except I think I just fucked up my knee. Man, I was bouncing about like a ping-pong ball.'

'How far down are you?'

'Another ten feet down from Joe.'

Ben secured the rope. 'Can you move at all?'

'Don't know,' Ross said. 'I've got my foot on a kind of ledge here. I'm not gonna fall any further if I keep absolutely still.'

'Joe?'

'If you can pull on the rope, I could try front-pointing up,' Joe said. 'It's narrow down here, shouldn't be too hard. Be a lot easier if it wasn't for this fucking great weight on the end of the line . . .'

'Me, you mean?' Ross said.

'That's right, you evil bastard.'

'I lost twelve kilos over the last week.'

'No shit? That's OK then.'

Ben listened to their banter, knowing that both were scared shitless. Any moment the two of them could plunge to an icy and irretrievable death. Their bones might lie on

164

the mountain for eternity, and there would be nothing he could do about it. He remembered Lisa weeping, asking him to take care of himself.

'OK, guys,' he shouted, thinking furiously. 'We're going to have to work together on this one. One foot at a time. Joe front-pointing, Ross using his ax. You still got the ax, Ross?'

'How do you think I'm hanging on here?' Ross said.

'Lose your pack, for starters.' Getting rid of Ross's gear was a calculated risk: if Ben managed to get the two men up from the crevasse and they then found themselves having to bivouac between here and the camp, it could mean death from hypothermia. But he knew that, weighed down, he wouldn't have the strength to help them both up.

After a moment, Ross shouted, 'Done.'

'Now you, Joe.'

'And make fucking sure it doesn't land on my head,' Ross said.

'I'm going to set up a Z pulley,' Ben said. Making himself safe, he cautiously approached the edge. Shrugging off his pack, he managed to force one end of it under the rope which led from the embedded ice ax down into the crevasse. Snow stung the exposed part of his face and whipped against his goggles, making it difficult to see. He fumbled for a couple of prusik loops and a few carabiners and pulled them off his harness, then, using the ax, constructed a simple pulley system. It took time, but it would make it much easier to get the other two to the top. When he was ready, he shouted, 'On the count of three, Ross lifts his ax and sinks it. At the same time, Joe moves up.'

'Can you handle it, Ben?' Joe sounded clearer-headed than he had for many hours. He too must have been calculating the odds.

'No sweat, man,' Ben said. ''Sides, I don't have any choice. Think of Ross's grandkids.'

'Guys . . .' It was Ross's voice, shaky now, frightened. 'What?'

'Look, I can hang on here for a while. Why don't you cut the rope and leave me here, go and get help?'

'Why don't you shut up?' Ben said roughly.

'That's not an option,' said Joe.

'If I wasn't on the end, you'd find it much easier.'

Ben thought about it. 'He's right. And once you're up, Joe, we can send down a fresh rope.'

'Right. Between us we shouldn't have too much problem hauling the fat bastard up.'

'What do you think, Ross?' Ben asked, though he knew the answer. Ross would be thinking how easy it would be to fall. Ross would be thinking that once his lifeline was cut, maybe the two of them would leave him to die. Ross was thinking that this blue-green ice-crack might be his tomb.

'Makes good sense,' he said.

Even with the rope cut, and Joe front-pointing, it took Ben nearly half an hour to pull him to the top. Above his head the wind screamed. Snow blew horizontally into his face, obscuring his vision. At one point he nearly lost his footing but managed to stop himself falling. Finally the top of Joe's helmet emerged and a few seconds later he lay spreadeagled on the snow, gasping, his face an ominous waxy white. Then he got to his knees and vomited copiously. 'Jesus,' he said. 'Jesus H. Christ. I really thought that was it,' before he collapsed and lay without moving.

Ben paid out a rope to where Ross waited further down, precariously anchored by one foot on a tiny ledge, his ax sunk into the ice wall, and only one of his legs operational.

166

Waiting for Ross to call up that he had secured the fresh rope round his body, Ben felt an overwhelming urge to sink down beside Joe and go to sleep. He thought of Lisa and tears came into his eyes. Fighting nausea from exertion in the altitude, he struggled to maintain control of his senses. He yelled at Joe, but there was no response, which scared him. He would have to do this alone and he wasn't sure he still had the physical stamina.

'Ross!' he shouted. 'What the hell are you doing down there?'

There was no reply.

'Ross?'

Nothing.

Jesus. Had he passed out? Fallen? If so, had he managed to secure the rope first?

'Ross?' he screamed. 'Where the fuck are you?' He tugged gently at the rope and found that there was weight on the end of it. Ross must have fainted from the pain of his shattered knee. But if he was unconscious, unable to help the ascent by sinking his ax into the walls of the crevasse, how the hell was he going to get him up to the top quickly, unless Joe helped? He kicked his friend as hard as he could. 'Joe!' he shouted. 'I need help here, you fucking bastard.' But Joe was out cold.

Bracing himself, Ben gritted his teeth, groaning with effort. Lisa flashed into his mind. He'd been a rotten husband to her, he realized. He loved her but he had never quite come to terms with staying in one place all the time and putting down roots. The baby might have ensured that – *would* have ensured that, he told himself, in the bleak hostility of the mountainside, both his friends out of it, no-one else around, only the eerie screams of the wind, the frozen granules of snow in his face, the semi-darkness of the blinding cloud which enveloped him.

The muscles round his ribs yelled for mercy as, inch by inch, he used the Z pulley to get Ross to the surface. His lungs felt as though they were on fire each time he drew breath in through his clenched teeth. How much longer could he keep this up? If he stopped, then all the precious inches he had fought for would go for nothing.

And Ross would die.

If only someone would come down the trail, making for the safety of the lower camp. Or some foolhardy climber would come up, hoping to find a weather window in which to push for the summit. It was so damn difficult with one. Especially someone who'd summited and come down again without any rest to speak of. He calculated that they must have been climbing for close to twenty-one hours non-stop.

Mucus oozed up from his throat, filling his mouth. He spat and saw the snow redden briefly before it was covered again. Joe was half-hidden now under a blanket of snow. If he didn't rouse himself soon . . .

The thought lent Ben new strength. He heaved on the rope again. And again. He was too far from the edge to see what progress he was making. He pulled. And pulled once more. There was something damp in his mittens which he knew must be blood from his split fingers.

'One,' he gritted. And tugged. 'Two.' And tugged again. He wasn't even sure that Ross was alive. It was well over an hour since he'd fallen: by now he might have succumbed to the cold. Yet, inch by inch, the rope was coiling at his feet.

There came a point when he knew it was all over. He could not make one single more effort. All he could do now was to give up, to let go of Ross, hanging so precariously on the end of the line. If he was unconscious, he'd never even be aware that he was plummeting to his

168

death. And then he, Ben, could lie down beside Joe and fall into a deep sleep. He pulled once more. He was almost done for.

. . . love you too, dreamboat. Out of nowhere, the phrase floated into his head. He thought he could see the letters blazoned on the snow, blue and green and red, like a neon sign flashing through the storm *Love you too . . .* Lisa, with her little hands and her shiny black hair, *love you, dreamboat, love you . . .* silver spoons and yellow roses, Joe's voice saying mountains and babies didn't mix, Lisa, Lisa, my darling, the baby, the lost baby, sunlight on the lake, *love you too, dreamboat . . .*

If he couldn't make one last effort, then all three of them were finished. He must not let that happen. Not with the possibility that Lisa needed him, that somewhere in a sane and quiet world far from here she waited for him, her fragile face turned to the door, listening for his footsteps.

And then he heard the voice. Ross's voice. Pain-filled. Exhausted. Spurring him onward. 'Think I lost it there for a while. Way to go, Benjamin. Almost there. One more try. One more. You can do it, you know you can do it.'

The tug on the pulley rope lessened slightly, as Ross used his ax in the ice walls of the crevasse. Nauseous with effort, his bones at cracking point, his muscles torn with fatigue, Ben finally saw one of Ross's mittens scrabbling at the surface, then the other, gave one more body-crunching pull, and another, and saw the top of Ross's red hood, his face, his shoulders.

'Jeez, man.' Ross dug his elbows into the snow and pulled himself forward, while Ben, walking backward, rapidly shortened the rope. 'Oh Jeez.' His voice was full of tears. 'Thought that was it, down there. Th-thought it

169

w-was all up with me.' He lay with his face pressed into the snow and his shoulders heaved.

Ben too sank down, and hung his head, fighting waves of nausea. The efforts they'd already made weren't going to be enough. There was more to come.

'Your knee – what's wrong with it?' he managed.

'Smashed, I think. Hit the side of the crevasse when I fell.'

'No chance you can walk?'

Ross turned over and sat up. He cradled his knee with both gloved hands and let out a sharp exhalation of pain. 'No way.' Despite the incipient frost nip on his nose, he sounded almost cheerful. He looked at Ben from under frost-caked eyebrows. 'Hey, man . . .'

'What?'

'You know.'

'What?'

'Thanks.'

'You'd have done the same for me.'

'I might have tried. Don't know if I'd have succeeded.' Ross glanced at Joe. 'What's with him?'

'Hypoxia. Hypothermia. By now, could be anything.'

'What're we gonna do?'

'We're gonna drag you over there.' Ben nodded at a slight mound in the snow, a rock no more than a couple of feet high. 'We're gonna dig you in. Put you inside my sleeping bag, cover you up as best we can. Then I'm going to get Joe down to the camp and fetch help for you.'

Ross was worried. 'Can you manage all that, man? On your own? You'll have to lower him down.'

'No other way.' A huge weariness filled Ben. He turned his back to the wind, hunched over himself, pulled some chocolate from the front of his parka and stuffed it into his mouth. 'Here.' He handed the rest to Ross.

'Are you OK?' Ross said anxiously.

'I'm fine.' He wasn't, but he couldn't give up now. With his ax, he set about cutting a shallow hole at the base of the rock, lined it with his sleeping mat, then put his hands under Ross's armpits and dragged him over to it. He stuffed his friend's legs into his own sleeping bag, ignoring Ross's groans, and pulled it up right over his face.

'Don't move,' he said. 'Don't move one inch from here.' He looked down at Ross's face, saw the fear the other man was trying to hide. 'And don't worry. I'll be back. Whatever happens, I'll be back.'

'Yeah, man. I know you will.'

Kneeling beside Joe, Ben lashed his arms to his sides, roped his legs together, round and round until he looked like a mummy in the snow. When he was ready, he began the long clamber down, paying out the rope attached to his belt, lowering Joe little by little, the trussed-up body sliding along the top of the snow like a sledge. He'd told Ross he would be back. He hoped it was true.

He had no idea how long it was before he had dragged himself and his burden down to fourteen thousand three hundred feet. Staggering into the camp, he wasn't even sure if Joe was still alive: he was half-dead himself. But after relinquishing his friend to the ministrations of the staff in the medical tent, pausing only to swallow almost a liter of hot tea and gather a small group of volunteers, he set off again up the mountain. By the time they reached him, with drinks, splints, food, Ross, though conscious, was in pretty bad shape. He rallied a little as he saw Ben looking down at him, and was able to give a tired twitch of the lips. 'Knew you'd make it, Benny boy,' he whispered. 'You fucking hero, you.'

* * *

171

'No,' Ben said sharply, as the hospital aide came towards him, syringe in hand.

The man was brusque. 'I've been told to give you this.'

'It'll put me under, won't it?'

'Probably.'

'Then I don't want it.' Ben backed away, but, in the small cubicle, there was nowhere to go. 'I've got to get back home.'

'Sorry.' With a swift lunge, the man grabbed Ben's arm and with practiced efficiency had swabbed the vein with alcohol and was plunging in the needle.

'Hey.' Dimly Ben heard Ross's voice. 'He told you he had to get home.'

'Shouldn'ta left it in the first place, should he?'

'His wife's sick, you friggin' jerk.'

'So's he. Or he will be, if he doesn't watch out.'

'He's just tired, is all.'

'He's also got two broken ribs, severe internal bruising and all the signs of someone suffering from exposure.'

'That's not serious stuff,' protested Ross, and then Ben was out of it, resistlessly swimming into a wave of snow, a sea of white cloud, Lisa somewhere calling him. He heard voices, Ross and Joe, a nursing orderly, a doctor. He drifted in and out, anxiety sitting somewhere inside him, growing increasingly urgent, though he couldn't concentrate for long enough to discover what it was about. Then he was gone.

He woke up, disoriented and aching. Every inch of his body felt agonizingly sore, as though he'd been worked over with a meat tenderizer. He had no idea how long he'd been asleep.

'Lisa,' he said, trying to prop himself up on one elbow

and falling back with a gasp of pain. Glancing sideways, he could see Ross in the next bed, his leg in traction, bandages covering both hands.

'How long have I been asleep?' Ben asked.

'A day and a half, off and on.'

'Jesus!' Ben smashed a fist down on the bedclothes. 'I *have* to get out of here.'

'Joe's telephoned your place a couple of times to explain what happened,' said Ross. 'But there was nobody home.'

Ben remembered Mel's voice floating thinly across the airwaves from another world. Lisa was OK, he told himself. Calm down, she was *OK*. 'My wife'll be going crazy, wondering what the hell I'm doing, why I'm not with her.' He pushed back the covers. 'Any idea where my stuff is?'

'They took it away. Mine too, even though I told them there was no way I'd be taking off, not with my leg strung up like this.'

'Going to be OK, are you?' Ben asked belatedly.

'Sure.' Ross waved his bandaged hands. 'Might lose a couple of fingertips.'

'I'm sorry.' Ben looked around. 'Where's the damn phone?'

'Out in the lobby.'

Ignoring his body's protests, Ben heaved himself out of bed and made his way to the little lobby. He called the operator to make a collect call, listened to the phone ring and ring, the woman's voice explaining that there was no response.

Fuck it! He slammed down the receiver. Where was Lisa? With her father? With friends? With . . . Mel Sherman? Hands unsteady, he called Enquiries, got Mel's number, dialed.

173

Again he listened to a telephone ringing in a silent house. Again he waited for a response, even an electronic one. But if Mel had an answering machine, it was switched off. There was no way he could let Lisa know where he was and why he hadn't come home.

CHAPTER ELEVEN

Mel picked Lisa up from the hospital. 'I'm taking you to Maple Street, OK?' she said.

'It's not necessary.'

'That way I can keep an eye on you.'

'I'll be OK on my own,' Lisa said dully.

'You probably will. However, tonight *I'm* in charge.' Mel reached across and squeezed Lisa's hand.

Later, after Lisa had pushed food around her plate, refused a glass of wine, swallowed two sips of coffee, Mel said, 'Let me call someone. Ben's mother? Your father?' She hated the way Lisa seemed to have shrunk inside herself, like a snail retreating deep into its shell.

'My dad wouldn't . . .' Lisa's voice trailed away and she was silent for so long that Mel thought she had fallen asleep. Then she said, 'Why hasn't Ben called?'

Remembering Ben's voice, *I can't just walk off the fucking mountain at a moment's notice*, Mel said, 'It was a pretty bad line. Maybe he's been trying and can't get through. Or he's called home, and you weren't there.'

'Or maybe he just hasn't tried.'

She looked so forlorn that Mel wanted to weep. 'I can't bear to see you so unhappy,' she said.

Lisa put her head back and closed her eyes. Tears

squeezed between her lids and slid down her face. 'The nurses in the hospital kept telling me it was just one those things. They said it was for the best. For the *best* . . .' Her pale cheeks flushed briefly. 'What's that supposed to mean?'

'Did you ask them?'

'One of them said, "Better to start over. Better to have an undamaged child." Another one kept telling me I was young, I could try again. "You'll have some more," she said. And maybe they're right. Maybe I will.' Lisa pressed her fingers to her forehead. Her voice wavered. 'That doesn't make it any easier to d-deal with the fact that I can't have the one I wanted, that *this* child, my d-daughter, is dead. Oh Mel . . .'

'I know.' Mel took her hand. 'I know.'

'I wanted this baby so *much*.'

And so did I, Mel thought.

'I can't believe that somehow I'm supposed to forget about her, just have another baby to replace her.'

'Did you see her?' Mel asked. Her own voice was unsteady. 'Did you get to hold her in your arms before they . . . before they took her away?'

Lisa shook her head. 'I asked but they'd already . . .' She clasped her hands together so tightly that the knuckles gleamed white. '. . . already done whatever it is they do with . . . with . . . what was the marvellous phrase they used? A non-viable pregnancy.'

'They have so much else on their minds, Lisa.'

'They were kind. They were very kind. But they just didn't understand that to me, she was a little girl, *my* little girl.' Lisa began to weep again, harsh sobs which shook her slight body. 'Ben and I made a child together, felt it grow, longed for it, planned a future for it – and to them it was nothing more than a non-viable pregnancy.'

176

Mel thought of the doctor she had spoken to. 'I'm sure they realized how you felt even if they didn't have time to show it.'

'She was . . . oh God, I can hardly bear to think of it . . . They told me she'd been dead for two weeks.'

'The doctor said.' Tears blurred the familiar room where they sat and Mel brushed them away.

'Dead . . .' Lisa twisted her hands together. 'I *knew* something was wrong, I knew it. Can you imagine the horror of that, Mel?'

All too easily, Mel thought. She could not get the images out of her own mind. 'Oh, Lisa, honey . . .'

'If it's OK, I'll take a shower and go to bed,' Lisa said.

'Anything. Anything you want.'

'Ben?'

'He'll get through, I know he will.'

Lisa gave a small smile. 'Dear Mel. Don't worry about me.'

'How can I not?' Mel said wretchedly.

While Lisa was in the bathroom upstairs, the phone rang.

'Ben Andersen here,' a voice said when Mel picked up.

'Thank God!'

'Where's Lisa? I've been telephoning my house and there's never any answer.'

'She's here with me. I've just brought her back from the hospital.'

'How is she?'

'Not too good.'

'But not sick . . .'

'Not physically sick.'

'I've been desperately worried about her,' he burst out. 'Stuck here . . . Your phone call . . . I couldn't hear what you were saying.' His voice dropped. 'I've been so afraid that she was . . . that she . . .'

'Where are you?'

'I'm still stuck in Alaska.'

'You should be *here*,' Mel said angrily.

There was a silence. Then he said, 'I'd like to speak to my wife.'

'She's taking a shower,' Mel said. 'Call back in ten minutes. She's desperate to talk to you.'

'I'll try,' he said wearily. 'But there are queues ten miles long to use these phones.'

'Where are you?' Mel asked again.

'In the local hospital.'

'What's wrong with you?'

'Nothing much.'

'I'll tell Lisa you called.' Mel replaced the receiver and went upstairs to the bathroom. 'That was Ben,' she said through the open door. 'He'll telephone back in ten minutes.'

Lisa turned off the faucet and grabbed a towel. 'When's he going to get here?'

'He – uh – wasn't sure.'

But although Lisa sat by the telephone for the rest of the evening, he did not call back.

'My wife is sick,' he said. 'For chrissake, how many times do I have to tell you?'

'It's not advisable,' the doctor said firmly. 'You should be under observation for at least—'

'If you won't discharge me, I'll discharge myself,' he shouted. Last night he'd waited hours to use the phone and by the time his turn came again, it was the middle of the night. 'You can't keep me here against my wish.' Remembering that his clothes were gone, he swallowed.

'Please.' He hated the whining note in his voice. Hated himself. These *friggin'* bureaucrats, playing everything by the book . . . 'I feel absolutely fine. There's nothing wrong with me beyond a few bruises.'

'I agree that your injuries aren't life-threatening,' the doctor said. 'But we can't be held responsible for any further—'

'Give me the damn forms,' he said. 'I'll sign anything, just so long as I can get out of here.'

It took another hour of argument before they agreed to discharge him. He signed waiver forms, used credit cards, made calls to the airline, to a taxi company, said goodbye to Ross and Joe.

And at last he was on his way back to Lisa.

'Come to the gallery with me,' Mel urged the following morning. 'I don't want to leave you alone.'

'I'm fine,' Lisa said. 'I'm OK.'

'You don't look it. You look . . .' Mel swallowed. Lisa was drained and muted, her eyes deep-shadowed in her sallow face. She was wearing a dark brown skirt, a dull red top. The colors of blood, Mel thought. The colors of birth. Or death.

'I'm sad.'

'Of course you are.'

'I mean, it's the sadness that makes me look so awful.'

'Apart from that, how are you feeling?'

'Sore. My boobs ache. I feel . . . empty.' Lisa stared at Mel, her mouth trembling. 'So empty.'

'Lisa . . .'

'I wish Ben would call.'

'The line was terrible when he phoned last night,' Mel said, finding excuses for Lisa's sake. Surely, somehow, he

179

could have found a way to telephone. 'Maybe it packed up altogether.'

Lisa pressed her fists to her chest. 'Maybe something's happened to him.'

'We'd have heard,' Mel soothed.

'I hate it when he's gone and I wake up in the night and think that he might have fallen, that he might already be dead and I don't even know it.' The silent tears spilled again. 'Where is he? What's he doing? Why doesn't he come home?'

She seemed to be growing more wounded, not less. The house was filled with the rawness of her pain; Mel found herself taking shallow breaths, as though to ward off infection.

Meeting Joanne at lunchtime, she said, 'I don't know what to do with her, how to help. It's like she's . . . given up.'

'Maybe she needs that.' Joanne slathered butter onto her roll. 'Not to have to think about anything. She just lost a baby. At more than five months. Think of the physical changes she's been through in the last few days, the hormones all racing round inside her with nowhere to go.'

'I feel so useless.'

'You're doing a great job, Mel.' Joanne ladled thousand island dressing over the lettuce garnish to her hamburger. 'Only way to make the stuff edible,' she said.

'I wish I could be of more help.'

'If I'm to believe you – and I'm still not sure – then you've been through something similar yourself. You know it isn't something you get over easily. Imagine how much worse it's got to be if you go through all of that pregnancy shit, and then end up with nothing to show for it.' Joanne bit vigorously into her hamburger.

'I'll be sure to pass that message on.' Mel felt a sudden surge of anger.

'Now, now.'

'The poor girl's in a bad state. Especially with Ben not here.'

'You'll probably think me callous for saying this, but a miscarriage isn't the end of the world.'

'You're right,' Mel said coldly. 'I *do* think you're callous.'

'Lisa may not want to believe it, but she'll get over it.'

'Which doesn't make it any easier right this minute.'

'Don't get snippy with me, babe. Whether you like it or not, life carries on. And it will for Lisa, too, even if she can't accept that right now.'

It wasn't your baby, thought Mel. You have three healthy children: I have none. I wanted this baby. *I* wanted it. She bit hard on her lip to prevent it trembling. Last night she had woken thinking she heard a shriek of pain. When she slept again, she had dreamed of Ben, his eyes the color of ice, his face remote.

'For fuck's sake!' Ben exploded. 'How much longer?'

'I'm sorry, sir.' The woman behind the counter lifted her chin at the weather beyond the windows of the airport. 'There's nothing we can do about it.'

'There must be *something*, surely. The country can't just close down every time there's a storm.'

'A bit more than a storm.' Ben could see that she was used to dealing with angry passengers anxious to be on their way to somewhere else. 'Freak weather. The back end of a hurricane. Even if we could get you up into the air, I don't know where you'd land, since airports are closing down all over the area.'

'A bus, maybe?'

181

'You can try. But even if you could get a seat, the roads are likely to be blocked.'

'What's the forecast?'

'More of the same, I'm afraid.' She looked at the man in the queue behind him and he turned away, seething with frustration. His shoulder ached, his ribs hurt, his stomach felt like raw hamburger. It looked as though he'd just have to sit it out.

Coming back from the gallery that evening, Mel discovered Lisa in the living room with the lights off, tears falling slowly down her cheeks.

'Lisa. Honey.' Mel switched on the lamps, closed the drapes.

'I can't go on,' Lisa said, turning away from the sudden light.

'You can. You will.' Mel held her close, remembering Joanne using the same words after Eric died. 'There's nothing else you *can* do except move on. It just takes time.'

'I wish Ben . . .'

'He's on his way.' At least, Mel thought, I hope he is.

'I can't work. I can't do anything. I called a cab this morning and went by my studio. I dug out some clay from the bins and thought about throwing a pot – and I couldn't.' Lisa waved her hands helplessly in the air. 'I simply couldn't imagine where to start. The whole process, it was like a mystery, something I'd never known about.'

'That'll change.'

'It all seemed so pointless.'

'It'll come right.'

'It won't. It won't. Nothing will.' She dragged an arm across her wet face. 'I'm not being melodramatic, Mel. I'll

182

go on functioning, of course I will. I'll probably be able to throw pots again. But it won't come right. I have to live with this for the rest of my life. I can't escape it.'

Mel took hold of the younger woman's hands. Lisa had removed the rings she habitually wore: the little diamond engagement ring, the thin gold wedding band, the silver love knot from Mexico. 'Remember that you're not alone.'

'I am. Without Ben, I am.'

Ben rang again. He was at the airport, waiting for a flight out. The weather was atrocious, flights were cancelled, he was on standby.

Lisa wept into the phone while he tried to comfort her. 'I can't believe you said that!' Mel heard her exclaim, as she slammed down the phone, ran upstairs to the guest room and closed the door behind her.

Ben called back. 'What the hell's happening?' he said angrily. 'She just hung up on me.'

'What did you say to her?'

'I was just . . . I said we could try again.'

'Exactly what a woman who's lost a baby wants to hear.'

'I suppose it was tactless.'

'Of course it was bloody tactless,' snapped Mel. 'And cruel.'

He drew a sharp breath. 'Doesn't she realize how much I want to be there with her?'

'I've no idea what she thinks. For the moment, she's all curled in on herself, like a wounded animal.'

'Look . . .' He broke off. Started again. 'Lisa knows that if I could walk from here to there, or swim, or ski, I'd do it, to be with her. But I can't. As soon as there's a flight, I'll be on it.'

'Fine.' She put down the telephone before he did.

183

* * *

When she came home at lunchtime the next day, she found a note on the kitchen table. *Don't worry, I'm OK*, Lisa had written. Knowing how far from the truth that was, Mel wondered if this was her way of asking to be left alone.

But whether she liked it or not, Lisa should not be by herself. Mel spent an uneasy afternoon at the gallery, and, in the end, left Carla to close up while she drove to the old Adams place. Late afternoon sun dazzled on the window-panes and warmed the mellow tiles on the peaked roof. Herbs – chives, parsley, thyme, mint – flourished beside the barn door, and geraniums gushed from the pots Lisa had planted. It looked as it had only a week ago, yet so much had changed.

Stepping into the hallway, Mel called Lisa's name. There was no answer.

She went upstairs. 'Lisa?' she called softly, increasingly apprehensive. Wishing she had not waited so long, she hurried down the passage to the room which had been intended for the baby, and stopped in the doorway. Her throat constricted as she saw Lisa sitting on the floor, rocking back and forth, clutching a tiny T-shirt to her breast, sobbing aloud.

'Lisa . . .' Running to kneel beside her, gather her into her arms, Mel recognized a grief that was almost un-containable. 'Honey, sweetheart, darling . . .' she murmured. Was this what it would have been like, if she had had a daughter? This shared ache, this mutual pain?

'Oh God, oh *God*,' Lisa screamed, the sound wrenched from some deep and empty place inside her. 'I can't . . .'

'Sssh . . .' Mel rocked her like a baby.

'She haunts me, Mel. *Haunts* me.' The words were a howl of pain. 'I *want* her. I need to hold her. I . . .' Lisa

184

pressed her knuckles hard against her mouth. 'And I can't reach her, Mel. I can't touch her.'

'Don't . . . don't . . .'

'I miss her, Mel. I never even knew her but I m-miss her s-so . . .'

'I know . . .'

'I used to think about her all the time. I'd see her paddling in the lake, or watching some stupid kids' video, or sitting in the ice-cream parlor with a strawberry vanilla scoop, getting it all over her face and me leaning over to w-wipe her clean with a p-paper napkin.' Lisa's voice began to shake. 'I . . . I imagined photographs of the three of us, and Ben carrying her on his back in one of those s-sling things, playing with her. Just ordinary things that any p-parent might th-think of. And now . . .' She looked down at the small garment in her hand and began to sob again.

'Darling Lisa . . .'

'The baby was so real to me, and now she's *dead* and I absolutely c-can't get my head round it.' Lisa bent her head again and cried, snot and tears and saliva dropping from her wet face. 'At the hospital they acted like it was nothing special. Like I was just supposed to go home and carry on as before. You'd have thought I was doing something really perverted when I asked about it, tried to make sense of what happened. And even . . .' She moaned, wrapping her arms around herself. '. . . even some of the women from my antenatal group – they've called up and . . . and they say the same things. They don't seem to realize that . . . that I *hurt*.' Sobs shook Lisa's slight body.

'Perhaps they don't know what to say.'

'They don't have to say what they *do* say.'

'They're probably terrified it could happen to them.' Mel looked round the room. At the quilt Lisa had sewn

185

for the baby's bed, at the white muslin curtains she had decorated with green leaves to match the ones Ben had stencilled on the sanded pine floor, at the white chest they had found at an auction up in the hills and the mobile of glittery butterflies which danced and sparkled in the sunshine, at the egg-yolk yellow walls. So much anticipation had gone into this room. So much love. And now it held nothing but broken promises.

'And I feel so guilty.' Lisa's face contorted, made ugly by grief. 'Maybe it happened because of something I did.'

'That's a natural reaction. But it's wrong,' Mel said forcefully.

'Wedging clay,' Lisa continued, as though she had not heard Mel. 'Maybe that's why it happened. Or because I didn't eat the right things.'

'There's no system of checks and balances,' said Mel. 'It wasn't because of anything you did.' She held Lisa tighter, feeling the thin bones beneath her shirt, the precarious knobs of her elbows, the fragile ribs.

Lisa laid one hand on her stomach. 'Perhaps I just plain didn't deserve to have this baby. Or maybe I wanted it for the wrong reasons. As a way to keep Ben at home, or to cement my marriage.'

'That's not *wrong*.'

Lisa shook her head.

The shine had gone from her hair, Mel noted. The webs of skin between her ringless fingers seemed almost transparent. She took Lisa's hand. 'Let's go back to Maple Street,' she urged gently.

After supper, Cheryl, a woman from Lisa's antenatal class, dropped by. She was some years older than Lisa, expecting her third child. 'Tell me about it,' she said softly.

Lisa shook her head.

'It would help to talk about it. Was the baby a girl or a boy?'

For a moment, Lisa pressed her lips together. Then, reluctantly, she said, 'A girl.'

'My husband and I lost our third son,' said Cheryl. 'When people ask me how many children I already have, I always say three.' She paused for a moment, looked down at her wedding band. 'There's Robert, and Richard. And there's Ralph. He wasn't with us very long, but I don't ever forget that he's part of the family.' She smiled. 'He had red hair, just like my other boys.'

'You mean you've had . . . I didn't know you'd . . .'

'He died three weeks after he was born. We were able to hold him, even take photographs of him. Our doctor took handprints, footprints. It's all we have of him.' Cheryl's soft voice was steady. 'We were luckier than you. We were able to have that time with him. We still miss him, think about him every day, wonder what he would have been like. He's part of our family, and always will be.' She leaned forward and took Lisa's hand. 'Did you give your daughter a name?'

After a long pause, Lisa nodded.

'What did you call her?'

Lisa lifted her shoulders, dropped them again. 'I called her . . . I *would* have called her, if they'd given me the chance . . . Rosie. My mother's name was Rosemary.'

'That's a lovely name for a little girl,' said Cheryl.

The child who might have been danced into Mel's mind, wearing a rose-pink dress, her hair tied back with a green ribbon. 'Naming is an important thing to do,' she said, so forcefully that the other women looked at her in astonishment.

'Naming makes her exist,' said Lisa.

When Cheryl left, Lisa said, 'I should go home. I've

187

invaded your life for long enough.' She looked much less stressed.

'You know you're welcome to stay here as long as you want to.'

'It's time I took up my own life again. Besides, I have to get ready for Ben coming back.'

'At least stay until he's home.'

Lisa's smile was brittle. 'It's like they said at the hospital: I'm not an invalid. I'm young and healthy.'

'I can't force you to stay,' Mel said.

'No.' Lisa hugged her. 'Thank you, Mel. For everything.'

Chapter Twelve

Seeing the needle of the speedometer flicker at over 100 mph, Ben stamped his foot down hard on the brake. The car he'd hired at Logan slid across the road, tires screeching, and finally stalled. Cursing, he banged the steering wheel with his fist, then turned the key in the ignition and restarted the engine. He felt around on the passenger seat and shook a couple of painkillers from the unstoppered container he'd placed there, crunching them down without water.

It was a week now since she'd lost the baby. Perhaps if he'd been there, it wouldn't have happened. But he hadn't. I fucked it up again, he thought bitterly. I could rescue Ross, but I couldn't rescue my baby. Tears loomed at the back of his throat and he swallowed, forcing them back. '*Big boys don't cry, Benjamin.*' His father's voice echoed in his head. 'But they do, Dad, they do,' he had thought when he was a kid, and he thought the same now, as he hunched over the steering wheel.

As he came over the top of Wilson's Notch, a bird flew heavily across the sky. The hills were gloomy in the vanishing daylight, ridge after gray ridge rolling somberly towards the horizon. Rain swept bleakly across the fields below him, blotting out cow-studded fields and red barns, the blunt domes of silos and square white church towers.

Coming off the winding hill-road to the long tree-lined stretch which led to the town, he put his foot down again. It was almost dark down here in the valley and he switched on his headlights. Rain beat against the windshield. As he came nearer home, grief settled more heavily on him, impenetrable as the cloud on Denali. The loss of the baby was a sorrow he only occasionally dared to probe. He couldn't afford to yield to his own pain when Lisa was going to need every ounce of love and support he could give her.

Quite apart from wanting to be with her, what the hell must she think of him? He'd tried to explain about the hospital, but when she wasn't slamming the phone down on him she sounded so totally wiped out, so down and depressed, that to start yapping on about trivial stuff like ribs and bruises had seemed redundant.

Jeez-us!

Once again he stamped hard on the brake. His tires squealed on the road as the car swerved, fishtailing on the rain-slick hardtop. He skidded in loose gravel and ended up with the two nearside wheels furrowed into the sandy soil at the side of the road. The ends of his broken ribs grated agonizingly together as he fought with the wheel. Christ, that hurt! Meanwhile, the fox which had suddenly appeared in his headlights continued its purposeful jog, reddish-grey, its thick tail held low behind, the white tip gleaming. Damn thing didn't even look at the car, just disappeared among the dripping trees on the opposite side of the road.

He cursed again as, for the moment, his wheels spun on the gravel, then he was able to pick up speed again, and carry on through the darkness.

* * *

When he finally reached the circular driveway of the Adams house, there were no lights on. He tried the front door and found it locked, as though Lisa wasn't expecting him. Had she gone back to Mel Sherman's house? He felt under the nearest flowerpot for the spare key and let himself quietly in.

He walked through the silent rooms, smelling the familiar fragrances of the old place. In the dining room, he stopped. Oh God . . . he bit his lip. The table had been set for two, with the wedding present flatware, the best glasses, linen napkins. In the middle of the table there were two red roses in a crystal vase. She'd prepared a homecoming dinner and he hadn't shown up for it.

He carried one of the roses upstairs with him. At the far end of the passage, the door of their bedroom was ajar, though the lamps were off. In the moonlight from the window he could see her face on the pillow, looking so frail that he hardly recognized her. In one hand she held the silver rattle he had bought – when? It seemed like years ago. He could see the faint marks of tears on her cheeks. 'Oh, Lisa,' he whispered. He laid the rose on her nightstand.

In the bathroom he showered, brushed his teeth, swallowed more painkillers, then eased himself into bed.

'Ben?' she murmured.

'I'm home, darling.'

'I thought you weren't going to come.'

In the darkness, he frowned. 'You knew I would.'

He felt her shake her head. 'I wasn't sure. Not any more.'

Wincing at the unspoken reproof, he put his arms carefully around her and felt her cringe away from him as though afraid of being hurt. He thought he could smell her sadness, rising like smoke from the narrow ranges

191

of her slight body. His own grief stifled him. After a while, he leaned up on his elbow. Looking down at her beloved familiar face in the half-light, at the new sad lines around her mouth, he felt a shiver of misgiving.

She was up in the morning before he awoke. He lay listening for the sounds he had grown used to over the years of their marriage: the birdlike swoops of excited chatter as she talked on the phone, the sound of her singing along to the radio. But the house was silent. He wanted to talk about the baby, to share their burden of loss. He needed catharsis; he assumed that she did too.

In the bathroom mirror, he examined himself: the marks across his shoulders, the deep bruises under his ribs and down his legs, the still raw places on his arms and legs. If he moved too quickly, his entire body protested. On his way downstairs, he paused outside the baby's room. The door was shut. There was something so final about that closed door that he felt cold. He put out his hand and touched the doorknob, then drew back. He wasn't sure he had the courage to walk in. The full force of what had happened hit him like a blow to the stomach.

'Lisa!' he shouted. He went down the stairs two at a time. 'Lisa!'

She wasn't in the house. He walked round to the barn, calling her name, but there was no sign of her. Dumped beside the herb garden she had planted earlier in the summer stood a garbage sack full of broken pieces of unfinished pots. On top of them lay the rose he had placed beside her bed the night before.

He found her at the end of the garden, standing motionless among the stunted apple trees. She was wearing black trousers, a grey top, colors he had never seen her in before. The swell of her belly, still in a state of prenatal distension, moved him unbearably.

192

When she turned her head to look at him, he had the illusion that she had disappeared, not physically, but emotionally, that Lisa herself was no longer there and only an outer casing remained, fragile as eggshell. 'Sweetheart,' he said.

'I should have insisted,' she said

'What?'

'On bringing her back here. The baby. We could have buried her under the trees.'

'Oh, Lisa . . .' He took her into his arms where she stood passive, unengaged.

'I called her Rosie,' she said, her lips moving against his shirt.

Sensing that he was stepping into dangerous territory, he tried not to show his confusion. 'Rosie,' he repeated.

She stepped away from him. 'After my mother. Isn't that what we agreed?'

He didn't know how to respond. 'Did you tell your father?' he asked. 'He might be glad to know.'

She made an impatient sound. 'My father wouldn't give a damn.'

'But surely—'

'Haven't you realized that about him yet?' Her voice was scornful. 'That he doesn't connect? Not even with me? Especially not with me.'

'I hadn't, no.'

'When my mother realized she was dying of cancer,' Lisa said flatly, 'she moved out of the room she shared with him, into the back bedroom of our apartment. She knew he wouldn't like it if she made a noise, so when the pain was too much she would bite on the pillow. I remember as a little girl standing at the end of the bed, staring at her while she lay there doubled up with agony, gasping with it, her face a kind of yellowy-white. And she'd look

193

back at me and put her finger on her lips, telling me to be quiet. He didn't want to know: he didn't want his normal routines interrupted. She died as quietly as she could, so as not to disturb him.'

'You've never told me that before.' He'd always seen Peter Tan's detachment as a virtue.

'I try not to think about it. About the kind of relationship they must have had.' She stared up at him as though he were a stranger. 'Our daughter died quietly too.'

Looking down at the part in her hair, he wanted to weep. Her distance alarmed him. 'Lisa!' he cried, stricken by the gap which had sprung up between them. 'Come back.'

Slowly she turned her eyes on him. Once he had imagined he could see the future in them but now they were as black and opaque as ink. She lifted the corners of her mouth: he could not imagine anything less like a smile. 'I'm here,' she said.

'You're not. You're *not*. You're shutting the doors on me,' he said, desperate, thinking of the baby's room, the door he hadn't dared to open. 'Let me in.'

'She'd been dead for two weeks,' Lisa said, in a conversational way.

'The baby?'

'Rosie, yes . . . when I lost her—'

'*We* lost her,' he said.

'She'd been dead for two weeks,' Lisa said again. She turned her head away and her body began to shake.

He stared at her, appalled. She had been carrying a dead child around inside her womb for two weeks. Fourteen days. He tried to imagine it and could not. 'You mean . . .' He put a hand to his mouth. 'Oh God . . .'

'Horrible, isn't it?' she said.

'Why didn't you tell me?'

194

'I didn't think you'd be interested.'

'That's a terrible thing to say.'

'When I was in the hospital, I met a woman who was told that the baby she was carrying was dead, and to come back after the weekend, to have a scrape. Can you imagine knowing that you were carrying something dead? I guess I was lucky,' Lisa said, wiping her eyes. 'At least I didn't know until afterwards.'

'It's monstrous. That poor woman.' His voice was hoarse. 'How absolutely . . .' A flush of horror powered through his blood. A dead child, inside his wife's body. He held Lisa tight against him, heedless of his cracked ribs and screaming muscles, seeing only blackness and despair.

'Sometimes I wake in the morning,' she said. 'And for a moment, just a split second, I think she's still there inside me. I think that I must have woken up because . . . because she was kicking me.'

'Oh honey . . .'

'It's like an amputee who can still feel the phantom limb. And then it sweeps over me again. She's gone. I'm empty, there's nothing to show that I was pregnant. No-one will ever know that I was expecting a baby.'

'I'll know. *We'll* know.'

She went on as though he hadn't spoken. 'People will pass me in the street, talk to me in the stores, pull up beside me at traffic lights, sit next to me at the movies, and they'll see a young woman in jeans and a sweater, an ordinary woman buying groceries or driving through town and they'll never realize that I was pregnant once, and now I'm not. That I went to the hospital full and came back empty.'

'Who cares what other people think or don't think?'

Tears gathered again in her eyes. 'I was going to have a baby and now I'm not.'

He looked at her with frustration. 'She wasn't just your baby, Lisa. She was ours.' Sadness had formed a hard lump in his chest.

She stepped out of the circle of his arms to stare at the garden. After a while, she said, 'I'm sorry.'

'Let me help,' he said, desperate, meaning: *Help me. Oh please, somebody, Lisa, help me, too*.

'You can't,' she said quietly. 'I wanted Rosie more than anything in the world. She meant everything to me. I was going to be the most wonderful mother ever. I wasn't going to leave her, like my mother left me. And now . . . now I don't know who I am, or where I'm going. You've always known who you were—'

'No.' He shook his head. 'That's not true.'

'You can't possibly understand what that's like. Nobody can. All they'd think, even if they knew, is that there's a very simple solution: just have another baby and everything will be fine.'

He'd had the same thought himself. Lying in the hospital bed, drifting on a sea of painkillers, he'd told himself the very same thing. 'I do understand,' he said, wanting to purge himself of the knowledge that he had been away while she was losing their child. He thought of Mel Sherman's strong clear features. 'Have you talked to Mel?'

'A little.' Lisa made a helpless gesture. 'And she's kind and lovely. But she's never had children. She can't really share any of this.'

He breathed a sigh. 'Let me try.'

She shrugged as though it didn't matter, though both of them knew how intensely it did.

'Let's walk by the river,' he said.

'I don't want to.'

He grabbed her hand. 'Come anyway.'

She followed where he led, putting one foot in front of another, staring down at the ground. The fresh air brought a little color to her face but no sparkle to her eyes. He walked her down to where the river leaped. 'Look,' he said, wanting to show her that there was still a world out there, beyond her misery. 'Deer tracks.' He pointed at the delicately slotted marks in the sand.

'Yes.'

'Did you know there are bears in these woods?' he said. She shook her head.

'They come down to the water's edge to fish.' Once, he would have tried to share it with her, the small black bear, balanced on a rock, one paw scooping water. Once she would have listened, her eyes alight with pleasure.

'Do they?' she said.

'I saw one myself, last time I came down here.'

'Hey, Ben . . .'

'Yes?'

'Like, I really need a nature lesson right now.'

A few weeks back, he'd led a group of rock-climbers, up in the Northeast Kingdom. Trekking through the lower woods, they'd seen elk, fox, hares. And then suddenly, unexpectedly, they'd come across a couple of moose standing motionless among the trees, monumental in the early morning mist.

'Aren't they beautiful?' one of the women had said on an indrawn breath. 'As though they were carved out of the rocks. Part of the mountains.' She'd grinned at him, hands hooked round the straps of her backpack. 'Isn't it a wonderful world, eh?'

'You said it.' He'd smiled back.

A wonderful world . . . 'I just thought you'd be interested,' he said.

'I'm not.' She began to walk away from him down the

riverbank. 'I couldn't care less, if you want to know.'

'Lisa . . .' He wanted to ask if she was glad he was back with her, he wanted to say how sad and sorry he was and that from here on in he would be there to love and protect her, but she stared at him with such hostility that he couldn't continue.

'Let me fix you something,' he said, when they got back to the house.

'Nothing, thanks.'

'Anything. Just name it. Anything you like.'

'I'm not hungry.'

'Eat something,' he begged. He took her cold hands in his. 'How about pasta – you know you like pasta.'

'I'm not hungry,' she said again, on a rising note. She pulled her hands away and pressed them to her stomach.

'I could make some pesto sauce,' he said. 'Remember us making it, when I came round to your apartment that first time?'

'I remember.' She sounded as if she was somewhere else, living an alternate life.

'Or we could try a takeout pizza. You know you love pizza.'

'For Christ's sake, Ben, leave me alone.' There was an hysterical note in her voice. 'How many times do I have to tell you I don't *want* anything?' She walked out of the room as though she couldn't bear to be in the same place as he was.

God, he was tired. He'd expected that she would be depressed. He had been prepared for her sadness. But not for this strange evaporation of self. Somehow she had disengaged herself from him and from the life they used to share. Even from herself.

He heard a door slam, the sound of her car starting up, the swish of tires on gravel as she barreled down the drive and onto the road. He closed his eyes and wearily rubbed his forehead. He wished he could simply lie down and go to sleep for a week. There had to be light at the end of this particular tunnel. He just wished he could see it.

Chapter Thirteen

'I don't know what's wrong with me.' Lisa sat on Mel's swing seat, staring at nothing, endlessly swinging back and forth. 'I think I'm going mad.'

'You can't expect to be—'

'I just felt like I couldn't stand to be in the same room with him for another second.'

'Why?'

'I don't really know.' Lisa fumbled in the pocket of her drab brown skirt. 'And this morning I went to the supermarket and I suddenly had this terrible fear that everything on the shelves was closing in on me, the cans of beans and the boxes of tissues and the economy-size detergent were going to rush at me and crush me to death.' She pressed a wad of tissues against her eyes. 'Oh God, I'm sorry, Mel, I shouldn't be offloading all this stuff on you.'

Mel remembered the feeling that the world was no longer stable, that any moment it might tip her off, that inanimate objects – chairs or books or buildings – wished her harm. Only much later had she understood that she had probably had a minor breakdown. Lisa was presumably undergoing much the same sort of emotional crisis. 'Don't let the miscarriage change things between you and Ben,' she said.

'Whether we like it or not, things *have* changed.'

'But you still love him.'

'I guess.'

'Of *course* you do.' Mel was surprised at the panic she could feel surging at the base of her stomach. Although she could not properly have described her feeling, it would have been something along the lines of a sense that if Ben was no longer loved, was now *un*loved, then a dangerous vacuum would have been formed. And vacuums need to be filled.

'I *know* I love him,' Lisa said. 'It's just that I can't *feel* it any more.'

'Give it a chance. It'll come back.'

Lisa shook her head. 'No. It's gone. I don't mean the love, but the . . . the joy. The lightness. I don't know how else to describe it. We can never go back to the way we were, Ben and me.' Her voice began to waver into incoherence. 'I f-feel like a line's been . . . like m-my marriage . . . it's g-gone, it's . . .' She drew in a deep shuddering breath. 'Last night, he was supposed to be home by eight. I waited up for him but . . .'

'Why should that mean your marriage is threatened?'

'I was so angry. So hurt. I sat at the table I'd set for dinner, and watched the hands on the clock going round and round and I realized that I couldn't assume any more that I come first.'

'That's ridiculous, Lisa. The flights from Alaska, the delays . . . I'm sure he got home as soon as he could.'

'I'm not saying he didn't. But I feel that the mountains, his male friends, they'll always be more important than I am. The ironic thing is, it was the climbing that attracted me in the first place. When he was on the construction sites, in New York, the way he could work up there, day after day, miles above the city.' Lisa grew briefly animated, waving her hands as she spoke. 'It was like he was an alien, existing on a different planet from the rest of us. What he did seemed so exciting, so . . . *heroic*. Sometimes I'd go down and stand on the sidewalk and just stare up at him, way up there in the sky. I hadn't a clue which one was him, but it didn't matter. I got a terrific buzz from knowing he was up there. He'd come home at night and I could hardly wait to get him into bed. The danger of it . . . there are accidents all the time: men losing their balance, or being knocked off by a load swinging too hard, or tripping on something and falling over the edge. They're supposed to use harnesses up there, but a lot of the guys don't bother because they get in the way.' The animation drained abruptly away. 'That's gone,' she repeated.

Mel took hold of Lisa's hands. 'Listen to me,' she said firmly. 'What's happened has been dreadful for you. You'll never forget it, and you shouldn't even try to. But Ben must be deeply upset about losing the baby too. You should be helping each other to get through this.'

'I don't want his help,' Lisa said painfully.

'Why not?'

'Because . . . because there isn't any help to be given. No-one can take over someone else's pain. It's something I have to get through by myself.' She began to sob again. 'It all started off so wonderfully, Mel. We were so happy. So much in love. Now . . . now I can hardly bear to be near him. He should have come back when he heard about the baby, and he didn't, and I really resent him for it.'

'Aren't you being a bit unreasonable? We all read about the freak storms up there, the airports closing down.'

'I know. I know all that, in my head. But in my heart I feel that if he'd set off as soon as he heard about the baby, he'd have been out of there before the weather changed. And in a way – I know it's awful of me but it's the way I feel right now – I don't want him to be justified for not being with me.'

'Darling Lisa, listen to me. This is the first real crisis you two have had. It's a terrible one, probably the worst you'll ever have. But there'll be others over the years. Love doesn't always turn out the way you expect it to.' Mel remembered her fourteen-year-old self, the smoothness of the paper under her hand, the sense of significance as she wrote on the clean white page of her journal. *I am waiting for my true love.*

'You're right.' Lisa looked away, then down at her hands. 'Absolutely. And I know it doesn't help to scream and shout. Poor darling, he looks so bewildered when I get irritated.'

'Why do it then?' Mel could imagine the expression on Ben's face, the puzzled frown between his sun-bleached eyebrows.

'I can't seem to help myself.'

'Why don't you tell him how you feel about him? About yourself?'

'Whatever I say, he can't possibly understand how it was.' Lisa squeezed her eyes shut and buried her face in her hands. 'How could he? He wasn't the one lying in that hammock, feeling the baby pushing out, knowing that something was terribly wrong.' She shuddered. 'It's like a nightmare from which I can't ever wake up.'

Jamie Mayfield came cycling up the drive. 'Hi,' he said, dragging his trainers along the cement hardtop instead of using the brakes, then sitting on his mountain bike at the foot of the porch steps, looking up at them. 'I was just at the library, and I thought I'd stop by because I wanted to ask you something.'

'Go ahead,' Mel said.

Jamie pushed his glasses up his nose. 'It's Mom's birthday soon, right?'

'Right.'

'And she likes things we make for her much better than something we've bought, right?'

'Right.'

'But I can't sew or paint or anything, like Tom and Lucy can. And the other day I was thinking about maybe being a chef when I grow up, so I started reading recipes and there was this one for a lemon cake and it didn't look too difficult and Mom likes lemon, so . . .'

'Last week you were going to be a paleontologist,' Mel said.

He grinned at her. 'I'm keeping my options open.'

'A cake sounds like fun,' Lisa said.

'That's what I thought. Unless . . .' He looked hopefully at Lisa. '. . . I could come by your place and throw a pot for Mom. You said I could one day.'

Lisa's pale face flushed. 'No, I . . . I don't think I . . . not at the moment,' she said. 'I'm sorry, Jamie, but no.'

'That's OK,' Jamie said. 'I don't expect you feel like it much. Mom told me you'd lost your baby, so you must be very sad.'

'Yes,' Lisa said. 'I am.'

'After the first death there is no other,' Jamie said.

Lisa stared at him, her eyes wide. 'What?'

'It was the title of my A book, this time round,' explained Jamie. 'By Robert Cormier. It's from a poem.' He nodded. 'It's kind of an interesting thought. But I don't expect it's much help, is it?'

Lisa bit her lip. 'Not really.'

'Anyway, my teachers keep telling me I lack co-ordination,' said Jamie, 'so I'd probably've made a mess potting.' His dimple showed. 'And I'd rather make a lemon cake, because Mom's bound to give me a bit.' He turned to Mel. 'One of those with vanilla cream in the middle.'

'Fine.'

'I'd need to practice first, though. And maybe if it turned out good, we could freeze it until Mom's birthday.'

'Good thinking,' said Mel. 'Want me to pick up the ingredients?'

'No, otherwise it wouldn't really be a present from me, would it?' Jamie dropped his bike on the ground, dug into the pocket of his shorts and fished out a piece of paper. 'I wrote them down, and I thought I could buy the stuff at the store on the way home tomorrow – if tomorrow's OK with you.' He looked at Mel. 'It's just the technical assistance I need. I can't do it at home or it won't be a surprise for Mom.'

'The technical assistance,' Mel said gravely.

'The methodology.'

'Right. But I ought to warn you, Jamie, that making cakes is not something I'm good at.'

'You've got to be better than me.'

'Don't count on it.'

'Are you going to put frosting on it?' Lisa said. Her tense features had relaxed a little.

'Definitely.' He wrinkled his nose. 'It'd be sort of great to have a bookshop or something on top, but I don't know how that would go.'

'You could make an outline in icing,' said Mel.

'Maybe in the shape of a book cover,' Lisa said.

'Put *Happy Birthday Mom* on it, like a title.'

'And Jamie Mayfield underneath, like he's the author,' said Jamie. 'Hey, that'd be cool.' He picked up his bike and did a few wheelies in front of them. 'So see you tomorrow, Mel, OK?'

'Don't forget to tell your mom you're going to be home a bit late.'

'I won't.' He raised his hand. 'I'm outta here.' He sped off down the drive.

'He's a cute kid,' Lisa said, looking after him.

'Clever, too.'

'What does it mean, after the first death there is no other?'

'I imagine the idea is that once you've experienced a significant death, gone through all the grief and adjustments and so on, none of the deaths which come after that can have the same impact on you. Something like that.'

'I wonder if it's true.'

'Hard to say,' said Mel, thinking of Eric, thinking of her baby, and the cold afternoon when her mother had died. Different deaths. Different griefs.

Lisa stood up. 'I guess I better get back.'

'Lisa . . .' Mel touched her hand. 'Don't blame Ben for not coming back. Don't spoil your relationship with him.'

Lisa nodded. 'You're right, Mel. I know you're right. I'll make a real effort.' She walked down the porch steps and Mel heard the sound of her car pulling away from the kerb.

In the kitchen, the phone buzzed. Mel went into the house and picked up. 'Mel Sherman.'

'Carla here. Guess what.'

'Tell me.'

'The *New York Times* was just on the line,' Carla said. 'They want to speak to you about the Koslowski show.'

'That's great!' If she could tempt some of the bigger reviewers up here, it would guarantee the success of the exhibition. Which in turn would mean that she could be even more ambitious for her next one.

'It certainly doesn't hurt to have a reputation like

Koslowski's,' Carla said. 'Didn't he push someone through a plate-glass window once?'

'It was him who was pushed.' Mel remembered the scene, an aggressive guy fronting up to the sculptor at a preview, throwing a glass of wine at him, then lunging at him, sending him backwards through the window. 'Man Pushes Sculptor Through Window is less exciting than the other way round.'

'Six weeks to go and counting,' Carla said.

'Where did you go?' Ben said.

'To Mel's.'

'Didn't you think I might be worried about you?'

Lisa stared at him without speaking.

'You're not the only one who hurts, you know,' Ben said loudly. A clot of pain and loss was lodged inside his chest. 'I wanted this baby, too.'

Again Lisa made no reply.

He threw down the book he'd been pretending to read. 'You could at least *answer* me. Why do you have to look at me like I'm some kind of retard every time I open my mouth?'

'I'm sorry.' She closed her eyes for a moment and took a deep breath. 'I'm sorry, honey.'

'Don't be fucking *sorry*.' Anger crouched between them. 'Answer me. Talk to me.'

'I . . . I haven't got much to say.'

He got up and seized her by the shoulders, hating the way she stiffened at his touch. 'Lisa, Lisa . . . I hurt too.'

He watched her try to relax, try to smile. 'I know, Ben.'

He remembered how she had been earlier in the summer, the brilliant colors of her clothes, her black hair bobbing in a ponytail or pinned up with bright clips, and was aware of a desperate sadness. She'd been slopping around in the same dark top for the last three days. Her hair was dull and lifeless; sometimes she didn't even bother to brush it when she got out of bed.

She looked away from him. Inside his chest, the tears he wanted so badly to shed felt as though they were slowly being turned to pebbles.

He grabbed her hand. 'Come with me, Lisa.'

'Where?'

'Just come.' He drew her towards the foot of the stairs. 'We're going to talk about this. We *have* to.'

'No,' she said. 'No. I don't want to. I can't.' Her voice was suddenly fearful.

'We have to face up to it,' he said. 'Together.'

He pulled her after him up the stairs and along the passage to the door of the baby's room. She hung back, a dead weight on the end of his arm. The muscles of his shoulder and abdomen protested but he took no notice. For a moment he paused outside, thinking of the hours they'd spent sanding down the broad pine planks, the smell of planed wood and wax polish, Lisa looking up and smiling at him, sawdust in her hair. He remembered the soft sweetness of her face as she told him she was pregnant, the delight oozing out of her like syrup. And buying the rattle in the dusty antique shop, ringing the silver bells, imagining it in his baby's hand. All that joy was gone, he knew that, but surely, *surely* the pain didn't have to be wasted. Out of the loss there had to come some kind of resolution.

He flung open the door. It was all as it had been when he left for Alaska. The quilt she'd made. The chest he'd painted. The willow leaves stencilled on the floor.

Without warning, the tears came, pouring from his eyes, thick and bitter. He let go of her and leaned against the wall, his face on his arm. 'Oh God. Oh Lisa, what are we going to do?'

There was no response, and when he lifted his head she was standing there, watching him, her own tears streaming down her face, as though there was an invisible wall between them, a sheet of ice through which neither of them could break.

The following afternoon he came back from the supermarket to find her in the barn, staring at the peacock-feather dishes which were supposed to be finished in time for the wedding in Texas. The studio smelled of fresh oil paint and he felt a sudden rush of optimism, until he saw that she had taken the tops off all the metal tubes of paint and squeezed the contents into the bin which stood beneath the sink he had set into the counter.

'Lisa,' he said. 'Oh, Lisa. What have you done?'

'I called the Peacockes,' she said tonelessly. Her voice echoed slightly, as though coming from the bottom of an empty vessel. 'Told them I couldn't finish the commission.'

Looking round the studio, he saw that she had removed the damp cloths from the clay, opened the sacking so that the clay would dry out.

She stood up. When he tried to hold her she pushed him away. 'Yesterday Jamie Mayfield asked if I'd help him make a pot for his mother's birthday – and I refused.'

'Why?'

'It wasn't just the thought of the clay on my hands, or the wheel . . . it was *him*. All I could think was that he's not *my* child.' She stared at him. 'What's happening to me? What kind of person have I become that I wouldn't even help a kid like that?' Her voice shook. 'And although

209

I try, I can't forgive you for not being there when . . . when I lost the baby.'

'Don't you understand that I can't forgive *myself*?'

Lisa pressed her lips together to stop them trembling. 'I can't forget that you were in the mountains instead of with me.'

He hardly recognized her as the girl he had married. 'Would you like me to move out?' he asked quietly. 'Would that make it easier for you?'

For a moment she sat still, her mouth quivering. Then she collapsed against him. 'I'm sorry, Ben,' she said into his chest. 'Dearest Ben. I'm so sorry.'

Both of them were appalled at the cracks, the crevasses which had suddenly appeared in their marriage.

She was lying on her side, her back to him. The bedroom smelled of her jasmine perfume. Through the open windows he could see the spotlit spire of St Andrew's Episcopal Church, the floodlights which lit up the high school football ground. A moth fluttered in the circle of light cast by his bedside lamp, drifting away for a moment only to return to the seductive glow. He slid into bed beside her and put an arm round her slight body, wanting to hold her, to protect her from any further harm.

'Don't!' she screamed suddenly, flailing wildly at his arm.

'What?'

She whipped round to face him. 'Don't touch me.'

'For God's sake, Lisa . . .' He moved away from her, alarmed by the hostility in her eyes. Her lips were drawn back from her teeth. 'You're being ridiculous.'

'I know you want to fuck me,' she said.

'Of course I do. You're my wife. But not until you're ready. Not until you want me to.'

'But it's not because I'm Lisa, is it? It's because I'm a female body lying next to you and you haven't had sex for a while. That's all you want, my body, not my . . . my mind or my heart. You don't give a damn about *me*, do you? You don't begin to understand how I feel.'

'If you'd tell me, I could at least try,' he said steadily.

'You?' she said. In the lamplight, her face was bitter. 'Ben Andersen, Action Man, understand?'

Pain and anger flared in his chest. He grabbed her arms and pulled her closer. Looking down at her, he thought that she resembled some wild animal. 'Is that really what you think of me?'

'That's just the b-beginning.'

'This isn't good for us,' he said.

'What don't you like?' she demanded. 'The fact that I'm not behaving like a nice little Vermont wife ought to?'

He tried to rein in his resentment, remembering what she had been through. He was acutely aware of the silver clock on the bedside table, a box of tissues, the edge of the lampshade, a trinket box carved into the shape of a heart where she put her earrings at night. 'I don't expect you to behave like anything except yourself. What I can't cope with is that you act as if you actually dislike me.'

'Maybe I do.'

'You don't mean that.'

'Don't I?'

He let her go and turned over. The moth fluttered and danced, flew away and returned, beating at the sides of the lampshade, its powdery wings growing ever more ragged. He felt as though there was a hole in his chest where his heart used once to fit. He wanted to weep for all that he had lost. He thought how cold and perilous were the mountain ranges of grief.

* * *

Time inched by. The two of them seemed locked in some stark and barren place, empty, cold, colorless. He thought of the bright existence they used to have, full of shape and pattern and sound.

'Lisa,' he said, on the tenth evening after his return, as they sat opposite each other, their plates untouched. The effort she made to lift her head and look at him was almost audible.

'Yes?'

'Talk to me, darling.'

'Uh . . .' She drew in a deep breath. 'Tell me about your climb.'

'I already did.'

She seemed surprised. 'Did you?'

'Half a dozen times.'

'Oh.' A pause. 'I'm so sorry, honey. I guess my mind's been on other things.'

'Yeah.' He smiled at her, encouraging. At least she was trying.

'So?'

'So what?'

'It was good, was it? The climb?' He watched her reach into her recent memory bank. 'You summited out, didn't you?'

'Yes.' He remembered it again, that sense of flawless purity, his sorrow that he could never share that immaculate beauty with her.

'I'll bet Joe was pleased.'

'That's one way of putting it.'

'And then you had to spend time in the hospital.' She lifted a lettuce leaf to her mouth and chewed it slowly. 'Are you OK? Do your ribs still hurt? You'd think that by now they'd have come up with a way to strap them up while they heal, wouldn't you? It seems all wrong just to

212

let them be. My dad broke a rib once, years ago, tripped over someone's dog in the street, and it was the same thing with him, no treatment, just had to put up with the pain until it healed.'

'And it did, of course.' Her babbling was almost as painful as her silence.

'What did?'

'Your father's rib,' he said carefully. 'It healed.'

'Oh. Yes, in the end. Dad was mortified. That's the only time he's ever fallen over, which, in the circumstances, is quite something.'

Her face was tight with anxiety as she made desperate attempts not to talk about the one thing which occupied her mind to the exclusion of everything else. He was overcome with tenderness; he longed to reach across the table and stroke her cheek, tell her to relax, it was OK. 'He's a remarkable man,' Ben said. 'With a remarkable daughter.'

She produced a brief smile. He could see her casting about for something else to talk about. He got up from the table. 'I'll do the dishes,' he said.

'I'll wash, you dry.' It was an exchange they'd had a hundred times before, but now it sounded like nothing more than a false note in a marriage which was just the skeleton of what it had once been.

As Lisa laid each piece of washed cutlery on the draining board, he dried it and put it away in the drawer.

'Honey,' he said, breaking the heavy silence. 'Don't hate me for saying this, but . . .'

'But what?'

'We could . . . I mean, it's not . . . we're . . . one of these days we can try again.'

She swung round from the sink and stared at him. '*What* did you say?'

As usual, when he tried to explain things, the words

213

had come out all wrong. Words were like that: they drifted away from you before you'd got a proper hold on them, they squeezed out between the gaps when you weren't looking. He cleared his throat. 'We could . . . think about another baby. When you're up to it, I mean. When you want to.'

'Don't say any more,' she said, through gritted teeth. 'I don't want to hear it.'

'But it's true,' he persisted. He was suddenly frightened.

She leaned on her hands and stared out of the window into the night. 'Stop,' she said loudly.

As she flung a handful of spoons onto the draining board, he picked three of them up and began to dry them. 'I know you need time to get over this,' he soothed.

'What do you mean, *this*? Just what do you think I need to get over?'

'Losing the baby. It'll come right. You'll see.' He wished he could be sure.

'It will never ever come right,' she said. She looked at him with fierce eyes. 'It *can't*.'

'We can . . . try again,' he repeated. He knew it was dangerous ground but he ploughed on. It needed to be said. It *had* to be, unless she was going to remain forever stuck in a time warp of loss and pain. 'It can't be the same, I know that, it couldn't ever be, but—'

'But what?' She slammed her fists into the water in the sink, sending a wave of suds over the draining board.

He swallowed. 'Other women have lost their babies and still gone on to . . . to have families.'

The air round her was suddenly raw. 'What do you mean? That I should just get on with it? Pretend it didn't happen? Snap out of it?'

'I didn't say any of—'

'After all, I'm young and healthy,' she said rapidly, her

voice getting louder and louder. 'There's no reason why I shouldn't have another perfectly normal pregnancy. Is that what you're saying? Is that what you want to tell me?'

He started to put the dried spoons into the cutlery drawer and abruptly she was screaming at him. 'For Christ's sake, Ben, you know the spoons are supposed to go the other way round.' She snatched the dishtowel from his hand. 'You *know* that.'

'Does it really matter?' He picked up two more spoons.

'Of course it matters!' She was shrieking at the top of her voice now. 'That's the way we always do it. The bowls are supposed to be *this* end so you can tell as soon as you open the drawer whether they're spoons or whether they're forks. You know that. You fucking *know* it.'

'I don't really give a shit how they're supposed to go,' he said. 'Nothing matters except you.'

She tugged at the drawer, wrenched it out of its casing. 'Everything matters.' Her voice broke around the words. 'Everything.'

'Lisa . . .'

As he moved towards her, she flung the drawer at him. 'I've told you a hundred times about the spoons!' Forks, spoons, knives cascaded around his head.

'Have you gone raving mad?' he said, trying to shield his face and get hold of her at the same time.

'*Everything* matters,' she shrieked again. 'Can't you see that?'

'Stop it, for chrissake!' he shouted. 'Stop yelling like that.' Cutlery crashed and jangled on the stone floor. Even in his anger, he was able to register amazement that they possessed so many forks. 'Get a fucking grip, Lisa.' He tried to seize her wrists but she twisted away from him.

'How dare you?' Her face was red, distorted. She

looked like a madwoman. 'How *dare* you tell me we can have another baby?'

'Calm down, will you.' He reached for her but she put her small hands on his chest and, with surprising force, pushed him away. The ends of his broken ribs grated agonizingly against each other. Gasping, he slipped, lost his balance, grabbed at the counter top, landed on his butt among the cutlery, sending a shock of pain up his spine.

'I don't want another baby,' she screamed, her mouth wide. 'Are you so fucking insensitive that you can't see I don't *want* another baby? I want the one's who's gone.'

'We have to move on,' he said. 'If we started thinking about having a second baby . . .' He tried to scramble to his feet but she pushed him down again, twisting the muscles in his still unhealed back.

'I want Rosie,' she said. Tears streamed down her cheeks and dripped onto the front of her T-shirt. 'I want Rosie.' She wiped her nose messily with the back of her hand. 'How can we have another baby when the first one is dead?'

'For God's sake, Lisa.'

She picked up a mug from the counter and flung it at the wall. 'Dead, damn you! Don't you understand anything at all? Rosie, my baby, is *dead*!' Snatching up a knife from the draining board, she lunged at him, catching him just below the eye, nicking his cheek.

'Jesus!' He grabbed her ankle, pulling at her so she fell awkwardly onto one knee as he tried to take the knife away from her. Her eyes were wide and unfocused, her mouth contorted. 'What the hell do you think you're doing?' He put his hand up to his face, felt blood sticky on his fingers. 'If you're not careful, someone's going to get hurt.'

'I'm already hurt,' she said. 'I am seriously fucking

216

hurt.' She put both her hands over her face and began to sob, her shoulders heaving. 'Oh God, Ben. You do not have the faintest *idea* how hurt I am.'

'Lisa,' he whispered. 'Oh, Lisa . . .'

She struggled away from him wiping a palm over her cheeks, smearing flecks of his blood over her wet face. Then she stood with her hands hanging by her sides and sobbed as though her heart was breaking.

CHAPTER FOURTEEN

He got up early the next morning, while she was still asleep. Jogging along the empty country roads, he wondered if it were possible to run off sadness, sweat away guilt. Above his head the trees whispered. His feet pounded in time to the dull thud of his heart. Would they ever be able to find a new way of living together, of forgetting the old?

When he got back, Lisa was going through her closet. 'I'm sorry. I'm so sorry,' she said as, breathing hard, he leaned against the door of their bedroom. 'I don't know what's happening to me. I don't seem to be able to hold onto things any more.'

'What're you doing?'

'I thought it was time to clear out some stuff.' She sounded almost like her old self and a huge relief swept over him. Maybe their fight the evening before had been worth it. She was putting books into some of the supermarket cartons lined up against the wall, clothes in others.

He looked at the bright tumble of colors. 'Don't you want those any more?'

'Maternity clothes,' she said briefly.

It wasn't an issue he was going to push. If they ever . . . they could buy new ones, start over. One day. Some day.

Showered, dressed for work, he said, as he always did, 'I love you,' and, this time, she gave him a smile, nodded at him. 'Love you too, dreamboat.'

Driving back to Butterfield the following evening, he thought of how things used to be. These days, he found himself dreading the thought of getting home. His own misery squatted under his heart, subdued and unexpressed, but Lisa's lived in the house with them like an unwanted guest, sat at their table, slept in their bed. Surrounded her like a briar hedge, preventing him from getting near. He touched the place under his eye, where she'd cut him with the knife. Jesus!

On the other hand, this morning, she'd seemed more cheerful. He crossed his fingers against the steering wheel. Maybe, just maybe, they could start looking forward again, instead of simply marking time.

There were lamps on all over the house when he finally pulled into the drive, beams of light rolling like rugs across the dark gravel. Another good sign. At least she wasn't sitting somewhere in the dark, weeping, as he'd found her doing two days ago.

He pushed open the front door. The hallway was full of cooking smells and his heart lifted even further. She'd cooked for them. She was – she must be – better. Or recovering. More than anything in the world he wanted her to be happy again. To see her smile. 'Honey,' he called. 'It's me.'

There was no answering cry, but that didn't bother him. In the week since he'd come back from the mountains, he'd grown used to living with a ghost. He went into the kitchen and saw a casserole sitting on top of the stove. When he lifted the lid, it was cold: she must have made it that morning. 'Lisa?' he shouted. 'Where are you?'

219

No reply. Maybe she was showering. He bounded up the stairs, two at a time, feeling almost light-headed with relief. In their bedroom he saw that the cardboard cartons had gone, another good sign. The bed was neatly made, the closets closed, her dressing table tidied up, everything put away for once. He smiled, remembering how it used to be: the easy chaos of jewellery and tubs of cream, hair-brushes and lipsticks missing their tops.

'Darling,' he said, opening the bathroom door.

But although the light was on, she wasn't in there. Perhaps she'd gone out to the studio. Perhaps – he clasped his hands together as though praying – she was back at work. Perhaps she'd changed her mind about the Texas job, driven to the art shop in Burlington and bought fresh paint, was working overtime in order to get it done in time for the Peacocke wedding. His horizons, which over the past week had dwindled about him, expanded again.

He poured two glasses of wine, then carried them out of the back door and through the apple-scented darkness to the barn. Using a foot, he pushed open the big door. There was a light in the studio. 'Lisa,' he called. 'I'm back.'

But she wasn't there either. Carefully he set down the wine, trying not to panic. She wasn't there, she didn't seem to be in the house. Where could she be?

He thought of the river which ran along one edge of the property. He thought of pills, of razors. He told himself not to be stupid. He ran back to the house and searched the ground floor, peered into the old-fashioned larder and the big utility room. He went upstairs and looked methodically through the three spare bedrooms, the big linen cupboard, behind the doors in the damp old bathrooms. Outside the baby's room, he hesitated. 'Lisa,' he called softly, anticipating despair, his earlier hopes falling round him like ashes.

When he pushed the door open, the room was empty. Stunned, he stared about him. The chest which he had rubbed down to the wood and then repainted had disappeared, along with the crib. The windows were bare. The quilt, the butterflies, they'd gone too. Only the sunshine-yellow walls and the stencilled leaves on the floor remained.

'You mustn't do that,' he said aloud. 'You can't erase her.' He'd suggested that they might one day have other babies but that didn't mean they had to obliterate the one they did not have. 'Oh God,' he said, and covered his face with his hands while, inside him, something broke.

Coming slowly down the stairs, he saw the mirror which hung in the hall. It had belonged to the Adams sisters, had been in the family for generations; when he and Lisa had moved in they'd said you have it, we can't take it with us, it belongs with the house. The frame was carved mahogany, all bursting pomegranates and bunches of grapes; the silvering was old and tarnished.

'You can't see yourself worth a damn in it,' Lisa had said, 'but I love it.'

Now he saw that there was writing on its surface, red writing. He peered more closely and glimpsed behind the lipstick marks on the glass his own stricken face, indistinct, as though seen through pond water.

I can't stay with you. And, underneath, an *L*.

He stared at the words. *I can't stay with you* . . . He remembered their wedding day, how she had looked up at him when they exchanged rings, the glow in her black eyes, the sense he'd had then that the vows they'd made to each other had a physical existence, like a chain of golden links, binding the two of them together for all their lives.

What had she said yesterday, packing up those cartons? That she was clearing out some stuff. That's what it was – or had she said simply – the thought now made him shiver – that she was clearing out? A whole different meaning. Nerves jumped along his jaw. She'd said she loved him. *Love you too, dreamboat* . . . She wouldn't have said that if she was planning to go, would she? If she loved him, she wouldn't leave him.

Would she?

The red words danced on the cloudy mirror. *I can't stay with you* . . .

'But I love you,' he whispered. Beyond the lipstick letters, his mouth moved.

'Lisa!' he shouted, suddenly desperate, voice cracking. 'Lisa! Where have you gone?'

The echoes of his voice ricocheted around the empty hall, bouncing up the stairs, beating at the walls. He went out of the kitchen door and back to the barn again. The two glasses of wine were on the counter where he'd left them. He drank them both, and felt the cold liquid slide through his body like icy rain.

He punched in his father-in-law's number. 'It's Ben here,' he said, when the receiver was lifted. 'How are you, Peter?'

'I'm just fine.'

'Good.' Ben envisaged the old man – old enough to be Lisa's grandfather – in his sparse apartment, reaching for things he could not see. 'Peter—'

'Isn't it rather late to be calling me?'

He looked down at his watch. Eleven thirty. He'd searched the house again, the barn. Run down to the creek at the end of the garden. Driven up and down the roads, looking for a parked white car, a stumbling figure. 'I guess.'

222

'What's wrong?' Peter Tan asked. 'Is Lisa sick again?'

'I . . . I don't know.'

'What are you saying?' The old man's voice was calm.

'She's not here. I wondered if she was with you but obviously she isn't.'

'Perhaps she has gone to visit friends.'

'Why would she leave without telling me she was going?'

'Lisa has always been a law unto herself,' said Peter. 'She will call you, I'm sure. If I hear anything from her, I will let you know.'

'Thanks.'

'Did you have a good time in the mountains?'

'Yes.' Ben waited for his condemnation for leaving Lisa alone.

'I would love to have climbed a mountain,' Tan said. 'It must truly be a magnificent experience to stand so high above the world.'

'It is.'

'Something few people aspire to, and fewer people still ever achieve. I would think it takes a special kind of person to do what you do. A hero, perhaps. But I believe that is what you are. Because I can't watch television, I listen a lot to the radio. I hear your name mentioned many times.'

'I don't know what that stuff means any more . . .' He heard the words echoing in the empty silence as he hung up.

He thought of calling his mother, his brother, but he knew Lisa would not have gone to them. Where else would she go? He pressed the numbers for Mel Sherman's phone. He could feel the rapid beating of his heart as he waited for her to pick up, adrenaline still surging through his body.

223

'Mel Sherman.' She sounded cool.

'Ben Andersen here.'

'Hi, Ben, what's the—'

'Is Lisa with you?'

'No, isn't she—'

'Any idea where she might be?'

'None. What's happened?' Alarm filled her voice.

'She seems . . .' he said carefully. 'It looks like she may have . . .'

'May have what?'

'She's gone.'

He heard her give a kind of moan.

'She wrote on the mirror.'

'Wrote?'

'Said she couldn't stay with me.'

'Oh, Ben. I know she's been in a terrible state but I never dreamed . . .'

He swallowed something thick and bitter at the back of his throat. 'There wasn't even a proper note. Just lipstick on the mirror.' He had a vision of a distracted Lisa looking round for a pen, for paper, finding it too much effort, grabbing some clothes and running out to the car, taking off. He saw her racing down the freeways, over the mountains, away from pain, away from *him*.

'She probably just wants some time alone. A couple of days, maybe, and she'll be back.'

'She's packed up her stuff. All her stuff, her clothes, books, make-up, it's all gone.' He swallowed again. He made a sound which could have been a sob. 'Oh God.' He drew in a deep breath. 'I'm sorry I called you so late.' He replaced the receiver before she could say anything further.

He was suddenly overwhelmed by a sense of emptiness. Was this what Lisa had felt, was feeling, with the baby gone from inside her, this chilling loss?

The baby. He thought of the terrace he had been working on, up at the lake, so his mother could watch over the grandchildren. Not one of his, though. Not any more.

He went out through the front door and stood under the apple tree, feeling the night warm and thick around his head. The windows of the house spilled gold light into the darkness, and he was reminded of the *Titanic* going down in a blaze of lights.

'Rosie,' he said, 'Rosemary,' seeing her for the first time, his daughter, black-haired like Lisa, with the same almond-shaped eyes and tiny body. He saw himself tucking a little girl into bed, reading her a bedtime story, changing her diapers, strapping her into her car seat when they drove down to see his mother, swinging her high to the ceiling the way he swung his nephews, Neil's boys.

He sobbed aloud.

Without Lisa, without the baby, there was nothing.

Chapter Fifteen

Mel woke with a heavy sense of foreboding. The shapes of furniture loomed dimly in the shimmering summer dawn. The house was quiet. As so often when caught off guard, her father's voice echoed again in her mind. *I'm afraid I don't.* Even after all this time, she did not understand how he could have said something so brutal. She clenched her fists. If only it was possible to go back, rewrite the moment. The burden of being an unloved child still weighed heavily on her.

I wish things to be other than they are, she thought. I want . . . I don't know what I want but something more than I have. I want another chance at life. I wish I did not feel so lonely, so unloved. The arbitrariness of things hovered at the edge of her vision. Even her house, her long refuge, was acting up, the furnace going out one night, a crack appearing in one of the bedroom windows, rust spots marking the tub.

Over the years, she had fashioned for herself a life which allowed the layers of her existence to lie undisturbed, but now she could see that leaving things undisturbed, unaired, made them more dangerous. You think they're safely stashed away somewhere at the back of your head and all of a sudden, when you least expect it, you encounter something – a photograph in a magazine, a pregnant girl – and they refuse to lie still. They start to take on a life of their own. Start to haunt your dreams.

'How're the kids?' Mel asked. She and Joanne were sitting at one of the five café tables in the coffee bar Joanne had added to the bookstore last year.

'Fine. Tom's handed over the direction of that darn film to Lee, so it's all onto his mom now, instead of me, thank the Lord.'

'What happened to the bomb?'

'No bombs. Lee's decided to set it in Alabama during the 1920's.'

'And Lucy?'

'In seventh heaven. On cloud nine. Walking on air. She's going to the Prom with Carl Hanson, which is who she now says she always wanted to go with.'

'And Jamie?'

Joanne frowned. 'I don't know. Maybe it's pre-adolescent angst: he's acting so . . . furtive is the only word. I don't know what he's up to, but it's something. Keeps calling from school to say he'll be home late.'

Mel reached for her coffee. She and Jamie still had not produced a lemon cake which Jamie deemed acceptable for his mother; sometimes she wondered if that was so he got to eat up the failures. 'At least he's calling you first.'

'If he were older,' Joanne said, 'I'd suspect that he'd fallen in love, but . . .' She shook her head slowly. '. . . surely my innocent baby can't have reached that stage yet.'

'Unless some strumpet's got her claws into him,' suggested Mel. 'Or an older woman.'

'One of those thirteen-year-old temptresses, you mean?'

Mel spooned cappuccino foam into her mouth. Looking up she saw a figure slouching across the Common, shoulders hunched, staring at the ground, gaunt and unkempt.

Joanne followed her gaze. 'Poor Ben. He looks a complete wreck.'

'I called round there a couple of times,' Mel said. 'Just to see how he was doing.'

'And how was he?'

'I never found out. I'm sure he was home, but he didn't answer the door.'

'Where do you think Lisa's gone?'

'Who knows. The way she was, last time I saw her, I don't think it would matter where it was, as long as Ben wasn't there.'

'What is it, ten days since she walked out?'

'Over two weeks.'

'Any word?'

'Maybe to Ben. Nothing to me.' Mel shrugged. 'I can't pretend I'm not disappointed, but I guess she felt she needed to get away from anything connected to Butterfield.'

'Talking of which, I'll tell you who I'm inviting to the Big Five Oh party,' Joanne said. 'That nice guy from the college, Paul Tilney.'

'The history prof?'

'Yeah. He came into the store this morning and managed to bring you into the conversation at least three times.'

'Joanne, honey. I'm not interested. Not in him. Not in anyone.'

'You're way too choosy. In the guy sense, I mean.'

'Perhaps I'm not that desperate for another man.'

'You can't hide behind that thorn hedge for the rest

of your life. You've got to start living a little.'

'I'm living plenty, thanks.'

But Mel knew it was not true. It had been once. What frightened her, when she allowed the thought into her head, was that it might never be true again.

Mel knocked again, louder this time. Despite the fact that the lights were on in the Andersen house and she could hear music playing behind the closed drapes, there was no response. She banged once more, listening for footsteps. There was no sound. Nothing.

Irresolute, she stepped back and took a couple of paces towards the side of the house. Maybe Ben was out in the studio.

The night was unexpectedly warm and full of scents. Damp leaves. Apples. Something tangy, sage or thyme, from Lisa's herb garden.

A voice suddenly spoke from the darkness behind her. 'Hello, Mel.'

She whirled, clapping a hand to her heart. 'Lord!' she gasped. 'You startled me.' She could see him there, ghostly in the dark, not coming any nearer, standing back from the edge of the circle of brightness cast by the security lights. 'I saw the lights on, so I stopped by.'

When he did not reply, she said, 'Any chance of a coffee? Glass of wine? Cup of tea?'

He gave a twisted smile. 'All or any of the above. But if I invite you in, you won't want to stay long enough to drink them.'

'I'm a big girl,' said Mel. 'I can handle most things.'

'Well . . .' Reluctantly he walked towards and past her. 'Don't say I didn't warn you.'

As Mel followed him inside, she tried not to show her dismay. The place smelled of decay and neglect. There was a crumpled sleeping bag on the sofa in the front room, and a number of mugs on the floor beside it. Dirty clothes lay where he had tossed them: shirts and sweat pants, muddy trainers, jockey shorts. His mountaineering gear lay scattered across the rug, as though he had dropped it when he arrived back from Alaska and never bothered to clear it up.

Overloud music filled the room – Mozart, a piano concerto she recognized but couldn't quite identify. Seeing him in the light, he wrung her heart. He looked as though he were on the point of collapse. There was several days' growth of beard along his jaw, and his eyes, deeply set into their sockets, were raw and red, as if he had been weeping for days.

He looked around and grimaced. 'Sorry,' he mumbled. 'I haven't . . .' He did not bother to complete the sentence. Instead, he turned down the music then went into the little kitchen. Mel followed him.

'Coffee, you said.' He pulled a mug from one of the cupboards then picked up a jar of instant coffee and stood holding it, as though not sure what to do next.

There was a garbage sack on the floor, half full of empty cans. More stood on the counter. A cereal bowl held baked beans covered with a layer of white fungus, slices of stale bread spilled from a plastic bag, half a dried-up apple lay on top of the remains of a grapefruit which had gone green with mould. The sink was full of dirty dishes and pans. He had tossed trash indiscriminately on top of them: tea bags, banana skins, egg shells. A trail of something sticky lay across the floor, marked by a line of ants: a couple of dead flies floated in a glass which was half full of what could have been apple juice or iced tea, or even stale beer.

'You're not coping very well,' Mel said.

He laughed harshly. 'I'm not coping at all.'

'Would it irritate you if I cleaned up a bit for you?'

He shrugged. 'It won't make any difference.'

'It might make you feel a bit better.'

She opened the small dishwasher under the sink and wrinkled her nose, trying not to retch. It looked as though the dishes inside had been there since Lisa's departure. Maggots were moving slowly about, like fat white seeds, and the plates were covered in a greenish fungus.

The refrigerator smelled sour. There were two opened yogurts inside, both with a thick topping of mould, some butter, some greenish cheese and a wrinkled tomato. Mel rooted through the drawers and found a roll of garbage sacks into which she threw the lot.

Taking the dishes out of the sink, she stacked them in the dishwasher. She carried in the dirty mugs from the living room, the empty glasses, the crusted saucepans and added them, then switched to the Heavy Load setting. The cycle would probably have to be run twice. While she cleaned up, Ben sat at the table, staring at nothing. When the kitchen finally looked reasonable, she opened cupboards and doors until she had located the vacuum cleaner, brooms, furniture polish and dusters, then she started on the living room and the hall, cleaning around him as best she could. Finally she located the linen closet and found fresh sheets and pillowcases. Feeling invasive, aware of the intimacy of the action, she stripped his bed and remade it with clean linen, then put the musty sheets into the washing machine and turned it on.

She went out to her car, rooted among the groceries she had bought earlier and brought some of them in: fresh milk, honey-roasted ham, a bag of apples and a loaf of wholemeal bread. She fixed a ham sandwich, put it on a plate with an apple, made coffee for them both and put it

231

down on the table. She pushed a mug and the sandwich across to Ben and sat down opposite him.

Ben stood up. 'I appreciate your kindness in coming round.' He gestured helplessly. 'And you're right, it does look better. Polished furniture. Nice disinfectant smells in the kitchen. Fresh sheets on my bed that don't smell of my wife, who hated living with me so much that two weeks ago she just up and left.'

'Lisa loves you.'

'Funny way to show it.'

Mel took a deep breath. 'Ben, losing the baby wasn't your fault.'

Abruptly he sat down again. He stared at her, his expression bewildered, holding her gaze.

Mel's throat thickened. 'Oh, Ben.' She reached over and took his hand. 'You think it was.'

'If I'd only stayed home . . .' He bent his head. 'I knew she wasn't feeling good.'

'It wouldn't have made the slightest difference,' she said. 'The baby was dead. Even if you'd been standing right beside her, you couldn't have changed anything.'

There was another long silence, then Ben said, 'It was a girl.'

'I know.'

'I keep seeing her, this tiny little girl, with – with black hair and black eyes, just like . . . like Lisa . . .'

Mel squeezed his fingers. He smelled sour, as though he had not bathed for a long time. He rested his elbows on the table. Not knowing how to offer comfort, she stroked the back of his hand, reflecting on the limitations which courtesy demands of near-strangers, especially those separated by age and gender. Despite his deep distress, she dared not offer him the comfort of her arms.

'I love her so,' he said, clearing his throat. 'So much.'

232

'Things happen. You can't change them. You can't anticipate them. All you can do is absorb them. And go on.'

'I don't know if I can.'

'When my husband died,' said Mel, 'my friend, Joanne Mayfield, wrote me a letter.' She smiled. 'She only lives a mile from me, but she wrote me because she wanted me to remember what she had to say. She said that however unfair it might seem, the earth wouldn't stop. She said: "*Dust will continue to gather in corners. Moons will wax and wane. Flowers will bloom and fade. Rivers will go on running to the sea. Life goes on.*" It may seem monstrous to you now, Ben, but she was right.'

He looked at her, his gray eyes bleak. 'And did life go on for you?'

She wanted to say: my life stopped years ago, long before I met Eric. 'Of course,' she said. 'It's the way things are.'

His fingers tightened round hers.

'At the time, I didn't want to believe it, but it's true.' Mel sighed. 'It's just the way things are.'

'Sometimes I think I'm losing my mind,' he said. 'I know I have to make some kind of an effort to get my life back on track but . . . I feel completely numb.'

'Have you heard from Lisa?'

'Yeah.' He squeezed his eyes shut. 'A letter. A couple of days ago. She said she wasn't coming back.' He gave a kind of grunt, as though he had just been kicked in the stomach.

'Did she mention any plans?'

'She might head for California, she said. Or Chicago – she's been offered a job there. She said . . . she . . .' His voice began to break. '. . . that she . . . she loved me but . . . it was a mistake . . . we shouldn't have gotten . . . married.'

Did she really mean that, Mel wondered? Or was it just a way to put some space between the two of them? She remembered Lisa in the studio which Ben had created, her whole body smiling as she made her declaration of faith, surprised at the easiness of it. *What it all boils down to is that I love him. Simple as that.* It was hard to believe that she could have changed so much in so short a time.

'Where do you think she is?' she asked.

He shook his head. Shrugged. 'New York seems the likeliest place.'

'Why don't you look for her,' she said. 'Go to New York, to the places where you used to hang out, visit your friends.' She pressed his fingers again. 'Don't let her go without even trying, Ben.'

He nodded, but without conviction.

'Listen, Ben.' She held his hand. 'I did it once. I left someone I . . . someone who was the entire world to me. And I've regretted it ever since. All my life since. Which, if you think about it, is a terrible waste, don't you agree?'

He stared at her with astonishment and she realized that she was talking much too loudly.

'Don't just let her go,' she said. 'Don't waste all the love which I know you had – still have – for each other.'

CHAPTER SIXTEEN

Ben had tried to pretend that Lisa was simply away for a while. At first he'd made an effort to keep the place tidy, thinking of her reaction if she came back to find it a mess, but eventually it didn't seem to matter much and anyway, he couldn't be bothered. She'd taken a lot of her things with her, but he drew comfort from the stuff she'd left behind, among it the pair of silver spoons he'd given her when they first met, a crystal dolphin she had fallen in love with in a shop window, the rainbow quilt they'd bought together at a craft fair, which she'd always said she wanted to be buried in.

What an image that brought to mind. He thought of the baby: what happened to the ones who never made it? Did they get buried? Were they considered worth burying or were they just scraps of flesh, thrown into a garbage sack, consigned to some incinerator? The question haunted him. He found the number of a woman called Cheryl on the noticeboard and called it, but there was no answer, just the phone ringing in an empty house, and he had a sudden vision of what the woman would think if she'd been there, picked up, heard him ask such an unnatural question.

Mel's visit roused him from his despairing lethargy. He

travelled down to New York the very next day, spurred on by the passion in her dark blue eyes, the way even her hair had seemed to blaze as she urged him not to sit tamely at home and let Lisa go.

He wondered who he was, the man who had meant the whole world to her. Obviously not her husband. Ben recalled him on summer evenings up at the lake, a big pompous man who always had a drink in his hand, a man incapable of accepting that he might be wrong about anything, from a baseball score to the correct way to pronounce Latin. Professor Andersen had loathed him.

In the city, he found a room in a cheap hotel in their old neighborhood, remembering, as he hung a clean shirt in the rickety wardrobe, how he and Lisa had always promised themselves that they would spend a night here, just to see if it really was as squalid inside as it looked from the street. 'It *couldn't* be,' Lisa used to say, every time they passed it.

If anything, it was worse. A thin coverlet on the bed, sheets from which nameless stains had been inadequately laundered, cockroaches scurrying out of his way when he went into the bathroom. If she'd been with him they could have laughed about it, outdone each other in discovering the room's defects: as it was, he felt that the degrading surroundings were all he deserved.

Tormenting himself even further, he spent hours in what had been their favorite coffee shop, nursing a cup of cappuccino, staring at the door in the hope that she would come in, her black hair swinging on her shoulders, trying to believe that she would smile when she saw him, join him at the table, take his hand. The woman behind the counter remembered him, asked after Lisa, and he had a momentary urge to unburden himself to her, might even have done so if another customer hadn't come in, demanding coffee and doughnuts.

On the off chance that he might find, run across, bump into her, he walked the streets for hours, stood on the sidewalk opposite the deli where they used to buy their breakfast Danish in the morning, lingered in the little store where they shopped in the evening when he came home from work. He sat through five performances of *The Wedding Banquet*, which was playing at their local fleapit theater, because it had been her favorite movie. He knew his search was futile – why would she want to come back to the places they had shared, when he had so obviously not made her happy? – but desperation kept him looking. And all the time he was assailed by memories of her laughter, haunted by her smile, her eyes crinkling at him, her hand tucked into the crook of his arm. She had flashed into his life like a hummingbird and he had not been able to save her from despair. Which was pretty ironic, considering the number of other people he had managed to rescue, so many of them, but not the one – the two – who meant most to him in the world.

One afternoon he dropped by Lisa's former apartment, now sub-let to a friend of hers, climbing up the many flights of stairs because the elevator was – as it always had been – out of order.

Sara had been at their wedding. When she opened the door, he tried to remember what she did – a photographer, he thought. 'Ben,' she said, smiling, her eyes moving over his face then shifting to look behind him for Lisa. 'This is a nice surprise. What brings you to the Big Apple?'

He tried to smile back. 'Just visiting.'

'Thought you hated the place.'

'I do.'

'And Lisa's not with you?'

'No.'

She surveyed him thoughtfully. 'Want to come in?'

'OK.' But doing so, sitting down on the striped futon, he knew that he was wasting his time: if Lisa had come here, Sara would not have invited him past the door.

'How's life up in the sticks?' she asked brightly, sinking cross-legged on a big floor cushion in front of him.

'Fine.'

'You look awfully miserable. What's up?'

He shrugged. 'Nothing.' He found it impossible to speak to this semi-stranger about something as intimate as the loss of the baby, the breakdown of his marriage.

'Really?' Sara rose fluidly and underneath his misery a little chip of memory reminded him that she was not a photographer but a dancer. She sat down next to him and put her arms round him. 'What's happened? Has Lisa left you?'

When he nodded, she took his hand. 'When did this happen?'

'A couple of weeks ago.'

'Lisa's a city girl. None of us really thought she'd manage to come to terms with those country ways,' Sara confided. 'She said she'd give it her best shot, but she wasn't sure if she'd . . .' Realizing she was being tactless, she shrugged. '. . . you know.'

Ben was pierced by this small sidelight on his wife's expectations. Had the move to Vermont been no more than a gamble for her? Some kind of risk she'd been ready to take, weighing up the odds but not prepared to be devastated if it hadn't worked? Had leaving him really been an option, during the months they'd spent in Butterfield? When they left New York, he'd always assumed that Lisa had been as committed to the move as he had.

238

Sara leaned forward from the waist to touch his leg with her finger and he remembered her coming on to him once, years before, at some party, in some kitchen, kissing him on the mouth, pressing herself against him with her hand on the front of his jeans. God, you gorgeous hunk, she'd said, or, you gorgeous beast, something like that. He'd tried to pretend it hadn't happened, and hoped now that she had forgotten the incident. 'You two were always so . . . I don't know, *together*,' she said. 'If anybody was going to make it, you were the ones.'

'Yeah.' Awkwardly, he got up, awkwardly returned the hug she gave him.

'She'll come back,' she said, squeezing his shoulder. 'Especially if you move down to the city.'

Is that what it would take? Passing a pub on the way back to his fleapit hotel, he heard music belting out, spilling onto the sidewalk like an audible stain. It was music he recognized, edgy, swaggering stuff, with an insistent pounding beat which sounded exactly like a thousand other mediocre rock bands he'd heard over the years. On impulse, he went into the dimly lit space and slid into a booth at the back. When the waitress came over, he ordered a double Scotch on the rocks and let the raucous sounds wash over him. The performer was one of Lisa's city friends; he hadn't liked him when they'd lived here and he didn't like the music now. But he listened because it brought back the early days of their marriage, the nervous blinking of the neon sign outside the window, the smell of wet streets in the summer, winter frost glittering along the edges of the sidewalks, coffee and gasolene and the sharp scent of urine in doorways. He had felt so potent then, convinced he could rule the world if he only wanted to, sure of Lisa, sure of love. Now he was sure of nothing.

The voice snarled and screamed above the line laid down by the amplified guitar. Ben remembered the guy sitting hunched over a guitar in their apartment. His face had been heavily pierced with silver rings and studs; there was even a tiny cross dangling from one eyebrow.

'All that ironwork, it must weigh a ton,' Lisa had said later, as they lay in bed.

'I'm amazed he manages to lift his head from the pillow in the morning.'

'I know I've got pierced ears, but what makes someone mutilate themselves like that?' Lisa shuddered. 'A stud in your tongue – *gross*.'

'The guy can't even talk properly any more.' Ben pushed his mouth against Lisa's. 'Kith me, thweetie,' he lisped. The two of them had clasped each other, laughing.

He knew she'd been reluctant about moving to Butterfield, but he hadn't realized how little faith she'd had that it would work out. Lisa, the city girl. Lisa, my love. His heart seemed too big suddenly to be contained inside his chest.

Words flooded him. Lisa, heart of my heart, apple of my eye, light of my life. Yet if she were there beside him, he could not have spoken them. He buried his face in his hands. He'd believed they loved each other – was he wrong about that too? Surely she could never have doubted his feelings for her.

Many whiskies later, exhausted, dispirited, he staggered back to his hotel and fell across the grungy coverlet, not bothering to take off his clothes. He thought back to Sara's words: '*She said she'd give it her best shot, but she wasn't sure if she'd . . .*' The inference was obvious. '. . . *she wasn't sure if she'd really be able to hack it.*'

The '*but*' tainted his memories. He'd thought they were happy together, and all the time he'd been on trial. He lay

240

restless, alcohol parching his throat, staring at the cracked and dirty ceiling, hearing the rustle of cockroaches in the bathroom, sirens whining on the streets, someone in an adjoining room cursing monotonously, on and on, the crude litany a fitting counterpoint to his wrenching thoughts.

It was pointless to stay on here. He would go back to Vermont in the morning.

Before he left, he dropped by Peter Tan's apartment.

'How are you Ben?' the old man said, standing aside at the door, his dark glasses seeming no more than a quiet eccentricity.

'Bad.'

'Lisa has still not returned?'

'No. She's been dreadfully depressed since … since she lost the baby.'

'This is to be expected.'

'If she shows up here, Peter, please tell her I'm worried about her.'

'I'll do that.' The old man walked confidently towards his little galley kitchen.

'Would you like some tea, Ben?'

'Thanks.'

The living room was full of light, its windows overlooking a small park where children played. The apartment smelled, as always, of the mingled fragrances of soy sauce and joss sticks. Heavy furniture brought from China, jade horses on a chest beneath the window, carved sandalwood statues. A sofa, a couple of chairs, a round cherrywood table with a bowl of water on which the old man floated white camellias. Always white ones.

Why would a blind man have ornaments and flowers, Ben thought. What possible difference could it make

241

whether the camellias were white or colored? Would he realize if the florist gave him pink ones instead?

The bowl was one of Lisa's. He envisaged her strong fingers pulling the clay, the whirr of the wheel, her hair falling over her face as she concentrated on the piece taking shape. Perhaps she'd have been wearing her pink smock. Or the peacock-blue one. She'd have tied her hair up in a yellow scarf, or a crimson one, and be singing along to something loud on her personal stereo.

Sudden tears pricked his eyes, and he blinked them away.

'Be patient, Ben.'

Ben looked up quickly to find Peter's dark glasses turned in his direction, almost as though he could see. 'What other choice do I have?' he said.

'None. At the moment.'

The old man brought over a tray with two translucent porcelain cups and a round black pot with a straw-wrapped handle, and sat down. 'So, Ben. Will you be climbing again soon?'

'No. Not for a while.'

'Why not?' Peter filled the two cups and pushed one over towards Ben.

'Because . . .'

'Because what?'

'A friend of mine maintains that all mountaineers are selfish shits,' Ben said. The tea was green and fragrant. If he shut his eyes, he could almost imagine that he and Lisa were paying one of their regular visits to the old man.

'Maybe they have to be, in order to survive.'

'I don't like being a shit. I don't . . .' Ben struggled, the words for what he wanted to say scattering as he tried to grasp them. 'I have to climb, you see. The mountains are the only place where I feel . . . where I feel like

242

myself.' He shook his head. 'I'm not making any sense.'

'You are.'

'The people I climb with know who I am, what I'm about. Nobody else does, not my family, not even Lisa. How can they? The thing is, Peter, up there, I know exactly who I am. Everywhere else, I don't seem to be able to . . . to get it together.' He looked down at the delicate cup, the drowned jasmine flowers floating.

'You are mistaken.'

His voice rose almost to a shout. 'I should have been there with Lisa.'

'But you were not. And if you had been, would things have turned out any differently?'

'I let her down.'

'I don't think so, And sooner or later, Lisa will see that. Meanwhile, you have to carry on.'

'I don't want to,' Ben said simply. 'Not without Lisa.'

'So you just give up? Ben, you are a better man than that.'

Driving back up to Butterfield, he wondered if it was true.

Another Saturday morning. Lisa had been gone more than three weeks. The lushness of July was giving way to the dusty greens of August. He couldn't get used to the way time carried on carrying on, nor how abruptly their lives together had fragmented. In retrospect, it was as though one day they seemed to be blissfully happy, the next she had gone. Yet he knew it had been a longer drawn-out process than that. Moments of Lisa's discontent came back to him, moments he had noted but ignored, not thinking them important.

Examining his reflection in the bathroom mirror, he scarcely recognized the gaunt face, the bony cheeks and sunken eyes, as his own. It was time he tried to re-establish some kind of order in his daily routine. He couldn't remember when he'd last had a proper meal. If he was going to get his life back again, he'd better start eating properly, instead of living off junk food, snatched sandwiches, takeout pizza. Mel had brought him ham, apples, fresh milk . . . when was that? It seemed like years ago.

He drove down to the Farmer's Market. He bought a Cornish Rock hen, new potatoes, lettuce, big slicing tomatoes, red onions, an avocado. There were fresh peaches on the fruit counter and, thinking of Mel, he purchased half a dozen. Nothing he'd bought was particularly exciting, but it was real food, it smelled of the earth, of leaves, of its origins, rather than stuff from the freezer or easy things like hamburgers. Pushing his trolley to the checkout, he bumped into Sarah Mahoney, exchanged smiles with one of the assistants from Joanne Mayfield's bookstore.

There were people out there. Even though his own world had come to a full stop, the earth went on turning.

It was still only mid-afternoon, but he coated the chicken with a mixture of olive oil, salt and pepper, fresh herbs, and French mustard, and placed it in the oven. He opened a bottle of Chardonnay. Later, he would start the potatoes boiling and make a salad of tomato and avocado, sprinkle them with chopped basil and French dressing made with real Dijon mustard, honey and luscious green Spanish olive oil.

Sipping the cool wine, he flipped idly through a cookbook, stopping to read recipes here and there. There wasn't enough time in each day to wander through the more esoteric branches of gastronomy, but shrimp teriyaki, crown roast of lamb, risottos, poached salmon, omelets; he could handle those. He'd always enjoyed food, as a child had spent far more time in the kitchen with his mother than Neil ever had.

He came across a color reproduction of a peach tart, the fruit halves set in some kind of custard, the whole thing caramelized, burnished with glaze. It must have been the recipe Lisa had used: there was a smear of butter on the page, two or three grains of sugar trapped in the fold. He licked his finger and collected them up, put them into his mouth, thinking of her standing in the kitchen in a washed-out pink denim skirt and a white sports top, stirring, adding, tasting, scattering sugar here and there, dropping a buttery knife onto the cookbook.

The telephone shrilled and he leaped for it, wishing, hoping that it might be her, knowing already that it would not be. Maybe it was his mother: fielding her distress was almost as hard as dealing with it himself. He picked up, his heart tied into an intricate knot of longing and loneliness, but he resolutely pushed both emotions to the back of his mind.

'Ben Andersen.'

'Oh, hi, Mr Andersen. How're you this evening?'

'Fine.' Did he recognize the voice?

'OK, now let me say first that I'm not trying to sell you anything, but you might be interested in—'

The treacly wheedling tones of a cold call salesman. 'I'm not.' He put down the receiver.

The kitchen began to fill with the smell of roasting meat and he poured himself another glass of Chardonnay. There was a glow in his stomach, a golden glow, the same color as the wine, as he walked into the living room. Lying in a drawer, under a packet of paper napkins left over from Christmas, was a tablecloth they had been given as a wedding present, made of fine lawn hand-embroidered with green-leaved yellow daisies. 'It's gorgeous,' Lisa had said, kneeling on the floor and scrabbling around for the card which told them who had sent the gift, 'but my *God*, talk about high maintenance.'

'What does that mean?'

'That we'd bankrupt ourselves with laundry bills if we ever used it. There's no way this could go through the washing machine, it'll have to be sent to a specialist cleaner.'

The result was that it had never been used. He shook it out and spread it across the table. He laid two places, found a couple of green wine glasses, set out two matching green glass plates to act as place mats. He picked up a photograph of Lisa which a friend had snapped on their wedding day, an informal portrait of her turning her head, laughing, her black hair, longer then, trailing across her face like the Botticelli painting of Venus, fresh white flowers in a crown across her head.

He piled books on the chair and set the photograph on top. Then he saluted it with his glass. 'Lisa,' he said, by now slightly drunk. 'I love you. I will always love you. I miss you. I need you.' He put a pair of candlesticks on the table and lit them.

The tomatoes were warm and plump in his hand. When he lifted them to his face, he could smell an echo of their promise, but they weren't the same as the ones his mom used to grow. Slicing them, sprinkling them with oil, cutting basil leaves over them, he remembered summer evenings, being sent out to pick tomatoes just minutes before the family sat down to eat, remembered the smell of the vines, feeling for the plump fruit among the leaves, the scent of summer heat on the rich red skin. Maybe next year he would plant some out in the back, maybe grow corn, too, there was nothing like fresh-picked corn.

He took the chicken out of the oven and carved it, laid out slices of dark and light meat, added the unpeeled potatoes tossed in butter and chopped parsley. He stirred some of his white wine into the drippings in the pan and added it, then carried his plate to the table, brought over the salad and dressed it, then sat down. She laughed at him across the table, insubstantial in the flicker of the candle flames. He missed her. So much. Was it the tears in his eyes or the wine he had drunk which made her image shift and blur? 'Lisa,' he said. 'I love you.'

He picked up his knife and fork, poured more wine. Ate.

Carrying on.

Later, the telephone rang again and he reached for the receiver, raising it without hope to his ear.

'Benjamin?'

'Oh, hi, Peter.'

'How are things with you, Benjamin?'

'OK. How about you?'

'I am very well, thank you. I am telephoning because I had a call, yesterday evening.'

'From Lisa.'

'Yes.'

Ben was surprised at the detachment with which he managed to absorb this piece of news. Only a short time ago his heart would have begun to vibrate like a tuning fork, waiting for Peter to relay some message from her, hoping to hear some special phrase which he would know was an indication that she still cared for him. Now he knew better. 'How is she? Is she well and . . . uh, happy?'

'She's well,' Peter said. 'I'm not sure about happy. She tells me she is moving to California.'

No! he thought. *It's too far.* All this time, knowing there was no hope, he had nonetheless gone on hoping that she would return. That he would come home and there she'd be, curled up in the corner of the sofa or stirring something in the kitchen.

Imagining her wide smile, the toss of her hair, he jammed the receiver hard against his shoulder. So this was it. She was going away. There really was no hope left. 'Where in California?'

'She didn't say.'

'Are you sure?' Ben found it hard to believe.

'Of course I am sure,' Peter said tartly. 'It is my eyes which do not work Benjamin. My ears are just fine.'

'I'm sorry.'

'She knows that to me, it does not matter. I would not travel to see her. I could not. Besides, as you will have discovered, in some ways she is a very reserved young woman, almost, you might say, distant.' Peter spoke with a catch in his breath. 'She did not have a conventional upbringing. Circumstances forced her into independence. And she was always different from her peers.'

'It was the difference that I loved.'

'Me too,' said Lisa's father.

'Did you ever tell her that?' Ben said, impulsively.

'There was no need – she knew.'

'I don't think so. She believes you don't love her. That she doesn't matter to you.' A month, a week ago, he couldn't have imagined daring to speak to his father-in-law in such a personal way.

There was silence at the other end of the phone. Then Tan said, his voice faint, 'That is nonsense.'

'Whether it is or not, it's what she thinks.'

'I see.'

Silence hung between them. 'If she goes to California, will you be all right?' Ben asked eventually.

'As right as I always am.'

'I could always come and visit, if you want me to.'

'It is kind of you to think of such things,' the old man said, in his high precise voice. 'But I have many friends. A routine which I have fine-tuned over the years, a home with which I am familiar. A pleasant way of life.'

Ben found it hard to believe that anyone who had lost their sight could really describe their life as pleasant.

As though he could read his thoughts, Tan added, 'Losing one's sight does not have to be a disaster, you know.'

'Of course not.'

'And you, Benjamin . . . how are you coping on your own?'

'Coping is probably a good word to describe it.'

'My daughter has things to work out.' The old man cleared his throat. 'We must hope that it does not take her too long to find her solutions, eh, Benjamin?'

'Why do you say that?'

'Because I do not think you will wait for her for ever.'

He wanted to respond with denials, insist that he was prepared to wait for Lisa for as long as it took, but he could not see beyond the wall of pain created by her absence.

'I love her,' he said quietly. 'And I loved our baby. Tell her that, next time she calls you.'

CHAPTER SEVENTEEN

On the other side of the covered bridge at Parris, the road began to deteriorate and the houses to thin out. Ben drove past shabby clapboard Victorians on unkempt lots, red-painted farms sentried by the blunt shape of their silos, an occasional church, an auction barn where, in the early summer, he'd bid for a rocking chair of turned maple, picturing Lisa holding the baby to her breast, motivated by a memory of the thump and squeak of his grand-mother's rocker on the wooden floor of her house in Concord, wanting the same involvement with tradition as he himself had grown up with. He had spent days on the chair, scrubbing off the crud which had accumulated over the years, sanding it down to the grain, oiling, rubbing, oiling again until the grain glowed through.

The mountains began to close in. As he climbed higher, boulders pushed up out of the earth, trees crowded to the very edge of the road, runnels of water fell between rocks from the higher ground. At this time of year they were no more than a thread of moisture; in the mud season they would be sizeable falls.

At Weston Notch, the mountains stretched away from him, layer after layer of green trees already touched with the colors of fall: bronze and yellow and the first flush of crimson. Between the trees, the silver line of the lake was distantly visible. Coming upon these perspectives, he used to wonder how Lisa did not experience the same soaring of the spirit as he did. Now, removed from her, he understood that this simply wasn't her landscape. Why should it have been? He flushed, remembering how he had refused to believe that a place so significant to him did not have meaning for her too.

He pulled up beside the little country store at Hallam's Cove, turned off the ignition and got out of the car.

Frank Oates, the storeowner, was standing by the potbellied stove in the middle of the floor, talking to one of the rangers from the National Park. 'Brings you up here, Ben?' he asked.

'Checking the place out,' Ben said.

'Summer's just 'bout over.'

'So they say.'

'How's things, anyway?' Frank's face was full of sympathy.

'Fine, Frank. You?'

'Gettin' by, thanks.'

Ben picked up a wire basket. 'Need a few stores,' he said. 'Kind of last-minute decision to come up.'

'They say the snow'll be here early this year,' the ranger said.

'That's what I heard.'

'Mind you, they're bringing the plows up here in the winter now. Never used to. Olden days, we wuz cut off for months.'

'Got kind of desperate sometimes,' said the ranger.

'Sometimes had to eat the dogs in them days, keep from starvin'.' Frank grinned at Ben, showing a mouthful of yellowed teeth. 'Before your time, Ben.'

251

'And if the dogs ran out,' said the ranger, 'they started in on the kids.'

'Or the wife.'

The two men snorted with laughter while Ben walked round the crowded shelves, taking bread from the bins, bacon and a packet of link sausages from the refrigerated case, orange juice and apples, eggs and a carton of milk. There were canned goods up at the house, and stuff in the freezer; he wouldn't starve.

The turn-off was two miles further along the highway. A flutter started up in the pit of his stomach. This was the first time he had been back to the lake since Lisa had left. Perhaps, in some parallel universe, there still existed the Ben Andersen he had been then – mountaineer, husband, soon-to-be-father – but here, today, there was only the shadow of that Ben, frayed and fragile.

He signalled, although the road was empty, and bumped off the blacktop onto the dirt track, past the bunched mailboxes and the boards painted with the names of those who owned places on this part of the lake: Andersen, Forster, Sherman, Abrams, Cheney. When they were young, he and Neil and Rory had played all summer long with the Cheney boys, with Howie Abrams and Dickie Forster, making camps, smoking illicit cigarettes, talking dirty, crouched in the bottom of the heavy old rowboat which Howie's dad kept tied up to his rickety dock at the edge of the water. They'd been closer than brothers then, but he hadn't seen either Howie or Dickie for years. He vaguely remembered hearing that Dickie had married a French girl and gone to live in Paris, that Howie had been involved in a car accident and lost the sight of one eye. The particular scent of all those summers came back to him: warm skin, suntan oil, sun-bleached wood, smoke from barbecues. So many shared evenings, the kids playing elaborate games among the trees while Dad and Mom and Aunt Evie drank martinis, and hamburgers sizzled next to foil-wrapped ears of corn and chicken legs.

His life.

The track was soft with the accumulation of years of fallen leaves. He drove carefully, the remembered taste of potato salad and barbecue sauce sharp on his tongue. He pulled up in front of the house. The stretch of water behind it glittered in the afternoon sun. Hoisting the paper sack of groceries from the back of the car, he felt for the keys in his pocket and opened the door.

The house was stifling, heat clinging to the wooden walls and under the ceilings. The shabby living room looked as it always had done, for as long as he could remember. Sand on the window sills. A heart-shaped stain on the hearthrug. A sleeping bag rolled up behind the couch. Dog-eared paperbacks. Full of memories. He had hoped that Lisa would become part of the place, as Neil's wife had done. But she had wanted something else, and Rosie, now, was never going to swing in the hammock, or dig sandcastles on the shore, or plunge into the summer lake or try to catch the eels beneath the water's surface.

He dumped the groceries on the kitchen counter and opened the door out onto the deck. The hammock still swung between two trees. That's where it happened, he thought. That's where she was when she lost the baby.

He stepped down and walked slowly across pine needles towards the hammock. Closer, he could see a dis-colored patch of grass, a few still-stiffened spikes, a small fir cone dark with blood. Her blood. Lisa's. Or Rosie's? He forced back the images which threatened to overcome him: Lisa lying here, dozing perhaps, and then suddenly the pain, growing stronger, contractions maybe, as her

253

small body tried to expel the child she was carrying, nobody there to help, the blood streaming from her, congealing on the grass and her not daring to move in case it made everything much worse, not yet knowing that the baby was already dead.

He turned abruptly away. At the foot of the steps to the porch, he pulled a twig from the bush of rosemary. The harsh scent reminded him of all the lost and golden summers. Of his father's voice: *big boys don't cry*.

But they do.

Joanne stood with one hand on the car door, inspecting the cabin. Sun slanted down through the glowing leaves of birch and maple, lightened the trunks of the pine trees. 'I'd forgotten how terrific it looks, set against the water like that,' she said.

'I know.' Mel began unloading bags from the open hatchback. Arms full, she walked along the wood-chip path between the hardtop parking and the entrance.

Joanne picked up their hiking boots, balanced a carton of groceries on her hip and followed. Inside the cabin, Mel set the cool-box on the kitchen counter and began unpacking it.

'At one point, Eric wanted us to move up here permanently, did you know that?' she said.

'Christ, what a nightmare.'

'That's what I told him. He was even talking about growing our own food, digging our own potatoes. Can you imagine?'

'Frankly, no. What did you do, put your foot down for once?'

'For once, yes. Said the only thing I really need to know about a potato is whether it's going to be French-fried or baked, with sour cream and chives,' Mel said. 'On top of that, for about five months of the year it would have been impossible to get down to Butterfield, and I wasn't prepared to cut myself off for so long.' She paused. 'Not even for a few days, actually.'

'Did he see the force of your argument?'

''Fraid not.'

'So?'

'So . . . so I said he could live up here by himself and I'd stay in town.'

'You bold thing, you.'

'I know.' Mel laughed uneasily, not wanting to remember the nights of argument, Eric's face dark with anger, his bewilderment that, for the first time in their marriage, his wife was refusing to go along with something he wished to do.

She took a bottle of white wine out of the cooler and began searching through the drawers for a corkscrew. 'It's not too early to start drinking alcohol, is it?'

'Honey, it's never too early.' Joanne looked appreciatively around. 'You've done a lot since my last visit,' she said. 'Rather . . . um . . . unEricy things, if I can put it like that.'

'We always had slightly different ideas about decoration.'

'I like yours better.'

'So do I.' Pulling at the sliding doors, Mel went out onto the terrace and dusted off two Adirondack chairs. The two women sat back, the wine on a low slatted table between them.

Heat crushed them, soaking into the shingles and walls of the cabin so that they could feel the strength of it at their backs. They sat with their bare feet up on the railing of the deck, while the sun blazed down on water which glittered like a spill of diamonds.

'God, it's hot out here.' Joanne wiped her face with her sleeve. 'Must be up in the eighties at least.'

'It'll get really cold once the sun goes down.' Mel gazed upwards. 'Funny, isn't it, that the sky is actually bluer in the fall than in the summer?'

'That's the difference between you and me,' Joanne said. 'I don't notice things like that.'

'Isn't it glorious?' Mel spread her arms. 'I love to feel the earth under my boots, and smell the woods. Maybe we'll see a deer – the woods are full of them. And foxes: there are lots of foxes. Last time I was here, I saw a whole family playing right in front of the cabin.'

'And there's not another soul for miles,' Joanne said wryly. 'Doncha just love it?'

'There are more people around than you think. When it gets dark, you'll see all sort of lights in the woods and round the lake. You're not really worried, are you? We've been up here before, just the two of us.'

'I know. Hated it then too.'

'You did not.'

'Did so. I only came to keep you company.'

'I'd never realized you were actually frightened,' Mel said.

'Guess it's agoraphobia.'

'You should have brought Jamie with you, like I suggested.'

'He wanted to go see his dad again.' Joanne gave a gusty sigh. 'You know, I never thought I'd ever say this, but looking back, I can see that in his bumbling insensitive way Gordon was a pretty good guy, and even if he did run off with Miss Bubblehead, maybe I didn't give him enough credit.'

'*What?* That's got to be the first time I ever heard you say anything even halfway positive about him.'

'Could be I'm mellowing.'

'Oh, Joanne, honey, please don't mellow. I couldn't stand it. Just go on being the crabby old broad you've always been.'

'OK.' Joanne grinned. 'Wanna go swimming?'

'The water'll be freezing.'

'In this heat, can't be too cold for me.'

'No swimsuits.'

'Who cares?' Joanne was already peeling off her shirt.

'OK.' Mel stood up and tore off her T-shirt, undid her bra, pulled at the fastening of her jeans. 'Last one in gets to make dinner.'

Naked, she ran down the steps of the deck towards the edge of the lake. The ground was soft underfoot, slick with pine needles. Flat rocks, crusted with golden circles of lichen, were embedded in the bright green moss. Joanne pounded along behind her as she reached the pale finger-nail of almost white sand which formed a tiny beach, and raced across a tangle of twiggy debris into the water.

The chill was sudden and stunning, like an electric shock. Her breath caught momentarily in her throat. She held herself tightly together, unwilling to yield another millimeter of her body to the cold, and then, making up her mind to it, launched herself onto the dark water. With a couple of clumsy strokes, she swam out further until she was waist deep.

'*Ya* da da *da* dah,' she sang. She winced away as Joanne splashed in, sending a shower of drops of molten cold over her. 'I won!'

'You said *you'd* make dinner,' accused Joanne, panting, laughing. 'Only reason I'm here.' She turned a circle in the water, beating at the surface with flat hands until spray fountained around her. 'Gaaahd, it's *freezing*.' Her hair stuck out from her face, the ends rat-tailed, darker than the rest. Her heavy brown-nippled breasts and bountiful hips, her abundant thighs, reminded Mel of the baths in Budapest, those naked women with their prodigal, nurturing bodies. Looking down at her own familiar body – the goosebumps on her skin, the pale curls of her pubic hair below the surface, the white drift of her thighs down into the sherry-brown water – she felt sad.

On shore, the hammock was still slung between the two pine trees. She tried not to think back to five weeks ago, Lisa's death-pale face, the slow drip of her blood onto the pine needles.

As though following her thoughts, Joanne said, 'Still no word from Lisa?'

'She contacted Ben, but I haven't heard anything.'

'I wonder where she went.'

'Who knows?' Mel spoke lightly. She saw movement at the kitchen windows of the Andersen house. The sun was hot on her back as she cupped water in her hands and hurled it at Joanne, the bright drops golden against the sun. She did it again so that Joanne, lurching backward to avoid them, staggered and nearly fell. Rainbows glittered through the air.

'Why, you . . . !' Joanne lumbered through the shallows, her generous mouth wide with laughter as she reared out of the water and launched herself at Mel. The two of them clung to each other for a moment, trying for a foothold on the muddy lake bottom, fingers sliding along water-slippery limbs, clutching at dolphin-sleek skin, until, shrieking, they both tumbled, in a tangle of shivering flesh, into the deeper water.

'Omigod!' gasped Mel. 'Oh, *Lord*, that's cold.'

For a moment they clung to each other, faces touching, mouth close to mouth, eyes laughing, breast brushing breast. Then Joanne shrieked, 'I'm outta here.'

'Me too.'

Breath huffing from their mouths, hair plastered against their skulls, they splashed towards the shore, hopping over the stones and across the ground to the warm steps of the deck.

'*Jeez*-us, that water's like ice.'

'Where are my feet?' moaned Mel.

'If I don't get my clothes back on, I'm going to die of pneumonia.'

'You can have first dibs on the shower,' said Mel. 'I'd just hate to have you pass out on me.'

He watched them for a while from the kitchen window. He had never seen women of their age naked before. He was touched by the way they frolicked with the unself-consciousness of children, faces turned to the sun, light bouncing off their wet bodies, catching the shape of a shoulder, the curve of a breast. He recognized Joanne Mayfield from the bookshop, a big undisciplined woman twice the size of Lisa— he stopped the thought, since he'd come up here expressly to lay some ghosts. Mel Sherman's hair glinted in the sun. Spun gold, corn silk. Above and below. Her breasts were . . . He felt himself blushing. He tried to look away but found it difficult not to stare.

If she had been up here alone, he might have plucked up the courage to go over later. Apart from Peter Tan, she was his only link with Lisa. Suddenly Mel looked up at the house and he stepped quickly back. He hoped she hadn't seen him; he didn't want her and Joanne coming over, offering sympathy he didn't need, gazing at him with those tolerant, understanding expressions on their faces. He wondered if he was losing the ability to interact with other people. Even his own family. The few days he had just spent with his mother down in Boston had been uneasy, claustrophobic; he had longed to be back up here, away from people. When he'd told her he had to get back to Butterfield, she'd taken his hand in both of hers. 'Don't go just yet,' she'd said. 'Stay a while longer, Ben.'

'I can't.'

'But it's all so new and raw . . .'

'Mom,' he said. 'I have to go home.'

Her face had shrunk a little. After a moment, she had said gently, 'Of course you do.'

He understood that, without meaning to, he had hurt her. For all of his life, her home had been his home, the family's home. He guessed it was hard for any parent to face up to the fact that children grew into adults and made their own homes. Aware of her loneliness, now that his father was gone, he had begun to appreciate the small heroisms of the life she had built for herself: the bridge club, the garden club, the locum work she undertook.

Unwilling to meet her loving anxious gaze, he turned away. 'I really need to get back, Mom. I've got some commitments which I can't ignore any longer.' He didn't say that he was due to work on one of Kim Bernhard's building sites, not wishing to see her wince away from him . . . *my son, the construction worker*.

'But after what you've . . .' She had bitten her lip, longing to help him, to make things better for him. 'You can explain. They'll understand.'

He felt like asking how anybody could possibly understand what he was going through. 'Understanding doesn't pay the bills,' he said.

'You know I'd be glad to help out.'

'Thanks, Mom. But it's not that simple.'

She looked at him sadly. 'Nothing's ever simple.'

Outside, the two women laughed and shrieked and he felt a sudden unfocused anger. Part of him envied them, another part wanted to run to the edge of the lake, to yell at them, to ask them how they dared to be so happy when he was in such pain.

Further round the lake, tiny in the distance and darkened by the haze of heat on the water, he could see someone sitting in a rowboat, a fishing rod extended over the side. A bird circled, close above the water, then suddenly dived, vanished, reappeared with a frantic gleam of silver in its beak. Hugging the shore, two kids came poling a home-made raft, and the sight made him remember the summer that he and Neil and Rory had made their own raft, lashing the planks together, launching it onto the water, watching it sink below the surface then rise again, the excitement as they scrambled on board, huddled precariously in the middle while Neil tried to push them off, Rory demanding a turn with the pole, saying it wasn't fair, falling into the water, the three of them laughing, laughing . . .

He squeezed his eyes shut against the memories of the past – and against the future which now would not be.

The kitchen window sill was dusty. Mel Sherman's voice sounded in his head: *dust will gather in corners . . .* is that what she'd said? *Moons will wax and wane.*

A dead branch stood in a glass jar, along with a black and white feather. Mugs were turned upside down on the draining board. He recalled what he had been doing last time he was here: hamburgers, canned soup. Someone must have been in and tidied up, cleared everything away. All the reminders. Mel Sherman again? He stroked the feather across his arm. Earlier in the summer he and Lisa had found it lying on the fine sand near a pile of lake debris – sodden twigs, the hollow, half-rotten tubes of golden rod, fragments of freshwater mussel shells – which had accumulated at the water's edge.

261

'It's an eagle feather,' Lisa said.

'No, darling, it's from a hawk or a heron or something.'

'It's an eagle,' she insisted. 'I bet you. Look, it's black at the end. It's like Injun chiefs used to wear.' Laughing, she had stuck it behind her ear. 'Do I look like a squaw?'

'No,' he said. 'You look like the most beautiful person in the entire world that I'm just about to kiss.'

Was the rest of his life going to consist of memories of her? If Lisa had been there, he would have told her that he didn't really care where they lived, that they could move back to New York if she wanted, go anywhere she chose, anywhere, just so long as she would come back to him, and they could be together again.

He should have been more sensitive to her needs. He could see that now. She'd said so often that she didn't like being away from the city, that she felt lost and exposed up here in the hills. And he'd said she'd get used to it, that he was there to take care of her, would always be there. He'd never taken her seriously, had assumed she was exaggerating, that her complaints were part of the sweet banter between the two of them.

What terrified him was the thought that he might never have a second chance. I'd do it so differently next time round, he told himself, stepping into the bedroom they'd shared. The bedlinen had gone; the duvet was rolled up at one end of the bare mattress, the pillows laid on top of it. He turned away, studied his unshaven face in the mirror, noted the rough hair and bloodshot eyes.

In the greenwater depths of the mirror, he looked like a drowning man. He wondered if Lisa ever thought of him in her new life, whether she had the faintest idea how much he missed her.

It's just the way things are, Mel had said. He pictured moons falling away over the rim of the earth, the silent

262

fall of dust, he saw flowers bloom and die, rivers endlessly reach the ocean.

He squeezed his eyes shut, while, outside, the women played.

Nine o'clock. Rain had begun to fall, a gentle patter on the shingles, a tap against the big windows which formed either end of the cabin. Wrapped in rugs, the two women sat close together on the huge sofa opposite the fireplace, staring into the fire which Mel fed from time to time from the logs which were stacked to one side of the hearth.

'That was truly delicious,' Joanne sighed. 'I shan't move for a month. You're such a great cook.' She slid down so that she was almost horizontal, feet stretched towards the flames. 'You know what you should do?'

'What's that?'

'Open a restaurant. We could really use some place nearer than Burlington. You'd be crowded out every night of the week.'

'I'd never have time to enjoy somewhere like this.'

'I guess not. If you could travel anywhere in the world,' Joanne asked lazily, 'where would you go?'

'This, right here, wouldn't be a bad place.'

'No, seriously.'

'I *am* serious.'

'C'mon, Mel. *Here?*'

'What's wrong with it?'

'It's just up the road from where you've spent the last twenty-five years, that's what's wrong with it. Not exactly adventurous, is it?'

'I leave that to others.'

'But you shouldn't. You've only got one life, girlfriend, you should get out there, do stuff, have adventures, *live.*'

'Maybe I like not being venturesome.'

263

'That is *so* pathetic.'

'This is the very last time I top up *your* glass.' Mel leaned across and poured more of the Zinfandel she had brought from the cellar at home.

'OK. New question: that abortion thing?'

'I don't want to talk about it.'

'Nor do I. I just wondered what other secrets you haven't told me about.'

'They wouldn't be secrets if I had.'

'It's not fair. I tell you everything.'

'The smallest book in the world,' Mel said.

'What is?'

'The one called *Joanne Mayfield's Secret Life*.'

'Well, at least I don't *hide* stuff.'

Mel got up and went into the kitchen. When she came back she had a bottle of champagne in her hand and two clean glasses. From behind the cushions of the sofa, she pulled a small soft package wrapped in fancy paper and trailing long streamers of ribbon.

'What's this?' asked Joanne.

'Your birthday's coming up. Had you forgotten?' Mel thought of the lemon cake sitting in her freezer back in Butterfield, the fourth one, the only one which Jamie had finally decreed was good enough for his mom. He had eaten the others. The plan was to defrost and decorate it the day before Joanne's party.

'Forgotten that I'm hitting the Big Five Oh?' said Joanne. 'I wish.'

'Aren't you the one who keeps insisting that the older women get, the better they are?'

'Yeah, but it's different when it's me.'

'That's why we all love you, Joanne. Because we can see the marshmallow beneath the cement.'

Joanne laughed. 'All I can see is the marshmallow

264

beneath the marshmallow. And over it. And round it.' She pulled at the flesh above her waist. 'Gawd, I've put on so much weight in the past few years.'

'Which makes no difference to the essential you.'

'Maybe not. Trouble is,' sighed Joanne, 'I'm running out of local guys who're young enough to be worth fucking but old enough to be interesting.'

'Horsefeathers. Anyway, I thought we'd have a little preliminary celebration, just the two of us.'

'What a sweetheart.' Joanne leaned over and for a moment rested her hand lightly on Mel's sleeve. 'My darling friend.'

'Open this first.' While Joanne ripped the folds of ice-green tissue paper, Mel tore off the foil cover of the champagne bottle and began to untwist the metal guard.

'Oh, Jeez,' Joanne said on an indrawn breath. 'Oh Mel, it's gorgeous.' She let the hand-dyed silk scarf trail over her fingers. 'It's beautiful.'

'I bought it when we went to Boston,' Mel said. 'While you were trying to recover from a vodka hangover. It just screamed "Joanne" at me.'

'Nasturtiums,' said Joanne. She reached across and hugged Mel, kissing her on the cheek. 'My favorite flowers. Yellow and orange: my favorite colors, too.'

Mel savored the feel of her friend's big body, the raw truthful smell of her skin, her weathered face. 'It would look marvellous with your silk jacket. Or just with your green shirt.' They knew each other's wardrobes as well as they knew their own.

'Wouldn't it, though?' Joanne tied it round her neck. 'I *love* it.'

Mel eased the cork out of the champagne bottle. 'Here's to birthdays. And to the warmest, wisest, wittiest woman in the world.'

'Me? I'll drink to that.' Joanne moved the glass back and forth. 'Don't you love the way the bubbles go up in such straight lines?' She wrinkled her nose. 'Does this mean I don't get anything next week?'

'I told you: this is just a warm-up party. Next week there'll be people round and you'll be occupied. I thought it would be good to be just the two of us, so you'd actually listen when I said thank you.' Mel tipped her glass at Joanne. 'For everything.'

Before they went to bed, Mel stepped out onto the deck outside her bedroom. The cold sky was full of stars. There was a new moon hanging over the mountains, a pale lemon-silver curve in the dark blue of the sky, frail as a thread. The melancholy of the changing seasons folded over her. To her left was the dark shape of the Andersen house, invisible against the greater black of night. A light had popped on: one of the family must be up for the weekend.

The lake was silver. She thought of how good she always felt up here. How strong, how secure within herself. She thought of lost loves and youth and wasted opportunity, and the compensation that maturity brings.

The wooden planking vibrated faintly as Joanne came to stand beside her.

'New moon,' she said. 'What're you wishing?'

'I don't know.'

Joanne slipped an arm around Mel's waist. 'Wish something for me, then. And I'll wish something for you.'

Mel leaned back against Joanne's shoulder, her heart thickening with love. 'I'll wish everything for you,' she said. 'Whatever you want.' Her friend. Her dear friend. She wanted to tell Joanne how much she loved her, that she wished for her every good thing it was possible to have. 'And neither of us will ever tell, right?'

'Right.'

She awoke from troubled sleep, torn anew by loss. She turned her head into the pillow and felt the sobs gather like storm clouds. Grief spilled from her like water. Secrets, told and untold. So much that never was, so much that might have been. How can you grieve for someone you have never known?

And yet you do.

CHAPTER EIGHTEEN

It was damp underfoot because of the overnight rain, and much cooler. Though the sky was unclouded, Mel and Joanne wore fleeces as they began to hike along the narrow track which bordered the creek feeding into the lake. It was easy going at first, following the course of the stream as it dashed and tumbled over and round the big boulders which had been thrown down from the hills in some paleontological upheaval half a million years ago.

After a while, the sides of the banks began to rise. The track veered away from the creek as they climbed higher, the angle of the slope gradually increasing, giving way to striated cliffs which grew closer and deeper until Mel and Joanne found themselves walking along the lip of a shallow ravine. Above their heads the trees – mostly pine and ash now – closed in so that the sky was only sporadically visible; the air grew crisper. Below them, the racing water sparkled and swirled.

An hour in, Joanne began to puff and wheeze. 'I'm not used to this. How much further?' she gasped. Her face was red and beaded with sweat.

'Not much.' Mel spoke over her shoulder. 'Any minute now we'll hear the sound of the falls, which'll mean we're practically at the top.'

'I definitely feel a heart attack coming on.' Joanne doubled over, clutching her chest. 'Why don't I find a nice boulder to sit on and wait here until you come down again?'

'What if I told you there's a McDonald's up there,' Mel said, laughing. 'And you can have a Big Mac with double cheese and all the French fries you can eat?'

'I'd call you a lying sadist.'

'Honestly, Jo, we're almost there. Just a couple of hundred yards more. Then it's along the flat.'

'I guess at this stage I've put in so much effort I might as well keep going,' Joanne said resignedly.

'Look up there,' Mel said. 'Isn't it spectacular? Water, rocks, trees.' And floating in the sky above them, an eagle, so close they could see the soft white feathers of its belly ruffle in the wind.

'Terrific.' Joanne stepped close to the edge of the gorge and, holding onto the slim trunk of a birch, leaned out to look at the water far below.

Mel grabbed the back of her mimosa-yellow polar fleece. 'I wouldn't get so close to the edge if I were you. It's quite slippery after the rain. And on top of that, those thin trunks can sometimes just snap in two.'

They walked in silence for a while, one behind the other. 'You never used to be this kind of a fresh air freak,' Joanne said.

'It wasn't until Eric died that I discovered how much I liked walking.'

That was when she first began to hike the mountain trails, enjoying the therapeutic act of putting space between her and the empty places in her life. She had found it hard to start with but gradually learned to adjust her body to the different surfaces she covered, to enjoy the stretch of her calf muscles, the integration of hip and thigh and foot. At first, she could only walk a quarter of the way round the lake before she had to turn back. Her feet blistered, her muscles ached. But gradually she had found that her body could undertake all she asked it to do, and more. One morning she had set off early, and on her return was astounded to discover, by measuring the distance on a map of the area, that she had walked over twenty miles. Little by little she had renewed her acquaint-ance with her single self, after all the years of being half of a pair.

'If I come back to earth again,' Joanne broke into her thoughts, 'I'm going to ask to be fifty pounds lighter.'

'Next time round, I'd be happy with non-sloping shoulders, so my bra straps don't keep sliding off.'

'I might put in a plea for longer arms, while I'm at it. I don't think I've bought a jacket or sweater in my entire life that didn't hang right down over my hands. You wouldn't believe the amount I've spent on having my sleeves shortened.'

As the path took a bend to the right, they heard the subdued drum of tumbling water. 'It's not the Niagara Falls,' Mel said. 'But it's still quite spectacular.'

'It better be, after the effort I've put in to get here.'

'We're there.' Mel rounded a boulder which protruded across the path and said, as Joanne caught up with her, 'Take a look at that.'

In front of them, across a deep circle carved out of the cliffs, a gush of water rolled over the edge and dropped ninety sheer feet or so to a dark brown pool before bounc-ing and skittering along the gorge towards the lake. A rainbow shimmered across the ravine where sunlight caught the spray.

'There's much more water in the spring, of course, when the rains come and the snow melts.' Mel sat down on the boulders above the falls and reached into her backpack. 'Here. Smoked salmon and cream cheese bagels. Grapes. Dried figs.'

'Wonderful.' Joanne eased her back against a rock and unzipped her jacket. 'You were right, Mel, this is really great. Just look at that rainbow.'

'Rainbows mean good luck, don't they?' Under Joanne's jacket, Mel caught a glimpse of the silk scarf she had given her the previous evening. 'Hey, I didn't buy that at L L Bean's,' she protested.

'I know it's not exactly an outdoor-activities-type scarf,' Joanne said, her expression guilty. 'But it goes beautifully with this jacket.'

'It cost a bomb: don't lose it.'

'OK, Mommy.'

They ate in silence for a while, then Joanne said lazily, 'The one thing I hope it will say on my gravestone is that I grabbed life by the balls.'

'You do that, all right.' Mel laughed. 'And life's not the only thing.'

'Bet your sweet life, baby.'

'Though, when you come to think of it,' Mel said, 'for all your talk, here you still are in Butterfield when you could have gone anywhere, done anything. Maybe I'm not the only loser round here.'

'Bullshit,' said Joanne.

'OK: if *you* could go anywhere, where would *you* go?'

Joanne was uncharacteristically silent. Then she said slowly, 'When I was a kid, we had an exchange teacher at school, a girl from New Zealand. She used to tell us about this place over there called Rotorua. She said it was amazing, full of hissing geysers and mud-pools puking and these boiling hot lakes, and steam coming out of the ground right in front of you. And the

271

whole place smelled of sulfur. She said it was like hell without the pitchforks – that's always stuck in my head.'

Mel smiled. 'Why didn't you go years ago?'

'Why don't we do half the things we want to? The fare out there isn't exactly cheap, plus the cost of hotels, and car hire . . . and once Gordon and I split up, it left me kind of tight. Besides, I still had a living to earn, the kids to raise.'

'A regular little Mother Courage,' Mel said. She looked at her watch and got to her feet. 'Come on. Guess we'd better start back.'

Joanne groaned. 'You're so restless. I was just getting comfortable.'

'We still have to pack the cabin up,' Mel said.

'That won't take long, will it? We can just pile everything into the car and drive off. Back to civilization, thank God.'

'Don't pretend you haven't had fun.'

'With you, darlin', I always have fun.'

'Me too.' Mel slung her pack across her shoulders and started back down the trail.

Joanne followed. 'Hey, slow down, will you?' she said. 'We aren't running a marathon here.'

'Sorry.' Mel paused to allow her friend to catch up.

'I feel so goddamned healthy,' Joanne complained. 'It's definitely not good for me.'

Mel stopped and breathed in deeply. The sun had now climbed to the top of the sky and the warm scent of resin was intoxicating. Despite the crash of water from the falls behind them, the forest was tranquil. Something rustled in the undergrowth beside the path and she turned to see what it was.

'Gawd,' Joanne pushed past. 'Nobody ever tells you it's

just as hard going down as it is coming up. My knees are killing me.'

'You should come up more often. You'd soon get in shape.' Mel watched Joanne's broad backside move on down the trail, thinking how comfortable they were together, how well they knew each other, almost like an old married couple. Below them, in the little ravine, the invisible water spun and gushed on its way to the lake.

'Next spring,' Joanne said, over her shoulder. 'I'll be up every weekend, I promise.'

'You said that last year.'

'I'll say it next year, too.' Joanne disappeared around the outcrop of granite which jutted out onto the trail. Following her at a leisurely pace, Mel lifted her head to glimpses of sky, drawing the scent of leaf and fern and moss deep into her lungs. If Joanne had not been with her she would have continued to climb beyond the falls, on and on into the higher ground and then down over the crest of the trail, into other deep woods like these, at one with them, part of it all.

She too rounded the overhanging boulder. Above the muted boom of the falls, she heard the long-drawn-out shriek of a bird. Ahead of her the trail descended steeply for another two hundred feet.

For a moment she walked on, then came to an abrupt stop. Where was Joanne? She should have been ahead and was not. To the right was the sheer edge of the small canyon, to the left an almost vertical slope of boulder and scrub. Mel turned to look back up the trail and her eye was caught by the orange wound of fresh-snapped wood. The lower half of a slender trunk still leaned out over the ravine, the rest of it had broken off.

Not a bird but . . .

'Oh God! Joanne!' Mel threw herself down on the brink

of the gorge and edged forward. Damp grasses. Little long-leaved ferns. Bright green of star moss, yellow green of sphagnum. Her hands clutched, her throat clenched, as she peered down.

Forty feet below, spread across the rocks at the stream's edge, was the yellow of her friend's jacket, like a smudge of mustard powder. Joanne's legs lay half in and half out of the water. Even from here it was obvious that one of them was broken. She was not moving.

'Joanne!' Mel screamed again, even though she knew she could not be heard. 'Oh, my God!' Her voice floated out over the sunless spaces of the ravine and the bright golden stain on the rocks, to lose itself in the thunder of the falls.

It was all too easy to follow Joanne's descent by the broken tree stems and the torn bushes at which she must have clutched. Shreds of clothing fluttered from the twigs and vines, from the gray tree skeletons which lined the side of the gorge. It would be impossible to climb down the steep cliff.

Instead, Mel ran further down the trail, boots slipping and sliding on the damp soil, feet catching on the small rocks which protruded from the path, so that several times she tripped and almost fell. As she ran, her thoughts played and replayed what must have happened. She could see it all too clearly: Joanne leaning out to look down at the water, going too close to the edge, grabbing at a tree trunk for support as her feet slid on the damp surface, only to have it break off and send her hurtling downwards.

Remembering that brief glimpse of yellow jacket, outflung arms, denimed legs scattered so carelessly on the rocks, Mel's breath caught in her throat. Her mind clamored with catastrophe. Joanne with a broken back, with smashed ribs, punctured lungs, fractured limbs, head wounds. Maybe dying. Maybe – the possibility was too terrible to contemplate – even dead. But Joanne was not – *could* not be – dying. The height from the trail was less than fifty feet; the undergrowth must have broken the speed of her fall. Surely, surely she could be no more than stunned. Groggy, perhaps. Concussed. With a broken leg. But otherwise all right.

When it reached the level of the river bed, the trail flattened out. Breath catching in her throat, Mel turned off the path and scrambled down onto the slippery black rocks which formed the narrow shore. She started to clamber across them, then paused, irresolute. Instead of trying to make it back upstream to Joanne, would it not be more sensible, more useful, to leave her lying where she was and find help? But that would mean running back to the cabin, which would take at least twenty minutes, then waiting for the emergency services – a ranger, or the medical people from the nearest hamlet? – then leading them back up the trail, all of which could take hours.

What should she do? Go for help or check on Joanne first, at least move her a little so that she was clear of the river, offer comfort, offer love? It was not a hard choice. *We were meant to be back at the cabin by two*, she thought, looking up at the cliffs and impassive sky as though they accused her, tiny by the river's edge. *Back by two, that's all*.

Breath ragged, she began to make her way back upstream. It was cold down here beside the water. Although it was nearly noon, the sun did not seem to have infiltrated the defile, and the once-blue sky was now covered in gray clouds. Joanne hated to be cold. What was she thinking, lying there? She would know that Mel would come. Whatever else happened, she would be certain of that. If she were still capable of such thoughts. If she were still alive.

This should not have happened. Did she say it aloud, or merely think it, as she scrabbled at spray-slicked rocks, lost her footing, reached for handholds which rolled under her grasp? Once she slipped and fell heavily onto one knee and, for the tiniest fraction of time, the forest was silent except for the hammering of her heart, the pumping of her lungs, the push of blood in her veins while excruciating pain burned through her body. She tried to stand and felt her leg begin to give way.

Afterwards, she had no idea how long it took before she finally saw the smudge of Joanne's fleece ahead. 'I'm coming!' she screamed now, lungs straining against the sound of the tumbling water. 'Hold on, Joanne, hold on, darling.'

Slipping, stumbling, cursing, she clambered the last few yards and knelt on the stones beside her friend. There was a huge amount of blood splashed across the rocks. Joanne was still lying in the same position, but when Mel took her hand she slowly turned her head and smiled. One cheek was gashed and torn.

'What took you so long?' she said weakly. Blood oozed thickly from her wounds. Her eyes looked odd, as though they belonged to another woman, to a different race.

Relief rendered Mel speechless.

'Thought I'd snuffed it, didn't you?' Joanne's lips were almost invisible against the clammy greyness of her skin. Her yellow fleece and the white T-shirt she had been wearing underneath it were ripped, the ragged ends of material edged with blood.

'Not for a moment,' Mel lied. Joanne's left hand hung

floppily from her wrist; both her palms had been torn and were embedded with earth and leaves. Mel stooped over her. 'Can you move?'

Joanne shook her head. Her eyes were terrified. One of them was grossly dilated, the pupil huge against the almost invisible iris. 'My back hurts.'

'I'm going to move your legs out of the water,' Mel said distinctly. 'I think you broke one of them.'

'Can't feel anything,' Joanne said.

Mel's heart went cold. Carefully she moved around Joanne's body and lifted first one leg out of the water onto the rocks and then, hands under thigh and calf, the other. She could clearly see the jut of broken bone under the bloodstained denim which covered it. As she moved it, Joanne coughed. Blood-flecked foam appeared at the corner of her mouth, and Mel felt her own face blanch. One of Joanne's lungs must be punctured, probably by a broken rib. Just as she had been with Lisa, she was overwhelmed by her own helplessness. She did not know what to do, what there was she *could* do.

She pulled off her backpack and then shrugged out of her fleece, which she laid tenderly over Joanne. 'Listen,' she said, trying not to show her fear. 'There's no way I can get you out of here on my own. I'll have to go and call for help.'

Joanne's fingers clamped over hers with surprising force. 'No,' she said. 'Don't leave me alone.'

'It's the only choice we have,' Mel said. She took the end of the silk scarf she had given Joanne last night, in a different, safer world, and gently wiped away the bloody foam. 'Even if someone was up on the trail above us right now, they'd never hear me calling over the noise of the water.'

'Should've brought my cellphone,' Joanne said. Her

277

grin was ghostly against her pale face. 'Nearly did.'

'It wouldn't have been much use down here.' Mel tried to disengage her fingers. 'Let me go and get help. I'll come right back, I promise. Straight back.'

Joanne clung more tightly to her. 'I'm going to die, aren't I?'

'Don't be *ridiculous*,' Mel said angrily. 'Of course you're not.'

'Don't let me die, Mel.'

'I've no intention of doing so. But I'll have to leave you for a while.'

'I don't want to die alone.'

'Listen to me.' Mel put her mouth close to Joanne's ear. 'You are not going to die, you hear me? I won't allow it. It's your birthday next week. You've got a party to go to at the bookstore. And don't forget the tickets I got for us for that concert in Boston.'

'Can't miss that,' Joanne said, and this time her smile was lost somewhere before it could properly form.

Although she wanted to weep, Mel forced herself to grin. 'Sorry, but I'm afraid dying's not on the agenda.'

'I'm frightened,' Joanne said. Her face crumpled, lips pulling back from her teeth, a tear oozing from one of her eyes and falling down the side of her face.

'I'm here, darling. I'm here.' Through Mel's mind rushed images, a scrapbook of their friendship, the two of them eating oysters in Bar Harbor, sobbing over *Now, Voyager*, trying on hats in Boston, clapping in time to the beat at the Montreal jazz festival, planning, sharing, laughing about so much. About everything.

'Don't let me die alone,' Joanne repeated.

Her voice sounded weaker, and Mel strove for calm. 'Will you just hush up? Think of the kids.'

278

'My poor kids . . .'

'Think of . . . of New Zealand, that place you wanted to visit.'

'Rotorua,' Joanne murmured. She coughed slightly and more froth bubbled from her mouth, redder this time, darker.

'Just let me go and find help,' Mel said, her voice unsteady, her lips trembling, as she wiped it away again. 'Please, Joanne. Because if you don't . . . if you don't . . .' There were hot tears on her own face and she brushed them away with the back of her hand, at the same time pulling the other out of Joanne's grip. She took off her sweatshirt and with infinite care inched it under her friend's head. If Joanne had injured her back, she did not want to risk damaging her spine still further. Reaching for her backpack, she took out the extra pair of socks. Gently she pulled them over Joanne's cold hands.

'I'll be back, sweetheart,' she said, as though Joanne were a child. 'Just as quickly as ever I can. Just wait for me. I'll be back, I swear it.'

Joanne closed her eyes. 'Hurry.'

From the kitchen window, he'd watched them set off. Both in jeans and hiking boots, Mel carrying a small backpack, Joanne in a yellow fleece. Not the kind of gear you'd take for a daylong hike so presumably they only planned to walk for a couple of hours or so. Especially given the meteorological forecast that morning. It was as automatic as breathing for him to check it. To note that despite the fine start to the day, more rain was predicted, followed by a cold front and high winds coming from Canada.

He spent the morning doing nothing very much. Walked down to the store for the newspaper. Swept up the leaves which were beginning to fall. Steeled himself to go out and unhook the hammock, soak it in the lake, hang it to dry from the hooks on the porch.

By early afternoon, the sky was clouding over and the tops of the trees were tossing. Small white caps ruffled the surface of the lake, rolling in towards the little beach below the house. He started to watch a football game, drank a beer, picked up a year-old copy of *National Geographic* and read about the decline of the Great Barrier Reef, fiesta time in Seville. He glanced at his watch. It was none of his business, but the habit of noting what was happening on the mountain kept half of his mind listening for the sound of the two women returning to the Sherman house.

Restless, he stood on the back porch, looking across the lake to the higher hills. None of his business ... but, ultimately, it was. He'd spent too many summers as a part-time volunteer for the Rescue Service, had been trained and tested too often for it not to be almost a reflex to watch out for people in the mountains. He looked again at his watch. They definitely should have been back by now.

In the end, he laced on his boots. The temperature had dropped and he added a couple of sweaters to his pack before setting off along the trail to the falls which the two women had taken earlier. The going was slippery, the track still slick after last night's rain. At every bend he expected to meet them coming down, but there was no sign of them. As the track began to climb more steeply, curving up the mountain away from the river, following the edge of the ravine, he quickened his pace, made uneasy by the silence and the solitude.

His attention was suddenly caught by a sapling snapped in half at the side of the gorge. Closer, he saw crushed grass, a scrap of material. Heartrate speeding up, adrenalin beginning to rush, he put down his pack and carefully leaned forward to peer over the edge. Nothing to alarm him. Digging in his heels, he bent further. Almost directly below where he stood, he saw Joanne Mayfield, arms outflung, her yellow fleece half-concealed by Mel's green sweatshirt. No sign of Mel: was that good or bad?

He inched himself backwards until he was safely on the trail again and then, snatching up his pack, began to jog back the way he had come. As he ran, he reached into his breast pocket for his mobile phone and tapped out the numbers for the ERS, though he knew the chances were slim that it would work here, deep under the tree canopy.

Ahead of him, Mel Sherman suddenly emerged onto the track. Supporting herself against a boulder, she bent double, trying to bring her breathing back to normal. Glancing up the trail, she saw him coming towards her. Her mouth opened and she said something he couldn't hear. Her face frantic, she started up towards him, then tripped and almost fell.

He reached her. Took her arm. He could smell her sweat. And something else. He recognized it immediately. The acrid stench of fear. 'Are you OK?' he said.

'I'm fine,' she said, labored breath rasping from her strained lungs. 'It's Joanne Mayfield. She fell, just up the trail. She's—'

'I saw. What sort of condition is she in? Can you tell?' Again he pressed buttons on the phone. Propelled Mel forward as he spoke. 'Is she conscious?'

'Sort of. Definitely got a broken leg. Something much worse, too. Her back, I think.' Mel's face was full of terror. 'There's a lot of blood. And her head . . .'

'What about her head?' His voice was calm, authoritative.

'Her eyes are strange. And she says she can't feel anything. I think . . . I really think . . . I'm afraid she may . . . she might . . .' Mel pressed her fists to her face, trying to force back the thought. '. . . might die.'

He shook his head, frowning at his cellphone. 'I'm not getting any response. I'd better get to her quickly. She may need stabilizing.'

'Oh God.' She was sobbing now, tears streaming down her face. 'Oh God, Ben . . . I'm so. . .' She started to shiver, her entire body shaking, her teeth chattering.

He put his hand on her arm. 'You're doing fine, Mel.' He swung his pack from his shoulder and took out a sweater. 'Put this on.'

'I-I c-can't.' She seemed to have lost control of her body.

He pulled her forward and with one arm held her against his chest while with the other he swiftly slipped the sweater over her head, then pushed her arms into the sleeves. He hugged her briefly and let her go. 'I'll go ahead, and you follow me, at your own pace,' he said. 'Once I've had a look at your friend, and can assess the damage, I'll leave you with her and then find a place where the phone works and I can call the ERS, OK?'

She nodded. 'OK.'

She had never felt so cold in her life. She watched him move sure-footedly along the edge of the river. Her body seemed incapable of action.

'Mel,' he called sharply, looking back at her across his shoulder. 'Get moving. She needs you.'

'All right.' If she had to move another foot she was certain she would collapse.

282

'She'll need you with her,' he said again. 'Don't let her down.'

'I'm coming.' Chest tight, legs already aching, she started after him.

How could I have allowed this to happen? she thought. It's my fault. I made Joanne come up here with me, I bullied her, she only came to make me happy, to stop me nagging. She hates walking, she hates exercise, she'd much rather have sat on the deck, drinking coffee and reading, but I *forced* her, my friend, my dear friend who may be dying, who may already be dead.

The pebbles along the river's edge gave way to rocks and boulders. She clambered across them. Her knee was swollen and painful. Ahead of her, Ben leaped from rock to rock until he reached the spot where Joanne lay. He knelt down and laid his head against her chest, then reached into his pack and brought out a red first-aid kit. As Mel joined him, he began probing Joanne's body: neck, head, chest, legs, his fingers delicately cautious.

'Well done,' he said, rising to his feet. His eyes assessed the broken debris at the foot of the cliff. He picked up a sturdy branch and with a knife stripped it of twigs and leaves. He looked at Mel. 'Not perfect, but the best we can do under the circumstances.' Carefully he pulled the bloodstained silk scarf from around Joanne's neck and began to tie her twisted leg to the branch.

'How do you think she is?' Mel asked, unconsciously whispering.

'Not too brilliant. But her vital signs are steady, which is good.' He smiled at her.

He seemed so confident that she felt a load lift from her heart. 'What can I do?'

'Check her pulse.'

Mel felt for a pulse on Joanne's wrist and found it

beating erratically, just below the skin. There was much more blood than there had been earlier, a thin rivulet of it snaking between the slick black rocks towards the river. Laying a hand against Joanne's cheek, she was horrified by its chill.

Ben found two more branches and began to strip them. 'I'd like to have improvised a stretcher,' he said. He glanced at Mel and then at Joanne and shook his head. 'But she's probably too heavy for us to manage. Besides, with the injuries to her head, it would be too dangerous without a third person to maintain stability of her neck. Give me your hand towel.'

'What?'

He gestured at the small towel clipped to her waist which she used to wipe sweat from her forehead. 'Luckily I brought one too.'

Folding the two together to make a thick wad, with infinite care he eased them under Joanne's neck and brought the ends round to overlap under her jaw. He held out his hand. 'Your belt, too.'

She undid the buckle, slid her leather belt out of the loops of her pants and watched him inch it round and then secure the two towels with it. 'Cervical collar,' he explained. 'I'm not sure how badly she's damaged her spine, but we can't take any chances.'

He took his pack and shoveled some rocks into it. 'You do the same,' he said.

Mel filled her own pack and pushed it over to him.

'She mustn't move,' he explained, setting the heavy packs on either side of Joanne's head.

He pointed to the water's edge where wood and branches had been tumbled down from higher upstream. 'Bring that driftwood log over here, Mel. And then that one.'

She was more than happy to let him call the shots. She

grabbed one end of the tree trunk he indicated, dragging it across the stones, panting with the weight, went back for the other. He put them on either side of Joanne's body, as close as he could, anchored them in place with more stones. Then he folded his jacket into a long roll and placed it between Joanne's legs, from thigh to ankles. With a bandage from the first-aid kit, he tied her feet and ankles together so that she was now almost immobile.

'If I ever find myself in real trouble, I'll know who to take with me,' Mel said, trying to joke, trying to mitigate the sense of disaster which lay like a spreading stain at the edge of her mind.

'You'd be a good person to have along.' He smiled at her, reassuring, encouraging. 'You did a fine job, keeping her warm, moving her legs out of the water. If it wasn't for you she'd be in much worse shape.'

'If it wasn't for me, she wouldn't be here at all,' Mel said. She bit down hard on her lip, determined not to break down in front of him.

He turned cold eyes on her. 'What, you pushed her, did you?'

'No, but—'

'Then don't be ridiculous.' His brusqueness was more comforting than any words of reassurance would have been. 'Stay here and keep Mrs Mayfield company until I get back. Whatever happens, don't let her move, OK?'

'OK,' she said, her voice unsteady.

He started walking swiftly downstream towards the track, then turned. 'Her neck must stay absolutely still,' he called.

Mel knelt behind Joanne and put a hand on either side of her head. She spoke her friend's name, wondering if she was doing the right thing. Maybe it was best for Joanne to remain unconscious.

285

'I told you I'd be back,' she said, not sure if Joanne could hear her, hoping to reach into her head, call her back from wherever she was. '*Told* you, and now it'll be all right, they're coming to take you out of here. Would you believe I found Ben Andersen on the trail, and he's gone for help?'

Joanne's eyelids fluttered.

'He's gone to call the emergency services. They're going to airlift you to hospital and put you back together again.'

'Like Humpty Dumpty,' Joanne murmured, the words slurred and heavy.

Mel's heart jumped with relief. '*Not* like Humpty Dumpty,' she said, 'because they *couldn't* put him together, could they? But they'll patch you up OK.'

'My leg . . .'

'Yes, you've broken it, but that's nothing, you can hobble around in a cast and everyone will feel terribly sorry for—'

'I can't feel it. Can't feel anything. Can't *move*.' Panic spread across Joanne's bloodied face. She began to struggle feebly.

'Keep still,' Mel said, pressing her hands more firmly against Joanne's head, feeling warm blood on her fingers, the strands of hair slippery under her fingers. 'Ben wants to keep you rigid until they can check out your spine.'

'What did he . . . ?'

'*Don't move.* Ben's put logs and rocks and all kinds of stuff round you,' Mel said. 'He's been fantastic.' She remembered the gentle way he had touched Joanne, the care he had taken over her.

'So stupid . . .' Joanne said.

'What is?' The rocks were beginning to dig painfully into Mel's knees.

'You told me not to . . . just wanted to see the river . . .

286

it's not your *fault*,' Joanne said, her voice suddenly stronger. 'Not your fault, you hear?' She coughed, then moaned. Blood glistened on her hair. Fresh blood, darkly crimson. 'Know what I wished last night?'

'You said you'd never tell.'

'Wished you'd fall in love again.' She closed her eyes.

Mel could feel her slipping away again. 'I'll come to New Zealand with you, if you like,' she said. 'We could go together. To see those mud pools. It'd be much more fun with two of us.'

Joanne did not reply.

'And I'll tell you what. After we'd gone to bed yesterday, I thought of somewhere I'd really like to go. When you asked me last night . . .'

Last night . . . unimaginably long ago. Since the previous evening, time had stretched, grown long and thin. The safe zones of the past had become inconceivably distant, compared to this terrifying present. '. . . I couldn't think of anywhere I wanted to go but I'd love to do some really long hikes, the Appalachian trail and the Rockies and maybe over to Scotland, or even the Andes. Wouldn't that be something, to walk up there in that thin air with the sun pouring down and snowy mountains all round and the llamas and people in tall hats and . . . and . . . oh, Joanne, wake up, speak to me, Joanne.'

There was no response. Mel could hear the muted crash of the falls further up the river, and, nearer, the rush of water over the boulders. High above was a slash of sky, and the tossing treetops. A bird circled lazily overhead, then drifted away. She shivered. She could feel the thin pulse of Joanne's heart. For the rest of her life she would remember the wet pebbles, the fissured cliff face on the other side of the swirling brown water, the seeping springs which spread across its surface like tears. She would only have to close her eyes to be there again, listening to the rush of the river, with her friend dying in her arms.

'Joanne!' she urged. 'Wake up. Come back.'

Nothing.

The absence grew. Emptiness, total and absolute, filled her. And anger. She wanted to scream, to smash, shatter, destroy. Life. Fate. Something. Anything.

'Joanne!' she said again, more sharply this time.

There was movement in the body she held so close. 'My legs.'

'What about them?'

'Can't move . . .'

'I already told you, Ben's got you trussed up like a chicken.'

'Can't feel . . .'

'You're cold, that's why.'

'. . .'s bad sign.' Joanne's words were slurring. She tried to turn her head but Mel increased the pressure of her hands. 'Couldn't . . . wheelchair . . . rather die.'

'You're not going to die,' Mel said sharply. 'Don't keep saying that. I told you Ben Andersen's calling the emergency services. They're on their way.'

'Ben?'

'Yeah. I *told* you.' God, had the fall damaged Joanne's brain?

'Poor Ben . . . 'n' Lisa, too.' Joanne sounded as if she were almost asleep.

'I know.'

'. . . not your fault . . .' murmured Joanne. 'Always was . . . clumsy bitch . . .'

'Oh, Joanne.'

'Gotta grab it . . .'

'What?'

288

'Grab it . . . by the balls.' Joanne opened her eyes. 'Don't . . . forget.'

'I won't be able to, with you around to remind me,' Mel said. Tears filled her eyes.

'Thirsty . . .'

'Hang on.' Carefully, Mel reached for the bottle of water lying beside her on the stones. She leaned over awkwardly and held it to her friend's lips.

'Secrets . . .' Joanne said, after a moment, sounding stronger.

'What about them?'

'Kept them.'

'I've kept secrets too,' Mel said. 'Things I should've told you.' Would it have made it more bearable, she thought now, with her friend's grey and bloodied face cradled between her hands, if she had talked about the abortion years before, as she had so much longed to? Would it have made the slightest difference if she'd let it out, instead of keeping it lodged inside her until so recently in Boston?

''S OK. I . . . didn't tell . . . either,' Joanne said thickly.

'Tell what?'

'Don Cunningham and me . . .'

'What? Did you have an affair with him?'

'Yes.'

'I don't believe it,' cried Mel, pretending outrage.

'How else . . . think . . . could afford . . . bookstore?' A ghost of Joanne's old grin shivered on her mouth.

Mel could not bear to look at her friend's fluttering eyes, at the face from which life seemed almost visibly to be ebbing. 'Not smelly old Don Cunningham. I just do not believe it!'

Trying to keep back her tears, she looked down at the wound on Joanne's head. The sweatshirt she had put under there earlier was black with drying blood. A clear liquid was leaking from one of her ears. Oh, Joanne . . . my friend. My loved one.

She could not stop shivering. The cold she felt was not just of the water and the wet sunless rocks, it was bone-deep, heart-deep. 'Not Don,' she whispered, as if it was that which mattered and not the terrible sense of loss which cut through her, the unstoppable flow of grief.

CHAPTER NINETEEN

Ben came with her to the lounge attached to the Intensive Care ward.

'You don't have to,' she said, jittery with anxiety.

'I'll stay until the doctor comes out,' he said. 'See what he has to say.'

They sat in the drab little room, together but not together, waiting. A shiny-leaved rubber plant stood in one corner, a bright green fern cascaded from a stand near the door, both of them unwanted reminders of health and vigor. On the walls there were framed photographs of local scenes, a spinnakered sailboat skimming across Lake Champlain, a country road in the fall, a sugar shack. Above their heads the humming fluorescent lights cast a dead glow which drained the color from the walls and floor, from clothes, from skin, reduced everything to a uniform mushroom white.

Ben leafed through a shabby magazine, tossed it down on the table, picked up another, slapped it down, got up and walked around with his hands in his pockets, stretched, sat down again and reached for another magazine.

'There's no need for you to stay.' The words drifted from Mel's mouth, light as air; she was not even sure she had spoken them until he shook his head.

291

'I want to.'

'I'll be all right.' In the distance, Mel could hear a murmur of voices, a sudden burst of laughter from somewhere. Wheelchairs were occasionally propelled down the corridor. A young man, his face covered in blood, was pushed by on a gurney. Time passed, heavy with dread. Once they heard someone cursing at the top of his voice, and a nurse shushing him.

Seized by a chill from somewhere deep inside her which spread until her teeth began to chatter, Mel started shivering.

Ben watched her in silence, then went down the hall to the coffee machine and brought back two plasticized paper cups, one of which he handed to her. She took a sip and grimaced, about to put it down on the scarred coffee table in front of her, but he stopped her. 'Drink it,' he said.

'It's way too sweet,' she complained. 'I don't take sugar in my coffee.'

'Drink it,' he said, and obediently she drained the contents of the cup, and felt the sugar and caffeine work their way through her bloodstream, restoring her depleted energy.

She wrapped her arms around her chest, holding onto herself, trying not to shout her terror aloud. Joanne would be fine, she had to be, nothing else was possible. She saw again the yellow jacket on the wet stones, the blood, the odd way Joanne's eyes had looked. But that was natural, that was what happened when you hit your head. Concussion, she told herself. Joanne was concussed. People get concussed all the time, and recover without any problem. She dug her fingers into her palms. Joanne would be OK. She *had* to be.

The stainless steel doors which led to the emergency

theater swung open and a gurney appeared, pushed by an orderly. Mel stood and took a step forward into the passage.

'Joanne?'

But the body lying on the gurney belonged to somebody else, a blond boy of ten or twelve with golden eyelashes, the longest lashes Mel had ever seen. At the far end of the corridor a fat woman appeared, mouth ugly in her distraught face, holding out both her arms, calling at the top of her voice, 'Baby, baby, my baby, is my baby all right? Is he OK?' Behind her were two other fair-headed boys, older, torn between embarrassment at their mother's uninhibited display of anxiety, and apprehension at the state of their younger brother.

'Baby, my baby . . .' The sobbing woman disappeared down the passage; the squeak of the wheels died away.

Ben took her arm and led her back into the lounge. Mel sat down again, dropping onto the Naugahyde sofa, her body lax and unco-ordinated, flesh coming loose from the bones, limbs slack. She sat forward, covering her face with her hands. She tried to pray, unformed words parading through her mind, '*please*' and '*help*' and '*let her be OK*' and '*please*' again, shamelessly begging. She saw the syllables, like pale blue butterflies, spiraling slowly upwards towards some indefinite notion of God.

It was another two hours before the surgeon appeared, a gray-faced man in green scrubs with a surgical mask hanging round his neck. It was late by now, nearly two o'clock in the morning, and he looked as if he had not slept for several days.

Mel stood up. 'What's the news?' she asked. Shivers rolled through her body again.

'Are you family?' he asked brusquely, too tired for courtesy.

293

'No – I was – we were with her when the accident happened.'

Ben moved to stand next to Mel. He nodded at the doctor. 'Hi, Jim. You look tired.'

'Oh, Ben. Didn't see you there. Yeah, I'm bushed. It's been a long job.'

'Mel here is Mrs Mayfield's closest friend,' Ben said. 'So tell us what's happening.' He took Mel's hand in his and, comforted by its rough warmth, she was happy to let him handle things, take over the questions, ease a little of the burden.

'What can I say?' The surgeon rubbed at his eyelids with two fingers. 'We've stabilized her. Stopped the internal hemorrhaging, given her a blood transfusion to replace what she lost. Put her back together as best we could. Pinned her leg. Had to remove her spleen. Gave her a shot of adrenaline at one point, when the blood pressure dropped, but it's back to one-ten over eighty.' He scanned Mel's face. 'Does this mean anything to you?'

She shook her head. 'I just want to know if she's OK.'

'She's alive, if that's what you mean. OK is something else entirely.'

Mel closed her eyes. What shredding of Joanne's life was she responsible for?

'She's in the recovery room right now,' the surgeon said. 'She'll stay there until she's come round from the anesthesia and we're satisfied with her condition – not that we're expecting any post-operative problems – and then she'll be moved into the ICU.'

'After that?' she asked nervously. 'What's the long-term prognosis?'

'We can't say at the moment. Not for at least twenty-four hours. That was quite a fall; she suffered some fairly extensive damage to both the head and the spine.' The

294

doctor turned, as another gurney was wheeled by. 'I'll be right there,' he called after the orderly who was pushing it.

'Will she be able to walk?' Mel said.

'We won't know for a while.' He shook his head. 'What we're more concerned about is the head injury. For a while there, while we were working on her, there was a certain loss of blood circulation.'

'What does that mean?' Mel sensed her own blood draining from her face, causing a sudden feeling of nausea, dizziness. She swayed and felt Ben's hand on her elbow.

'There was a . . . Due to a considerable drop in blood pressure, circulation of blood to the brain was compromised.'

'Oh, my God.' Visions flashed past her: Joanne in a wheelchair, head lolling, eyes dead, a vegetable, unable to do the slightest thing for herself, spoon-feeding, *diapers* for God's sake, Joanne would *loathe* that. 'Are you telling me that Joanne might be . . . be brain-damaged?'

'It's a possibility. Loss of blood to the brain lasted for a very limited period, but nonetheless we have to face the fact that she might – in a worst-case scenario, which hope-fully we won't have here – when the anesthesia wears off, she might still not be fully alert.'

'What are you saying?'

'That she . . .' He hesitated, brushed his sleeve, looked at Ben. 'She just might be in a coma.'

She clutched at his sleeve. 'A coma?'

He nodded morosely. 'It's too early to say. But we – you – the family should prepare themselves for the possibility.'

'But . . .' The word blocked her throat. How could this have happened, two friends walking in the woods,

295

enjoying the sunshine, laughing? And suddenly, this *horror*.

He moved away from her, acknowledging her anxiety with a tired smile. 'I'm sorry but I can't say anything more at the moment. We'll simply have to wait and see.'

'What are her chances?' asked Ben. He tightened his grip on Mel's hand. 'Overall.'

The doctor coughed, looked at them, looked away. 'She's in a critical condition. I can't hold out a lot of—'

'Percentage-wise,' Ben said.

The intern rocked his hand from side to side. 'We're doing our best . . .'

'Come on, Jim.'

'No more than fifty, sixty per cent, I'm afraid. She could go either way. We'll hope to have a better feel twenty-four hours from now.'

'Fifty per . . .' Mel was afraid she was going to faint. 'Oh God.' She pressed her hand against her mouth. 'Will she be able to . . . to get around again?'

'It's possible.' The doctor nodded. 'It's entirely possible. Not at first, of course. But eventually, with some extensive therapy, it's more than possible. Like I said, we won't know anything further for a few hours yet.' He pulled at one of his ear lobes. 'Do you live locally?'

'Yes.'

'Then I suggest you go home, come back later.'

'I don't know.' Mel looked at Ben. To go would seem as though she were abandoning Joanne. On the other hand, for the moment there was little she could do here. She stared down at her watch, not seeing the numbers. 'That'll give me the chance to call her family. It'll be easier from my house.'

'Like me to drive you?' Ben asked.

About to refuse, she realized that he wanted – needed – to do something. 'That would be very kind.'

They walked towards the parking lot. 'I can wait and bring you back here, if you like,' Ben said.

'All right.'

He took her arm and guided her towards his Jeep. As he opened the door on the passenger side, she caught his eye and for a moment the two of them stared at each other without speaking. She cleared her throat and started to say something as he took a step towards her, spoke her name.

'Mel . . .' His fingers tightened round her arm.

'Ben . . .'

The silence lengthened between them again. Finally Mel turned her head away. She climbed into the Jeep and sat staring straight ahead while Ben got into the driver's seat and, without looking at her again, engaged the gears and eased his foot down on the accelerator.

Arriving at her home, she fumbled with the keys and opened the front door. 'Coffee?' she said, walking into the empty house. 'Or something stronger?'

'Do you have any brandy?'

'Over there.' Mel waved a hand. 'Help yourself.'

'Not for me,' he said. 'For you.'

'I have to call Joanne's . . . her ex-husband.' She raised her shoulders and dropped them. She picked up the telephone, then replaced it. She covered her face with her hands. 'How am I going to tell him? And Jamie, too. He's staying with his father.'

'There's no easy way to break bad news.' Ben put a glass of brandy in her hand. 'Drink that first.'

'Dutch courage?'

'Right.'

She dialled Gordon Mayfield's number. When he finally answered, clearly roused from sleep, she said, 'It's Mel Sherman.'

'Something's happened to one of the kids,' he said, instantly alert.

'Not the kids.'

'What then? At this time of night it can't be good news.'

Mel's throat seized up. Although her mouth formed words, no sound emerged.

'Hello?' Gordon said. 'Mel . . . are you still there?'

She made a tiny strangulated sound. 'I-I . . .'

'Joanne,' he said flatly.

'It's . . . yes . . .'

'Take your time,' he said, the city lawyer, used to clients who were under stress.

'She's . . . she's . . .' Mel began to sob.

'She's dead.' He sounded tired; there was a catch in his voice as he added, 'Why do I feel as if I've been dreading this ever since I left?'

'No. It's not that. Oh *God* . . . she's not dead.' Somehow Mel managed to explain what had happened.

There was a long sigh at the other end of the line. 'How am I going to tell Jamie?' Gordon asked.

'I can't imagine.'

'Do Tom and Lucy know?'

'Not yet. Tom's in New York and Lucy's with a friend in California.'

'I remember.'

'Do you want me to call them?'

'I guess I'd better do it.' Another deep sigh. 'You must be devastated yourself,' he added quietly. 'I know how close you and Joanne are.'

'Yes.' Devastated, demolished, destroyed.

'Is there someone with you? Someone you can talk to?'

'Not really . . .' A void suddenly yawned. There was no-one to giggle with, to feel schoolgirl-young again with, to

laugh with. She heard Ben moving about in the kitchen.
'Well . . . sort of.'

'I'll drive up tomorrow,' he said. 'Will you be all right
until then?'

'Yes.' What choice did she have? What else could she be
but all right?

It seemed like only minutes later that the telephone
rang. It was Tom. 'What *happened*?' he cried, his voice
cracking.

'We were out hiking in the woods, and your mom fell.'

'I don't understand.' Behind Tom's words were tears
waiting for release. 'What was she doing up there in the
first place? She hates the whole outdoor bit. What was she
doing?'

'She was staying with me, at my cabin,' Mel said,
braced for reproach.

He broke down. 'Mel, *why*?' And then he was sobbing,
weeping like a child, and she was trying to soothe him, to
comfort him, but it was impossible, what could you say,
what could you possibly say when a seventeen-year-old
wept on the telephone, saying *Mommy* in the voice he
must have used in childhood, saying *Mom, Mom*, terrified
he might never again see her as she used to be, as she
always had been?

'Tom,' she said quietly, her throat aching. 'Tom,' while
he wept into the telephone receiver.

'Mom,' he said again, his voice tiny at the other end of
the phone. 'I can't . . . I can't take it in, I just can't believe
it.'

'I'm sorry, honey. I'm so sorry.'

'I can't understand it,' said Tom, his voice breaking. 'I
loved her,' as though his love should have protected,
should have rendered his mother inviolable.

When she'd put down the receiver, she sat with her

299

hand on the telephone, staring unseeing at the wall. The one thing she wanted to do above all else was to call Joanne, as she had so many times over the years, to talk this terrible event over with her, to hear her robust and comforting reaction.

Ben Andersen appeared from the kitchen with a mug of coffee in his hand. He had made sandwiches – ham and tomato – and she suddenly realized how long ago it was since she had eaten.

'Thank you,' she said, grateful for his consideration. As she took a bite, she saw blood, dried and flaking, on the back of her hands. Joanne's blood. She ran into the kitchen and turned on the tap, watching the discolored water fall into the sink and flow away. Joanne's lifeblood. Suddenly nauseous, she pressed a wet hand to her mouth, trying not to retch.

When she turned round, Ben was standing there, watching her. He held out his arms and silently she stepped into them, laid her head against his shoulder, accepted the support he offered.

'If it hadn't been for you,' she said, voice muffled, 'she wouldn't still be alive.'

'Maybe she'll wish she wasn't.'

'Don't say that.'

'I wish there was something I could do,' he said. 'Something I could say.'

She felt light, insubstantial, as though she might float away from him if he let her go. The solidity and warmth of his body was comforting. 'I can't bear it,' she whispered, weeping into his chest. 'She was such a . . . *giving* person. She had such a generous heart.'

'I know.'

The phone began to bleep. 'I'd better get that,' she said, not moving.

'OK.' He still held her.

His eyes were like water, sea water, lake water. 'Thank you for being here with me,' she said. 'Thank you, Ben.' Gently, reluctantly, she disengaged herself and went towards the telephone.

Chapter Twenty

Gordon Mayfield and his children arrived the following day and drove straight to the hospital. Exhausted, distressed, Mel waited for them in Joanne's house. When they finally came through the door, all of them looked as though they had been bludgeoned. Tom, who had filled out over the summer vacation. put his arms round her. Mel hugged Lucy, the girl's head burrowed into her neck. When she held out her arms to Jamie, he pushed his spectacles up his nose and frowned, his lower lip quivering, then burst into tears.

'Mom,' he wailed. 'Mom.'

'Oh, honey,' Mel crooned, holding him tight against her breast. 'Oh, my little Jamie,' remembering him as a toddler, at four, at seven, solemn, precocious, never without a book. She thought of the lemon cake in her freezer, which might never now be set with candles. 'Do you think there are different kinds of love?' he had asked her a week ago, owlish in his round glasses, his mouth smeared with frosting, 'or is love always the same?'

'Of course not. Think how you love your mom, and your sister—'

'Some of the time,' he broke in.

'– and Gargery. It's all love, but you can see it's not the same kind.'

'I guess.'

'The point really is that you should seize it when you have it, because whatever form it takes, love is precious.'

Now, he looked up at her, sniffing. 'Is Mom going to die?' he said.

'She's going to be fine, Jamie,' Tom said, touching his little brother's hair. He seemed finally to have left boyhood behind and stepped into adulthood. 'You know Mom.'

Was it her imagination, Mel wondered, or did Tom avoid her gaze? She thought that she would never lose the images of the water-dark stones, the gushing river, the abundant leaves, and that sulfur-yellow stain at the bottom of the gorge, bright as springtime, acid with dread.

Gordon Mayfield put both his hands on Mel's shoulders. He was a big, still-handsome man with a fine theatrical head, a sweep of heavy gray hair, a summer tan. 'This is so terrible,' he said. 'I don't know how we are . . . Lying on that hospital bed, she looks so . . .' His kind eyes were red-rimmed. He sat down heavily on the shabby old sofa and his children gathered around him, Lucy leaning her head on his shoulder, Tom upright, Jamie burrowing into his lap as though he were a baby again.

Superfluous, Mel went out to make coffee. She was stabbed by the familiarity of Joanne's yellow-walled kitchen, which the two of them had redecorated last Easter weekend. The absence of Joanne's big ebullient personality was made worse by the memories: the Sabatier knife Mel had bought her, the ugly-face mug which Joanne always swore reminded her of Sarah Mahoney, the corn dolly tied with a red ribbon, the antique cherrywood salt box they'd found at a garage sale.

Mel set the tray with mugs of coffee, a glass of juice for

303

Jamie, and carried it back to the living room. The others did not appear to have moved. She put the tray down on the battered coffee table then stood in front of them, her hands clasped, her palms slippery with nervous sweat. Lucy blinked at her, trying to keep awake after her long flight from the West Coast. She began to cry, her mouth open, sobs shaking her shoulders.

'I'd just like to . . .' Mel wanted to confess her guilt over having taken Joanne up to the lake. But as she took a breath to continue, she realized how unfair it would be to burden them with her pain when they had so much of their own. She was going to have to bear this extra ordeal alone. '. . . to say that if there's anything at all I can do to help . . .'

'Thanks, Mel.'

She poured coffee, handed it round. Were they blaming her for what had happened? Did they hate her?

Gordon seemed worried. 'What's the best way to handle things like the bookstore?'

'The two assistants, Karen and Wendy, are pretty clued up,' Mel said. 'They'll be able to carry on as usual. It won't matter much until it comes to reordering: they know how to cope with the day-to-day stuff.'

Tom suddenly lost his composure. 'I just can't take it in,' he said. His voice wavered and cracked. 'Mom, in a wheel-chair. That's what they said at the hospital. She might be in a—' He bent his head and his shoulders shook.

Gordon glanced at his elder son. 'Might it be better just to . . . to start trying to sell the store? If she's not going to be able to . . . to get about, I mean. Later. I don't necessarily mean right away, but . . .'

'Dad, let's not give up on her before we start, OK?' Lucy put a hand on her father's knee.

'Until we know for sure, we shouldn't assume the

worst,' said Mel. She was aware that all of them were concentrating on Joanne's possible loss of mobility, in order not to have to think about the much worse options. 'Actually, she *was* thinking of selling up. Or, at least, of changing direction.'

'Changing?'

'We were talking about it quite recently and she said that maybe it was time to move on, do something else.'

'Like what?'

'Well, you might not believe this, but she was seriously talking about opening a health-food store.' In spite of her misery, Mel could not help smiling.

'Joanne was?'

'Mom selling organic vegetables?' Tom said.

'Scrunchy little apples and herbs and stuff like that?' Jamie pushed his glasses up his nose. 'Doesn't sound like Mom.'

'I can't believe it,' Lucy said, eyes full of tears, mouth curving in a smile.

'I can,' said Gordon, 'for about three minutes!'

And then suddenly all of them were laughing, roaring, falling about in their seats, the images bright and clear: Joanne with her wild hair, surrounded by sacks of pulses, buckets of basmati rice, organic wholefoods, Joanne doling out knobbly carrots and weird-shaped tomatoes, carob-covered raisins and soy-bean nibbles and sugar-free muesli.

'Can you imagine?' gasped Lucy, her face red with laughter. 'Mom selling tofu?'

Mel nodded, tears of mirth squeezing from her eyes. 'Quark,' she managed.

'I *beg* your pardon,' said Gordon.

'Vegetarian cheese!'

'Yucky carob chocolate.'

'Herbal *tea*!' Lucy said, trying to catch her breath. 'She hated – *hates* – the stuff.'

Laughter turned quickly to tears.

When the others went back to the hospital, Mel returned to her own home. The house was full of dead shadows as she walked unsteadily through the dark rooms to the kitchen. The clock on the stove glowed a gentle green, out of synch by twenty, thirty, forty seconds with the clock on the microwave. Opening the refrigerator, she looked in at milk cartons and mayonnaise jars, at a pot of blueberry butter she had bought from the Farmer's Market last week, at lo-fat spread and some wax-wrapped ham from the delicatessen on the far side of the Common, at the mottled nakedness of chicken thighs lying in a blue polystyrene tray. She knew she ought to eat something, but the thought of food, the physical acts of preparing and eating it, nauseated her. She closed the door, took a banana from the fruit bowl on the counter and began slowly to strip it, until once again revulsion choked her. She folded it together again and laid it back on top of the oranges and apples.

In the living room, she stood looking out at the dark front yard. A street light, diffused through the leaves of the big maple tree, cast a dim orangey glow across the japonica and the roses. She needed to talk, but there was no-one to talk to. She needed reassurance, a hand to hold. She had friends, plenty of them, in and around Butterfield, but nobody who could ease her pain and guilt, nobody who would understand that if anyone had to lie in a hospital bed, it should be her, not Joanne, that although she was grateful not to be, she would never to able to forgive herself for what had happened.

She thought suddenly of Ben.

She hesitated, hand above the telephone, then slowly dialed his number. Would he mind? Would he understand that she needed comfort? Anticipating, she heard his supportive voice in her head *I'll come round right away* and immediately felt calmer.

The phone rang, fifteen, twenty, thirty times before it finally clicked off into a raucous buzz and she replaced the receiver.

Tubes. Dozens of tubes. Up the nose, in the mouth, attached to the arm, snaking under the covers to feed and monitor. Surreal. A work in progress. Installation art.

Mel's head was way too heavy for her neck. It kept falling forward onto her chest. She blinked awake again. Her eyelids felt like sandpaper and her mouth was dry and foul. How long had she been sitting beside Joanne's bed? Hours? Days? A lifetime, waiting, talking, hoping for some signal, some sign.

A couple of times Joanne had sneezed, little snickerings which shook the sheet covering her chest. Occasionally she turned her head on the pillow, muttered something, her lips whiffling briefly outwards. Once it sounded like a word: '*don't*' or '*won't*'; once, like '*no*'.

She looked terrible. Her color was bad, a waxy gray that reminded Mel of cold boiled potatoes. One side of her face was encrusted with thick red scabs and her eyes were swollen shut, the skin around them startlingly purple against the paleness of her cheeks. Most of the hair had been shaved from her head, leaving her skull – where it was visible – as vulnerable as a baby's. Bandages. Plaster. And those darn tubes, so many of them it was difficult to find Joanne under all the yards of plastic piping.

Seeing her for the first time since surgery, Mel had felt as though she had been punched in the stomach. How could anyone expect to recover from such injuries? What hope was there that Joanne could ever take up the life she had lost? Yet, over the following days, the nursing staff remained positive.

They came and went, checking Joanne out, feeding her, washing her, dealing with the necessary bodily functions. Funny, Mel sometimes thought, how even when the mind was absent, the body went on requiring food and water, needing to evacuate. 'The vital signs are stable. Her response to external stimuli is the same as it was,' they said. 'We're not seeing any change for the worse.'

'But she's not waking up. She's . . . not *there*,' Mel said wildly, after a long night of sitting beside her friend's bed, holding the limp hand, watching the expressionless face.

The nurse, a girl half Mel's age, Beverly, glanced across at Joanne and laid a finger on her lips. 'Hearing sensitivity is very acute in coma cases,' she said softly. 'Let's try and be positive. Just accept that she's there, somewhere.'

'Is she?' Is she still the friend I once knew? Mel wanted to ask. 'How can you be so sure?'

'Trust me.'

'But how do you *know*, Beverly?'

'Gotta have faith, Mel!' Beverly moved on, her mind obviously on something else. 'Gotta have faith.'

Faith: Mel was not sure if she had enough faith to restore Joanne to health again, or if any single person could possess that much faith. She had worked out a visiting rota with Gordon, but in between her own sessions at Joanne's bedside, she was unable to sleep. Now, she cranked up her eyelids again. Exhaustion coated her. Occasionally, she hallucinated, seeing white owls walking through the door of Joanne's room, a tiger under

308

the bed, conducting conversations with people who weren't there – Hillary Clinton or the English Prime Minister, once even with Galen Koslowski. Disjointed sentences sometimes came out of her mouth when she talked to the nurses and they would look at her then with a professional compassion, as though they had seen all this before.

They were all cookie-cutter versions of each other, she reflected, her brain buzzing more and more slowly as though powered by a run-down battery. Trim, slim, blonde, neat little butts, big feet. Probably the white shoes they wore made their feet look bigger than they really were. Sometimes she wondered if her mind was going, if this unremitting wakefulness was eroding her brain cells, inducing dementia.

She shifted on the vinyl-covered chair and heard the cushion squeak, as though her movements had caused it pain. It was an uncomfortable chair, unyielding, with strips of rubber for arms. After the past few days, it was beginning to feel like a second skin.

Desperately she wished to get back to normal, then wondered if there still existed a normal to get back to. This room, this chair, this figure in this bed, Joanne and yet not Joanne, was her normality now. She had offered to move into the Mayfield home, to take over the role of carer of the family, to make dinner for them at night, pack Jamie's lunch box, but Gordon had shaken his head, squeezed her arm, his eyes full of compassion.

'Concentrate on Joanne,' he said. 'I'll cope with the kids. They need some continuity at the moment,' and, though she knew that had not been his intention, she had felt excluded again, all the years shared with her friend meaningless now.

Going home to eat, shower, change clothes, she would

sometimes look round at her familiar possessions and not recognize them. Running her fingers over the smooth wood of the little statue in her bedroom, or taking a familiar mug from the kitchen cupboard, she would find herself wondering where they had come from, what sort of person they belonged to, who had chosen this particular cushion or that toothbrush. She scarcely slept in her own bed, slumping down, instead, on the couch, falling instantly into a deep and consuming sleep, only to start up after a couple of hours, knowing she should be at the hospital, standing briefly under the shower, pulling a comb through her hair, fretting that Joanne had awakened at last, was calling for her, was calling for something, for anything.

She found time to drop in at the gallery, sign a few letters, agree with whatever Carla suggested, but the Koslowski show seemed remote and inconsequential, something that no longer had any relevance.

Now, she took her friend's hand and lifted it to her mouth, kissed it. It would have felt silly if Joanne had been there to see her do it. But she was not.

Sometimes Mel read aloud from *Great Expectations*, always top of Joanne's list of books she would want if marooned on a desert island. Sometimes she just talked.

'I wish you'd wake up,' she said now. 'I want to hear you laugh, not that you've got much to laugh at, I know that, God, don't I know, but I just wanted to tell you about Gordon, about the way he made a pot of tea last night when we came back from visiting you.'

She felt as though she had been talking like this for days. Her throat was raw and scratchy, but she was sure that if only she could press the right button, hit the password, then Joanne would be able to drag herself out of whatever mental quagmire she was mired in and respond.

310

'What he did was, he put two tea bags in the pot and then filled it with cold water from the tap and then, *then* he stuck it in the microwave for three minutes. I mean, can you imagine? Is that cute, or what?' Mel pressed her friend's fingers. 'What a way to make tea. And the worst thing was, it didn't taste bad, it really didn't, not like a properly made pot with a pinch of that Earl Grey we bought last time we went down to Boston, do you remember, Joanne, can you hear me, but certainly not as bad as I thought it would be, and a whole heap better than we had at that dreadful place on the road to Burlington.'

There was no reaction from the still figure on the bed. Sometimes, during her vigils, Mel thought there was a flicker of movement in the hand she clasped in her own, a flutter of an eyelid, a twitch of the mouth. But if there had been, it was too faint, too brief, to be taken as a response to anything she had said.

'Oh, Joanne,' she said softly. 'I miss you so much, so much you can't imagine. I miss your laughter and your wit and your raunchiness and your – let's face it – your big mouth, and if you can hear me, Jo, if you object to what I'm saying, or you've got something of your own to say, don't hesitate to butt in. I mean, when did interrupting somebody ever stop you shoving in your oar? Like that time we went to New York for the weekend, and you got into a fight with that guy in the bar of the hotel, the St Regis, as I recall, because he was going on and on to the friends he was with – complete strangers, if you remember, never seen any of them before in our lives – going on about books or writers or something and you just had to break in, didn't you? The two of you had a real humdinger of an argument about Ernest Hemingway – remember? – and you ended up telling him he should have been drowned at birth and he took a swing at you, both of you drunk as skunks, and the manager came out and tried to reason with you and you decked *him* one. Oh Joanne, the shame of it, and I tried and the bartender tried, even the damned bellboy tried but you, oh no, you weren't going to listen to anybody saying anything nice about Hemingway. Calling him a male chauvinist pig is an insult to pigs, you shouted, and in the end . . . Oh Joanne, answer me, because I want to tell you all sorts of stuff and if you're not listening, I don't want to waste my breath, especially when I could be doing something useful like running my art gallery which, *by* the way, is doing very well, thank you, very well indeed in the run-up to Christmas, not that it's Christmas yet, of course, but like they say, it starts earlier every year and my Koslowski exhibition is coming up, and the preview party won't be any fun if you're not there.'

She took a sip of water from the glass on the night-stand. Thank god for Carla, who was dealing so efficiently with the last-minute details of the exhibition.

She paused, drew a deep breath, started once more. 'Tom cut the grass in your backyard yesterday,' she continued, 'and I personally raked up the leaves under that big old maple and if you don't believe me, I've got the blisters to prove it, and as I've said to you before, that tree definitely needs to be trimmed down a little before a branch falls onto someone's head and kills them. Especially since, in the nature of things, it's bound to be me. Oh, I wish you would wake up, Joanne, I really wish you would come back to me and be my friend again.'

Tears filled Mel's eyes. It was the sort of thing a kindergarten kid might say. *Will you be my friend?* She reached for the glass of water again; her throat was beginning to seize up and her chest felt tight. Gordon Mayfield would be in to spell her soon, and then she would be free to go back to her empty house and sit on the couch, alone, wrapped round with guilt and regret, until it was time to come back again.

She had not known she could keep up a verbal barrage like this for so long. At first her brain used to run ahead of her mouth, desperately searching for something to say, trying to shape sentences, to make sense. But latterly she had simply let the thoughts emerge in whatever order they wanted, talking to Joanne in the easy freewheeling way that had developed between them, each confident that the other would be able to follow the connections between one subject and the next, or meander effortlessly down the conversational byways without losing the thread. She had no idea whether it was doing any good or whether she was simply wasting her time. She concentrated on words like *Gordon* and *Jamie* and *bookstore* and *New Zealand*, trigger words, verbal prompts which she hoped would penetrate the fog occupying Joanne's brain.

'Do you remember,' she began once more and suddenly tears were splashing down her cheeks and grief rose inside her, a huge heavy ball of it, swelling, stifling her.

So many *do-you-remembers*. So many things shared.

'Oh, Joanne, wake up,' she whispered. 'Squeeze my hand, blink, smile, *anything*, so I know you can hear me. Please wake up so I can stop feeling so terribly *guilty*, because it's tearing me apart. Wake up, Joanne. *Please.*'

But there was no response. No squeeze. No flicker. No twitch. Nothing to show for all the words. Nothing to ease Mel's misery.

CHAPTER TWENTY-ONE

He had bought flowers for Joanne. Roses, orangey-brown ones, with a sprig or two of some white lacy-type thing and some green stuff to set it off. She wouldn't know, of course, wouldn't give a damn whether he brought her anything or not, but he'd decided, driving home that evening and passing the florist shop, that it might comfort the family to know that people cared enough to bring flowers.

It was late as he drove into the hospital parking lot. He turned off the ignition and gazed up at the sky, sprinkled with the hard clear stars which announced the coming autumn. Fall used to be his favorite time of year. He'd liked the sense of things closing down, days getting shorter, darkness wrapping itself around the earth. He'd liked the crisp days, the bite of frost in the air, the way things smelled sharper, seemed clearer. And the colors, so many reds – wine, crimson, scarlet, cranberry – and yellows, everything from palest lemon to amber to mustard, and oranges like fire or copper . . .

His mouth twisted. Who gave a rat's ass what season it was? Spring, fall, summer, winter, what the hell did it matter, without Lisa there to share it?

He walked down long passages, glanced in at darkened

314

rooms. He knew that Joanne was still in Intensive Care, still in a coma. How was Mel handling that? The ward was quiet, most people either asleep or out of it on medication. No-one asked him what he was doing; perhaps the flowers he was carrying spoke their own message.

When he reached Joanne's room, the lights were on and he could see Mel sitting by the bed, her back to the door. She was holding her friend's hand and had her head down on the covers.

He wondered what to do. Then he tiptoed in and laid the flowers on the high hospital table which had been pushed to the end of the bed.

As he turned to leave, Mel lifted her head.

'Ben.' She sounded absolutely whacked.

'Hi.' He was shocked at the change in her. She seemed ten years older than she had only a few days earlier. There were deep smudges of shadow under her dark blue eyes, and she looked like she'd lost quite a bit of weight.

'You've brought flowers,' she said, and he wasn't sure if she thought they were for her or not. Maybe he should have brought her some: she'd enjoy them more than Joanne could.

'How is she?' he asked.

She stared at him as though she hadn't heard, then gave herself a small shake. 'They don't know. There might be brain damage. There might be . . . they don't really know.'

'When she wakes up,' he said awkwardly, picking them up again and laying them down on the end of the bed, 'she might like to see some roses.'

'She loves roses,' Mel said. 'They're her favorite flower.'

'Good.' There were dozens of vases in the room, already full of flowers, and for a moment he felt ridiculous, standing there. 'I guess the last thing she wants is more of them.'

'Can anyone ever have enough roses?' She smiled tiredly. He could see the exhaustion in her eyes. 'Or apricots,' she said. A blank expression crossed her face.

'Apricots?'

She stared at him and he realized that for a moment she had actually fallen asleep with her eyes open, that the words had spiraled their way upwards from her unconscious self. 'What?'

'You said something about apricots.'

'Did I? I love them. Love apricots. Peaches too.' She sounded as though she were speaking to him across an ocean of weariness.

'Right. Well . . .' Lifting his hand in farewell, he walked away. Under the soles of his boots, the polished floor squeaked. From the darkened rooms on either side came a variety of sounds: groans, sighs, odd phrases. Mel was obviously exhausted. Even her hair looked tired, not so much blond as colorless. She probably hadn't even noticed he'd left. A coma, brain damage . . . Poor Mel. Poor Joanne, too, of course. And she had children, he remembered. Two in high school, plus a younger kid he'd seen at the bookstore, curled up on a sofa, reading.

Peaches . . . Briefly he smiled. Where had that come from? He was reminded of the slices of peach tart that Lisa used to bring back from her favorite deli in the Village. And the cobbler she baked for him once, a couple of months after they'd married.

'I bet I know what this is,' he'd said, peering at it, not quite sure.

'Can't you tell?'

'Almost.'

She pouted, her dimples moving like shadows on her cheeks. 'It's a peach-and-passion cobbler.'

'Exactly what I thought!' He'd cut himself a huge slice.

'How did you know that's my absolute favorite kind?' He'd reached for the little pitcher in the center of the table. 'And I'll bet this here is some of that genuine lo-fat whipped love to put on top.'

'Oh, honey,' she said. 'You're just so smart.'

Don't think about her.

Don't think . . .

He used to dream of her returning to him, but, as time went by, the possibility of a second chance for them faded with every passing day.

Pulling into the short driveway of his house, he saw that there were lights in the upper rooms and his heart began to bounce like a piledriver. Surely he hadn't gone out leaving so many lights on. Someone else must have switched them on . . . She was back! She was inside, waiting for him!

Leaping out of the car, he pushed eagerly at the front door. But it was locked and he had to fumble for his keys. His mood flattened as he dropped them, bent to pick them up, knowing that she wasn't back, that she was never coming back. He let himself into the house and, reluctant to let go of the fantasy, took the stairs two at a time, calling out her name, 'Lisa! Lisa!' tears cutting his voice like broken glass.

Maybe she came back sometimes, when he was at work. He pictured her running beneath the apple tree to the front door, stepping into the hall, bright as a butterfly in the noonday sun. He imagined her moving through the house, touching objects with her small blunt fingers, straightening the pictures, looking at herself in the glass in the hall. Maybe she hoped her reflection would linger there, so that sometimes, as he passed, he would catch, from the corner of his eyes, a glimpse of her smile. Maybe she stood outside the windows in the evening, looking in

317

at him. Maybe she listened when he played Mozart for her, and remembered what the two of them once had.

But he knew none of this was true, and though he checked the rooms he found nothing before he stumbled into the bedroom and collapsed across his bed, falling into black desolation once again. He longed for her quick bright presence in his life, for the moth-light touch of her lips. Even for the arguments they had. Oh, to have her here again, feisty and beautiful, with her sardonic take on life, on love, on *him*.

That night he dreamed of his daughter, a tiny black-haired creature who smiled at him but who, when he bent to pick her up, began to swell like some monstrous bloated fish, her limbs and features gradually disappearing, consumed, swallowed by ballooning bloodstreaked flesh.

Disconcerted by the nightmare, he got up and stood at the window of the bedroom he and Lisa had once shared, looking out into the gathering dawn. Usually, he saw her inhabiting a kind of mist-shrouded limbo, empty of landmarks or other people, a vague Chicago, a nebulous California. Now he tried to propel his longing and his need in her direction. Lisa ... where are you? What are you doing? Are you happy or unhappy? Do you miss me as I miss you?

The shapes of the objects below him – the car, the apple tree, the edge of the barn – were blurred in the shadowy light. The sky was purple-gray, heavy with moisture although it had rained during the night. Just above the town, the cloud layer had split open, a bright-edged wound across the sky, revealing a dazzling slash of gold and apple green which was reflected in the wet roofs. Beautiful, he thought. Further lay the hills, their intense green, now touched with autumn, suffused with the milky light which heralds a coming storm.

Over the past weeks he had felt hollowed out, as though misery were a scoop which had scraped him clean, so that at first he failed to identify the emotion which now swept over him as pleasure. Having done so, he was unnerved. He pushed away the feeling, astonished and guilty that he could experience esthetic satisfaction in the middle of pain. He thought of Joanne. What kind of a future lay in store for her? Or her children? He had no right to complain, when he was alive and well, when there were such things as sunrises and good wine and mountains still to climb. At least he could *feel*. What was going on inside Joanne's head? Anything? He recalled the feel of Mel inside the circle of his arms, her pale head resting on his shoulder, needing comfort when there was no comfort to give.

Once, years ago, he'd been up at the lake with his dad, the two of them relaxed on the porch with beers in their hands, watching the swallows skim the water and the divers go through their busy rituals. It was one of those sultry early-summer days, too hot to do much; they'd been out in the boat and come back with sunburn on their shoulders and a string of bass, feeling pretty good about it. And idly, not really considering what he said, he'd asked, 'Are you and Mom happy?'

'I'd say so.' Professor Andersen had smiled to himself. 'Yup, I'd say we were happy.' He was silent for a while. 'But happiness isn't in the destination, it's in the journey, which makes it a fairly elusive commodity. Start trying to pin it down, and it's far too easy to come up with caveats and limitations, reasons why this moment is less happy than that one, whether you were happier last week or last year than you are now, until suddenly you've lost it.'

'I guess what I really meant was, are you *conscious* of being happy?'

'All the time. That's what I meant about it being elusive. Don't analyze it, just accept it. Recognize it as a gift, and don't ask too many questions about where it came from.'

'I guess you and Mom have a pretty good marriage, don't you?'

'I'd say. Pretty good, considering.'

'Considering?' Alarmed, Ben straightened in his chair. 'How do you mean?'

'Oh, there were times in there when things got kind of difficult,' his father said.

He'd wanted to ask what kind of things, but was afraid. He'd taken for granted the serenity of the relationship between his parents. To learn, in this oblique fashion, that it had not always been plain sailing alarmed him; cowardice prevented him from questioning further, in case his simplistic vision of his childhood was unavoidably altered by revelations he had been unaware of and did not want to know about: other women, other men, illegitimate children, financial irregularities, shameful admissions which would irrevocably alter his vision of his own childhood if his father was to speak.

But parents did not have a duty to be happy, or to be the demigods their kids would like them to be. He remembered the seminal moments when he first realized that his father was fallible, when he first saw his mother cry. Terrifying, that sense of something going wrong which could not be put right. He had known then that having once glimpsed their vulnerabilities, he would never be able to think of them in the same way again.

CHAPTER TWENTY-TWO

Another week went by.

The first delivery of Koslowski's work arrived at the Vernon Gallery. The UPS man carried the three big crates into the gallery and set them carefully down on the polished maple floor. Handing over a sheaf of papers to be signed, he reached into the pouch he was carrying and pulled out an envelope. 'There's this too,' he said. 'Special Delivery, supposed to go with the other forms. The guy was real insistent about it.'

'Which guy?' Mel said.

'Where I picked it up from. This place in SoHo. His studio.'

'You mean Mr Koslowski?'

'Yeah. Him. Real impatient sort of guy. Follows me all the way down the stairs. Yells at me. "You gotta hand it over personal," he says. "I'll hold you directly responsible if anything goes wrong." I'm like, look mister, I'm just the messenger boy here, but he's not listening. "Hand it over personal," he's going, real loud, with people stopping to see what's goin' on, like it was a stick-up or something.'

'He's quite a character,' agreed Mel.

'I'll say. Wasn't even dressed. Standing there on the

sidewalk in his bathrobe like it was six o'clock in the morning instead of gone noon.'

'The artistic temperament,' Carla said.

The UPS man nodded. 'I'll say. No shoes on his feet, hair all mussed – and nothing on under the robe, either, as I can personally testify to. Any how, here's the letter and I'm handing it over personal, like he said.'

Mel took the white envelope and looked down at the ungainly black script – *TO WHOM IT MAY CONCERN / / /* She was surprised by the complicated sensations which swept over her. She remembered notes stuck to the door of Galen's studio, sudden postcards from Rome or Calcutta when she had believed him to be in Oregon, angry letters fired off to critics who had failed to understand his work. She remembered his smile, his tender hands. And how, back then, she had never felt so unhappy – or so alive.

In the office at the back of the gallery a phone rang and Carla hurried to answer it. While Mel dealt with the paperwork, the UPS man inspected the paintings on the walls. 'I like the way this guy hasn't painted the snow white,' he said, looking at a swirling mass of color depicting Mt Mansfield under a blanket of snow. 'Which it isn't, when you look at it. Real snow isn't white at all.'

'I know.' Mel signed the delivery note, added her signature at the bottom of various pages.

'Funny, all those blues and greens and kinda mauves, they look like white, don't they?'

Mel smiled at the man.

The UPS guy nodded. 'Yeah. I could live with a painting like that. Guess it's kind of expensive, isn't it?'

'Not as expensive as it'll be five years from now,' Mel said. She opened a drawer and rummaged through it. 'Here. I know it's not the same, but it'll remind you.' She

322

handed him one of the brochures which had been printed up for her last exhibition. 'Page 4. There's a reproduction of that painting.'

'Hey, thanks!'

While Carla fixed coffee for them both, Mel sat down at the table in her office and opened the envelope the UPS man had brought. A sheet of A4, torn from a pad, strong black letters, a mass of exclamation marks. The sculptor had jabbed at the paper so hard that in places he had gone right through.

TO WHOM IT MAY CONCERN she read.

All the pieces have been labeled very clearly.

Do NOT mix them up ! !

Contour IV is to be displayed in a corner ie between two walls.

Harbinger should stand in water.

These conditions MUST be met!

And the flourishing signature: *Galen Koslowski*

'What do you think of this?' Mel said, handing it to her assistant.

Carla scanned it. 'Well, that's telling you.' She laughed. 'He sounds like he's kind of off the wall.'

'He's eccentric, but not nuts. He's . . . he's actually one of the kindest people you could ever meet. He just gets very frustrated.'

'What about?'

'Like a lot of creative people, he feels that nobody really understands his work.'

Carla dropped a heavy hand onto Mel's shoulder, made a severe face. 'Mind you don't go making a mistake, now, Ms Sherman. Stick *Contour IV* in a bowl of water, instead of *Harbinger*, for instance. What does he mean, anyway, displayed in water?'

'It's something he does. He's probably packed in a

marble or granite basin which we'll have to fill.'

'Will plain water from the faucet be acceptable?' said Carla. 'Or does it have to be designer water? Should I lay in a stock of Evian or something? And – oh my! – should it be still or sparkling?'

'I'm amazed he hasn't specified it,' Mel said.

'I had another call from that couple up in South Burlington,' said Carla. 'They got the invitation to the preview and are going to bring some art-dealer friends who're over from Paris.'

'Terrific.'

'And the *Boston Globe*'s confirmed that they're coming and want to do an interview.'

'I'm sorry you've been landed with so much of the load while I deal with my ... my crises. First Lisa Andersen, now poor Joanne.'

'Don't give it a thought.' Carla patted Mel's shoulder. 'Much better you should be with Mrs Mayfield. Anyway, I love it, you know that.'

'When this is all over, we'll have a talk, get things on a better footing, yes?'

'Fine by me.'

'OK. Let's get the new stuff unpacked.'

It was gone eight o'clock at night, but Mel was still prowling through the gallery, inspecting the exhibits. Now that so much of his recent work was assembled in one place, it was easy to see how Koslowski's style had evolved over the years. Initially jagged, dark, full of twisted fluid shapes which forced the viewer, however unwillingly, to participate in horrors of which he might have no personal experience, the early Koslowskis had spoken to the dark places of the human soul. There had followed a period of exuberance, perhaps even joy, when his pieces had

324

flowered like roses, before he began to get fussy, unfocused, less pure in form. Now, as though he had made a conscious decision, he had abruptly abandoned the new style and turned to a sparer kind of work.

She stopped in front of a heavy piece of black basalt. *Woman*. A female body, squat and heavy, cut off at the thighs and the shoulders. The stone was undressed, except for the heavy breasts and distended belly, which had been polished to a high sheen. The sculpture was strong and stark, clearly influenced by primitive fertility symbols and yet unmistakably by Koslowski.

Another recent piece caught her eye. Called *Birth*, it was simply a face, reaching out of the stone, contorted by an expression which could have been anything: agony or grief or ecstasy. Or perhaps all three.

She wondered whether to add *First Love*, her own sculpture, to the show. A tender, personal piece, he had made it specifically for her; she was not entirely sure whether it would fit in with the other work. She would have to think about it some more before she decided.

Butterfield continued its usual routines: the Craft Fair, the historical pageant, civic council meetings, events in which Mel would normally have taken a part. But since Joanne remained comatose, her own life had been reduced. Occasionally she shopped for essential supplies; otherwise she divided her time between home, the hospital and, when she could, the gallery. She was home now. A fire burned in the hearth of her living room; outside, a strong wind was tugging at the turning leaves and smacking them against the windows.

Jamie was curled up on the sofa beside her, looking at a picture book. 'Mom told me I'd enjoy something called *Orlando*,' he said, looking up at her. 'By this English writer called Veronica Woolf or something. No, not Veronica . . . Virginia.'

'You're on O's now, are you?'

'Yes, but I couldn't . . .' He looked at the fire and bit his lip. 'I know she didn't mean *Orlando the Marmalade Cat*, which anyway I've read hundreds of times, but . . . at the moment it just seems sort of less complicated to read something I already know.'

'No demands,' said Mel.

'Right. And also, I really like the pictures. They're kind of . . . comforting, aren't they?'

Oh, my poor little Jamie, she thought. At least, when your world turns upside down, you can always bury yourself in a book. 'When I was little, I loved the way Orlando wears his watch on his tail,' she said.

Jamie's eyes rounded. 'Wow! He's been around since *you* were a kid?'

'You ageist swine, you.' Mel snuggled him closer to her. 'How's Gargery doing?'

'He's pretty sad,' Jamie said. 'I took him for a walk this morning and he just walked. Normally he . . . he . . .' Jamie pressed his lips together, holding back. '. . . he runs about all over the place.'

'Want something to eat?'

'I had a hamburger at the hospital.' He closed the book on his knee. 'Mel. Is Mom going to get better?'

So many things she could say. So many lies she could tell. 'Honey, I just don't know.'

'What will happen to us if she . . . if she dies?'

'You've got a loving dad. You and Tom and Lucy would probably go and live with him.' She knew this because she and Gordon had discussed it as a worst-case scenario. 'So you'd still be together.'

Jamie gave a deep sigh, started to say something but

choked instead. Suddenly he was sobbing against her, shaking his head from side to side. 'I don't want her to . . .'

'Jamie, Jamie.'

'I dream about her all the time. Sometimes she's there, but not really. Sometimes she's falling, falling . . . Sometimes I'm falling with her. And when I wake up I can hear Lucy crying or Tom. Or me.' Blindly he burrowed against her, questing for comfort.

Mel held him against her breasts, rocking back and forth. She cupped her hand over his skull as though he were newborn, soft against her palm, and her tears fell onto his hair. He was too young to have to bear this burden, but who else could bear it for him?

They were sitting like that when Lucy and Gordon arrived. 'How is she?' Mel asked, already knowing the answer.

'The same,' Gordon said. 'Just the same.'

Lucy dropped her bag. She looked at her little brother and her forehead creased as she tried not to break down in front of him. Distractedly, she ran her fingers through her long loose hair.

It was a gesture Mel had seen a hundred times. Joanne had always shared her children, as she had shared so much else, leaving Mel a legacy of memories associated with them: Lucy in her first long dress, going to the Prom, Tom taking first place for his clarinet-playing in the State musical competitions, the tears and histrionics when Carter Longstrom dumped fourteen-year-old Lucy, Tom falling out of a tree in the backyard, mealtimes and picnics and trips to the ocean and pick-up games of baseball.

Gordon leaned over the back of the sofa and put his hand on Mel's shoulder. 'We're so lucky to have you,' he said. Gently he touched his son's head.

327

Mel wiped her eyes with her free hand. 'I'm the one who's lucky.'

'We've always thought of you as family, you know that,' Lucy said suddenly, talking in disconnected sentences, the way they all were at the moment, twining memories of the past into words of the present. 'Christmas, Thanksgiving, birthdays, tobogganing on Hammer Hill. All those picnics in the summer.' Her shoulders lifted in a sob and she turned away. 'I better get down to the hospital and take over from Tom. You coming with me, Jamie?'

Jamie hesitated. Then he stood up and squared his shoulders. 'OK.'

Lucy took his hand and moved towards the door. 'We'll see you later, Dad.'

'Sure, honey.'

At the door, Lucy hesitated, turned back, stood with bowed shoulders, staring at the floor. 'I hate this, Dad.'

'We all do, sweetheart.' Gordon went over and put his arms around her and Jamie.

'Oh Dad . . .' Lucy leaned into his shoulder. 'Oh, God, this is so terrible. Mom lying there, like she doesn't exist any more. I can't bear it.'

'It's OK, hon.' He smoothed her hair, kissed her ear. 'It'll be fine. It'll all come right in the end.' The ritual words of childhood, a magic incantation left over from the days when children believe their parents to be omnipotent.

'Dad . . .'

'Women like your Mom don't give up easily. She'll be back with us before we know it and then we'll all miss the peace and quiet.'

'Da-ad . . .' But Lucy was half-smiling now, wanting to believe him, longing to be convinced. Jamie said nothing.

His face was set. He knows, Mel thought. He's prepared for the worst.

'She may not be the mom we're used to,' Gordon said. 'But she'll be back, one way or the other.' He held his daughter at arm's length, his hands on her shoulders. 'Apart from anything else, we're coming up to party season, and you know how much your mom loves a party.'

'I so much want to believe you.' Lucy planted a kiss on her father's cheek and pulled open the front door, letting in a swirl of cold air.

'You better.' It was the voice dads used to ward off the demons and Mel could see that even Lucy was half convinced.

'See you,' she said, then she and Jamie were gone, slamming the door behind them.

Gordon sighed. 'When she was little and fell over, scraped her knee or hurt her finger, she'd come running to me and I'd blow on the sore place, tell her it was magic and it was cured. Darnedest thing was that ninety per cent of the time, it worked.' He sat down again. 'My kids are everything to me,' he said simply. 'They're my whole life.'

'You're lucky to have such a good relationship with them.' Mel could see little resemblance in this tired, sad man to the demon that Joanne had so often painted.

'Joanne is a generous woman. That's why she moved here after the divorce, so that they wouldn't be too far away from me. I doubt if she's ever said a bad word about me to them.' He turned and looked directly at Mel. 'She probably saved it all for you.'

'Well . . .'

'It's OK, Mel. I can imagine. I know what she's like in full flight.'

They sat in silence for a while. 'Joanne always wanted

329

to go to New Zealand,' Mel said as another unconnected thought rose to the surface. 'I was thinking that maybe I could go with her when . . . if . . .'

'There's no reason why she shouldn't have gone long ago.'

'Except money.'

'Money?' He raised his eyebrows.

'The bookshop doesn't exactly lose money, but there's not a lot left over by the time she's covered the overheads. She can't afford the flight.'

'Baloney.'

'What do you mean?'

Gordon picked up his coffee cup. 'I've lost count of the number of times I've offered to buy her a ticket to Auckland.'

'Oh?'

'I'm not short of money, Melissa,' he said. 'And I've got all the material comforts I need. The most important people in my life are the three children and – whether she likes it or not – Joanne. Why wouldn't I want her to do the things she'd like to do?'

'Perhaps she didn't want to be beholden.'

He lowered his head and glanced at her from under his eyebrows. 'Truth is, she's afraid to travel on her own.'

'*Joanne* is? I don't believe it.'

'She's afraid of a lot of things.'

'Spiders I knew about,' Mel said.

'Life,' Gordon said succinctly.

'But she's always telling me to grab life by the balls, get out and live, that sort of thing.'

He smiled tiredly. 'And no doubt told you any number of times that she was going to sell up the bookshop, take French lessons, trek across Africa, learn to play the saxophone.'

330

'Yes . . .'

'How many of them did she ever do?'

'Not many.' Mel thought about it. 'None, actually.'

'Joanne always thinks there's a more perfect life somewhere over the rainbow. Nothing's ever quite good enough but she never wants to go for the dreams, in case they turn sour on her.'

'The bookshop was a dream she went for.'

'Buying the bookshop was the biggest decision she ever took, but she was terrified it would fall apart in her hands. In the end, she only went ahead because I said I would underwrite it for her.' He gave her a quizzical look. 'I bet you didn't know that either.'

Mel made a movement of the head which could have been a nod. But in fact, no, she had not known.

He leaned back against the arm of the sofa. 'Oh God, Mel, when I think of the way I've wasted my life. All these years with my kids lost because of a single moment of madness, chasing off with some bimbo from the office. God knows what possessed me. I knew the day I left that it was a terrible mistake, that the one I really loved was Joanne.'

'She was coming round to realizing that,' Mel said, thinking, I know all about mistakes. 'Maybe she even felt the same way, though she'd never admit it directly.'

Gordon wiped his hands over his face. 'Jesus. We make these stupid, spur-of-the-moment, life-changing decisions without really thinking them through, and then we suddenly discover the value of what we've lost, and by then it's too late. It's impossible to get it back.'

'Difficult, maybe. But not always impossible.'

He smiled and briefly put his hand over hers. 'Guess I'd better get along to Joanne's place and make sure there's something for Tom to eat when he gets back from the hospital.'

At the front door, he patted her shoulder. 'She'll be back with us soon,' he said. 'I know she will. The same old feisty Joanne, bossing us about, telling us how to run our lives while making a mess of her own.' He suddenly looked uncertain. 'She *will* be back, won't she?'

Mel nodded at him. 'Of course she will.'

The telephone bleeped and she ran to answer it, while Gordon still hovered in the open doorway. 'Hello?'

'Mel! It's Lucy! Oh Mel, guess *what!*'

'What?'

'It's Mom . . . she woke up!'

'That's . . . oh heavens, that's *wonderful*! That's just so . . .'

Jamie pulled the phone from his sister. 'Mom woke up. Just like that. She said hello, Jamie.' His voice swooped like a swallow, bubbly with joy. 'She asked me what I was reading.'

'Hang on, honey. You can tell your dad all about it.' Mel handed the receiver to Gordon, who had come back into the room and was now standing beside her. The air inside her chest seemed to have expanded to such an extent that she feared she might explode. Joanne awake, alive? It was almost too much to take in.

'Oh my . . .' Gordon said, his eyes shining as he listened to his children. A tear rolled down his cheek and he brushed at it. 'Did she really? Isn't that typical of . . . Yes, I'm absolutely . . . I'll come right over . . . Yes, give her a kiss from me, sweetheart, I'm on my way.'

He put down the telephone and drew a deep breath. 'Oh, God, Mel,' he said. He steadied himself against the back of the living-room sofa. 'I've been putting a brave face on things for the sake of the kids, but all this time, I didn't really . . . I honestly feared the worst.'

'I did too.' Mel seized his hand. 'I can't believe it.'

'Lucy said she and Jamie were sitting there, either side of the bed, talking about some girl in Lucy's class, Suzie something or other, and Joanne suddenly opened her eyes and said she'd never liked Suzie's mom, and then asked Jamie what he was reading.'

The two of them looked at each other, smiles splitting their faces. 'I'm off to the hospital – come with me,' Gordon said.

'No. It's a time for family.'

'You *are* family, you know that.'

'I'll go in later.' She pressed her hands to her mouth. 'Oh Gordon, I'm so happy.'

'Me too.'

When he had gone, Mel walked through the house, picking things up, setting them down again. She looked at the phone, needing to share her joy with someone. She called Ben's number, but there was no answer. As she replaced the handset, she heard a car pull up in front of the house and someone running up the path, leaping the wooden steps onto the porch, rapping at the door using the heavy brass knocker, over and over until she opened the door.

'Joanne's OK!' It was Ben.

'I know, I know!'

'I dropped in at the hospital to check up how things were going,' Ben said, coming inside and shutting the door behind him. 'They told me she'd just, like fifteen minutes ago, come out of the coma.'

'It's marvellous!' Mel hugged him. 'Miraculous!' She sobered suddenly. 'Is it going to last?'

'Who can say, Mel. But it has to be a good sign, doesn't it? Which is why I brought some champagne.' He waved a bottle at her.

'It'll be all fizzed up if you shake it around like that.'

'Who cares!'

Mel laughed, whirled around the room, wanting to jump, to leap, to fly, feeling as though she had been given back the world.

In the kitchen, Ben opened the bottle over the sink while Mel held two flutes under the neck, managing to catch about half the contents.

'To Joanne,' Ben said, taking one of the glasses from her. 'To . . . I don't know . . . life and love and . . . happiness.'

'I'll drink to that.' Mel raised her glass to her mouth. 'Oh, Ben, I can't really believe she's woken up at last.'

'It's only a first step,' he said, suddenly cautious.

'I know. There's all sorts of stuff still to go through. Tests, prognoses, all that. I know we're not out of the woods yet. But all the same . . .' She held out her glass for more champagne. 'She's been unconscious for so long that it's worth celebrating.'

Ben pressed the switch on the player Mel kept on one of the counters. Something jazzy filled the kitchen and he pranced around the table, snapping his fingers, his hips undulating. 'Yeah, *man*!' he growled, guttural as Mick Jagger. 'Go, baby, *go*!' while Mel leaned against the counter top, laughing. She had never seen this side of him, never even suspected that he could be so light-hearted.

The music changed to something slow and sweet and he strummed a few bars on an air guitar, then came over to Mel. He took her champagne out of her hand, set it down on the table and put his arms around her. Together they swayed in time to the music. 'I feel so darn good,' he said. 'So . . . what's the word I want?'

'Unreal?'

'That'll do.'

His hand was on the small of her back, pressing her against him. She laid her head on his shoulder, smelling his sweat, and closed her eyes. 'Mmmm,' she said.

He held her away from him. 'Sometimes in this sorry life, things do actually come good, don't they?'

'Sometimes. Maybe.' Mel still could not entirely believe it.

Lightly he kissed the tip of her nose. 'Hold the thought.'

CHAPTER TWENTY-THREE

Mel read aloud two more chapters of *Great Expectations*. Sometimes, in the gritty gray hours at the heart of the night, Pip and Miss Havisham and Estella seemed to have more reality than she herself did. Sometimes it seemed as if there had never been anywhere else but the four peach-colored walls of this hospital room, filled with flowers Joanne could not see, books and magazines she had not read. There was a magnum of champagne standing on a table under the slatted blinds of the window, an act of faith, now that the hopelessness had fallen upon them once more.

Mel came back from one of the occasional breaks she allowed herself during the harsh span of time between midnight and dawn, to find Beverly frowning as she marked something down on Joanne's notes. 'She's not doing so good,' the nurse said. 'Pulse rate's way down.' She looked worried.

'What does the doctor say?'

'They're thinking of operating again, take out some of the fluid, relieve the pressure.' She flipped the watch on the front of her shirt, squinted down at it. 'I'll be back soon as I can.'

Mel pressed her fingers against her temples. 'But you

told us she was holding her own.'

'She was, honey. Just took a bit of a downturn this morning.'

'Is she going to be all right?' Joanne lay quiet on the bed, her face smooth and expressionless, all emotion wiped away.

Beverly looked at her. 'Gotta have faith, Mel,' she said, her voice gentle.

It seemed unbelievable that only two days ago Joanne had roused herself, spoken to her children, made a feeble joke. By the time Mel and Ben, merry with champagne, had driven to the hospital, it was to be told that she had relapsed. She had remained in a coma ever since. 'Just closed her eyes,' Gordon had said, helplessly, 'and never opened them again. The kids were devastated. All of us were.'

'I so wish I'd been there when she woke up.'

'I know.' Gordon had rubbed wearily at the stubble on his chin. 'At least Lucy and Jamie got to speak to her. We'll just have to go on hoping it'll happen again, and for longer next time.'

Mel pulled the chair up to the bed, sat down, took hold of her friend's hand. The shaven side of Joanne's head glinted a little: leaning closer, Mel could see the hair beginning to grow back in.

'Joanne!' she said urgently, squeezing the fingers so tightly that they cracked. 'Joanne, wake up! Come back!' But, as usual, there was no response from the still figure on the bed, nothing but the faint bleeping of the monitor and the occasional liquid belch from the bottle attached to an IV pole on the other side of the bed.

Sometimes Mel felt it would be easier to give up, to acknowledge defeat and just let Joanne float away. But that would be like a second betrayal. Wearily she reached

337

for the book she had left on the nightstand and opened it at the bookmark advertising Mayfield's Bookstore. '*Great Expectations*,' she said. 'Remember we'd got to the bit where Mr Jaggers arrives to inform lovely Joe Gargery – talking of which, Gargery the beagle is looking so damn sad these days that Jamie can't stand it, so do please make an effort to come back to us again, will you, for his sake, if not ours? Anyway, Mr Jaggers explains that Pip has great expectations and tries to compensate Joe for the loss of his apprentice.' She smoothed the pages down with one hand and began to read.

' "*Pip is that hearty welcome,*" *said Joe,* "*to go free with his services, to honour and fortun', as no words can tell him. But if you think as Money can make compensation to me for the loss of the little child . . .*" ' For a moment Mel could not speak. ' " – *the little child what come to the forge – and ever the best of friends!*" ' she said with difficulty. She laid the book on the bed. 'Ever the best of friends, eh, Jo?' she said softly.

'Bes' of frens . . .' The voice was hoarse and weak, but the words were unmistakable.

'Joanne!' Mel was instantly alert.

The woman in the bed cleared her throat with a visible effort. Her head was turned on the pillow and her eyes were open, staring at Mel.

'You . . . you *spoke.*' Mel was trembling, on the verge of tears which had nothing to do with sorrow, flooded with an upsurge of emotion so profound that she could scarcely contain it. Giving birth must be pretty close to this almost orgasmic sense of triumph and relief. 'You're back again . . .'

Gently she took hold of the hand which lay palm upward on the cover. Where the dark crusted scabs were beginning to heal, the skin was rough, ridged with scar tissue. Squeezing the fingers, she felt pressure in response.

Joanne's pale face crinkled infinitesimally in what was recognizably an attempt at a smile. Her tongue moved slowly over her cracked lips and Mel reached for the plastic tub of lanolin on the nightstand and smoothed some around her friend's mouth.

'Wha's go'n' on?'

'You're in the hospital, darling.'

Lines of incomprehension gathered between Joanne's brows. 'My kids . . .'

'They're OK, Jo. Missing you like crazy. Lucy's looking gorgeous, Jamie's grown at least an inch, Tom's got a new girlfriend. But it's no fun without you there – for any of us.'

Joanne's hand moved faintly on the bed cover. 'Hos . . . pit'l?' Her forehead creased again.

'Yes.'

'Why?'

'Do you remember coming up to the lake with me?' Mel asked.

A faint nod.

'You had a fall,' Mel said. She glanced at the dark square of the window. It was lighter now, dawn was approaching. Already she could see the palest flush of rose above the roofs of the town, and the outline of the white spire of the Episcopalian church. First light. The hour when the body's defenses are at their lowest ebb. The hour at which people die.

As though she were recounting the plot of a film, she went through the sequence of events which had led from the falls, from blue sky and birdsong and the deep murmur of the leaves to the slippery grass at the edge of the cliff and a stain of yellow on the black stones below, Ben Andersen's efficient ministrations, the helicopter swinging up into the sky.

339

'Ever the best of friends,' Joanne said, very clearly.

Mel smiled at the pale face on the pillow. 'Oh, Joanne, I can't tell you how . . . I just can't begin to . . .' She sniffed. 'Wot larks, eh?'

'Wot larks,' echoed Joanne faintly.

Her hand tightened on Mel's fingers and relaxed. Then, while Mel continued to smile at her, unaware, she went away. Gently, like a swimmer striking out from the shore, heading for deeper waters, pushing further and further towards a greater silence, she moved away until finally she was out of sight.

Ben sat nursing a mug of coffee. Last night, as most nights, he had fallen asleep on the sofa and woken to a chilly room, gray ashes, dawn light seeping through the drapes. Right now, that was the way it went. No point going to bed. He'd made himself coffee, thinking that next week was his birthday. He guessed he'd spend it alone this year. Last year, he was still in New York. Lisa had taken him out to dinner and when they'd gotten back to the apartment, opened the door and snapped on the lights, there'd been thirty or forty people in the living room, all yelling 'Surprise!' He'd never seen most of them in his life.

He heard a car turn in off the road and crunch up the short drive, circle the apple tree, pull up at the door. He frowned. Kind of early for visitors. Getting up, he drew back the drapes and saw Mel standing on the porch, holding the collar of a navy blue topcoat close under her chin.

He ran to the door, tugged it open. 'Has she woken up again?'

'Ben.' She bent her head but not before he had seen the way her mouth was distorted by grief. She dropped her shoulders, trying for self-control. 'I wanted to tell you first because you . . . without you . . . you were there when . . .'

'Come in,' he said quietly.

Mel covered her face with her hand and squeezed her eyes shut. 'Oh, Ben . . .' It was a moan of pain. 'She died. She *died*.'

'When?'

'Two hours ago. Two hours . . .' She looked surprised, though whether because it seemed so short or so long a time ago, he couldn't tell.

'I'm *so* sorry, Mel.'

'She . . .' Mel pressed the backs of her hands against her eyes, looking utterly lost. 'She wasn't supposed to die.' She shook her head. 'My best friend,' she said, in a high childlike voice. 'And she's dead.'

'Come inside,' he said again. When she stayed where she was, he put an arm around her shoulders. 'Come on, Mel.' He guided her into the house.

'I just wanted to come and tell you.' Vaguely she looked about her. 'It's too early. I hope you don't mind.'

'Of course not, I was up, anyway.' He took her hand and led her into the sitting room. 'What happened? I thought she was doing OK.'

Mel sat down and began to pick at the material of her coat. 'One moment she was there in the room with me,' she said, sounding bewildered. 'The next she was . . . she was so *not* there.' She gave a small sob, a wet intake of breath, and then was silent. Under her coat she wore a blue cambric shirt; he could see a gold chain, the hollow at the base of her neck. 'I was sitting by her bed, and suddenly she spoke to me.' Mel's shoulders shook. 'And then she looked at me, and . . . and she went. I watched her, Ben, I thought she was going to talk some more and instead she . . . she died right there in front of me.'

341

He put his hands on her arms and gathered her against his chest. 'Mel, Mel . . .'

'I sat there,' she said, leaning back so she could look at him. 'I sat there, Ben, smiling at her, and all the time she was dying.'

'That could be a good way to go,' he said. He remembered a Chinese climber on Annapurna who had begun hallucinating as they huddled in their tents during a blizzard. They'd given him what oxygen they could spare but the cerebral edema was too far advanced. They all knew his chances of surviving the night were minimal, that there was nothing any of them could do. He would never forget the expression on the man's face as he waited for death among strangers. 'Remember that the last thing she saw was her best friend's face. Someone she loved.'

Mel stared at him. The whites of her eyes were the color of paper. The fatigue of the past few days was imprinted on her face. 'I hadn't thought of that.'

'Smiling,' he said. 'That's good.'

They sat quietly for a while, not speaking, nursing their separate griefs. She said simply, 'I loved her.' She gave a sad little smile. 'Far more than I ever loved my husband. She was . . . she was all the family I had.'

He made an inarticulate soothing sound.

Her hand plucked restlessly at the navy blue wool. 'At the beginning, you think it's all going to be straightforward. You think you can see the milestones ahead, and all you have to do is reach them, go past, on to the next one.' She shook her head again. 'It's not a bit like that. When you're young, you don't make allowances for the . . . the losses.'

'If you're lucky, you don't have to.'

'I'll never be able to go up to the lake again,' she said. 'Not after what's happened. First Lisa. Now Joanne.'

He put his hand over her restless fingers. 'That's why I was up at our place when . . . when Joanne fell. I needed to go back to where Lisa lost the baby. After she . . .' He gripped his coffee mug hard enough for the bones to shine through the skin of his knuckles. Below the ring finger of his left hand was a ragged half-healed scar, where he had caught the pad of flesh with a chisel. 'I had to. It'll be the same for you.'

'Maybe.'

He wanted to hug her, to comfort her, but she sat stiffly against his arm. Last time he had touched her, he'd been able – or so he hoped – to offer her some solace. She was trembling. The warmth of her body pressed into the sleeve of his sweatshirt. She smelled of vanilla and salt and ironed cotton.

She sniffed back tears, tried to wipe her face but he leaned in close, gently stubbed his thumb into the tears pooling below her dark blue eyes. 'Cry, Mel. Sometimes that's all there is.'

'I'm not just crying for myself,' she said, her voice unsteady. 'I'm crying for all of us. For Joanne. For her children. Lisa. Your baby.' She closed her eyes. 'For all the lost babies.'

She looked so defenseless. He felt a profound need to console and comfort her. When he pulled her closer, she shifted against him. He lifted her hand to his mouth. 'Mel,' he said. Her fingers were cold against his lips. 'Mel.'

He looked down at her, tucked into the curve of his shoulder. Her mouth was slightly open. He could feel the heat from her body, sense rather than see the beat of her heart beneath her shirt. Her hands were long and slender, the nails short-clipped and unpainted. She wore no wedding band, only the sapphire.

343

When she lifted her face and looked at him, a collage of images rolled through his mind: Mel leaning against a sunlit rock, her gleaming body as she played in the lake with Joanne, her mouth by candlelight, her smile, the vanilla smell of her. There'd been a party, somewhere or other, he'd been standing by a bookcase, thinking about a climb he'd done in Switzerland, remembering how his foot had slipped, his sudden realization that he'd made a mistake, that he might be about to die. He'd faced death many times on the mountains, knew that it was an inextricable part of climbing, that however careful you were, each step you took could be your last, but that didn't make those narrow escapes any the less heart-stopping. And he'd looked up to see Mel smiling at him, noticed her almost-navy eyes, thick white-gold hair, remembered that he'd seen her up at the lake in summers past, standing by the edge of the water, alone.

Unsurprised, he recognized that this moment had been building for a long time. She needed comfort and he sensed that he was the only one who could offer it. Putting his hand beneath her chin, he tilted her head. For a fraction of time, her lips parted, her body moved against him. The space between them was frantic with possibility. 'Mel,' he said.

'I want . . .' Moaning, she twisted her head away. 'I need . . .'

He turned her face up to his and gently kissed her wet eyelids.

Mel was stunned by the strength of feeling which had so suddenly swept over her. She wanted – *needed* – to feel his mouth on hers, to touch his gold-tipped curls. In that blink of time, she envisaged the feel of his skin, the way he would move in her white bedroom, his confidence in removing his clothes, the creak of the mattress as he climbed in beside her. She saw his head alongside her own, knew how fresh he would smell, how young.

Oh *God*. She longed to press onwards, to touch him, taste him, bury her grief in the wonder of their two bodies, drown her sorrow in desire. A dark warmth lingered in her belly. Her face burned. His mouth was on her mouth, his hands on her breast. She closed her eyes, felt his strength reach out to her, his cheek against hers, his searching mouth. Whatever it was he offered her, however temporary it might be, she wanted it. She thought of the white-shirted boy on her honeymoon, beckoning, crossing the bridge, disappearing under an archway to who knew what gardens of felicity.

He raised her hand to his mouth, kissed each knuckle, then turned it over and pressed his lips to her palm. He put his big hands on either side of her face and brought her closer to him. He kissed her, tiny kisses, on her forehead, her eyebrows, her ear, the hollow of her neck. The stubble of his chin rasped against her cheek. One of them moaned and she could not have said which. It was enough to be there with him, insulated for a while from the world and its numbing griefs.

Holding her face with his right hand, he slid his left one under her coat. His fingers were cold and she shivered slightly. His hand touched her breast, stroking the nipple through the lace of her bra, and she turned to look into his eyes, hardening under his touch.

'Ben,' she said. 'I need you.' And then again: 'I *need* you.'

He lifted the shirt over her head. Reaching behind her back, he undid her bra and slid the straps down her arms. Gravely, he looked at her breasts, then put out his hands and held them as though they were something infinitely rare and precious. He bent his head to caress them with his lips.

His tongue moved lightly across her body as she undid the buttons of his shirt. She was unaccustomed and clumsy; it was years since she had undressed a man. Yet how easily the actions of love returned. As she pushed the shirt from his shoulders, he pulled his arms through the sleeves so that his torso was naked. She embraced him, let her breasts graze his chest.

Undoing the zipper on her skirt, he gently tugged it down over her hips while she lifted her body towards him. She helped him out of his jeans, her hand brushing across his back and his hips and his buttocks. His belly was hard and flat, with a line of golden hairs running towards his groin. He pushed her down until she was lying on her back then stretched alongside her, the two of them lying naked, skin touching skin. He put a hand under her back and held her against him. His skin was smooth, almost silky. She spread her hand across his heart and felt the strong beat of it under her fingers.

She knew she ought to say, 'We shouldn't be doing this: you are married to another woman, this is wrong.' Instead, as he kissed her, his mouth moving over her body, across her breasts under her arms, down to her belly, she was filled with a hunger to possess and be possessed. She knew that someone had to be sensible – but why should it be her? Why was sensible supposed to be good? I need him now, she thought. I need him to show me that, however fleetingly, there can be something other than grief. She found herself saying things like 'yes' and 'oh' and 'please'.

Joanne was dead, but she herself was alive. Celebrate that fact, she told herself. Just for once, do not feel guilty.

Last night's wine was on his breath. He put a hand between her thighs and touched the wetness there. Slowly he slid a finger inside her and she felt that any moment now she would explode. When he entered her, she knew a thankfulness so enormous that when she came, rising to meet him, convulsing suddenly, then clasping him, holding him motionless inside her while she twisted around him, she sobbed aloud. Slowly he increased his tempo until he was soaring towards his climax and she felt the heat of him gushing into her body.

Silently she began to weep, tears falling down either side of her face. Yes, she was alive – but Joanne was gone. Joanne would never kiss her children again, or touch a man with love, with desire. Joanne lay still and cold, alone now, for ever.

'Don't cry,' Ben said.

'I can't help it. I'm here with you and she's . . . Only the blink of an eye separates life and death.'

She pulled his head down to her breasts. For years she had not dared to unzip her heart and permit herself to feel an emotion such as love, for love was dangerous. Love, if you allowed it to, could kill. Her marriage had offered her a niggardly sense of warmth but in the generosity of Ben's lovemaking, the rich scents of his body, she was aware of an overpowering sense of fulfilment.

She drove to the dam above the town. Nobody else was there on this cold leaden morning. The water was still, flat. Trees were reflected in the surface of the water, and gray rocks, perfect mirror images, smooth as paint on the reflected gray sky. They used to come here in vacation time, she and Joanne and the three children. Picnics. Barbecues. Kids splashing around, swimming, playing frisbee. Two women, three children. A family. Happy.

'You've got the husband, I've got the kids,' Joanne sometimes said, and Mel would think: I know which I'd rather have.

She remembered Eric newly dead, herself weeping, saying, 'Eric and I did everything together . . .'

And Joanne's matter-of-fact voice. 'Not true, sweetie. It's *me* you do things with. Always has been. Me, not Eric.'

Not Eric. Never Eric.

Her skin still held the aromas of lovemaking. It was less than an hour since she had left Ben's side but already she longed for him again, the scent of his hair, the long length of him beside her, the glint of golden stubble along his jaw. I want to touch, taste, smell, feel him all over again, and then again, she thought, breathless, rubbing her hands together against the cold. I want to *drown* in him.

Once she had had dreams. The world had been a place full of possibilities. All she had needed to do was reach out and catch hold of them. Joanne was more like me than I realized, she thought. For all her brave words, she was just as afraid of taking chances. Of making choices.

She was the friend of my heart, Mel thought, and now she lies on a shelf in the funeral home, bruised and damaged. I shall never see her wide smile again, hear her raucous laughter, her tuneless singing, watch her dancing to the radio with a glass of wine in her hand, see her tender with her children. Time would soften the grief but could never heal it.

A few autumnal leaves drifted across the heavy sky. A fish leaped, ruffling the surface of the dam. The water took minutes to return to its former flat stillness.

CHAPTER TWENTY-FOUR

What do you wear to your best friend's funeral? Your beloved fifty-year-old friend who liked to say that she was going to live to be a hundred if it killed her. The friend you would miss for the rest of your life. And another question: was it seemly to go to your best friend's funeral with a lover's caresses still warm on your body, your mouth swollen from his kisses? Smiling slightly, Mel rather thought that, given this particular friend, it was.

Rummaging through the clothes hanging in her closet, Mel recalled another funeral, Cath Delaney, dead of cancer long before her time, and Joanne defiant in a crimson leather coat with matching knee-high boots, a long pink scarf wound round her neck.

'You scarlet woman, you,' Mel had whispered at one point, as the mourners shuffled out of the church to stand round the rectangle dug in the soil. 'Sarah Mahoney's just noticed you and looks like she's about to pass out.'

'She's just jealous,' said Joanne. 'No-one's gonna wear red at *her* funeral. No-one's even gonna *come* to her funeral, miserable old witch. Anyway, black doesn't do a thing for me. I like bright colors.'

Mel found a silk scarf in delicate shades of mauve and purple. She let it slip through her fingers: she had last worn it when she and Joanne had gone to Boston.

'We had fun, didn't we?' she whispered, crushing the silk in her hand. 'Such fun.'

Life with Joanne had been a ball. There was always laughter when she was around, always the sense of being at a party. There were so many memories, indelibly part of the fabric of the life Mel had fashioned for herself. And now the ball was over.

Overcome, Mel wrapped her arms around her chest. She had not felt such devastating grief since her first arrival in Butterfield; she had hoped never to feel it again. 'Joanne,' she murmured. From the start, theirs had been a sustaining relationship, based on mutual support and affection. How would she survive without it?

From her closet she took out a skirt of lavender wool and a matching linen shirt. On the shelf above it sat the hatbox of watered lilac silk, edged with purple leather. She pulled it forward, took off the lid, lifted out the hat inside. The memory of violets drifted up from the dried bunch lying in the tissue paper.

Around her neck she hung the amethyst necklace which had been her mother's, and a gold chain with the heart-shaped locket which had been a gift from Joanne two years ago. Outside, clouds full of rain hung low on the hills, heavy as concrete. The trees shook in the wind. Last week, before Joanne died, it had seemed as though they were still at the end of the summer. Now, a cold autumn was upon them, with winter already hovering. Definitely not the weather for a straw hat. Mel dabbed her make-up on her face, found a lipstick and outlined her pale mouth, scrabbled in her drawers for a pair of sunglasses to hide her eyes.

She got into the car, switched it on and set the heater working. She laid her coat on the passenger seat. About to back out of the drive, she hesitated, pulled on the hand-brake, shook her head.

'*Wear it at my funeral . . .*' Joanne's voice came back to her, and her smile. Mel got out of the car, went back into her house and ran upstairs to her bedroom. Tears stung her eyes as she picked up the beautiful lilac and purple hatbox and took it out to the car.

As she parked beside the neat stone walls which bounded the graveyard, freezing rain blew into her face, stung her eyes, drenched the black slate headstones. A small flag beside a headstone snapped and cracked; leaves whirled in the sudden gusts of cold air blowing beneath the trees. Black coats, black cars grim under wet black branches, black umbrellas, a biting wind. Mel shivered. Joanne had hated the cold. She should have been laid to rest on a day of sunshine, with blue skies above and singing birds swooping through the air.

Mel pulled her coat closer round her body, wrapping the pain inside herself. She felt empty of all emotion but grief. That a simple hike through the woods should have ended in this bleak moment still seemed in-comprehensible. She walked between the graves to join Joanne's family. Lucy's hand touched hers, and she held it tightly as the girl began to sob. She still had not found an opportunity to spill out the corroding guilt she felt. On her other side, Gordon Mayfield took her arm while Tom stood with his arm around his sister, his hand on Mel's shoulder. Diminished by his loss, Jamie leaned against her, forlorn.

Beyond the graveyard, traffic was flowing along Main Street. As they began to lower the casket into the ground, the cars slowed down to watch. Mel wondered if any of them knew whose burial this was, whether they paused out of respect, or merely from curiosity. A red truck drifted by, tires hissing on the blacktop, a young guy at the wheel in a Grateful Dead T-shirt, lighting a cigarette as he stared out of the window. What did he see? What did he feel? Did he come anywhere near to appreciating the fact that this coffin contained fifty years of life and vitality, laughter and experience?

A fierce gust of rain battered Mel's face and she blinked, stepping back a little. Gordon's hand tightened on her arm, as though he was afraid she might collapse. On the other side of the grave, she saw Ben watching her from the back of the crowd, the strain of the past few weeks evident in the new lines around his mouth and under his eyes. The boyishness had gone from his face, along with something which could have been naivety, might have been innocence. She remembered him making love to her that morning, learning her with his mouth as she lay in the cradle of his arms, kissing his smooth skin. Could people tell that they were lovers? That neither of them had slept last night or the night before, that they were consumed by each other?

We are two hurt people, she thought, who have been fortunate enough to find and help one another. We are blessed. She smiled briefly at him. Love had come so unexpectedly that she scarcely recognized it. Now, she thought, I love you for so many reasons. Because you listen to what I'm saying. Because you put your head on one side and watch my mouth moving as though you can actually see the words emerging. Because when your eyes rest on my face, they are no longer remote. But mostly because when you touch me, I am not me, but someone made of fire and air, a creature of the elements. Because you give me back the Mel I once was.

What kind of a woman was she, to be thinking such thoughts as they lowered the coffin of her dearest friend into the unyielding earth? Joanne would have loved it. 'You heartless bitch!' she would have said, her eyes crinkled with laughter. 'Your best friend's dead and you're *happy*?'

As the final words were spoken, people began to drift away to their cars. Mel stood at the graveside for a moment, looking down at the earth-spattered wood, remembering once again the plunge from the trail, the smudge of yellow lying on the stones.

Goodbye, Joanne. My friend. My strength. My shield.

She turned and walked blindly away.

The room was crowded. It seemed as though half the town had come to say goodbye to the Bookstore Lady. Chairs had been set in a semicircle in front of Joanne's family, who sat together, holding hands.

'Joanne would have been delighted to know that she was held in such affection,' Gordon told them. His face was gray, rutted with care and weariness. 'She often said to me that there was nothing she wanted more than a full turnout at her funeral.' He gave a crooked grin. 'How she would have liked to be here, to check out how many of you showed up.' There was laughter. Lucy scrubbed at her eyes. Gordon spoke for a few moments, shaping for them a younger Joanne whom none of them had known but could easily imagine. Lucy recited a poem by Emily Dickinson, tears blocking her throat as she reached the final stanza; Tom read a piece he had written about his mother when he was in high school. Finally, Jamie stood. Unaccustomedly neat in a tie, a too-big jacket which had once been Tom's, shiny leather shoes, he pushed his glasses back up his nose. 'She's still my mom,' he said. His voice broke. 'And I love her. That's all I want to say.' He sat down again and stared at his lap.

Mel held the hatbox on her knee. When Gordon indicated that it was her turn to speak, she stood up and reached into the box. 'Joanne and I bought this together in Boston, earlier this year,' she said steadily. 'The minute she saw it in the window, Joanne told me I had to buy it, so I did, because, as you all know, she had the most phenomenal powers of persuasion – or do I mean coercion?' Laughter rippled warmly round the room. 'It's not a funeral hat, not a mourning hat. But that doesn't matter.'

She put the hat on her head, settled it there. Tears filled her eyes. 'I'm wearing this for her,' she said. 'And I just hope *you* all like it because *I* was never sure that it suited me, and . . .' She looked up at the ceiling. '. . . whatever you say, Joanne, I'm still not.'

She turned back to the people in front of her. 'I'm going to read a poem which I've always thought summed up Joanne as she would have been if she had lived.' She paused, smiled at the gathering, felt a sheen of tears in her eyes and blinked them away. 'It's called '"Warning."' She cleared her throat, her nose already smarting with tears.

'*When I am an old woman I shall wear purple,*' she read.
'*With a red hat which doesn't go, and doesn't suit me,*
And I shall spend my pension on brandy and summer gloves
And satin sandals, and say we've no money for butter.'

She cleared her throat again as she came to the end:

'But maybe I ought to practise a little now,
So people who know me are not too shocked and
*   surprised*
When suddenly I am old, and start to wear purple.'

She took off the purple hat and held it in both hands. 'She'd been practising for years,' she said, half-smiling. 'That was Joanne Mayfield. That was my friend.'

As she sat down, Gordon Mayfield stood again. 'We want to celebrate Joanne's life,' he said, 'as well as mourn it. She was an exceptional woman, truly a one-off, so if you have other memories of her, please share them with us.'

Someone from the Library Committee began to reminisce about Joanne's commitment to books and reading. One of Lucy's schoolfriends said how welcoming Joanne had always been. Others took their turn. It seemed a measure of the dead woman that most of those present spoke of her with affectionate laughter.

Later, wine was poured, food served. The noise level rose; Tom and some of his high-school friends started strumming guitars and singing softly, the songs of his mother's youth, the Beatles, Joan Baez, Peter, Paul and Mary. She had always liked things she could sing along with: people began to join in the well-remembered words.

Mel wandered around, spoke to friends, murmured. There is nothing you can say, she thought, not at a time like this, and yet we all try so hard, as though words can bring someone back, or soften the blow. She found herself next to Ben, felt his fingers brush hers, looked up at him.

'Mr Mayfield's right,' he said. 'We have to celebrate, as well as mourn. Not just death. Life too.'

'Yes.' She nodded and moved on.

As she passed the entrance, someone slipped into the

room. It took Mel a moment to realize who it was, then the blood rushed to her face.

'Lisa!' she said.

'I had to come.' Lisa put her arms round Mel. 'I only heard about Joanne yesterday. I'm so so sorry. I . . . what is there to say when something like this happens?'

'Nothing,' said Mel, shaking her head. 'There's nothing.'

'She was such a wonderful woman.' Lisa's small face looked strained and tired. Yet, at the same time, there was a new serenity about her, as though she had come to some kind of settlement within herself.

'Which makes the whole thing even worse.'

'Poor Joanne. Poor Mel. You must be totally devastated.'

'I am.'

'I'm so sorry. I should never have taken off like that without getting in touch with you.' Lisa gave Mel another quick hug. 'It all suddenly seemed more than I could handle.'

Mel tried to smile. 'And how is it now?'

'I'm managing.'

'Where are you living?' Mel found it hard to meet Lisa's black eyes. 'What plans do you have?'

'Plans?' Lisa gave a tight smile. 'I've given up on making plans. They always seem to go wrong.'

'And what are you doing at the moment?' Over Lisa's head, Mel saw Ben staring at them, his face grim.

'Teaching art and ceramics. In Montpelier,' Lisa said. 'At a little private school there.' She clutched Mel's arm. 'Please don't tell Ben where I am.'

Ben was standing now, pushing between the chairs, moving towards them. Before Mel could say anything more, he was beside them.

356

Lisa's face paled. 'Hello, Ben.' She did not look up at him.

'I can't believe you're here.' His eyes flicked to Mel's and for a second the corner of his mouth lifted.

'I'm not here for us, for you or me,' Lisa said. 'I'm here for Mel – and Joanne.'

'Lisa . . .' He put out a hand towards her and she stepped back. 'Can we talk?' He looked at Mel and she saw apology in his eyes.

'I'm not ready to discuss anything,' Lisa said.

'All right. OK.' He pulled back, putting space between the two of them. 'Any idea when you will be?'

'Maybe never.' She still did not look at him.

'I see.' Ben took a step closer to Mel. She felt the heat of his arm against her side. 'Should I . . .' He hesitated, looking down at Lisa. 'I'll have your things sent to your father's house.'

'Keep them.' Lisa's hands were gripped tightly together; she still kept her face averted. 'I already took everything I wanted.'

Color rose in his cheeks. He clenched his fists and his expression grew distant, hostile. 'That's fine by me.' He swung away from the two of them. The door opened and then closed behind him.

'Oh God.' Lisa bit her lip.

Mel was furious on Ben's behalf. 'You had no reason to be so . . . so mean, so spiteful,' she said. 'Seems to me you need to move on. Instead of being so angry, try forgiveness instead.'

'It didn't occur to me that he'd be here.'

'Of *course* he would. If it hadn't been for him, Joanne would have died right where she fell.'

'Mrs Sherman?'

Mel swung around. Two men were standing beside her,

357

awkward in shirts and ties, their sport jackets hanging from broad shoulders. 'Yes?'

The smaller of the two shook her hand. 'Jim Trotter. This is Bill Faraday. You won't remember us,' he said, 'but we were part of the emergency team who rescued your friend when she fell.'

'I'm so sorry she didn't make it,' Faraday continued. 'She looked pretty bad at the time, I must say, but you have to keep hoping. Ben Andersen did a terrific job.'

'But then he always does,' said Trotter.

'Thank you for coming,' Mel said. 'I know Mrs Mayfield would have appreciated everything you did for her.'

'We just wanted to tell you . . .' They moved off together.

'I wasn't exactly pleasant to Ben, was I?' Lisa said.

Mel merely raised cold eyebrows.

'I hardly recognize myself any more.' Lisa's eyes filled with tears. 'Ben looked at me as though he hated me.'

'Are you surprised.' Mel turned away from her. Across the room, Gordon Mayfield was chatting to Karen and Wendy, the two assistants from the bookshop, and behind him Jamie was standing alone, lonely and forlorn, tears rolling down his face.

'I better go,' she said. She started to move away, then turned back. Thinking how miserable Lisa looked, how wounded, she touched her arm. 'Good luck.'

The last mourner had left and the room was empty now except for the remains of the wake. 'I'll go now,' Mel said. Since Lisa's appearance and Ben's abrupt departure, she had felt restless and unsettled.

'Thanks, Mel.' Gordon put his arms round her. 'For everything. Not just for today.'

358

Jamie took her hand. 'Wanna come back and eat with us?' he said, looking at his father for assent.

'Yes, do that,' said Gordon. 'We'd like that.'

Mel shook her head. 'Thank you so much. But I'd rather just be by myself tonight.'

'Mom would have been pleased, don't you think?' Tom said. 'She always liked a party.'

'We gave her a fine send-off,' Mel agreed.

'Remember the good things, Mel.' Gordon said.

'I will. I do.' Mel lifted her hand in farewell.

Tired and sorrowful, she went out to the parking lot. There had been too much emotion these past few weeks. Too much soul-searching, too much resurrection of the past. She wanted to be with Ben again. She wanted not to feel anything except whatever it was she felt when she was with him.

When she reached the parking lot, he was waiting for her, leaning against her car, his expression bleak. 'Let's go,' he said.

'Where to?'

'Does it matter?'

'It doesn't matter at all.'

CHAPTER TWENTY-FIVE

When she realized where he was headed, she put a hand on his arm. 'No, Ben,' she protested. 'I'm not ready. There are too many bad memories here.'

'You'll have to face them sometime.'

'We only buried her today.' The horror of it struck her afresh: her generous life-enhancing friend was now no more than a decaying body lying in a wooden box beneath the earth.

Already she was regretting their impulsive departure from Butterfield. *This is not what I am about,* she thought. *I do not do this sort of thing.* But as Ben pulled out to overtake a pulp truck, as the skies darkened over the mountains, she heard Joanne's emphatic voice ringing in her head: *then it's high time you started.*

Ben reached for her hand and held it in his. 'You have to confront your demons,' he said firmly. 'Like that old thing of getting back up on a horse when it's thrown you. The longer you leave it, the harder it becomes.'

'Yes, but—'

'Think of it as therapy – for both of us.'

'Therapy . . .'

'For me, it's not . . . not just about Lisa,' he said.

'Who else?'

360

'My cousin.' Before she could ask what he meant, he had hurried on. 'Remember what you told me when Lisa first left? You said you can't change what happened, you have to let it become part of you.'

'I'm not ready,' she repeated.

'Too bad,' he said. 'We're almost there.'

She sighed, gave a little shrug, a crooked unwilling grin. 'OK.'

They stopped for supplies at the corner store in Hallams Cove, then drove on to Mel's cabin. Stepping out of the car, Mel looked up at the star-studded sky. A sliver of new moon hung above the green-black forest. It had been warm when she was last here: now the cold pure air struck her lungs like a spear.

Ben lit a fire while she sliced onions, grilled a steak, halved tomatoes, cut bread, poured wine into green glasses. He had lighted candles, too, which gave the dark room a soft and intimate glow. Moonlight lay in a thin silver line across water flattened by the cold.

They pushed one of the sofas close to the hearth, and ate in front of the fire. It seemed only a few short days since Mel was last here: she was surprised to realize that it was more than three weeks since Joanne's fall. She recalled the dolphin-feel of Joanne's naked body against hers in the lake, the strength of her arms as they stood on the deck in the moonlight, silk nasturtiums, champagne and laughter. Friendship. Things which would never come again.

Suddenly she broke into sobs.

Ben took her hand. 'What is it, my sweet Mel?'

'I wish . . . *so* much . . .'

'What? That it had never happened?'

'That I could have – have said something to Joanne's

361

family. I couldn't, I couldn't, when they were suffering so much but I so much wanted to apologize. To have their – their forgiveness.'

'What for?'

'It was all my fault, all my fault. If I hadn't made her come with me, she would never have been up here in the first place. She hates – hated hiking and the open air and being out in the country.'

'She was a grown woman,' Ben said. 'Nobody made her do anything she didn't want to. It was her own choice to come up here with you.'

'She wouldn't have come if I hadn't complained about being all on my own, not having a family like she did.'

'No-one could possibly blame you, Mel.'

'Except myself. Ultimately, I have to take responsibility for what happened.'

'Would it have been your fault if she'd had a car crash on the way to your house before you set off up here?'

'I – I don't know.'

'Or if she'd fallen down the stairs on her way out of the house to the car?'

'Perhaps, in a way.'

'Where do consequences begin? Maybe it's really your husband's fault that Joanne's dead, because he bought this place from my mom. Or should we blame Mom, for selling it to him?'

'You're being ridiculous.' She twisted the sapphire ring on her finger.

'No more than you are, for trying to claim responsibility for something you didn't do.' He tilted her face up to his. 'It's not a blame thing. You weren't at fault.'

'I am in my heart.'

'No.' He kissed the side of her neck, just below her ear.

'Remember what she wrote you, when your husband died?'

'*Dust will continue to gather in corners. Moons will wax and wane. Flowers will bloom and fade. Rivers will go on running to the sea,*' Mel quoted softly.

'That's right,' said Ben. 'And over the past weeks I've realized how true that is. For both of us. I'm an expert in this, believe me. I've blamed myself for everything that ever went wrong, for as far back as I can remember. But life carries on and instead of useless regrets, we have to learn to take the people we've lost with us into the future.'

He slipped off his shoes and socks and lay back against the cushions, holding his feet towards the flames. Two toes on his left foot were missing. Mel reached forward and caressed his foot with her hand, running her fingers along the ridged space where once there had been toes and now there was nothing. 'Frostbite,' he said, anticipating her question.

'When?'

'Three years ago.'

'Where?'

'In the Himalayas.'

'Does it hurt?'

'Sometimes. Not very often.'

She curled her fingers round his thumb, like a baby. 'I read a book recently about the 1996 Everest expedition. Is that what it was like in Alaska: the freezing cold, the fierce winds, the altitude sickness?'

'Pretty much.' He shifted so that he was sitting right up close to her. He held his glass up to the flames. 'Right now, I'm more interested in being here with you.'

She started laughing. 'Remember when you came out above Fitch's Gulley and found me sitting there?'

'Sure do.'

'You looked so mad.'

'Not mad, more astonished.'

'That a little old lady like me could have made it all the way up there?'

'No. Nothing like that.'

'It certainly looked like it to me.'

'What it was . . .' He smiled to himself. 'I hadn't realized until then how beautiful you were. Your hair in the sunshine . . .' His big hand covered the top of her head. 'In fairy tales, the princess always has hair like spun gold. Until I saw you that day, I never knew what it meant.'

Her stomach tightened. Little pulses, sharp as electricity, sparked across her skin. 'Oh Ben . . .'

'I saw you,' he said. 'That afternoon, you and Joanne in the water.'

'I guessed there was someone in the house.' With an ache in her heart she recalled that carefree rainbow-glittering moment.

He put a hand over her breast. 'When I saw you then, I thought how beautiful you were.'

'Do you still?'

'Now, I think you are more than beautiful.'

He kissed her and she tasted the wine on his tongue. Her throat contracted. This moment will stay with me for the rest of my life, she thought. The warmth of his palm, the shadows on his face, candlelight, moonlight, firelight, like sips of champagne from someone else's glass.

Except that this time, the glass was her own, even though the champagne was not.

She turned her mouth into his, desire clawing at her, insistent. She put her hands on his back, felt the knobs of his spine under his shirt, the shape of his shoulder blades.

She unbuttoned his shirt, watched the play of light and shadow on his torso, touched his ribs one by one, felt the solid beat of his heart. 'Ben . . . Ben,' she said. Under her hand his skin was cool, satiny. She pressed her lips to his belly, closed her eyes, drew the good scent of him into herself.

His hand burrowed into her hair. She could feel the heat between his thighs, feel the movement of his body. The years of desire repressed, of feelings denied, could never be regained or relived. She had thrown them away, accepted second best, knowingly exchanged the fires of her long-lost lover for the cold kisses of her husband. She had squandered her life. 'Make love to me,' she said fiercely, gripped by passion, scarcely recognizing her own voice. 'Love me.'

'I do.' He undid the buttons on her lavender jacket, lifted the cream silk shell over her head. Firelight warmed her naked breasts as he knelt between her legs. He moved his hands up her body, lingered on her hips, her breasts, her shoulders. He bent his head and kissed the corn-silk hair between her thighs. 'Beautiful beautiful Mel,' he murmured.

She grabbed his hair, pressed him closer to her body. Even as she lifted her hips to him, felt the urgent rush as he came into her, tears squeezed between her eyelids. 'Yes,' she gasped, arching as he held her, looked down at her, his mouth swollen. 'Oh yes.'

They got up late the next morning, having lingered for hours over each other's bodies, having strolled, sprinted, galloped, through each other's physical territories with as much certainty as if they had created them.

'We're going for a hike this morning,' Ben said, cutting bread, making toast for Mel, while she poured orange juice from a carton and pushed down the plunger of the coffee pot.

'Are you telling, or asking?'

'Let me rephrase that.' He paused, looked across the lake at the far mountains. 'I'm going for a hike this morning. Do you want to come along?'

'Yes. But I told you: I'll never be able to walk here again.'

'Mel.' He put his arms around her and held her close.

She shook her head. 'I can't. Not after what happened.'

'It happened here to both of us.' His face was suddenly sad. 'You must. *We* must.'

'More therapy?'

'Yes.' He kissed her fiercely. 'But this isn't. Nor this. Nor this.'

'What is this, then?' She was moist and boneless, saturated with desire.

'This is love.'

The word spun into her consciousness. Light as a bubble, heavier than concrete. It *felt* like love. She put her fingers over his mouth.

'It is,' he insisted. 'You know it is.'

She smiled at him, briefly moved her head from side to side.

'Say you love me,' he demanded.

She could imagine him as a child, eager, impetuous, demanding what he wanted and getting it. A child, sixteen years younger than she was. Child. Mother. Young. Old. She thought wearily: with all the love in the world, the years between us cannot be expunged. I have lived too much longer than he has, I started too much earlier, this relationship cannot last.

'I love you,' she said.

* * *

366

Her body was so different from Lisa's. Softer, more used. And yet so obviously unused. Overlaid with her past. She reacted to him in ways which were new to him. Looking out at the lake, he felt he had been granted an immense privilege. Mel. Melissa. He was younger than she was. So what? All that mattered was that she was Mel and he loved her.

He leaned against the counter top. 'Are you ready?' he said.

'For what?'

He loved the precision of her speech. 'Anything.'

'Absolutely.'

'But right now, to walk?' She opened her mouth to say something and he forestalled her. 'You have to, Mel. I'll be with you. And *I* have to, as well. So we can help each other through this together.'

'All right.'

It would be like the Stations of the Cross for her, he thought as they set off. First they would have to pass the fork at which the trail diverged from the river and swung upwards. Then they would reach the point at which she had seen him coming down the trail and had screamed for help. Then the place where Joanne had plunged off the edge of the cliff. And the falls further up, above the tree-line, where the two women must have sat and enjoyed the view before turning back.

He reached for Mel's hand and held it tightly. 'Don't be afraid,' he said. It felt so warm, so much smoother than Lisa's had ever been. He turned his fingers into the shell of hers.

'I'll try,' she said. Her face was trusting, like a child's.

They continued to climb towards the cold sunshine which splashed gold on the tips of the higher trees. Though the sun shone out of a cloudless sky, it was cold on the trail. Frost-edged leaves lay under the trees. At the turn where the path led upwards, away from the river, he squeezed her hand. 'I'm here,' he said.

Higher up, she stared along the path to where she had seen him jogging towards her. She faltered, stopped, shook her head. 'This isn't going to work,' she said. 'I just can't forget the ... the emptiness after she'd fallen. Looking around, back behind me, absolutely knowing she wasn't there and yet equally certain that she ... she *had* to be.'

'Keep walking,' he said.

When they came to the point where Joanne had fallen, he stopped. The broken sapling was still there, though the scar where it had snapped had weathered. 'I told her,' Mel said, her face crumpling. 'On the way up, she got much too close to the edge, and I told her it was dangerous. There'd been rain the night before and the ground was wet.'

'I remember.'

'I pulled her back,' said Mel. 'Grabbed her jacket and pulled her away from the edge.'

'You *told* her?'

'Yes.'

'But she did it again on the way down?' He smiled at her for a moment, with his head tilted. 'Your fault? I don't think so.'

Mel bit her lip for a moment. 'No,' she said, decisively. 'No.'

'Look!' Ben pointed. 'Did you see it?'

'See what?'

'A snowy owl. They're not often around during the day. And over there.' He pointed to an almost imperceptible shadow between the trees. 'Deer: these woods are full of them.' He put his arm round her shoulders. 'One of the things I love about you is that you're happy up here.'

As they climbed higher, the temperature rose until they were forced to shuck off their jackets. At the top of the trail, where the slope flattened out along the stream which came down from the higher hills to become the falls, and tumbled boulders led off into scree and scrub, they stood panting in the clear crisp air.

'It's so beautiful,' she exclaimed, easing off her pack. 'It smells like the very first morning of all must have done.'

Ben took off his own pack. He pulled her into his arms and nuzzled into her neck. His hands moved inside the insulation of her clothes and caressed the bones of her back. He tugged at her shirt, freed a shoulder, kissed it.

'Oh,' she groaned. 'I can't *not* do this.'

When he opened her clothes and closed his hand over her breast, she shivered with delight. He could feel her melting. Feel her caution, her habitual sadness loosening, pulling free, washing away on a stream of love. Always, before, he had stood outside, seen himself feeling. With Mel, he was part of a whole.

Before they set off again, she raised both arms to the sun. There was something pagan, something primitive, about the gesture. Seeing him watching her, she laughed aloud, then put her arms around his neck and leaned her head on his shoulder. 'You've given me so much,' she said.

It was two o'clock in the morning. They lay in bed in a tangle of bedclothes, holding hands, talking. Ben had brought champagne up from the refrigerator, and two glasses.

'Why didn't you have any children?' he said.

'My husband didn't want any,' she said lightly, as she had always done when the question was asked.

'And you let him decide?'

She opened her mouth to say yes, to let Eric bear the responsibility. But she found that here, with Ben, she had no desire for deceit. 'No,' she said. 'It was my decision.'

He sensed something important here. 'Why?'

'Because . . . I really don't want to talk about it . . . but years ago I had an abortion.'

He was astonished. '*You* did?'

She touched the side of his jaw. 'You must have realized by now that nobody is ever what they seem.'

'But why should an abortion stop you having a family – or was it one of those bungled ones?'

'Not as far as I know. It was simply . . .' She gazed down the telescope of the years. It was all so unimaginably long ago. '. . . simply that if I couldn't have children with . . . with the man I loved, then I didn't want them with anyone. Particularly Eric.'

'You still could, though, couldn't you?'

'I guess so. But I'm long past the stage of wanting to.'

All this time, she thought, all these years, and thanks to the man I love now, a man who is almost young enough to be the child I never had, I am astonished to discover that the raw wound has finally healed. She recalled her honeymoon, the little brown butterflies on the hills above Florence, when she had held buttercups under Eric's chin, thinking, with a sense of panic, what have I done, what on earth have I done?

Taking his hand in hers, she thought: but that's all over now. I am what I am. I have fashioned an alternative existence, one in which I need no longer grieve for my empty womb. I am content.

He poured more champagne for them and turned towards her.

'Tell me about your cousin,' she said.

He sipped slowly from his glass, resting it on his stomach. Beads of condensation rolled down the sides and onto his chest: the sudden chill brought goosebumps out on his skin. 'He was such fun, always planning something new: swimming by moonlight, picnics out on the lake in the middle of the night, getting drunk on white wine he'd stolen from the liquor cabinet.' He blinked away the tears which suddenly stung his eyes and rubbed his hand over his chest. 'He lived by his own rules, and I loved that. And then . . .'

Mel reached for his hand.

'Then he was killed.'

'How?'

'It was an accident. A stupid accident. We were on our new bikes, riding down the hill to the main road. He was ahead of me, and instead of slowing down at the corner, he picked up speed and went straight under the wheels of a truck coming the other way. I didn't see it, but I heard it.' He gritted his teeth. 'I'll never forget the sound. And then the silence.'

'Not your fault, Ben.'

'And after Rory died,' Ben said, as though he had not heard her, 'my aunt Evie went to pieces. It was terrible, watching someone disintegrate. In the end, she took an overdose.'

'You can't blame yourself for that.'

A complicated expression crossed his face. 'I knew that Rory's death wasn't down to me. I really knew that. But Aunt Evie . . .'

'Where do consequences begin?' Mel asked, quoting his own words back at him. 'Think about it, Ben. It's like you said about Joanne. It was your cousin's choice to go down that hill too fast, not yours. None of it had to do with you.'

He took a deep breath. 'I'm trying to believe that, I really am.'

'Is that why you climb, why you spent all those summers working with the Mountain Rescue people? Because you couldn't save Rory, you try to save the rest of the world instead?' She cupped her hand round his cheek, so tenderly, so full of love. 'Ben,' she said. 'My Benjamin.'

He turned his head so he could kiss the vulnerable veins on the inside of her wrist, lick the soft places between her fingers. 'Why do you look so sad?'

She half-smiled but didn't answer.

'You do love me, don't you?' he demanded.

'Yes.' Her voice was so low he had to bend his head to hear her. 'Always.'

'Me too.'

'But I have to go back tomorrow,' she said.

'No.'

'I must. I have a show to organize.'

'Another day,' he begged. He didn't want to return to the real world, to take up the frayed edges of his life again.

'I can't.'

'Call your assistant. Tell her you've broken your leg, or you've got flu, anything. But don't go back just yet. Please, Mel. Please.'

In the end, she telephoned Carla and said she was still too depressed after Joanne's death to think about work and would come in the following day.

She had forgotten that such uncomplicated happiness was possible. Somewhere down in the valley lay Butterfield, lay duty and expectation. For the moment, she was happy to stay here in the hills and let the world flow by. She willed herself to set aside everything else and simply give herself up to it, let the golden moments uncurl one by one.

Lisa, Joanne, the past and the future, did not for the present exist. Soon she would have to go back to work, to grief, to loneliness, but for a few precious hours she was able – she had the *right* – to lose herself in Ben. She watched him sleep. The shape of his face, the line of his mouth, the way his hair grew, gave her a pleasure so exquisite that she shook with it. He is part of me, she thought, reaching out a finger to touch the tip of a curl, or leaning close to draw into herself the fresh scent of his sweat, and always will be.

And yet, lying beside his big body the next morning – their last morning – her fingers entwined with his, she was seized once more with the thought that this joy was not hers to take. Rain spattered intermittently against the window. She could see the pointed tops of the fir trees against a waterlogged sky.

Ben leaned up on his elbow to look down at her, kissed her breast, lifted one of her hands. 'I love you.'

I love you too, she wanted to say. Oh, so much more than you can imagine.

'The stone in your ring is the exact same color as your eyes,' he told her.

'That's what the person who gave it to me said.'

'Who was he?' When she did not answer, he said, 'Not your husband?'

'Eric didn't believe in giving me jewellery.'

'What *did* he believe in?'

'Himself.'

'Did he love you?'

'I don't know.'

'Why did you marry him?'

'He was lonely,' she said. 'Like me. And . . . and completely different from the man I'd been with before him.'

'The man who gave you the ring?'

373

'Yes. Eric was very ordinary, very average and conventional.'

'Why would someone like you marry a man like that?'

'I think I thought that there might be a kind of sanctuary in ordinariness, in averageness. That being conventional could be more appealing than passion. And . . .' She hesitated.

'And what?'

'My father . . .' she said. 'My parents were quite elderly when I was born. He hadn't wanted me – any child, not just me. He didn't . . . he really didn't love me.' She tried to laugh. 'I know it's silly but once I ran home with a painting I'd done in class, a green horse. I was so proud of it. I said, "Look at my picture, Daddy, it's a horse." And he said, so coldly, "Horses aren't green." I was crushed. He didn't even look up, just turned the page of his book.'

'What a bastard.' He remembered suddenly how Lisa had felt about her father.

'I think I saw Eric as a father figure,' Mel said. 'One who'd love me, this time round. My second chance.'

'You're *my* second chance.'

'Oh, if only . . .' she felt like weeping.

'It's true, Mel.' He turned her face to his and kissed her, his mouth pressing into her, his hands gently holding her breasts. He danced his fingers down the scar below her breast. 'Where did you get this?'

'An accident, when I was seven or so,' she said. 'I fell off the big slide right onto a baby buggy which one of the other mommies had left there, and tore myself open.'

She could still remember the screaming, the blood, the look of terror on her mother's face, the fascination of the stitches laddering her flesh, the black threads begging to be pulled out.

374

'You'd have thought it would have disappeared by now,' he said.

'Wounds heal,' she said. 'Scars don't.'

The white light from the window glittered on the separate honey-colored hairs springing from his skin. She lifted his hand and began to stroke it, smoothing the skin over the knuckles, circling the scar on his thumb, outlining the shape of his nails.

His skin. His fingers, his body. 'All my life I've kept things bottled up inside me,' she said abruptly. 'I thought it was good to be controlled, not to burden other people with my messy emotions.'

'I'm like that too.'

'But a person can be too private, too self-contained. What I loved about Joanne was that she let it all out, all the time, and that made her happy, that made her able to get on with her life.'

'Surely some things should be kept to yourself.'

'But secrets can fester. Secrets can be like an abscess. If you lance it, you recover. If you don't, the infection can spread through your whole body.' Or sometimes, Mel thought, a burden simply grows too heavy to be borne.

'The man who gave you the ring,' said Ben. 'Did he know you were pregnant?'

Her answer was oblique. 'I would have died for him. From the moment we met, he was everything to me. He lit up my life. But, just like my father, he didn't want children. So I never told him about the pregnancy. I could *not* let a child be born to a father who didn't, wouldn't love it.' There were tears in her eyes. 'So I . . . *murdered* it.'

She had often thought the words but never, until now, spoken them aloud. Here, with the sound of the lake on the shore, the sound of rain on the roof, the swish

375

of wind in the trees, they sounded melodramatic, hysterical.

'Was it a boy or a girl?' Ben asked quietly.

There was a long silence.

'Melissa . . .'

'I don't know.'

'They didn't tell you?'

'I didn't ask.' Mel rubbed her hands roughly over her face. 'I didn't want to know. I just wanted it . . . to be over.'

'That's understandable. Forgivable.'

'How can it be? I killed the baby I was carrying, just because I was unhappy.' Mel remembered the roads speeding away behind her, the miles multiplying between her and New York, running, running, wanting a home, a place of her own, wanting somewhere she could curl up and be safe in. She could feel it all as if it was last week, the anguish, the loneliness, the way her body had felt as though it might split open, spilling her heart out onto the earth like a raw bruised plum.

'And you've never told the father?'

'It wouldn't have changed anything.'

'Are you sure?' He took her hand and raised it to his lips. Smoothed her damp hair behind her ears. Gestures of love.

'Yes.' She had to be certain she was right. 'Absolutely sure.'

But what would have happened if she had stayed in New York, instead of running away? If she had made a different choice, that awful afternoon, when the path her life was to take still hung in the balance. She had wanted to tell Galen, but a kaleidoscope of the years ahead, the remembrance of her chilly father, had passed through her head and she had kept silent. She had packed her bag and taken off, somewhere, anywhere, already knowing, as she took the empty roads north, that she had made an irretrievable mistake.

'Do you know where the baby's father is?'

Mel nodded.

'Maybe you'd feel better about all this if you told him about it now.'

'He's not the kind of person . . .' She broke off.

'How do you know? Maybe he's changed. People do.'

'Not him.'

'You don't know that. You've changed – why shouldn't he have done, too?' Ben caught her wrist and kissed the pale skin on the inside. 'I love you,' he said.

She touched his mouth with her finger. 'Me too,' she said.

Later, lingering over breakfast, she said, 'Have you heard anything from Lisa?'

'Nothing.'

'She's still trying to come to terms with what happened.'

'How long does it take?' He poured coffee, sipped his, shook his head. 'I've had a lot of time to think about her leaving. I know it would have been better if I'd been there when she lost the baby. But I wasn't. How many other husbands find themselves in the same position as I was in? There are situations where you can't just walk away. You know that. I came back the minute I could. I wanted to help, to share it with her, and somehow we couldn't seem to communicate.' He remembered Lisa's face, mouth open in a howl of rage and grief, and felt a tightness around his heart. 'I always thought we had such a strong . . . such an idyllic marriage. And when the first real test came, we failed.'

'Pain takes people in different ways.'

'Running away wasn't going to make things better.' The

377

way Lisa had spoken to him at Joanne's funeral still hurt him. '*I'm not ready to discuss anything*,' she'd said, and he had seen then that she would probably never be ready. Whatever there'd once been between them had come to an end. 'Let's not talk about it.'

CHAPTER TWENTY-SIX

Mel woke with a throbbing headache and a stiff neck, to find that she was out of coffee. The water heater seemed to have packed up so she was unable to take a shower and when she arrived at the gallery, aching and depressed, it was to discover that there was no coffee here either, not even a jar of instant. Foraging, she found a couple of Carla's camomile tea bags. Camomile, to start a busy day? Thanks, but no thanks.

After some thought, she had decided to include *First Love*, her own carving, in the show; she carried it into the office and set it down carefully on her desk. The light on the answering machine was blinking so she picked up the handset and jammed it into her shoulder, turning over papers on her desk as she listened to the messages. They were routine, except for the final one. Koslowski's agent. 'Something's come up. Call me. Doesn't matter what time.'

What the hell was it now? Almost certainly Koslowski was playing up again, wanting to impose more impossible conditions. Just what she needed. Angrily she pushed the numbers for the agent's cellphone, heard him pick up, told him who she was.

'You're not gonna like it,' he said.

'Try me.'

'You better brace yourself, Mrs Sherman.'

'Consider me braced.'

'Uh . . . how do I say this . . . ?'

'English will do.' She reached for a mug of coffee that was not there.

'Putting it bluntly, Galen wants to cancel.'

'Cancel what?'

'The show. Call it off.'

'You are joking, aren't you?'

'I wish I were,' the agent said heavily. 'I've told him he can't do that, but I might as well be talking to a wall.'

Furious, Mel held the receiver so tightly she was afraid it would crack. 'Any particular reason?'

'Some crap he came up with yesterday. Got these cosmic vibes or something—'

'What planet is this guy living on?' she snapped, mind racing with moves and counter-moves.

'– thinks there's something weird going on up there in Vermont.'

'Presumably there's nothing he can do about it if I ignore him.'

'Except you know what he's like.'

'I do,' she said. Only too well.

'He might sue.'

'I'd counter-sue.' Mel thought about it for a moment. 'Suppose I never got your message.'

'There wouldn't be a lot he could do about it, I guess.'

'I'm not even going to point out the costs I've already incurred, the time I've spent setting this up, because you know all about them, and if you don't, you can imagine.'

'Tell me about it.' The agent coughed. 'I don't know what he's on at the moment—'

'He does drugs, now?' He never used to. Not even a joint.

'Just a manner of speaking – far as I know he's always been clean. But he came round to my place last night, started talking about love and life and what's-the-point-of-it-all? sort of stuff. How he's wasted his life, never found the right woman, all that blah. And then he suddenly leans forward and says he's thinking of going up to Vermont and personally removing the pieces.'

'Just let him try.' Fruitlessly, Mel tried to massage the muscles of her neck.

'I know that. I told him. I'm entirely with you. I just thought I'd warn you.'

'Thanks.'

The agent's voice changed. 'You sound tired.'

'I *am* tired, dammit. I've put a lot of work into this show, and on top of that my . . . my closest friend just died and I really *really* don't need this kind of crap.'

'I'm sorry to hear that, Mrs Sherman.' He sounded genuinely concerned.

'An agent with a heart?' Mel said wryly. She paused for a moment, options racing through her mind. 'Is there any chance that you might be prepared to compromise your deepest principles for a woman you've never met?'

'You sound like a spunky lady. I guess I could put my dick on the line for you. Depends what you want.'

'Galen's phone number.'

'I can't do that. Client confidentiality – you know how it is.'

'Maybe, just for once, you could forget yourself.'

'You mean, like, get all confused, reel off some numbers purely at random?'

'That sort of thing.'

'It wouldn't be my fault if they turned out to be his phone number, would it?'

'Could happen to anyone.'

Impatiently she pushed buttons on her handset. Allowed the phone to ring, on and on. *Come on, damn you . . .* After a dozen beeps, the answering machine kicked in. She did not wait for the message, just rang off, redialed, rang off when the machine came on. She did this for five minutes, imagining him lying in bed, cursing, reaching down to the floor for a drink – except she had recently read a newspaper article in which he had claimed that he was on the wagon. In the accompanying photograph he had looked unlike himself, neat in a linen jacket over a purple T-shirt, shaven, hair tamed into a tidy ponytail. The interviewer had confirmed that he kept a glass of water in front of him throughout, no question of it being vodka, she had personally poured it for him.

Answer the darn phone, for Pete's sake . . . Mel dialled for the twenty-sixth time and, at last, someone picked up. *About time, you asshole . . .*

'What?' a voice barked. Koslowski's voice. 'Are you mad?'

'Extremely mad,' she said. A catch of the breath at the sound of his voice, a clutch at her heart.

'I am asleep,' he said loudly. 'Who is this?'

'Mrs Sherman. From the Vernon Art Gallery in Vermont.'

'What are you doing, calling me so early?'

'Your agent has just told me you want to cancel the show I've spent eighteen months or more setting up, and *I* want to tell *you* that if you lay so much as a finger on a single one of the sculptures which I'm exhibiting at my gallery for the next three weeks, then I will sue your ass off.'

'Those pieces are my children,' he said.

There was a sudden flare of pain in Mel's right temple. 'What pretentious crap.'

'Excuse me?'

'Your children? Are you kidding?'

'Why should I be?'

'They *are* for sale, right?' All she needed now was a migraine on top of everything else, she thought. 'I mean, if someone wants to pay you good money for them, you'd take it, wouldn't you?'

'Of course.'

'Mr Koslowski, I don't know how it is in Poland, which is where I believe you come from, but in this country, people don't usually sell their children every time they need money.'

A long pause. Then, sounding sulky, Koslowski said, 'I have to make a living.'

'So do I. And I've spent a lot of time and even more money on getting this show together and there is no *way* you are going to cancel it now.'

'But I have to.'

She could hear police sirens wailing in the background, the sound surging through his windows. 'You do not.' She pressed the receiver closer to her ear. Was that a sleepy voice beside him, someone stirring under the duvet, murmuring his name?

'There is something odd about you, Mrs Sherman,' he said. 'Something . . . unusual. I am wondering how safe my works will be in your care.'

'Whether they'll be safe or not, you don't have a lot of choice, Mr Koslowski. We signed an agreement, remember?'

There was another silence.

'What did you say your first name was?' he asked eventually.

'I didn't.'

'And you are from Vermont?'

'That is correct.'

'Have we met before? Your voice is . . .'

'No.'

'Well, Mrs Schumann from Vermont, I'm warning you that—'

She ran out of patience. 'And I, Mr Koslowski from New York, am warning *you*, don't start fucking me about of I'll fuck you about much *much* worse.' Mel slammed down the phone.

What was it Joanne always used to say: *Don't let the bastards grind you down*. Well, she wouldn't. If Koslowski came up here and tried to haul away any of the stuff, as she knew he was perfectly capable of doing, she would cause him some real damage. She contemplated the uproar that might ensue if it came down to a fist fight between her and the sculptor. Headlines. Pictures. Terrific publicity, even if not exactly the kind she wanted.

Her head was hammering. So was her heart. How well she remembered that voice from the past, those unchanged unmistakable mid-European vowels . . . and that blatant disregard for others. She used to think it was pure selfishness; perhaps she had been too blind, too naïve, to see that it was simply single-mindedness, a refusal to be deflected. Like Ben and his mountains.

Carla arrived, carrying a jar of coffee, cookies, apples, a couple of sandwiches from Chris's Place. 'I thought we might have to eat lunch on the hoof,' she said.

'All I need right now is coffee. There's none there and I'm suffering from severe caffeine withdrawal.'

'Here.' Carla thrust the jar at her. 'I didn't have time to buy any fresh yesterday.'

'Never mind.' Mel plugged in the kettle. 'It's only nine

thirty and I feel like I already worked a full day.' She leaned back in her chair. 'Guess what: Koslowski's trying to stop the exhibition.'

'You are joking, aren't you? You don't really think . . .'

'Even Koslowski wouldn't be that stupid.' The two women looked at each other. 'Would he?' Mel said doubtfully.

'Every time the door opens between now and opening night, I'm going to think it's him.' Carla rolled her eyes. 'Gif me back mein sculptures,' she said dramatically, in a heavy east European accent. 'Wouldn't it be fun, if he does show up and tries to haul the whole exhibition away?' She poured boiling water into the two mugs and handed one to Mel.

'For about five seconds, maybe,' said Mel. 'After that, it could get a little tiresome.'

'Great publicity, though.' Carla sipped her coffee. 'You do kind of wonder how a screwball like that actually manages to function in the normal world, don't you?'

'I wouldn't say he was screwy. Just eccentric.'

'Whichever, I pity his wife. Or wives. Personally, I like predictable a lot better than eccentric.' Carla glanced at her watch, took her feet off the table and pushed them back into her shoes. 'Give me my nice safe Walter any time. I like to know that every single morning, at exactly five after seven, he's going to yawn and then get out of bed and make himself a cup of coffee and bring one in to me, and then he'll ask me what kind of a day I've got ahead of me and then he'll look in the mirror and pat the top of his head, and say, "Honey, do you think I'm going bald?" and I'll say, "No, Walter, you are not going bald," and then he'll pull his suit out of the closet and say, "Honey, which tie should I wear with this?" and I'll tell him, every day the same, never varies. Sometimes I want

385

to say, "Take the day off, Wally baby, come back to bed and let's make mad passionate love instead," or I think, why don't I tell him to wear the handpainted tie with the nude cuties on that his brother Herman gave him six Christmases ago, but he'd be so bewildered, it would be like kicking a puppy in the teeth, or having a hurricane suddenly lift the roof off the house.'

'Carla . . .'

'Yes?'

'Ever been tempted to run off and join a circus or something?' Carla thought about it, her head on one side. 'Maybe once or twice, back in the days when I still had the figure for those pink spangled tights. But you grow out of that, don't you?'

'Do you?'

'Hey, it's called growing up. It's called coming to terms. It's called accepting your limitations.' Carla got out of her chair and planted a light kiss on the top of Mel's hair. 'Though I have to say you'd look fabulous in spangled tights.' She rinsed her coffee mug in the little sink and laid it on the draining board. 'OK, guys. Let's get to work. There's a show to put on.'

Mel reached for the telephone to start making back-up calls, reminding people, *you said you were coming, looking forward to seeing you*, reminding the press, *a terrific turnout, guy from the* Globe, *guy from the* Herald, *lots of cover*. Opening night was coming ever closer.

By half past seven that night, she was exhausted. Carla had gone home to her husband an hour ago, but Mel wanted a period of time to herself to relish the stillness, to walk round her gallery, see how the exhibition would look to the people attending, check that everything was as in place as it was possible to be.

386

She paused in front of *Harbinger*, a block of granite which had been highly polished on one side, left unfinished on the other. It was a powerful piece, but its full significance was only made clear when it was placed, as intended, in water in the carved granite bowl which the sculptor had provided. The reflected surfaces moved and changed with the faint but constant tremble of the water, the movements of the water rippled on the stone. She had trained a spot on the piece to emphasize the fluidity of the carving.

'Beautiful,' she said aloud. It was impossible not to touch it. She reached forward, slid her fingers along the polished planes, felt them snag on the rough ones.

It was one of the miracles of creation, of creativity, that someone like Galen Koslowski could produce such amazing work. Or were the inconsistencies, the mood swings, the unpredictability, an essential part of the creative process?

The telephone bleeped in her office and she hurried to answer it.

'Vernon Gallery.'

'I did not think you would be there so late,' a voice said.

Mel was suddenly breathless. 'Then why did you call, Mr Koslowski?'

'Because I had to know if you have mounted my work as I wish.'

'We've followed your instructions to the letter,' she said. 'Exactly as you wanted. You would be pleased for once.'

'For once?'

'You're not easy to please.'

'This is true.' He waited a heartbeat, then said gruffly, 'I apologize for my discourtesy this morning. And naturally I will not spoil your show.' He coughed. 'I hope very much that it will go well.'

387

'I'm in charge,' Mel said. 'Of course it will.'

She would have liked to prolong the conversation but she replaced the handset and went out to her car. The temperature was falling. She was always disconcerted by the sudden change from crisp fall to icy cold as each day dragged them nearer to the chilly beauty of a New England winter. Puddles froze overnight and frost lay thickly along the edges of gutters and sidewalks.

Back in Maple Street, she made herself some coffee. As she raised the mug to her lips, she thought, the hell with it. Down in the basement was rack upon rack of wine, dozens of bottles which Eric always said he was saving for a really important occasion. Mel took one from its resting place and carried it up to the kitchen. That just about sums up my life with him, she thought: waiting for special moments which never arrived.

She filled a glass and grabbed something to eat, then picked up the telephone and called Ben's number, but the line was engaged. My lovely Ben, she thought. His scent, his smile, his gentle fingers on her skin, the passion in his eyes.

In the living room she sank down on one of the sofas and pulled round herself the woollen throw which lay over the back. On the wall above the hearth, Grandmother Sherman stared down as she always did, eyes full of cold disdain.

So like Eric . . . selfish, controlling, cold Eric. Defiantly Mel refilled her glass, took a long swallow and got to her feet. Reaching up, she jerked the picture off the wall and carried it out into the hall, opened the front door and threw it out into the wet and chilly darkness. There was absolutely nothing the old witch could do about it: all that those baleful eyes were able to disapprove of now was the peeling paint of the porch. She ran up to her bedroom and lifted the calmly glowing icon off its hook between the windows. Downstairs again, she hung it in Grandmother Sherman's place and stepped back to look up at it. Perfect. Exactly right. Suddenly, she felt wonderful. She should have changed things years ago, as Joanne had always urged her to. Should have had the courage to acknowledge how much her marriage – her safe, uneventful marriage – had diminished her.

Now she had taken the first step, why stop at the pictures? Tomorrow she would call the Goodwill people, look at paint samples, think about new drapes. Joanne would have approved. She lay back against the sofa cushions. Maybe she would even contemplate moving, starting over again somewhere else. A week ago, she would not have considered such a thing possible. Now it seemed not only possible but inevitable.

The doorbell sounded, followed by the knocker. Ben? Smiling, she went out into the passage and opened the door.

Lisa was standing outside, right at the edge of the porch steps, as though poised for flight. A bag was slung over her shoulder. She wore a red woollen hat pulled down over her ears and a matching scarf round her neck. Despite the sharpness of the bones in her face, she looked like a child. 'I know it's late . . .' she said. Behind her, slanted against the yellow light from the street lamps, cold rods of rain fell heavily onto the grass.

'Come in.' Guilt flushed through Mel. Could Lisa smell the scent of love which rose from her like a precious balm? Could she see Ben's kisses on her body, the sweet glittering marks of his passion?

Closing the door, Lisa pushed Mel gently ahead of her along the hall towards the warm kitchen. 'You look tired. Let's have coffee,' she said, easy and familiar with

Mel and Mel's home. Like she used to be. Like a friend.

Or a daughter.

'I already made some,' Mel said. 'What are you doing here?'

'I came to talk to Ben,' There were lines below Lisa's eyes, new hollows under her cheekbones.

Mel felt the beat of her culpable blood. 'I see.'

'I thought about what you said. I wanted to apologize to him for the way I behaved at Joanne's funeral,' Lisa said, handing Mel a mug of coffee.

Mel raised the mug to her lips. I also have rights, she wanted to say. I deserve a measure of happiness. 'What . . . uh . . . what did he say?'

Lisa shrugged. 'He didn't want to know. He was angry, Mel. Really angry.' Lisa played with her spoon, nervously turning it over and over between her fingers. 'You know Ben . . .'

'Yes.'

'. . . he's not angry very often. But I guess in one way, I can't blame him. He wanted to help me over the miscarriage but he didn't know how, and instead of realizing that, I did my best to hurt him.'

'Did you tell him that?'

'I tried.' Lisa's mouth trembled a little. 'After I lost the baby, I felt so . . . *wounded*. I think I must have had a kind of breakdown. I did such silly things, cruel things. I left behind some things he'd given me, when we first fell in love, just to hurt him. And now he's fallen out of love with me. If you'd seen the way he looked at me – so cold and remote – it was like I was invisible.'

'So . . . uh . . . what are you going to do?'

'What can I do? I just have to admit that we should never have gotten married in the first place.'

'Do you really believe that?'

For a moment the younger woman stared at nothing. Then she said softly, 'No. Of course I don't.'

'Do you still love him?'

'Yes. I do.'

Mel cleared her throat. Somewhere at the very core of her she could feel a grief so monstrous that she was afraid it might split her apart. 'Then . . .' I can't do this, she thought. I cannot.

'Then what?'

'T-tell him.'

'He wouldn't hear me if I did.' Lisa raised her hands to her face. 'He's very stubborn. Once he's taken a stand on something, it's impossible to shift him.'

'Can you take a stand on love?'

'What?'

'Love . . . can one really take a stand?' Mel reached for a chair and sat down. 'I did once,' she said slowly. 'I've regretted it ever since. It was the most stupid, the most destructive thing I've ever done. It ruined my life. Some of the decisions I made because of it have haunted me ever since.'

Lisa stared at her, a frown between her dark brows.

'Don't make the wrong decision.' Mel pressed her hands to her heart. 'If . . . if you still love Ben . . . don't walk away from him.' Each word felt like a tombstone planted in the graveyard of her love.

'He said he'd found someone else. He had that look, Mel.' Lisa's face crumpled as though a cold wind had blown across it. 'You know, that kind of shiny look that people in love have?'

'Yes.' I know, I know. His hands on my face, the smell of his skin, his beautiful face above mine . . . Oh, can I give that up, can I lose that?

Lisa lifted her thin shoulders and dropped them again.

'I shan't come back to Butterfield. At least, not for a while. But I couldn't go without saying goodbye this time. I didn't get in touch after I left because I was afraid you'd disapprove. On top of everything else, I couldn't have coped with that. So I just . . .' She spread her hands, began rooting in the bag she had been carrying and took out something wrapped in tissue paper. 'I brought you one of my new pieces.'

Mel unwrapped it carefully. In her hands she held an oval-shaped bowl thickly glazed in a smooth honey-color. The sides curved outwards and in again, like a boat, then doubled back onto themselves so that the bowl almost seemed to be self-lined. Simple, strong, beautiful. 'Oh,' she said.

'It's quite different from anything I've done before,' Lisa said anxiously. 'Do you like it?'

Mel turned the piece in her hands and felt tears pricking behind her eyes. 'If you want my professional opinion –'

'Please.'

'– I'd say you've finally found your voice. This is simply stunning.' The prospect of grief receded as Mel's mind raced ahead, planning a show, writing a release, organizing publicity. 'Have you produced any other pieces like this?'

'Some.' Lisa hesitated. 'I used to think I had to decorate the clay but I've been experimenting with refining the forms down to something so basic and elemental that decoration becomes unnecessary. The clay itself is beautiful enough.'

'How do you get this marvellous glow from the glaze?'

'More experimenting. Recently I've been firing the pots as many as three times, to make them come to life.'

392

'Wonderful.' Mel turned the simple functional shape in her hand.

'I've made one for Ben too,' Lisa said. 'But I didn't want to give it to him when I was there earlier, in case he threw it at the wall or something. I wondered if you could – would you, Mel? – take it round sometime and give it to him.'

'Take it yourself.'

Lisa shook her head. 'The moment's long gone.' Raindrops sat like diamonds on her black hair.

The telephone began to trill and both women stared at it, startled, before Mel picked up.

'Melissa? Mel: it's me.' Ben's voice, urgent. 'Something happened tonight . . .'

'Hi,' Mel said, overbrightly.

'What's wrong?'

'I can't talk. I've got company.'

'Anyone I know?'

'No.' Across the room, Lisa was staring down at the piece she had made for Mel, the bones of her neck looking as fragile as those of a bird. 'I'll call you later.' Mel put down the telephone.

'Everything OK?' Lisa said. She smiled, and, for a moment, the skin bunching up under her eyes, dimples showing, it was possible to believe that she was the old Lisa once more.

'Just fine.'

'The show's opening any time now, isn't it?'

'Next week.'

'Will the sculptor – Koslowski – come up from the city for it?'

'I hope not.'

'Didn't you tell me you knew him once?'

'It was years ago.'

'I'll bet that was exciting.'

'It was.'

'Did he make you laugh?'

'Cry, more often than laugh.' Mel remembered that constant sense of life enhanced, of choices, dreams, magical possibilities. The bright expansion of normality. 'I had it,' she said suddenly.

'What?'

'I had it and I threw it all away.' Impulsively, she grabbed Lisa's hands, squeezed them hard. 'Lisa, don't do what I did. Don't let it go.'

'There's nothing left to let go.' Lisa gathered her things together, walked out to the hall and began to pull on her coat. 'It's best this way.' She tugged the hat down over her hair. 'Thank you for . . . for being my mom.'

'People don't just abandon their moms,' Mel said. She wondered how she could speak so calmly.

'Maybe we'll meet up again later. When I'm back on the path again.'

'I'd like to see more of your new work,' Mel said. 'I'd like to display it in the gallery. I'd like to think about an exhibition, when you've got enough to show. Not the one we talked about, earlier in the summer, but one of your own.'

'I'll be in touch.' Lisa flung her arms around Mel. 'I love you,' she murmured. 'I miss you. But for the moment, I'm still finding my way.' She opened the door and stepped out onto the porch, went down the steps to the path and walked towards the side of the house. She waved once and disappeared.

Mel picked up the telephone.

CHAPTER TWENTY-SEVEN

There was a light on over the porch, and more lights in the living room behind the drapes. Ben parked on the road and ran through the rain up the stone path. When Mel opened the door to him, he smiled happily and followed her into the living room.

'I was afraid I wasn't going to see you today,' he said. He stared at the icon on the wall above the hearth. 'You've changed this room around, haven't you?'

'Minimally,' she said. 'But crucially.' Her voice sounded strange.

'I see.' He sensed that there was much he did not, *could* not see. She stood on the other side of the room, looking severe, her pale hair pulled back from her face in a tight French knot, an unreadable expression in her eyes. He wasn't sure he wanted to know what message it contained. Remorse lodged in his chest: guilt about the way he'd acted earlier in the evening, when he'd opened his own front door to find Lisa standing there. She'd tried to apologize for her behaviour at Joanne's funeral but he hadn't wanted to listen. He'd told her he was in love with someone else and then been scalded by the look of anguish on her face. His instinct had been to go over and take her in his arms, comfort her, murmur that everything would be all right, but he'd forced himself to stay where he was.

'I can't do this any more,' Mel said, without preamble.

'Do what?'

Gray shadows lay above her cheekbones. 'You and me . . .'

'What do you mean?'

She leaned her head against the wall behind her. 'You and Lisa . . .' The sentence trailed away.

'What about us?' he said gently.

'You . . . the two of you have to start over.'

He could see the effort the words cost her. 'I don't think so.'

Mel's eyes were full of pain. 'I've thought about it, I can't think of anything else, and this . . . what we have between us . . . can't be.'

Ignoring the hand she raised to stop him, he went over and put his arms round her. 'I love you.'

'It's not *right*.'

'If I think it is, and you do, then it is.' Her body was as tense as a statue. 'Are you ashamed of loving me?'

'Never.' She closed her eyes. '*Never*. But you . . . don't you see, this is the second chance for you both?'

'Lisa and I are through.'

'We m-mustn't s-see each other again.' Her chin trembled.

'You don't mean it,' he whispered into her hair.

'I do.' She gave a kind of gasp.

'You will break my heart.'

'And mine,' she said. 'But . . . but hearts can be mended.' She stared at him, his lovely, clear-eyed Mel. 'We don't belong together. You should be with Lisa. And I –' She shook her head slightly. 'I'm not quite sure where I belong. But it can't be with you, Ben. Beautiful Ben. I'm too old for you.'

'Your husband was much older than you. What's the difference?' Yet, though he despised himself for it, he knew she was right.

Tears came into her eyes. 'That's one of the mean tricks that nature plays on women.'

'I don't give a shit about your age,' he said angrily.

'Maybe not now. Maybe not in a month, a year, even two years. But sooner or later, you will. You'll look at me and you'll wonder why you are in bed with someone old enough to be your mother. Why there are no children in the house.'

He was seized by dread, a sense of trumpets sounding, walls tumbling, destruction hurtling through the air. 'I've never for a single moment thought of your age,' he said.

'Which is why you're a good man.'

He remembered Lisa saying the same thing. *You smell like a good man*, she'd told him, her hands cupping his face. 'No.' He wasn't sure what exactly he was denying. Memory, possibility, the wilfulness of circumstance?

'You'll want children, Ben.'

'Not if you don't.'

'That's not true.' Mel put a hand on the back of the armchair. 'I lied to you when you called me earlier this evening. I told you I had company. I said it was nobody you knew. It was Lisa. She told me she wouldn't be coming back to Butterfield. She left that for you.' Mel nodded at something on the table beside him. 'It's a piece of her recent work.'

'I don't need this,' he said.

'Open it.'

'Please don't do this.'

'Open it, Ben.'

397

The bowl inside the wrapping was oval-shaped, with the round fullness of an egg. Like an egg, it contained a yolk, a softly fertile second layer in a different glaze, the two together combining to produce something powerful and solid, yet, at the same time, infinitely vulnerable. He held it carefully between his two hands. He pictured her at the turning wheel, her shining hair coming loose from the brilliant butterfly clips and falling over her face, her little hands emphatic on the wet clay. Lisa the potter. The artist. His wife. 'Oh God,' he said softly, feeling the future change.

'Isn't it superb?'

He hefted the pot in his hand. 'Her other stuff was beautiful, but this is so much more . . .' The right word eluded him.

'Mature,' Mel said.

He looked down at the pot in his hands. Something glorious was slipping from him, streaming away like the plume of ice crystals on Everest's summit.

'She told me you two had quarreled earlier,' Mel said.

He grimaced. 'That was good of her. The truth is, *I* quarreled. She didn't.'

'She wants to come back to you. She wants to come home.'

Home . . . . him and Lisa again, fitting together again. Home. 'You don't know what you're talking about,' he said harshly. There was an ache under his ribs, a hollowness.

'She loves you,' Mel said. The words were like acid in her throat.

'Did she tell you that?'

'Yes.'

'Love wasn't enough, last time round.'

'Give it another try,' Mel said. She had gone very pale.

398

'And another after that, if necessary. You had so much going for you.'

'Lisa isn't the person I married any more.'

'Of course she's not. After what happened this summer, how could she be?' Mel looked down at the ring on her hand. 'How could any of us?'

'I want *you*,' he cried.

'I told you once to go and look for her.'

'That was before.'

'And this is after, Ben. But the reason remains the same. You love her.'

'I love *you*.'

'Oh, Ben.'

'Our marriage didn't work.'

'It worked fine until she lost the baby.'

He spread his arms wide. 'It's too late.'

'It's never too late.'

He walked over to her hearth and kicked at the logs, sending up a plume of grey ash. 'Fuck it,' he said. 'Fuck it, fuck it.' He buried his face in his hands.

'Find her, Ben. Tell her you want her to come home.'

'Mel, I love you.'

'And I you. But . . .' She had to force the words out. '. . . but we weren't meant to be together.'

'How many times do I have to say it? It's over between Lisa and me. I even told her I . . . I was in love with somebody else.'

She brushed angrily at her wet cheeks. 'Ben,' she said sharply.

'What?'

'Promise me something.'

'Anything.'

'Swear that you will never, ever, whatever the provocation, whatever quarrels you have, you will not

399

ever tell her, Ben, that it was me. *Never*.'

He was taken aback by her vehemence. He tried to take her hand. 'The question doesn't arise, since she and I aren't together any more.'

'I know where she is,' Mel said abruptly.

'Oh?'

'She asked me not to tell you . . .'

His expression hardened. Blood drummed behind his ears. 'Doesn't that exactly prove what I'm saying?'

'. . . but I think you need to know,' she said.

'Much better not to break her confidence,' he said, angry now.

Picking up Lisa's bowl, he walked rapidly out of the room. He pulled open the front door and walked down the steps of the porch, light spilling like champagne across the wet front yard. He began to run down the cleared path towards the street. A rising wind churned the pine trees in the yard next to Mel's, and sent little scurries of water down the road. In the house opposite he could see people seated round a table in a room with leaf-green walls, a woman pouring coffee from a silver jug, someone's head thrown back in laughter.

As he climbed into his car, did he really hear her say 'I love you,' or was it just the blood pounding in his ears, the hammering of his heart, the need for her which he would never be allowed to assuage? Because he knew she spoke the truth, that there was no hope for the two of them.

He gunned the engine, pulled out from the kerb, the rear end fishtailing in the wet road, drove away with his shoulders hunched against her voice, against possibility and redemption.

She heard his car start up, saw the wheel of his headlights across the trees, and the redescending darkness. She

400

thought of his hands on the wheel, the way he raised one finger and tapped it up and down as he drove. She thought of his body, strong and scarred, the line of blond hairs on his belly. His face in repose, the sun-whitened eyebrows, the full mouth, the way his eyes lit up when he was happy.

These memories were to be her punishment. As she had once arranged to have her unborn child torn from her body, so now she had wrenched her lover from her heart. Then, she had acted without recognizing the value of what she was losing, without fully realizing the consequences: now she knew the value of what she had given away.

She was torn by a consciousness of the essential unfairness of things. I want my real life back, she thought – except that this *is* my real life and I have no choice except to live it. Real life was what happened all around you while you waited for it to begin, and if you were not careful, you might be too busy waiting to recognize it.

Closing the front door, she leaned against it. You are breaking my heart, he had said. She could feel the sound of her own as it chipped, cracked, fractured, fell into shards. Having done the right thing, why did the moral high ground hurt so badly?

I am waiting for my true love . . . she had written, thirty years ago. She had fled from one true love; she had just sent the other away.

That night she lay open-eyed, hungry for Ben. Moonlight drifted through the half-open windows; the muslin curtains billowed gently in the chilly breeze, in, out, in, out, like lungs pumping to keep a life going, a heart beating. But her heart was in hibernation: she was alive, but not living.

When she finally slept, she dreamed of flight, of wings sprouting from between her shoulders, carrying

401

her through the blue air to somewhere far away from him.

With the Koslowski exhibition opening in a few days' time, she was able to immerse herself in her final preparations, keep her head empty of him. But when the telephone rang two days later and she heard his voice, the thump of her heart was almost painful.

'Mel, I love you.'

She stared out at the rain falling in heavy sheets over the outdoor sculptures in the meadow at the front of the gallery.

'Don't do this, Mel.'

'Go and bring Lisa home.'

There was a long pause. Then he said slowly, 'I'd need to find her first. And since I haven't the least idea where she is, how can I?'

Rain outside, rain in my heart, Mel thought. With that question, he has given himself the answer. 'She's teaching,' she said. 'At a private school in Montpelier.' Gently she put down the receiver.

Don't think about him, she told herself fiercely.

Don't.

CHAPTER TWENTY-EIGHT

At first, he could scarcely believe she had been serious when she sent him away. He assumed that she would eventually change her mind. But he hadn't seen her now for more than a week. She refused to answer his calls. If he telephoned the gallery, her assistant told him she was not available. He'd gone to her house, but she wouldn't open the door to him. Once, sitting in his parked Jeep across the street, he saw her come into the living room, wearing a blue robe the same color as her eyes. He loved the way she moved about the room. At one point she had walked across to the window and stared out, a little smile on her face, but if she'd seen the Jeep, she had made no sign. Was she thinking about them, about the love that they had so briefly shared?

But gradually, with each slowly passing day, he had begun to see the value of what she had done, the sacrifice she had made for him and Lisa. Despairingly, he saw, too, that she was right. Especially since, somewhere deep inside himself, he'd always known that his relationship with Mel couldn't last. He would carry it with him for the rest of his life. It would mark his future, of that he was very sure. But it couldn't be part of his present.

Montpelier, he wrote, over and over again on the legal

pad in front of him. Yellow paper, blue lines, black ink. Black like Lisa's eyes. The black rug on the floor of her apartment in New York. Whatever happened to that? Or the black table and chairs? I was so much younger then, he thought. Running over with hope.

Montpelier. That's where Lisa was. Just an hour or so's drive away. An ember burning in the winter darkness.

If you wanted to find someone in Montpelier, the smallest state capital of them all – just as a kind of intellectual exercise, not because you really intended to start looking – how would you begin? First of all, you would have to get hold of a list of the private schools in the area – there couldn't be that many – and then you'd call them up one by one and ask if they had a teacher called Lisa Tan on the payroll. If you really wanted to find someone, that's what you would do.

Even if you *didn't* want to find them. If you just wanted, say, to write them a letter explaining things, that's what you'd do. Explaining what? That mistakes had been made but could be rectified? That because of one woman, he was at last understanding just how deeply he felt about another? *Montpelier*, he wrote on his pad. *Montpelier*.

He turned the page.

Dear Lisa. He contemplated the two words. Dear. Lisa. He drew a line through the word Dear.

I wish I knew where you were, and what you're doing, he wrote.

I wish you were here with me.

He stopped. Tapped the pen against his teeth. She had come to the house and gone away again. Because he had refused to hear what she was trying to say. And maybe that was what had been wrong with their marriage. They talked, but not to each other. They laughed and shared and made love, but deep down, maybe they

404

hadn't built a solid enough commitment on which to forge a lifetime's partnership.

When she left that night, she had looked back at him over her shoulder, and he had remembered then that once the shape of her cheek, the line of her jaw, had been able to move him to tears. She had told him that she'd changed but he hadn't listened. 'You told me to find another woman,' he'd said. 'And I have.' How could he have been so cruel?

She stared at him and then walked across the hall. He'd heard the front door closing behind her, a car starting up, tires crunching on snow. And he'd stood there, thinking: so this is how a marriage finally ends: with this quiet withdrawal, this lack of farewell, this emotionless departure. As if the intensity of the love they used to share had never been. As if he himself had no reality.

He laid down his pen, pushed back his chair, made himself another mug of coffee. If Lisa appeared at the door right this minute, would it change anything? He put a hand up to his head and felt the roughness of his hair, slid his fingers across his face, touched the scar under his eye. In one sense, her final leaving had come as no surprise: he'd never understood what she saw in him in the first place.

Yet Mel had insisted that Lisa loved him. Had urged him to go and find her. He sat down and looked at the paper in front of him. Picked up the pen again.

I miss you, Lisa, he wrote. It was true. He did miss her. But was that love? Was that enough reason to resurrect a marriage?

And Rosemary, our daughter. I miss her too.

He lifted his mug again. The words were there in his head. He could feel them moving about, words that said everything if you could only handle them. He thought of

Rory, quick and bright as a bullet, dead Rory who had haunted him for so many years. He thought of the curve of Rory's back in front of him, yellow and black, beetle-bright, speeding down the hill away from him, killed by a lorry through no-one's fault but his own.

I miss her too, he wrote, *I've only recently begun to understand that there will never be a resolution to what happened. All we can do is accommodate it. Live with it. Absorb it into our lives.*

He paused. Frowned. These were Mel's words, not his. Was this really what he wanted to say? For that matter, what exactly *did* he want to say? Did he want to say anything at all?

I wish we could all go back and start over. But you can't do that. You can't put your foot in the same river twice. I know you're not going to come back. I know it's over between us, and that I have to get on with the rest of my life. And you do too.
I hope that wherever you are, you are happier.

He stared at the page and wrote at the bottom: *I love you, Lisa.*

He tore the sheet of paper from the pad and scrumpled it up, tossed it towards the sink. *I love you* . . . He put his head in his hands. Was it true?

Mel and he had offered each other something immensely valuable. This too must be absorbed into the rest of his life. It would remain a secret that was not to be shared, one that only he and she would ever know about. He thought of her long feet, the pearly pink polish on her nails, the tentative splay of her toes as she crossed the floor. He thought of the knobs on her spine, her full breasts resting like fruit in his hands, the endearing curve of her belly.

And yet . . .

If it *were* Lisa he loved, if he *did* go and find her, he would want to tell her that from the moment he'd first seen her between the candle flames, he had felt there would never be anyone else for him. He had been wrong, but that was what he would say.

Memories came back to him: New York in the rain, Lisa's sleeping face on the pillow, an eagle feather on the lake shore, the brush of skin against skin, the sweet scents of lovemaking. The precise and particular textures of happiness. He would want her to know how she had made him feel. How . . . his mind hesitated over the thought. How they might make each other feel again.

Somewhere.

Sometime.

One of these days.

Maybe.

If he was lucky.

But can you quantify love? Can you express something so *sensed*? Words come from the head: love is in the heart. Words alone couldn't begin to convey the smallest amount of his emotions.

He looked down at the words sitting there in front of him. The inadequate ineffectual words. He thought: there has to be a better way than this.

He parked across the wide street from the Hanson School. Behind a wall broken by tall iron gates sat an imposing building in the style of an eighteenth-century French country house. A leafless chestnut tree stood on either side of the short walk up to the wide front steps and porticoed entrance; under them, traces of frost glittered in the cold late-afternoon sunshine. Girls spilled out of the grounds onto the sidewalk, standing in chattering groups as they waited to be picked up by their parents, or scrambling into the top-of-the-range vehicles which idled at the kerb. Ben rolled down the window into cold brisk air and heard female voices rising through the overhanging branches like the chattering of birds.

After a while, the kids thinned out until there were only a few older ones, heads bent together as they discussed something, or thrown back in sudden wide laughter. Adults began to hurry down the front steps, carrying books or papers, heavy bags slung over their shoulders. Faculty, Ben decided. Teachers. Staff. Whatever they were called at a school like this.

Would Lisa come? If not, he would come back the next day. And the one after that. If he didn't see her, eventually he would walk in and talk to the school secretary who'd originally told him on the phone that yes, they did have an art teacher called Lisa Tan on the staff. He would find out where her teaching room was and then hang about outside until class was over, the way he used to at the age of sixteen, when he had fallen in love with a cheerleader called Donna Partridge. He felt momentarily breathless as he remembered that long-ago blood-pumping love.

A man came out onto the top step, and paused, holding the door open for a woman behind him. The woman was Lisa. She looked up at the man, laid a hand on his arm.

Without thinking further, Ben scrambled out of the Jeep and ran across to her, dodging traffic, ignoring the angry toots of horns. 'Lisa,' he called. The air smelled fresh and clean, with an edge of frost to it; the sky was a pure unclouded blue.

She turned. She murmured something to her companion, who looked at Ben with interest, before nodding vigorously and moving away. She came slowly towards her husband, frowning.

'How did you know where I was?' she asked.

408

'Mel told me you were teaching in Montpelier.'

'I asked her not to.'

'Mel is . . . a very wise woman,' he said. 'She thought it was better for both of us if I knew. Is there somewhere we can go for a coffee or something? I need to talk to you.'

'Do we have anything to discuss?'

'Yes,' he said firmly, suddenly sure. 'We most certainly do.'

'There's a place on the edge of town,' she said. 'We might get a seat before the after-school crowd shows up.'

He took her elbow and guided her towards the Jeep. It was the first time he had touched her for months. Under her jacket her bones were small and fine. Two or three silver earrings arched along the curve of her right ear. He hadn't noticed them when she'd come to the house last week.

She directed him along suburban roads to a small shopping mall. He found a parking place behind a bank, and took a plastic bag out of the Jeep before they walked together, not speaking, across a rapidly filling parking lot, past a Blockbuster Video, an A&P supermarket, the dry-cleaners, a bookshop, a place with its window full of hand-blocked patchwork quilts and cushions.

They found a table and sat down opposite each other. A waitress came and took their order for coffee, latte for her, cappuccino for him.

'Well,' Lisa said. 'What do you want to talk about?'

'I wanted to say . . .' He hesitated. He wished she would smile, make it easier. Mel hovered at the back of his mind. 'I wanted to apologize. When you came by the other night, I didn't give you much of a chance.'

'No.'

He wanted to be somewhere else, not sitting in this steamy restaurant which was rapidly filling up with kids and their mothers. 'I should have listened to what you had to say.'

'It doesn't matter any more.'

'Why not?' Her indifference stabbed him.

Her black eyes were opaque. 'You told me you'd fallen in love with someone else.'

He recognized this as a defining moment. His future lay within his answer. Whatever he said, he would be betraying a woman he loved. Mel had pleaded with him never to tell Lisa about her but he wasn't the sort of man who misrepresented things. He was used to being open.

'I . . .' He lifted his coffee to his mouth, staving off the necessity for an answer, thinking of Mel. *You belong with Lisa . . .* how hard had it been for her to say that? 'I just said that because I was angry. And maybe a little bit drunk.'

A kind of tremor moved across her face, leaving the skin smooth and unwrinkled. 'You mean it's not true?'

'No, I . . .' He swallowed. 'I said it to hurt you.'

'Oh, Ben.'

'What happened this summer,' he said. 'The baby. We can never make it not have happened.'

He reached across the table and took her hand, knocking over his coffee cup. The hot liquid spilled across the table and onto his lap but he took no notice. 'Let's try again,' he said, not even knowing if he meant it. At the next table, two women sitting with their daughters turned their heads to stare at him.

At first she didn't respond. Then she smiled briefly at him. 'Do you think that's possible?'

Regret and longing clogged his throat, desire for the innocence they had once possessed, regret for what he was losing. For a moment he was afraid his eyes would fill with tears. He wished he could take the words back, so neither of them need be embarrassed.

'Do I think it's possible,' he repeated slowly. Yes. The word sounded inside his head. Mel was right. 'Yes. I do.'

'Ben—'

'I've been thinking about buying a plot of land. By the lake. I kind of had this idea that maybe we could build a house together and live there.' He looked down at the pool of coffee in front of him and dragged a finger through it, searching for the right words.

'I don't . . . I don't know.'

'OK,' he said. He wasn't going to push it. Beneath his ear, a pulse beat so loudly that the noise of the café temporarily faded around him. 'But there's something I'd really like to do. It means you'd have to come back to Butterfield with me.'

'Now?'

'Right now. This very minute.'

'Why?'

He lifted the bag he'd been carrying and put it on the table between then. 'Because of this.'

'What is it?'

'A last reminder,' he said. A crushing sorrow waited somewhere in his chest. Something he would have to deal with later. He wondered how it could all have come to this when there had been – still was – so much love. 'I want us to plant it together.' He pulled open the top of the bag and a sweetly pungent scent of herbs hung in the air between them. 'It's a rosemary bush. I thought . . .' His voice cracked. 'I thought it would be a way of remembering her. Remembering Rosie.' *There's rosemary, that's for remembrance.* He hurried on, not wanting to hear her make some scornful remark. 'I told you about my cousin Rory.'

'Yes,' she said gently.

'I always blamed myself though I've come to realize that

411

it was nothing to do with me. But my father planted a rosemary bush by our house at the lake, in memory of him and my aunt. And I thought . . . I thought we could do the same for our daughter. For Rosemary.'

'Listen, Ben. I really—'

He interrupted again. 'Whatever you say or do, please, Lisa, remember that I also miss her. She was my child too. And whatever happens in the future, she will always be my first child, our first baby. Always.'

She stared at him for a moment, then she shut her eyes. 'I know. And I never took that into consideration.' Tears squeezed between the lids and moved slowly down her cheeks.

'I didn't mean to hurt you,' he said, reaching across the table for her hand. So small. He rubbed his thumb across the wedding band she still wore.

She moved her head from side to side but said nothing.

'I never *ever* meant to hurt you,' he said.

She opened her eyes, bit down on her lip. 'Nor I you.'

The waitress came over with a cloth in her hand and began to mop up the coffee he had spilled. 'Your pants are all wet,' she said. At the other table, the mother and daughters watched avidly.

He brushed ineffectually at himself. 'That's OK.'

'Want I should bring some paper towels?'

'I'm all right,' Ben said.

'Give us the bill,' said Lisa. 'We're just leaving.'

The two of them walked down the length of the café to the till and paid.

'So . . . will you come with me?' Ben asked as they walked back to the Jeep. His wet trousers clung chillingly to his thighs.

She stood in the middle of the parking lot. A few cold raindrops drifted down. 'Is it really a good idea?'

412

'Yes,' he said.

'I guess I could spent the night at . . . the house.'

'I'll drive you back here tomorrow.' He looked up at the already darkening sky. 'We could plant the tree in the morning,'

'Or we could stop at a garden center, buy a pot and put it in there,' Lisa said.

'Transplant it next spring.'

'Yes.'

They looked at each other without smiling, then he opened the door of the Jeep, helped her up into the passenger seat. They drove down to Butterfield without exchanging more than a dozen meaningless words. Lisa sat quietly with her hands neatly folded in her lap. Ben was too full of heartache and regret to want to talk. If he kept silent, he could kid himself that everything was all right and they were a couple again.

Mel had been right. He flushed, despising himself in a way he had never felt it necessary to do before. He had taken from Mel and given so little in exchange. Yet, driving down the black wet roads, stars above them, he remembered her voice, her smile, and thought that maybe he was being too hard on himself. 'You've given me so much,' she had said. Perhaps, after all, there had been a mutual kind of healing.

As they neared the old Adams house, Lisa spoke. 'Is there anything to eat?'

'Not much. We could call in a pizza or something.' As they had so often done in the past, settling down on the rug in front of the fire to watch TV and gorge on a Romano or a Margerita with all the trimmings, accompanied by a bottle of cheap Italian wine. 'Otherwise I've only got eggs and cheese. And bread. And some tomatoes. And pasta, of course.'

413

'We could make a cheese omelet.'

'Or stop at the store, if you like.' He was hesitant to do this, in case they ran into someone they knew. He didn't want to try and explain that no, they weren't back together. It was too difficult. Too painful.

'Let's not stop.'

'The house is in a bit of a mess,' he said, as they turned into the drive.

'I was there the other night, remember? It didn't look bad then.'

He turned impulsively to her. 'I behaved like a spoiled child that night.'

'I've done that too.' She leaned towards him and for a moment he thought she was going to kiss him. 'We're all entitled to behave badly once in a while.'

'You wouldn't have said that four months ago.'

'I've grown up a bit,' she said.

'So have I.'

He parked under the apple tree, heavy now with over-ripe fruit that was turning rotten. The light was beginning to fade. A faint sliver of new moon already hung over the fields across the lane, colorless and bleak except for the thick green of the pines.

He set a match to wood in the fireplace, added scrumpled newspaper and a half-burnt log left in the ashes from last time. Lisa sat on the old blue-covered sofa, like a guest, watching him.

'Want something to drink?' he said. He felt absurdly shy, almost as though they were on their first date.

'A glass of white wine, please,' she said. She didn't make any kind of move to follow him into the kitchen, or find glasses. His heart dropped. The messages she was sending were loud and clear. *This is not my house any more. This is no longer my marriage.* He wondered how they were going to get through the rest of the evening. He'd better make up a bed for her in the spare bedroom. He flushed, imagining the mortification of her having to suggest it herself. He gripped his hands together and pressed them against his chest. 'Please,' he said, under his breath. '*Please . . .*'

Please what? He had no idea.

He took two glasses and a chilled bottle from the refrigerator into the living room. The fire was burning comfortably and Lisa sat on the raised hearth, feeding it with pieces of kindling.

'No-one can resist fiddling with a fire, can they?' she said.

'Two reasons for that,' he said, painfully aware that they were manufacturing conversation. 'One because fire is so elemental. The other because everyone in the entire world knows that no-one can make a fire work better than they can.'

She laughed. 'You're probably right.'

He removed the cork, poured for them both, handed her a glass. He sat down and tipped his glass at her in a kind of toast. 'Made any plans for Thanksgiving? Christmas?' he asked awkwardly.

'Christmas? It's kind of early, isn't it?' She looked down at her hands and twisted the gold band on her finger. 'What about you?'

'Mom wants me to go to Boston again. Neil and family will be there.'

'And will you go?'

'I haven't decided.' He looked away from her.

They'd planned to stay in Butterfield this year, just the three of them, him, Lisa and the baby. Last Christmas, Lisa had decorated the house with twigs she'd sprayed with white paint and something sparkly, hung baubles

415

everywhere, crystal and silver and a kind of mulberry red, decorated the dark stairway with tiny silvery lights, covered the surfaces with pale candles. Some of them had smelled of cinnamon and spices, and when they were all lit, the old house had taken on a warmth and glow it did not usually possess. They'd driven down to Boston on Christmas Eve to be with his mother, and left again the day after Christmas, eager to get home. As they turned into the snow-covered circle in front of their home, he'd experienced a sense of belonging so deep that his heart had felt like a balloon trying to burst out of his chest.

'Thanksgiving, Christmas – they're about families, aren't they?' she said.

Refilling her glass, he said, 'My fault, I know, but we didn't talk much last time you were here. So tell me about the new job, how things are going.'

'Just about OK.' She made a face. 'I only took it because they promised me unlimited use of the kilns and the wheels in the art studio. Turned out their idea of unlimited wasn't exactly the same as mine.'

'But you're managing to get some work done.' He picked up the bowl she had left with Mel. 'Some *great* work. This is the most striking piece of yours that I've seen.' He thought of Mel handing it to him, the pain which had shadowed her face. Thank you, he wanted to say. Thank you for everything. For loving me, for healing me. Thank you, my generous Mel.

Lisa inspected the bowl as though this was the first time she'd seen it. 'Yes, I'm pleased with it.'

'Are you hungry?' he asked.

'Very.' Carefully she put down her glass. 'Tell you what,' she said. 'We could make pesto sauce, if you like. That first time, when you came to my apartment, you said

416

anything could happen. I don't know about you, but it sure worked for me.'

There was a dimple in her cheek: it seemed like years since he had last seen it. *That first time* . . . It had been so easy then. Too easy, maybe. He put his arms around her and smiled into her upturned face. 'Sign me on,' he said.

'Boy, that pesto sauce.' Lisa pushed her chair back from the table, pressed a hand to her belly. 'I feel so full.' Her red mouth shone with oil as she stared at him through the candle flames.

'Me too.' He poured more wine into their glasses.

'Funny thing is,' she said, putting her elbows on the table and cupping her face in her hands. 'I have this weird feeling that, like you said, anything could happen.'

'Any idea what form this "anything" might take?'

'Oh, yes.' She laughed. 'Absolutely.'

She came round the table and bent to kiss his lips, her mouth slippery on his, fragrant and exciting. But when he reached for her, she slipped away.

When she went up to bed, he blew out the candles, hearing water rushing in the ancient plumbing system, the clank of radiators, the wheeze of the pump. In the living room, the fire was no more than a red glow, the logs crumbled in on each other. He turned off lights, locked the front door, slowly went upstairs. He wasn't dreaming. Lisa was back. The evening really had happened. And the rest, please God, would follow. *Might* follow. Mel's image, her moonlight-colored hair, her night-blue eyes, hovered briefly behind his eyelids. He felt no guilt, just a secret kind of loving. What had happened between them had been necessary, for both of them. The brief time they'd shared had enriched and strengthened them, given them the fortitude to go on with their real lives.

417

He lay in bed, alone, listening to the sound of Lisa in the other bedroom. Once he thought he heard soft footsteps in the passage, her bare feet on the polished floor, and hoped she was coming to him. Then he heard the door of the nursery open, and – after a while – softly close.

I shall never take this . . . this privilege for granted again, he thought. I shall never ever assume anything again. In the distance of his mind hung the mountains he had loved, remote, mysterious, eternal, forever trailing their banners of ice crystals, unconquerable. He realized suddenly that however many times he reached the top, standing as close to heaven as any man was able to, they would always remain unconquerable.

In Lisa's studio they found one of the cheap earthenware pots she loved to buy from the garden centers – 'such gorgeous glazes!' – and filled it with potting compound which was stored in the front half of the barn.

Together they planted the little rosemary bush, tamped down the compound round its roots, watered it with rainwater from the barrel behind the house. 'Ben,' Lisa said, holding his hand. 'This is a beautiful idea of yours.'

'It was the name,' he said. 'Rosemary for remembrance. From Shakespeare. Whenever we see it, we'll be able to think of her.'

'All the things she might have done, might have been.'

'That's what I thought.'

She looked at him with shining eyes. 'We can move on, Ben. Do you realize that?'

'Yes, I do.' He held her away from him. Took a deep breath. And another. 'Lisa.'

'What?'

'I promise I'll never go climbing again.'

She put a finger across his lips. 'Best not to make promises you may not be able to keep.'

'But I mean it.'

'Ssh,' she said.

CHAPTER TWENTY-NINE

Across the fields, trees stood against the clear sky, fiery, brilliant, and beyond them the encircling mountains. White birds rose suddenly and wheeled through the air, the sun catching the underside of their wings. A fox parted the long grass on the opposite verge and peered carefully out before trotting across the road, its brush momentarily vivid in a slice of sunlight. Mel could see its ruthless yellow eye, the shine of its wet nose.

Overhead, a gust of wind shook down a shower of flaming leaves then lifted them along the lane in front of her, scarlet, apricot, saffron and plum, like a flight of exotic butterflies. Her life in this place had been made up of countless small moments such as these, images laid down like paint on the canvas of her mind. These fields, those hills, that sky, were as familiar to her as her own reflection in the mirror; the pleasure they gave her had once been integral to her well-being.

Last time she had taken the road south from Butterfield, Joanne had been with her. This time she was going down to visit Joanne's children. When she had called Gordon to suggest it, he had been delighted, told her that they had missed her, hoped she would stay.

'Just one night,' she had replied. 'My exhibition is in

three days' time.' She did not add that along with her desire to see how Tom, Lucy and, above all, Jamie were doing, was the need to be doing something, anything that would prevent her from thinking about Ben.

'Jamie,' she said, sweeping him into her arms. 'Oh Jamie, sweetheart, how are you?'

'I'm doing OK.' He seemed taller than when she had last seen him, more reserved. He led her into Gordon Mayfield's designer kitchen, and, lifting an elegant chrome kettle, asked if she would like a cup of tea. 'Or coffee. There's a plunger thing here, and another gadget: Dad's kind of fussy about his coffee.'

'Tea would be good.' She pulled out a chair and sat down. The immaculate counters and polished floor were a far cry from the warm and homely kitchen he had grown up in. 'Do you like your new school?'

'It's OK.'

'What are you reading?' She delved into her bag and brought out a package. 'Here's a book for you. Save it until you reach the Cs again.'

He picked it up. 'Maybe I won't bother to wait. I already broke the pattern.'

'Is that good or bad?'

'Good, don't you think?' There was a new maturity in his voice. 'I was getting kind of set in my ways. Dad says that's OK when you're older but not so cool when you're twelve.'

'I think Dad's probably right,' she said gravely. 'So open it.'

He tore off the wrapping paper. His face lit up. '*Catcher in the Rye*: perfect. It's on my reading list.' He bent and kissed her cheek. 'Thanks, Mel.'

'How's Gargery liking it down here?'

'Sure doesn't like the traffic, but otherwise he's fine. Lucy's just taken him for a walk with her new boyfriend. Boy, what a geek *he* is.' He poured hot water into a pot, and took down two mugs, ones which Mel recognized from Joanne's house. 'Dad and I think Gargery's lost weight.'

'He certainly needed to.'

'Yeah.'

'And how is your dad?'

'He's . . . I guess happy isn't the right word 'cause of losing Mom, but he's real glad to have us staying with him.'

'I'm sure he is. And you, Jamie . . . are you all right?'

'I guess,' he said slowly.

'It'll take time,' she said. 'Maybe the rest of your life.'

'That's what I thought.'

'Do you know what your mom's very favorite book of all was?'

'What?'

'*Great Expectations*.'

'That's by Charles Dickens.'

'It's where she got Gargery's name from.'

'Is it?' He assimilated the information. 'Maybe I'll read that next. If you don't mind. Save *Catcher in the Rye* for the book after that.' He pushed his glasses further up the bridge of his nose. 'Dad says I might be old enough to have contact lenses.'

She felt a push of sentimental tears at the back of her throat. 'Nice tea,' she said.

'Yeah. Lapsang souchong, it's called. I'm kind of keen on different teas, at the moment. One of Dad's clients is a tea importer and he took me round his warehouses a couple of days ago. It was really interesting.'

Gordon and Tom arrived at the same time as Lucy. 'Oh

Mel, we've missed you so much,' Lucy said, flinging her arms round Mel. She looked well; she even looked happy. Tom too: like his little brother, he seemed to have gained a veneer of confidence in the past weeks. Despite the trauma of losing their mother, the three of them were travelling onward, as they needed to. As they must. Moving on, Mel thought. And I must move on too.

Lucy and the boyfriend, a handsome sophomore at Brown and not in the least geeky as far as Mel could see, had volunteered to cook supper.

'This is called *spana kopitta*,' Lucy said, putting an oven dish on the table in Gordon's formal dining room, 'and it's really really good.' The boyfriend produced a sophisticated lemony salad which contained, among other things, snap beans, artichoke hearts, mangoes and rice. They brought in garlic bread and baked potatoes topped with melted cheese, and sliced tomatoes with a pesto sauce. 'Vegetarian, as you can see,' said Lucy.

'Sometimes we get to eat steak,' said Tom.

'Especially when it's my turn to cook,' Gordon said. 'Steak's about all I can handle.'

'I make roast chicken when it's my turn,' said Jamie. 'With roast potatoes. Wicked.'

'Do you have plans, Mel?' Gordon said, taking the cork out of a bottle of wine.

'I can only think as far as my exhibition,' she said. 'After that . . . who knows.' She felt like a kite, free but tethered.

'You know what you ought to do, Mel?' Jamie said.

'What's that, honey?'

'You should go to that place Mom was always talking about. In New Zealand.'

She smiled at him. 'I don't think so.'

'Why not?' Gordon asked mildly. 'What's to stop you?'

She remembered him telling her Joanne had always been too scared to travel on her own. I'm scared too, she thought.

'No, really,' insisted Jamie. 'I've been reading all about New Zealand. That place, Rotorua, sounds totally wicked. Mud and steam and smelly pools. And they have these people called the Maori, who were there to start with, who have war canoes and cloaks made of feathers, and these fantastic carvings with their tongues sticking out. I wish I could go.'

'I'll take you one day,' she said.

'Will you really?'

'A graduation present.'

'That's cool.'

'You might not want an old lady along by then, of course,' she said, smiling at him. At his father and siblings.

'I'll always want you, Mel,' he said.

'Creep,' said Lucy, but she was smiling. 'You're part of the family,' she said, reaching out a hand to Mel.

'Thank you, sweetheart.'

Driving back the following day, she felt content. I need no longer worry about Joanne's children, she thought. Gordon was taking over where Joanne left off. They were good kids; he was a good father.

Wheels had turned, things had moved on. Despite the bad, there was some good.

On the morning of the exhibition preview, Mel arrived at the gallery to find a UPS truck waiting outside. The delivery man – a different one this time – walked in behind her, carrying a small wooden crate, and put it down on her desk.

'I thought we had all the exhibits,' Mel said.

He shrugged. 'I was asked to deliver this, is all I know.' While she signed the necessary documentation, he put an envelope in front of her. 'Plus this.'

When he had driven away, she sat down at the table in her office and opened the commercial envelope he had left. Inside was another envelope which contained another note from Koslowski. Like the first, it was scrawled on a sheet of A4, thick black writing enlivened by capital letters and exclamation marks.

MRS SHERMAN she read.
This is Lost Love, my most recent work.
I must emphasise that it is MY OWN PERSONAL
POSSESSION and is not repeat NOT FOR SALE / / / / /
Galen Koslowski

His most recent work! With extreme care, fingers trembling with anticipation, she broke open the crate and lifted the piece inside clear of its wrappings. She blew away sawdust, licked her finger and removed a tiny scrap of wood-shaving.

Lost Love. The breath caught in her throat, blood pounded in her ears. She looked at her own piece on the table, and then back at the new one. Despite the more than twenty-five years which separated them, the two were almost identical. On closer inspection, both revealed that what appeared at first to be little more than a block of curving polished wood was in fact a female torso, surfacing from the grain as though from sleep or from water. But whereas the first was a juvenile piece, produced when the sculptor had not yet fully realized his ability, the other was the work of an artist at the height of his mature creativity. And there was another more significant difference. The first figure was that of a girl, slight, barely

425

pubescent, while the second had been modeled by a woman of riper years, rounder of breast, curved of belly.

She picked it up and ran her hands over the wood. Below the left breast, running towards the inward crook of the waist, was a narrow, almost imperceptible slash. She pulled open one of the desk drawers and took out her loupe to examine the piece more closely. She had thought it might be merely a flaw in the wood, but it was clear it had been added deliberately, that it was an intrinsic part of the sculpture.

Lost Love: not, repeat NOT FOR SALE!!!

'Oh, Galen,' she said softly. She tilted the sapphire ring on her finger so that the stones caught the light from the window and blazed with blue fire.

One half of her mind was occupied in wondering whether she was wrong in reading a secret message there, a private code: one which said that while wounds may heal, scars never will. The other half was debating where to place the two pieces. Should her own be the first sculpture on view as people came in, with *Lost Love* as the final sculpture? Or should they be placed together, to illustrate the subtleties of passing time? She would have to act swiftly, change things around before this evening.

As though someone had taken a bite from her heart, she thought of Joanne, wished yet again that she was there to discuss it with. Almost more than anything else, she missed their freewheeling, light-hearted conversations.

Best not to think about Joanne. Or about loneliness. There was no time. Not at the moment.

'Did that go well, or what!' Carla eased her feet out of her pumps and propped them up on the table in the gallery office. The last invitees had left the gallery ten minutes ago, and finally they could relax.

426

'It was terrific. Absolutely terrific.' Mel poured the remains of a bottle of Chardonnay into a glass and handed it to her assistant. 'Here's to us.'

'And our future success.'

'At the moment, I'm just happy with the current one.'

The two women clinked glasses and smiled at each other. 'You're right,' Carla said. 'I don't believe I've got the energy to think about the future.'

'You've been doing far more than you should.'

'Well . . .' Carla lifted a shoulder. 'I feel as committed as you do. And if you should ever think of selling this place . . .' She let the unspoken question hang.

'I'll remember that,' Mel said. She looked at Carla with affection. 'You deserve a bonus.'

'I wouldn't turn one down.'

'We'll sort it out tomorrow.' Mel creaked back her chair and closed her eyes. 'Gaahd. I'm bushed.'

'Are you OK? If you don't mind me saying, you've been looking pretty terrible the last few days.'

'I've been sleeping really badly. Coffee and adrenaline are all that's keeping me going.'

'Maybe now the exhibition's launched, you'll sleep better.' Carla lifted her glass to her mouth. 'That piece which arrived this morning looked marvellous, right in the middle of the floor like that, especially with the other one you brought in. I never knew you already owned something by Koslowski.'

'That's partly where I got the idea of setting this show up.'

'If they'd been for sale, you'd could have sold them both five times over.'

'I know.'

'Did you realize that *all* the press people we invited showed up? Isn't that great?'

427

'I can't wait to see the reviews.' Yawning, Mel opened her eyes. 'Thank God there weren't any major disasters.'

'I thought there might be when Helen Wotsername, that woman from the gift shop, spilled red wine down the front of Lindy Kellerman's white suit.'

'She wasn't exactly thrilled about it, was she? Not that I would have been, either – I happen to know exactly how much Lindy paid for that suit because I was looking at the same one in burgundy.'

'*Well*.' Carla wrinkled her nose fastidiously. 'I don't know about *you*, but *I* was brought up to believe that no lady wears white after Labor Day.'

'Whoever said Lindy Kellerman was a lady?'

'You've got a vicious tongue on you, Miz Sherman, you know that?'

'Rita Bernhard looked stunning, didn't she?'

'She can afford to. That was Donna Karan she was wearing.'

Mel laughed. 'I think the worst bit was when Judge Mahoney backed into the water sculpture.'

'I really thought we were in trouble then. If Kim Bernhard hadn't been there . . . talk about quick reflexes. Sheesh! Can you imagine what Mr Koslowski would have said if he'd been there? *I vill sue, I vill sue!*' She looked at her watch. 'I better get on home.'

Mel reached up and clasped the other woman's hand. 'Thanks, Carla, for everything. You're an absolute star.'

She listened as Carla's footsteps receded down the wooden floor of the gallery. There was the creak and clank of the heavy old ring-handle, the bang as the door closed behind her. It was time she went home herself. But she stayed where she was. She tipped more wine into her glass and slowly consumed it.

God, she was tired. And, despite the success of the

evening, forlorn. Loss weighed her down. If only Joanne were here. Over the years there had been so many gatherings, so many parties, when the two of them had kicked off their shoes and sat down with the remains of a bottle of wine to pick over the details, relive the evening, post-mortem it. She longed to hear her friend's sharp observations, her pungent comments, the laughter they used to share, her lively take on things. Nothing was the same without her.

She validated my life, Mel thought. The way a parent does – or ought to do. *Look, Daddy, it's a horse*, turning the corner, sunshine tangled in the trees along the street, Rudy Howard's old dog asleep in the middle of the road. Is that, in the end, what a life is all about? Being able to show Daddy my painting?

My pain.

It was now over a week since she had last seen Ben. She had left a message on his answering machine, telling him not to come to the opening, and he had stayed away, although she had half-hoped he would defy her. Although she was exhausted, she was wired, elated, she wanted to talk, to exclaim, to describe. But there was no-one to share her excitement with.

Except . . .

Maybe . . .

Slowly she reached towards the telephone and as she did so, it bleeped, the sound echoing through the silent gallery, bouncing off the stone pieces, rippling the surface of the water sculpture. She snatched it up.

'Vernon Gallery.'

'Mrs Sherman.'

Her low mood dissipated, her weariness vanished. 'Mr Koslowski. I was just about to call you.'

'How did it go this evening?'

'Brilliant! Fantastic!'

'That's wonderful.'

'Three pieces were sold in the first half-hour,' she said. 'Isn't that marvellous? And at least four other people will almost certainly buy later.'

'You must be very good at your job,' he said.

'You're not so bad at yours . . . Plus, of course, the fact that I and my assistant – she's called Carla – have been working on this project for the last twenty months.'

'It sounds like it paid off.'

'I'll say. Three sales in the first *half-hour*? How good is *that*? And the show doesn't even officially open until tomorrow.'

'That's really something.' He sounded impressed. 'Did many people come?'

'Nearly two hundred.'

'Mrs Sherman, you are obviously a genius.'

She laughed. 'Thank goodness they didn't all show up at the same time. My gallery is quite small.'

'I wish I could have been there.'

'Mmmm,' she said, non-committal.

'You don't sound as though you agree. No doubt you've heard of my reputation as a wild man.'

Not just heard; I've seen you in action, she thought. 'Who hasn't?'

'None of it is true.'

'None?'

'As a matter of fact, I intended to come tonight. As a surprise. I even hired a car to drive up there, but – unfortunately I managed to clip someone's wing, and by the time the cops were through, it was too late.'

'I bet you're a lousy driver.'

'Yes, I'm afraid I am.'

'You missed a terrific evening,' she said.

430

'The extra piece I sent you yesterday, it arrived safely?'

'*Lost Love*,' Mel said. 'That was surprise enough.' She hesitated. 'I wanted to ask . . . who was the model?'

'There was no model.'

'I thought perhaps . . . someone you know.'

'Someone I *used* to know. I made it from . . . from the heart. From my memories. She was young then, we both were. I wondered how she might be now, changed by the years, grown older. This piece is the result.'

'It's a beautiful piece of work.'

'It's a nostalgic piece of work. Describe for me how you displayed it.'

'Well.' Mel tipped more wine into her glass and leaned back. 'I thought about it quite hard. Whether to have it as the final piece, you know, show people what you are currently producing. But in the end, I grouped it with the companion piece.'

'The companion piece?'

'Yes, they seemed to fit together so well, to illustrate the damage that time causes and how, despite that, even in middle age, a woman's body can still be beautiful.'

There was a long silence. She heard the clink of glass against glass, a deep-drawn breath, almost a sigh. Silence.

'Mr Koslowski?'

'The companion piece,' he repeated.

'Yes.'

'Mrs Sherman . . .'

'Yes?'

'There is no companion piece.'

'There is. It's a carving you did a long time ago.'

'Called?'

'Uh . . . *First Love*.'

There was another lengthy pause. 'Ah,' he said finally,

431

drawing the syllable out. 'I have often wondered where that piece was.'

The two of them sat without speaking, companionable. The polished floor of the gallery stretched away to dimness, lit by the occasional spotlights Mel had not yet switched off.

'She left me,' Koslowski said into the silence. 'The beautiful woman who was the model for that. I never knew why. It almost killed me. The stupid thing is that it was only then, in that moment of separation, that I realized just how much she meant to me. Without her, I couldn't work. I needed her. She was my inspiration.'

'Why didn't you go after her?'

'Where? Where would I start looking? America is a big place. She would have married, changed her name. Moved. She might even have gone somewhere like Vermont.'

'That's very possible.' Mel put her feet up on her desk. 'Nonetheless, you still went on producing good stuff.'

'Good, yes. But without a heart. And then, I realized that I could not waste the rest of my life waiting for her to return, or I would never produce anything worthwhile again.'

'So you're over her now.'

'What do you think, Mrs Sherman? Am I over her? You have seen my newest work.'

'Mr Koslowski, I . . .'

'What, Mrs Sherman?'

From her office, Mel could see the whole exhibition stretching in front of her. 'The piece called *Birth* is absolutely magnificent.'

'Was it one of the pieces which sold?'

'I bought it myself, before the show started.' She refilled her glass and laughed, for no particular reason.

'You sound happy,' he said.

'I do believe that I am.'

'Do you have children, Mrs Sherman?'

'No.'

'Why not?'

'I . . .' What am I doing? she asked herself. For a moment she hesitated. 'I had an abortion when I was young.'

'Oh no . . .' He drew a sharp breath. 'I see.'

'I've never forgiven myself. After that, I never considered that I deserved to have children.'

'I have none either,' he said abruptly.

'Why not?'

'At first because I thought I must not bring children into a world like this one. By the time I changed my mind, the only person I wanted children with was gone. I often wonder what sort of father I would have been. I love children, but maybe I would have found the responsibility of my own too much to handle. This woman whom I loved wanted to have children with me and I refused.'

'That's probably why she went.'

'I regret it now. I bitterly regret it.'

'Maybe one of these days you'll see her again.'

He gave a deep sigh. 'If I do, I shall certainly ask her to give me back the icon that she took from our apartment.'

Mel's mouth curved upwards. 'Are you sure you didn't offer it to her as a gift?'

'Only on the assumption that we would be staying together.'

'Indian giver.'

He chuckled, a rich warm sound. She heard wine being poured into a glass. 'Yesterday I had to go to a party.'

'Did you enjoy it?'

'Not in the least. Such a waste of time,' he said, and she remembered other parties long ago, his wild hair flying,

433

light catching his wine glass as he gesticulated, his head thrown back in laughter. 'However, I met a man just arrived from Poland, a gifted artist, he will go far, I'm sure. We talked about Warsaw, Cracow, what is happening over there on the art scene. And, listening to him talk, I thought that maybe I should go back to my homeland. At least for a visit. I've never had the courage before now.'

Do you still have nightmares, she wanted to ask. Do you still wake shuddering in the night to reach out for someone, to weep into her hair? Do you miss me, as I have always missed you, as I missed you still even as I lay in the arms of my young lover?

'You sound about as tired as I feel,' she said.

'Not tired. Just . . . old.'

'Not you,' she said.

'And I don't always sleep so well. Also – why do I tell you this? – I am lonely. What about you, Mrs Sherman? Are you also lonely? Or do you lead a life of social gaiety? I imagine you up there, surrounded by cows and buttercups, the queen of Butterfield, the hostess with the mostest.'

'A social butterfly? Hardly.'

'What about Mr Sherman?'

'What about him?'

'Perhaps he drags you to functions and business dinners, where you sparkle and shine.'

'Mr Sherman has been dead for some time.'

'I see. And, of course, you miss him.'

'The one I miss is Joanne, my dearest closest friend, who died a few weeks ago. She was the nearest thing I have to family.'

'So you are lonely, too.'

'Yes.'

'Sometimes friends can mean more than those who are supposed to be closest to you.'

434

'That's so true.'

'And I must have added to your worries at what must be a bad time for you.'

'That's the way it goes. Highs and lows. Ups and downs. The best you can do is enjoy the ups and endure the downs. Trouble is . . .' Mel pressed her lips together.

'Are you crying, Mrs Sherman?'

'Since you ask, Mr Koslowski, I guess I am.'

'If I was with you,' he said, 'I would hold your hand. It's not much, but it would show you that you still have a friend, even if it's only a crabby old shabby old sculptor like me.'

She found herself smiling again, despite herself. 'Are you crabby?'

'A little bit. There are so many things here in New York which drive me mad. Cellphones, for instance. Why must people walk down the street talking on the phone? Why can't they wait until they get home?

'Isn't that just the most irritating thing?'

'Something else I hate is the way in restaurants, the waiter tells you his name and then gabbles off the specials for the evening so fast you cannot remember a single one when he's finished. Where is the menu, I always ask them, these Ryans and Damons? I do not wish to hear a three-act play, I tell them, give me the menu and I will read for myself what you have. Not that a menu is much good these days: I don't understand what it is they are serving. Arugula – what is arugula?'

'Something green, I think.'

'The last restaurant I was in, I did not recognize half the dishes they wished me to eat. Arugula. Radicchio . . .'

'Carambolas,' said Mel.

'Poha berries.'

'Triticale.'

435

'Pompana. What are these things? Where do they come from? The other day I was offered a wilted lettuce salad, and I asked Damon – or maybe Ryan – I said, why are you offering me wilted lettuce? Lettuce should be crisp and fresh-picked, not wilted, not ready for the garbage can.'

Mel laughed aloud.

'You have a lovely laugh,' he said. 'What kind of cuisine do you like, Mrs Sherman?'

'Most sorts.'

'Me too. But the old dishes are my favorites, the ones with names I recognize.'

'I agree. Last time I went to Boston,' said Mel, 'I ate in a Russian restaurant.'

'I used to know a Russian restaurant in Boston – I wonder if it was the same one.'

'How many can there be?'

'Let me guess what you ate: *borzscht*, and *pirozhki*, no?'

'Pretty standard choices, Mr Koslowski. We had blinis, too. And some fish.' Mel giggled, wondered if she had drunk too much wine. 'No arugula, but a truly wicked amount of vodka.'

'Mrs Sherman!' he said. 'I don't want to call you Mrs Sherman. It's ridiculous to be so formal. By now we have become friends.'

'Have we?'

'I think so. I know I would like you. I already do. I feel I have known you for years. The formal Mrs Sherman. The formidable Mrs Sherman. The sometimes sad Mrs Sherman.'

She heard the creak of the chair he was sitting on. She listened to the wind shaking the trees outside, rain beating at the skylights overhead. A car passed, tires hissing on the wet pavement. 'People of our age are bound to be sad from time to time,' she said. 'We've lived long enough to have experienced loss and grief.'

'Of course. What keeps me going is the certainty that happiness is waiting for me around the next corner. Or the one after that.'

'Don't you think you have to expect less than happiness, in order to find any at all?'

'No, no. That is the wrong approach. You must always expect everything.'

'Do you believe in second chances, Mr Koslowski?'

'Absolutely. Without any question.' His chair creaked again. 'One moment.'

She heard hollow noises from the other end of the phone and then the sound of Mahler's Symphony No 2. When he picked up the receiver again, she said softly, 'The Resurrection Symphony – one of my favorites.'

'I thought it might be.'

Mel smiled secretly. They had been on the telephone for over forty-five minutes; she felt as though she could go on talking for the rest of the night. 'What are you working on at the moment?'

'Nothing. But I'm thinking about something.' There was a familiar rise in his voice, the excited lift which always preceded the start of a new work. 'I have this piece of marble, from South America. Green marble, with the most wonderful streaks of gold. I've had it for years, waiting for the right moment to use it.'

She remembered the warehouse full of blocks of stone, marble dust everywhere, sheets of granite, slate, lumps of sandstone, Galen's eyes lighting up as he saw what looked to her like just another piece of rock. 'And now it's come,' she said.

'Is coming,' he corrected her. 'For the moment, I'm just

considering it, trying to see what is hiding inside, waiting to appear.'

'Like Michelangelo.'

'I wouldn't put myself anywhere near him, but yes. Now tell, Mrs Sherman, what plans do you have for the future?'

'I'm still struggling to cope with the present.'

'Other exhibitions, maybe?'

'I have at least two I'm considering, rather like you and your piece of marble.'

'Anything more? A visit to New York, perhaps?'

It suddenly came to her. Excited, she sat up straight, put her feet down on the floor. Jamie's suggestion was exactly the right one. She could not imagine why she had not seen it before. 'No. Not New York. New Zealand.'

'But why?'

Mel wrinkled her forehead. 'Sounds kind of crazy, I know. But Joanne—'

'Your friend who died?'

'– yes. She always dreamed of going there, some place called Rotorua, and she never did, even though she had the chance.'

'Why not?'

'Her former husband told me she was too scared of traveling on her own.' And there's that other worry, Mel thought. The fear that the journey, once completed, can never match up to the expectation of it. That the reality will prove to be less than the dream. But that's the price you might have to pay, the risk you have to take. It was not her dream, but nonetheless she pictured blue skies, savage landscapes, birds with huge wings floating above lion-colored grass. 'I'm scared too,' she said. 'Traveling to strange places on my own . . . but I'm going. Yes, I'm going to go.'

Carla would jump at the chance to look after the gallery, a hike in salary, a chance to use her own judgement. The journey would mean closure. A fresh start. More than that, it would be a journey which might lead anywhere. Change hovered in front of her like a dragonfly.

'I could come with you,' he said quietly. 'If you're scared.'

'Oh . . .' she said. 'Mr Koslowski.' She remembered how once she had been so in love that, if she had wanted to, she could have reached up and touched the sky. There were tears in her eyes.

'Are you crying again, Mrs Sherman?'

'Yes, Mr Koslowski, I do believe I am.'

CHAPTER THIRTY

Before she left, she drove to the dam and stood looking down at the frozen water, hands jammed deep into the pockets of her coat. Her breath hung in the air like smoke, like melancholy. The wind hurled snow spray into her face, tiny stinging dots of cold. Dark birds flapped slowly above the water and disappeared among the black-spired pines. Cold had bleached the color from the trees, from the sky, the wintry hills. She used to walk here with Joanne and the children, on winter holidays. Now she saw her friend lifting away from her, propelled like a time-warping spaceship into the distance, further and further, until she was no more than a prick of light in a sky full of stars.

And Ben, too, was charting new territory. Sometimes she caught glimpses of him, crossing the Common, buying flowers. Lisa was often with him, enough for Mel to be aware that the two of them had moved into a resumption of their lives together. Sarah Mahoney had told her Ben was working with Kim Bernhard.

The air was sharp as glass. She imagined that she could smell the scents of summers past: roses, jasmine, lilacs. Deep down, like a silver fish on the bottom of a fathom-less pond, like an eel below the surface, she knew that if

440

she had the courage to go out and find them, choices, dreams, magical possibilities still existed. I've lived safely for too long, she thought. I shall be better at living in the future than I have been in the past.

From the airport, she took a cab into the city. At the hotel, she hung up her clothes, took the icon from her bag and laid it on the bed. She stared at her reflection in the mirror, saw her mother's face behind her own and – for the first time – her father's. Lifting her pale heavy hair from her neck, she felt the weight of it in her hands. The sapphire ring shone on her finger. She smiled at herself.

The familiar street had scarcely changed since she last walked away from it, twenty-five years before. At the deli on the corner she stopped to buy rye bread, the big Polish pickles Galen used to love, unsalted butter, curls of smoked ham, pastrami. She carried the brown paper sack to the familiar steps, took out the key she had kept all these years, let herself in. Two floors up she could hear the chip of hammer on stone. She started to hurry. Faster and faster. The stone stairs sped away from her feet. Running down the passage, she turned the handle of the door – *their* door – and found, as always, that it was unlocked. Pushing it open, she saw him against the window, head on one side, staring intently at the stone before him, green streaked with gold.

He looked up. Opened his mouth to say something, shut it again. He began to smile, wider and wider, lighting up the room. Lighting up the world.

'Mr Koslowski,' she said.

'Mrs Sherman.' He opened his arms to her. 'Melissa. My honeybee.'

THE END

THE COLOUR OF HOPE
by Susan Madison

All her life she had feared death by water . . .

Ruth Carter, her gentle husband Paul and their two children spend idyllic summers at their holiday retreat on the beautiful and rugged coast of Maine. But one year, as son Will celebrates his fourteenth birthday, a sailing trip goes tragically wrong and their beautiful, troubled daughter Josie is swept overboard. She disappears without trace.

Trapped in a spiral of guilt, grief and denial, Ruth finds her life beginning to fall apart. But fate has an even crueller trick up its sleeve, one which threatens to take from her everything that she holds most dear. The only thing she has to keep her going is hope – hope that a miracle will happen, hope that her family can rebuild their love for one another and recapture the joys of the past.

The Colour of Hope – a powerful and uplifting story of love, courage and hope for the future.

'An emotional roller-coaster of a novel, guaranteed to make you reach for your Kleenex'
Woman and Home

0 552 14772 9

THE SHADOW CATCHER
by Michelle Paver

EDEN. In the depths of the lush Jamaican forest stands a ruined house of haunting beauty – the last remains of a great estate founded on slavery. Abandoned for decades, it still casts its spell down the generations. A place of dreams, magic and madness.

Worlds away, ten-year-old Madeleine's untroubled Scottish childhood is cut short by a fateful encounter and a searing loss. Left alone to raise her new-born sister Sophie, growing up an outcast in Victorian London, she seizes her chance to escape and returns to the decaying Jamaican plantation where she was conceived. There she finds a people haunted by a savage legacy and a family torn apart by obsession and betrayal; but here too she finds Eden – where she must finally confront the shadows of her past.

0 552 14872 5

SONG OF THE SOUND
by Adam Armstrong

For Libby, expert in whale and dolphin communication, the job in New Zealand seemed perfect. She could provide a settled home for her daughter Bree, while she studied the marine creatures she loved in one of the world's last unspoilt places. And when she met John-Cody Gibbs, who had and understanding of the wildlife of the place so profound that it was almost magical, it seemed as if she might at last have found the man she could share her life with.

But John-Cody was still grieving the loss of Mahina, the woman he had loved for more than twenty years, and who had taught him all he knew. He had a dark secret in his past and enemies who were more than ready to use it to destroy his earthly paradise. It took a dangerous voyage into the mountainous seas of the Southern Ocean and a mystical encounter with the whales to give him the freedom Hamina had wanted for him.

'Fans of the mystical fusion of romance and wildlife lore in *The Horse Whisperer* and Armstrong's mesmerising début *Cry of the Panther* will be swept away by this New Zealand-set story'
Evening Telegraph

0 552 14812 1

THE SMOKE JUMPER
by Nicholas Evans

'A dazzling novel which unveils with rapid pace'
The Times

In a searing novel of love and loyalty, guilt and honour, the acclaimed author the international bestseller *The Horse Whisperer* creates another magnificent epic. . .

THE SMOKE JUMPER

His name is Connor Ford and he falls like an angel of mercy form the sky, braving the flames to save the woman he loves but knows he cannot have. For Julia Bishop is the partner of his best friend and fellow 'smoke jumper', Ed Tully. Julia loves them both – until a terrible fire on a Montana mountain forces her to chose between them and burns a brand on all their hearts.

In the wake of the fire, Connor embarks on a harrowing journey to the worlds' worst wars and disasters to take photographs that find him fame but never happiness. Reckless of a life he no longer wants, again and again he dares death to take him until another fateful day on another continent, when he must walk through fire once more. . .

'Evans is not only a cracking storyteller – he has the rare ability to tell his tale with great vividness and simplicity, an descriptions of such neck-grabbing power that you could feel you are sitting through a Hollywood blockbuster'
Daily Mail

'Captures the grit and splendour of the contemporary American West with compelling realism, His rhythm and observation are key and he demonstrates impeccable timing as he alternates between sweeping atmospheric overviews and intensely detailed character portraits'
The Times

'A rich, imaginative, tragic and heroic tale, told unashamedly straight form the heart'
Sunday Express

0 552 14738 9

A TIME TO DANCE
by Kathryn Haig

1968 – a year of revolution. Five girls join the army, five very different girls, but their friendship makes the hardships, the square-bashing and the petty humiliations of army life bearable.

Isa – determined and focused. She'd looked through the glass ceiling and saw what she wanted on the other side, and she'd do anything to get it.
Juliet – she just wanted to have fun.
Ruth – steady and dependable, she was expected by her friends to carry all their problems as well as her own.
Nell – her marriage to charismatic and ambitious Oliver gave her all the good things of life, but the glossy façade of the life hid a very different reality.
Hope – the odd one out. No one knew what Hope wanted. But when their friendship was threatened, Hope gave up her own future to save it and, in doing so, began a life of deception whose shadow reached out to touch the next generation.

Reunited after twenty-five years, the five woman discover that the past still has a grip on them, which threatens their stability and brings with it violent death.

0 552 14538 6

A SELECTED LIST OF FINE NOVELS
AVAILABLE FROM CORGI BOOKS

14783 4	CRY OF THE PANTHER	Adam Armstrong	£5.99
14812 1	SONG OF THE SOUND	Adam Armstrong	£5.99
14654 4	THE HORSE WHISPERER	Nicholas Evans	£6.99
14738 9	THE SMOKE JUMPER	Nicholas Evans	£6.99
14895 4	NOT ALL TARTS ARE APPLE	Pip Granger	£5.99
14537 8	APPLE BLOSSOM TIME	Kathryn Haig	£5.99
14538 6	A TIME TO DANCE	Kathryn Haig	£5.99
14770 2	MULLIGAN'S YARD	Ruth Hamilton	£5.99
14771 0	SATURDAY'S CHILD	Ruth Hamilton	£5.99
14686 2	CITY OF GEMS	Caroline Harvey	£5.99
14820 2	THE TAVERNERS' PLACE	Caroline Harvey	£5.99
14692 7	THE PARADISE GARDEN	Joan Hessayon	£5.99
14868 7	SEASON OF MISTS	Joan Hessayon	£5.99
14599 8	FOOTPRINTS ON THE SAND	Judith Lennox	£5.99
14603 X	THE SHADOW CHILD	Judith Lennox	£5.99
14772 9	THE COLOUR OF HOPE	Susan Madison	£5.99
14822 9	OUR YANKS	Margaret Mayhew	£5.99
14823 7	THE PATHFINDER	Margaret Mayhew	£5.99
14872 5	THE SHADOW CATCHER	Michelle Paver	£5.99
14753 2	A PLACE IN THE HILLS	Michelle Paver	£5.99
14947 0	THREE IN A BED	Carmen Reid	£5.99
14747 8	THE APPLE BARREL	Susan Sallis	£5.99
14867 9	SEA OF DREAMS	Susan Sallis	£5.99
14794 X	CRY OF THE CURLEW	Peter Watt	£6.99
14795 8	SHADOW OF THE OSPREY	Peter Watt	£6.99
14845 8	GOING HOME	Valerie Wood	£5.99
14846 6	ROSA'S ISLAND	Valerie Wood	£5.99